T0151928

Smooth Sailing

SUSAN X MEAGHER

Smooth Sailing

© 2011 BY SUSAN X MEAGHER

ISBN (10) 09832758-1-5
ISBN (13) 978-0-9832758-1-7

THIS TRADE PAPERBACK ORIGINAL IS PUBLISHED BY BRISK PRESS, BRIELLE, NJ 08730

EDITED BY: LINDA LORENZO
COVER DESIGN AND LAYOUT BY: CAROLYN NORMAN

FIRST PRINTING: JULY 2011

By Susan X Meagher

Novels

Arbor Vitae

All That Matters

Cherry Grove

Girl Meets Girl

The Lies That Bind

The Legacy

Doublecrossed

Smooth Sailing

Serial Novel

I Found My Heart In San Francisco

Awakenings: Book One

Beginnings: Book Two

Coalescence: Book Three

Disclosures: Book Four

Entwined: Book Five

Fidelity: Book Six

Getaway: Book Seven

Honesty: Book Eight

Intentions: Book Nine

Journeys: Book Ten

Karma: Book Eleven

Anthologies

Undercover Tales

Outsiders

To purchase these books go to

www.briskpress.com

Acknowledgments

Thanks to Stef for her advice on all things Dutch

Dedication

To Carrie. Always.

CHAPTER ONE

A LIGHT FOG descended upon the room. Fog? In her tightly sealed, air conditioned office? Laurie Nielsen blinked and tried to ignore what had to be some unfunny trick her mind was playing on her. She was too swamped to pay any real attention to anything but the six windows open on her monitor. She rapidly switched among them as small brushfires burned all around her. Metaphorical brushfires, of course, but each had the potential for a lot of real damage. The fog would just have to wait.

Another instant message popped up, signaling a fire bigger than all the rest. She mumbled, "Hang on, Hiroshi, incoming," before hitting the mute button on her cellphone. She then hit the mute button on the desk phone jammed into her neck. "Give me another minute, Andrea. Don't hang up." At the same time, she tried to find the numbers her boss was demanding in his instant message.

She opened another window and scanned her recent docs, finding the staffing needs projection for Osaka's food and beverage. The fog began to lift, only to be replaced by a tunneling sensation. There were the numbers that Fernando needed. They stood sharp in raised relief as everything else on the screen faded. Now only a single line of numbers grew and grew until a buzzing made everything disappear in a gray snow…

The next thing she was aware of was Wendy, her admin, gently holding her hand. Strange, they'd never held hands before. Laurie started to pull away when she realized she was lying on the floor and Wendy was kneeling next to her, looking down with alarm.

She tried to sit up but Wendy hovered over her. "No, no, don't try to get up until we know what happened."

"What…? When…?" Why was she lying on her office floor and why did Wendy look so worried? She hated being out of the loop, especially when something major was going on. But something was missing. How much time had passed since she'd…what had she been doing? Then her last conscious act came back to her, crisp and fresh. "Is Fernando still on the line? He needs some numbers ASAP."

Looking even more concerned, Wendy said, "He called me when you didn't respond."

Laurie tried to get up again, but her limbs failed to cooperate. "Why am I on the floor?"

"I think you had a stroke or a heart attack. Please try to stay still." Wendy's lip quivered and she began to cry, tears rolling down her cheeks to fall onto Laurie's tailored blue and white striped shirt.

"Don't be ridiculous." She focused all of her muscles and started to push herself up when two men with a gurney trotted into her office. They were on her before she got very far.

One of them gently eased her back to the floor and started taking her vital signs while the other helped Wendy up and questioned her.

"Was she unconscious when you got here?"

"Yes, yes," she sobbed. "She was just ly…lying there. I thought she was dead."

"I'm not dead!" Laurie growled, insulted by the very idea. "I must have tripped or something."

"What's the last thing you remember?"

"I was looking for something on my computer." She stopped and thought hard. "Then the room was foggy or something. It was odd." She shook her head and kept going. "Then everything got out of focus and… Wendy was here."

"Do you remember falling?"

"No."

"Okay," the paramedic said. "We're going to take you to Glendale General." He turned to Wendy. "Notify anyone who needs to know that, okay?"

"Wait!" A board was being slid under her, but Laurie wasn't going easily. "I've got work to do!"

The paramedic gently restrained her with light pressure on her shoulder. "Work can wait. You need to get checked out." Then they loaded her onto the gurney and she closed her eyes, unwilling to see the looks on the faces of her staff as she was wheeled out of her office, feet first.

—⁓—

The next morning, Fernando knocked quietly on her hospital-room door and entered. Laurie looked at her watch. It was five thirty. "I can't believe visiting hours start this early," she said, trying to sound as normal as possible. "You didn't have to waste the trip. I'm fine and I'll be in as soon as I can get my clothes back."

"No, you won't." Fernando lowered his very tall, very thin frame into a chair that seemed made for someone three times his width. His dark eyes scanned her quickly, and she could see him assessing her and making a decision even before he spoke. "I called your parents last night and they told me some things. Some things that have me worried."

"Oh, shit." You couldn't trust anyone with personal information. Even your parents would sell you out.

"They say you've been having problems with your vision and with your heart for months now."

"That's ridiculous. My heart races a little, but that happens to everyone when they're keyed up. And my doctor thinks the vision problem is just a form of migraine. They did every test in the world on me yesterday and they all said there's nothing wrong."

"That's not true," he said, his voice clear and strong. "They said you've been working too much. And that's my fault. I've been driving you too hard."

"No harder than you do yourself."

3

"That may be true, but that's my problem. We're talking about you. When was your last vacation?"

"Uhm…I…Christmas," she said, certain of her facts. "I went to see my family. I had a whole week."

"You weren't gone a whole week. I remember you going to Osaka just a day or two after Christmas."

"Yeah, but I had the weekend at my parents'. Including travel from here to Cincinnati and then back here and on to Osaka, I was out of the office a whole week."

"Travel days aren't vacation. Besides, that was almost a year ago. When was the last time you took a week to go somewhere relaxing?"

"Uhm…I guess that was Spring Break." Her gaze strayed from Fernando's face and she nodded. "College."

"You've never had a real vacation?"

"Sure I have. I visit my family three or four times a year. That counts."

"No, it really doesn't. You go on the worst travel days of the year and you're never gone long." He held her gaze for a few seconds, an expression on his face that showed he'd made a decision. "You've got to relax, and you've got to do it now."

"You can't be serious! I'm up to my ass in alligators, Fernando, and you, better than anyone, knows just how true that is. How can I relax when I know everything I ignore will be waiting to bite me when I return? Trust me. I'm much better off being at work than worrying about it."

He seemed to think this over for a minute. "What's your next deadline?"

"Since we're one hundred and ninety-four days from open, we need to have key personnel for every division online by the end of next week. Everything looks good from a hiring perspective, but then we have to start training them. I'm going to Osaka in two weeks to meet everyone."

"No go. You skip that trip and take a vacation. Two weeks." His thin mustache was almost completely horizontal, an undeniable signal that his mind was made up. When his mouth was set, his mind was too.

4

"No! I've got to make sure Hiroshi hires the right people. You know he's still green."

"You can send Aaron. He's your backup. Let him back you up."

"But Aaron's swamped. He's battling all of the problems going on with the government approvals of the rides. You know the build is full of issues."

"Then don't send him. Learn to trust Hiroshi."

"Oh, God, please don't do this. Please?" She'd never begged Fernando for anything, but the situation called for desperate measures.

"You've got to go on vacation, Laurie. It's time to take the training wheels off and trust the people you've hired. I did it with you, and now it's your turn." He squeezed her shoulder, then headed for the door. "Now get some rest, but try not to be late for the eight o'clock. Warren's gonna be there."

***

Two hours later, Laurie sprinted for the conference room, mildly chewing out Aaron, who was running right beside her. "You brought me slacks? For a meeting with Warren?"

"I didn't know what you wanted. I'm sorry, I don't pay much attention to what women wear at work."

She scowled at him. "This blouse looks stupid with these slacks. I asked you to get me a dress."

"It took a long time to get the locksmith to open the door and I didn't have time to look around. I grabbed the first thing I saw."

It wasn't easy, but she forced herself to be civil. None of this was Aaron's fault. Selecting an outfit for his boss was miles outside of his pay grade. "Don't worry about it. I'll get you a key. I'm sure you'll need it again at some point." She stopped outside the room, took a deep breath, flicked her hands through her hair and asked, "Do I look well?"

"You look great," he said with enthusiasm.

"I meant physically. I don't want my health to be an issue."

His brow knit as he gazed at her. She'd never seen him look at her in an assessing manner, and it was strangely uncomfortable. His eyes darted around her head a few times and she almost snapped "What?" while she pushed her hair around with her hand, trying to fix what he seemed unable to define.

He made a motion near the side of her head. "Your hair looks a lot longer."

He could have made a less important observation, but it was hard to think of what that might have been. "I didn't have a blow dryer or a curling iron."

"I didn't realize it was that long. It's past your shoulders."

Damn straight men and their long-hair hang-up. "Warren's not a hair stylist. I just wanted to know if I looked sick."

"No, you look good." His eyes slid to her hair again and she wanted to bean him.

"Don't speak without giving me a quick look for permission. Warren hates for meetings to go long, and he doesn't know you well enough to know he should listen to you." She put on a confident smile, nodded quickly to Aaron and boldly opened the door.

⸻

Later that afternoon, Fernando called her. "Talked to HR. They tell me you've waived over three months of vacation since you've been here."

"How much have *you* lost?" She knew the best way to get him to see the error of his ways was to point out that she was merely following his lead.

"Not that much. I take my kids to Puebla to see their great-grandmother for a week every year. And we go to Florida every spring break."

"How much vacation did you take before you had kids?"

The few moments of silence showed she'd won the point. She was feeling pretty smug.

"Well, that was in the past. HR says they're worried they'll be sued if one of us drops dead from stress and our families prove we weren't allowed to take vacations."

"We're *allowed* to," she protested. "We just can't. It's our choice. Larry Simkowitz took a month this year."

Fernando let the silence build for a few seconds, until Laurie said, "Okay, so he's hanging on by his fingernails and he wanted to get paid for the time he was job hunting. Still…no one complained."

"Warren was happy to have him gone. I think he'd have let him take our vacations just to be rid of him. But that's not the point," he said, all businesslike again. "HR is like a dog with a bone when they get on something, and they're on this. Go on your vacation and play the game."

"Fine." She sighed. "Maybe I'll go to Australia. I've always wanted to see it. Then, since I'll be halfway there…"

"Where did you learn geography?" He chuckled to himself. "I'm serious about this. You have to take a real vacation. No working. No side trips to Osaka."

"All right. I'll go see my family."

"Do something for yourself this time. How about Europe?"

"I'm not interested in Europe. It's all churches and museums. I hate that stuff."

"How about something outdoors? What do you like to do?"

"I run on the treadmill at the gym. Other than that…"

"Oh, come on. You don't have *any* interests?"

"What are your interests?"

A longish silence followed. "I like to be with my kids."

"Well, I like to be with my nieces."

"Aren't they in school?"

"Yeah, but they're home by four. I could…"

"No way. You're going to work all day while the house is empty, and call that a vacation. I'm going to plan this vacation for you, Laurie. Block off the first two weeks of December and leave it to me."

Her gulp was loud enough for him to have heard it.

—◆◆◆—

Laurie was so busy for the next two weeks it barely crossed her mind that she was going on a mystery vacation. But the Friday before she was to leave, the mystery was solved when she received a fat packet via interoffice mail. Wendy delivered it intact, tentatively offering it up. "I think this is your vacation information."

Scowling, Laurie took it from her, opening it while she continued to talk to Toshi in Osaka. "Yes, I understand that. But the rides won't be fully operational until February—if we're lucky." She got the packet open and couldn't stop herself from exclaiming, "Oh, fuck!"

She stared in amazement and disgust as the contents of the packet poured out onto her desk. Her stomach turned when she started to read about her two week cruise to seven exotic, fantastic Caribbean islands on Teddy Bear Cruises, where all your days are as sweet as honey.

CHAPTER TWO

AFTER HER SIX-HOUR flight, Laurie waited in a room the size of an airplane hangar for a chirpy, chipper woman to give the assembled masses their departure information. "We're going to send you in, one row at a time. Be ready when I call."

"I've been ready for an hour," Laurie mumbled.

"The kids got us up at five a.m.," the woman next to her said. "They were hyperventilating."

Laurie dragged herself out of her funk to focus on the family next to her, a fairly handsome dad, a fit, athletic-looking mom, and three cute kids: a boy, a girl and a baby of indeterminate classification. "I bet they're excited."

"Oh, it's bigger than Christmas. It's all we've talked about for three months. We had a big countdown calendar, didn't we, Lindsay?"

"Yeah!" the girl said, her voice filled with enough high-pitched excitement that she could have used it to etch glass. "It's today!"

"It sure is."

"You're alone?" the mom asked.

"Yes. My boss ordered me to take a vacation."

"Ordered you?" The woman looked skeptical.

"Strange, but true. I've been working on a massive project, and he found out I haven't had a vacation since I started working for Lux...the company."

"Do you work for Luxor?"

"Yes, I do." She hated to "come out" to strangers since they either wanted tickets to a park or made fun of her for working for a teddy bear, but since the woman was in line for the cruise, she could hardly throw stones. "Six years. One of the bad things about working for a family-entertainment conglomerate is that they've got a handy cruise ship to stick me on. That keeps me from working on opening the new theme park in Osaka, and that's supposed to be to everyone's benefit."

"Oh, I heard about that. I don't think I'll ever get over there, but I'd love to take the kids to the original park in LA."

"It's nice." Laurie smiled and let herself feel the spark of pleasure she got when a civilian expressed excitement about one of their parks.

The pleasure was destroyed in seconds. The woman caught her daughter's attention and said, "Lindsay, this lady works with Teddy Bear."

The little girl looked at Laurie with awe, as though she were about to bow down before her. "Teddy Bear?" she shrieked. "You know Teddy Bear?"

"Well, no," Laurie stammered. "I don't actually *know* him. He's…he's usually in…Florida and I work in California…" That should work, since the mother said they hadn't been to the original park.

"Teddy Bear?" Other, older children hesitantly approached, surrounding Laurie as though she were a creature under study. They launched questions at her with rapidity. "Have you been to his Bee Hive? Do you know Buzzy? How about his cousin Brownie? Elmer the cat?"

"No, no, really," she insisted. "I don't work near Teddy Bear. He's at the theme park…I mean, his house over here in Miami almost all the time."

The woman in charge called their row and the kids forgot about Laurie as soon as they began to move. She stayed right in her seat to allow a dozen kids and their parents and grandparents to move past her until no one in the line knew she worked with or for Teddy Bear and his ilk.

The procedure for boarding was crisp and efficient, as all Luxor brands strove to be. One thing you could count on with Luxor was efficiency, not to mention boundless friendliness. Laurie said hello to no fewer than fifteen friendly faces on her way to her cabin. Her steward caught her as she was going in and offered to do anything she needed at any time of day or night. With complete relief, she shut the door and leaned against it, hoping no one followed her in to smile and welcome her further.

She sat on the bed and took her laptop out, immediately following the instructions on the TV for ordering Wi-Fi. Her job didn't require a great deal of technical proficiency, but she was no slouch when it came to being a techie. After her tenth time trying to log on she took her computer up to the Internet Café and asked for help. A friendly, smiling young man whose ID labeled him "Terry" worked on it for several minutes, then said, "Oh, I see the problem. Your account has been locked. Did you or your husband ask us to shut off the Internet because you didn't want your kids using it?"

"No husband. No kids."

"Oh." He smiled again and continued running through procedures. "I'm trying to turn it back on, but it's still blocked. Would you mind if I worked on this a little later?" He discreetly eyed the line behind her and said quietly, "You understand we have to put non team members first, right?"

"Oh, yes, Terry, I certainly do." Terry had clearly been able to tell from her reservation that she was a team member. There was no anonymity at Luxor. You were all part of the group, and every member of the group came after every member of the public. She gritted her teeth and went back to her cabin, grumpily consigned to work on just her PDA and her smartphone. Luckily, she had a strong signal on both and she texted back and forth with her staff in Osaka, who were just getting in on Monday morning. Sometimes the sixteen-hour time difference between home and Japan worked to her advantage.

She worked until the horn blasted a noise loud enough to be heard in Cuba. "I'll call you right back," she told Toshi. Then she went to the balcony and watched the ship back out of its slip, amazed that the huge vessel could back up as easily as a cabin cruiser. The whole procedure was fascinating, and she spent a good half hour watching the skyscrapers of Miami fade into the setting sun. With a start, she called Toshi back, embarrassed that she'd been so taken with the departure that she'd forgotten all about him. They talked for a while, then the signal faltered, then stopped. She knew she wouldn't have another cell signal until they reached land: the Internet was now not a luxury, but a requirement.

Even though the public came first, she had her business card with her —the one that identified her as a vice president of the corporation. She jotted down her cabin number on it, planning to use it for dual purposes in case one of the technical guys needed to call her. She'd never used her position to get any special treatment, but today was an exception. If Terry tried to slough her off, she was going to show him that her place in the company was higher than his bosses' bosses' boss, and then some. It was a breach of every tenet of the Teddy Bear brand, but desperate times call for desperate measures.

Resolved, she strode back to the Internet Café to find Terry huddled with yet another earnest young man, both of them leaning over her laptop. "What's up?" she asked.

"Oh, hi, Ms. Nielsen," Terry said. He looked worried enough that he must have figured out she was a VIP. "We're having a heck of a time with your access."

"Well, I need it. I'll just use a desktop until you can fix it."

"Oh, sure." He walked over to a computer and instructed her in putting in her stateroom and name. But, once again, her access was denied.

It was very hard to keep her temper under control, but these guys were screwing with her life. "Terry, I don't have time to play with this. Give me an access code that will work. Now."

His eyes grew wide and he gave his companion a quick glance. "We're not allowed to let anyone use our codes. That's cause for termination."

"If you don't give me a code, the new park in Osaka might be delayed," she hissed quietly, making sure no one else could hear. "I've got things I *have* to do today. They're vital."

"I'll call someone in Miami," he said, almost shaking.

She cooled her heels for a few minutes, trying to think of a way to properly apologize for scaring the poor kid. But when he came back, he looked more puzzled than intimidated, and it slipped her mind. "Miami says you're not allowed to use the Internet, Ms. Nielsen."

"What?" Her shout made every head turn. "What?"

"I don't understand what's going on, but someone in Los Angeles put a block on your access. We're under strict orders not to let you use any of our computers." He looked sad, as though she were being fired and he was delivering the bad news. "I'm genuinely sorry."

She walked over to Terry's comrade and held out her hands. He put the laptop in them and she started to leave, then remembered her manners and said, "I'm very sorry for losing my temper. I've been under a lot of pressure. Please don't take it personally."

"I understand," he said, his smile back in place. "Have a super sweet day, filled with honey!"

———

It took a long time for her to calm down enough to convince herself not to jump overboard and swim to shore. Yes, she'd probably drown, but at least she'd have gone down with a fight. It was absolutely infuriating that this was supposed to be relaxing. It was like being forced to stand in the corner for two weeks. Human Resources was populated by people who'd never had a deadline in their lives, and they didn't know a thing about pressure. She'd clashed with HR too many times to count, and they were obviously using this vacation gambit to put her in her place. But no one in HR would be humiliated on two continents if the theme part didn't open on time. Only she'd get that honor.

Thinking about it just agitated her, but what else was there to do with no phone, and no internet? Her cabin, though nice enough, was small, and after a while the walls were closing in on her. With nothing to do until her eight-thirty dinner reservation, she went onto the pool deck and found an empty deck chair. Turning it to face the water, she thought about ways to smooth the opening of the park—her park—in Osaka. She was achingly lonely, like she was the only person around who realized how difficult it was to make tough things look easy. Suddenly, it hit her. She was among friends. Everyone working on the ship knew how hard it was, and it was their job to make sure the passengers did not. That's what made Luxor the respected brand it was, and she was inordinately proud to be one of the busy bees making sure the hive worked to perfection.

———

She'd filled out a few questionnaires about the cruise while waiting to board, and she'd made sure to request a single table. To her dismay, she was shown to a table with nine other travelers. "I requested to sit alone," she whispered to the captain.

"Yes, miss," he said in his soft Croatian accent. "But my supervisor informed me you should be seated with other guests who do not have children."

Not willing to make a scene, she gave him a tight smile and acquiesced. She sat down and met everyone: a young couple from LA who also worked for The Bear, as the cognoscenti called it; a group of three sisters from Toledo who loved all things Bear related and couldn't understand why there weren't more people without kids on the cruise; and four men who didn't explicitly announce they were gay but could have been picked out as Friends of Dorothy by the most oblivious passerby.

Everyone at the table was nice enough, and they all desperately wanted to converse, but it was very tough to make a contribution. Small talk was named that for a reason. People seemed to need it, but why? Who really cared where these strangers were from? Were they going to be friends after this trip? No. The last thing she needed was another person in her life that she'd be forced to ignore. She didn't even have time to call her mother! But maybe one of them had internet access and she could… No, somehow Fernando would find out and next he'd send her to a monastery.

Every person said something about him or herself, and when it came to her turn, she said, "I'm Laurie, and I'm trying to get my life back together after a"—she fixed each person with a cold stare—"a bunch of people messed me up. In the— Where I was for a while— They told me it's good to talk about what happened." She let her eyes dart from one set of startled eyes to another. "But talking isn't gonna change the past." She folded her hands neatly on the white tablecloth and mumbled, "Next." After a few minutes the rest of her tablemates found safe subjects to banter about, but for some reason, they studiously avoided her.

CHAPTER THREE

THE NEXT EVENING, the phone in her room rang right before dinner. "Hello, Laurie," Fernando said.

"What's wrong? Her heart raced, sure something catastrophic had occurred.

"I had to waste ten valuable minutes trying to smooth some ruffled feathers in Miami today."

"Miami?"

"Yeah. At the cruise-line offices. Guess why they're angry."

She didn't reply, knowing he liked to play cat and mouse.

"That's right, my friend. Some people don't like an outsider wasting their time, telling them how to improve their product."

"I'm not an outsider. I'm part of the Luxor team!"

"You don't know the first thing about the cruise line."

"I know plenty about F and B and hotel management. I was just trying to share some of my thoughts."

"I'm sure you were. But the theme parks are a different animal. We do things our way and they do things theirs. Those people are busy, and they don't have time to talk to an outsider. Besides, you're on vacation. No more work."

"Fine," she said, chastened.

"And don't even think about going to the buffet for your meals. I'm getting a report on your attendance in the dining room."

"Fernando, I'm here. Isn't that enough?"

"No. I want you to learn how to be a civilized adult. Learn how to talk about more than business. Play bingo; go to the bar; read a book. Just do something other than harass the staff."

"I wasn't harassing them," she grumbled. "It was that F and B manager, wasn't it? She was a bitch."

"It's her food and her beverages. Stay out of it. Now, go have fun."

Fun is work, work is fun. She thought it, but had the prudence not to say it.

—⁓—

At dinner, everyone dutifully asked her if she'd enjoyed her day in San Juan. When she said she hadn't gotten off the boat, no one asked a follow-up question, and she was left to eat her dinner. She intentionally stopped by the head waiter's area on the way out to ensure her attendance was noted.

—⁓—

Up before dawn the next day, she tried to trick herself into falling asleep again, but it was a waste of time She decided to go to the library to find something to read. She hadn't read fiction since college, and wasn't very fond of it then, but she figured as she had nothing else to do, she might as well give it a try.

Even though she was looking for a novel, the business section called to her. Regrettably, the management books were written for a general audience and gave elementary advice. Instead, she picked up the first mystery her hand landed on. After a quick breakfast, she went out to the pool deck to read.

She'd barely passed page ten when her head dropped to the right and she fell asleep, remaining in that exact pose until three. Despite a crick in her neck from her slumped position, she had to admit she felt a little more energetic after the longest stretch of sleep she'd had in weeks.

—⁓—

Laurie hadn't gotten to her position in the company by failing to follow orders. She decided to stop fighting, to listen to Fernando, and to try to relax. But how do you learn to relax when you've spent your entire adult life trying not to? It took a massive dedication to ignore her needs for the good of the project, but now that the project was off limits, her body started to speak, and she was forced to listen. Every part of her ached, and she slowly realized she wasn't sick at all, she was exhausted. Even "exhausted" was too weak a word for it, but she didn't have a better one. If Osaka was off limits, then getting herself ready for the final push would be the new goal.

She attacked the goal with her usual élan. She needed to fuel her body with sleep, and sleep she did. She slept at sea, she slept at port, she slept during the napkin-folding classes and the dance instructions. She slept on the deck at the adults-only pool for so many hours, she was surprised someone didn't call the ship's doctor. But after a solid week of nothing but eating and sleeping, she woke up early one morning, ready to begin her vacation.

At work, she was most concerned with looking professional. That had become the only thing she cared about, but she decided it was time to pamper her body, to get it ready to dive back into the shark's tank. Having made an appointment in the spa, she treated herself to a facial and a soothing massage, something she never took time to do. That night she dressed more carefully, spent a few more minutes fixing her hair, and put on some makeup. By the time she got to the dining room at least four men had noticed her, and the table captain so obviously checked her out it was funny. That felt surprisingly good. Rare, but good.

—•—

There were plenty of things to do after dinner, but sitting out by the pool, watching the moonlight glisten on the water was her favorite. It was warm and breezy, and the wind in her hair felt sensual, almost erotic. It had been so very long since anyone had caressed her that she'd almost forgotten what a gentle touch on her neck felt like.

With relatively nothing on her mind, she let her thoughts drift to her body and the dearth of touch it had experienced. She concentrated hard and tried to feel her erogenous zones. Her nipples stiffened against her bra and she rhythmically squeezed her vulva a few times. Everything was still there, but it had all fallen into a coma.

Actually, that was a little disingenuous. There wasn't a huge difference between now and any other time in her life. Sex had never been a driving force, and there was little reason to think that would change. Living with a man had been very satisfying, and being a couple made life easier on many, many levels. But the sex had been an add-on that didn't make or break the relationship.

It was uncomfortable to think about how often she'd lied to cover up her lack of interest, but the truth was that she had sex primarily to please men. It wasn't that she didn't enjoy it. It was really nice sometimes, and pretty nice fairly often. But her boyfriends always, always wanted it much more than she did. Her adult sex life had consisted mostly of boyfriends pressing for sex and her whittling down their needs. If they wanted it every day she tried to get it down to every other day. If that worked, then she'd try for every third. There had always been an unspoken negotiation going on, and she was both a party and the arbitrator. It really wasn't fair, but great sex was more likely when it was less frequent—at least for her. She was certain none of her past boyfriends had shared that idea.

Her sister the sex fiend had busted her many times, prying, in Laurie's opinion, about her lack of enthusiasm. Their mom had even joined in, asking if she might be a lesbian. But that wasn't it. That would have been apparent by now. The simple fact was that her drive just wasn't strong. Maybe it was hormonal, or biochemical, or just the way she was made. But even though she was feeling more sexual than she'd felt in a very long time, she knew she would go back to her cabin alone and go right to sleep.

—*~*—

Early the next morning, when the ship pulled into St. Maarten, Laurie got up and peered through her window to see a lovely tropical island surrounded by water a shade of turquoise she didn't know was possible. Energized, she put on a pair of shorts, a nice blouse, and an attractive pair of sandals, and spent some extra time fixing her hair. She looked good. Darned good. It was her vacation and she was going to find someone to at least buy her a drink. Teddy Bear ruled her world, but she couldn't anthropomorphize him into a decent date, and it had been too long since she'd had one. Luckily, she'd have to leave said date at four o'clock, and wouldn't have to have more than sparkling conversation—if she remembered how to do that.

It was just eight when she disembarked, and the day was bright and clear, with a salty-fresh scent in the air. Even though it was early, all of the shops were open in the tiny mall next to the cruise-passenger terminal in Philipsburg. They were quite upscale and she found a store that sold the small crystal animals that her mom liked. With Christmas coming, she was tempted, but she hated to buy anything without comparison shopping. That need led her to an Internet Café where she did the research, then read her personal mail. She couldn't get into her work e-mail thanks to Fernando the Evil, and no one was at the office in LA or Osaka at this hour, so she decided to go for a brisk walk like the ones her doctor had been recommending ever since she'd started having heart palpitations a year ago.

Laurie headed for the waterline to check out the short piers full of sailboats. Growing up in Cincinnati, she'd been on her share of houseboats and small speedboats, but had no experience with sailboats. For some reason they fascinated her, and she tried to compare one with the next as she walked along.

One boat she happened upon was decidedly different from its neighbors. *The Flying Dutchwoman* looked like two big, enclosed kayaks held together by a wide cabin of some sort. It resembled a spider or some other bug. Or maybe something from a sci-fi show. Its other attribute was a woman lying on a large piece of material stretched out between the front of the two kayak-like pods. At first Laurie assumed it was a regular owner taking a nap on a lovely day, but there was a sign hung on the side advertising "full day / half day / overnights" with a phone number and a website address. A boat for hire? What kind of crazy business practice was it to have an employee sleeping on the job? Or maybe she was the boss. Either way, the person was lazy and showed a complete lack of salesmanship. No one wanted to wake the staff to ask about going on a sail. She couldn't stop herself from saying, "This looks more like *The Sleeping Dutchwoman*."

The woman tilted her cap to expose her eyes, then raised a hand to shield them from the sun. Expressionless, she said, "Did you wake me for a reason?"

Laurie spent just a moment figuring out her archetype. If she was the owner, she was far from serious about her business, and you'd have to be very serious to earn enough to buy such a big craft. She was probably one of those women who dabbled at things. Pretty, bright, and talented, with lots of family money. There were hundreds of women like her in LA. Laurie'd met a ton of them when she went to Hollywood parties with Colin, her last boyfriend. This particular indolent woman was probably between advanced degrees, or maybe her father was trying to teach her a lesson by making her work for a while…after giving her a huge boat.

"I was just wondering why everyone else is over at the passenger terminal trying to drum up business. Does your way work better?"

The woman lowered the bill on her white baseball cap and let her head rest on her hands, which she'd linked behind her head, providing a low pillow. "I'm not looking for business."

"Your sign says you are. This is your boat, isn't it?"

"Yes, it is. Are you from the government? I have a license and I pay my taxes." She lifted her hat just an inch and said, "Or do you want to go for a sail?"

"Well, I wouldn't want to put you out…"

The woman dropped her hat again, completely covering her eyes. "Okay. Bye bye."

It was all she could do to not jump onto the boat, take that hat off her, and slap her with it. "Are you serious? How do you make a living with that kind of work ethic?"

"By sailing. I asked if you wanted to go."

"You certainly don't seem very enthusiastic about it."

The woman finally sat up and took a few seconds to settle herself. She crossed her legs and rested her elbows on her knees while gazing at Laurie with a puzzled look. "Who are you? Is this a joke?"

"I'm a potential customer."

"Everyone in Philipsburg is a potential customer, but you're the first one who's ever harassed me for taking a nap on my own boat. Do you hate naps that much?"

"No." She stood there for a second, thinking, "Well, yes, I do, to be honest. You sleep at night, you work during the day."

The woman showed a full, rich smile. The one she'd probably used to get her father or older married lover to give her the boat.

"You're funny. I'm not sure you mean to be, but you're funny. What ship are you on?"

"Who said I'm on a ship?"

"I did." She laughed at her own lame joke. "You're too pale to be local. You're either on a ship or a tourist just walking around. Which is it?"

"*Kingdom of Denmark*," Laurie said automatically, having noticed that ship in port. She wasn't embarrassed to work for Luxor, but she was a little embarrassed to be a single, adult woman on a ship named *The Teddy Bear*.

"Let's go for a sail. Half price."

"Half price? How can you make a living doing that?"

"Fine. Full price. Want to go?"

"How much is full price?" Listening to herself for a moment, she realized she was being an idiot. Not everyone was as focused as she was, even though she'd never understood why. "Never mind. I'll go. I don't care how much it costs."

"You are very, very funny." The woman scrambled to her feet, gracefully leapt onto one of the kayaks, then onto the dock, landing right next to Laurie. She extended her hand. "Kaat-ya Hoog-e-boom."

Must be a St. Maarten name. Were they called Maartenians? That was probably something to research later. "Laurie Nielsen."

"Swedish?"

"Half Norwegian."

Kaatje chuckled, clearly finding herself very funny. "I'll take you anyway."

They walked down the pier until they reached the back of the boat. Laurie was behind Kaatje and she spent the seconds available checking her out. Her opinion of her was changing, and she was trying to sort out her impressions.

Kaatje was probably gay or at least bisexual, and that had led Laurie to read her entirely wrong. She had that hard-to-define vibe some lesbians give off. An "I'm not trying to impress you" attitude that made her seem slightly haughty.

Adding to the puzzle, Kaatje was pretty enough to be a jet-setter, with her long, glossy dark hair and striking features. And she certainly had the build of a rich girl—tall, very thin and angular. But her excited smile when they decided to go sailing made that seemingly haughty façade disappear.

"Have you been on a cat before?"

"If this is a cat, no I haven't. Actually I've never been on a sailboat."

"Then you are in luck. A catamaran is, in my opinion, sometimes faster and always a lot more fun than a regular sailboat." Kaatje jumped on board and steadied Laurie as she followed. "I'll give you a very quick tour. This is the cockpit." She pointed at the thick vinyl-covered cushions in a U shape. "You can sit there"—she slapped the deck a foot and a half higher than the cushions—"or here. You can also go up where I was trying to sleep, but then you can't listen to me talk, and I'm pretty interesting."

Definitely a lesbian. She had that vaguely flirty attitude that could easily be explained away as mere friendliness, but it could also mean she was hitting on her. Lesbians could get away with much more of that than guys could, and some of them were shameless about exploiting it. "You sail this big boat by yourself?'

"I can, but it's easier if I have an assistant. I had one during high season, but she left a couple of weeks ago."

"Are you sure you can do it alone?"

With a smug smile Kaatje said, "Positive. I could use some help casting off, but if you don't want to, I can find somebody to help."

"I'll do it if you tell me how."

"If I don't tell you how to cast off properly, you'll get left on the dock and then I can't charge you full price. So, it's in my best interest to train you well."

"It's in your best interest to stay awake and try to find clients." She batted her eyes and gave her a big Teddy Bear smile.

CHAPTER FOUR

LAURIE WAS NOTHING if not fastidious about following directions, and she was a stellar cast-off mate. She nimbly hopped back onto the boat at the exact time Kaatje told her to, and managed to balance herself with the aid of Kaatje's steadying hand. "Well done! You've got good balance."

"I had years of gymnastics training. It's paid off."

"Ready to head out?"

She looked up at Kaatje who had climbed onto a wide bench that faced a big wheel and a dozen black gauges. "Yeah, but I won't be able to talk to you."

"Come on up. You can sit right here." She patted the seat next to her, trying not to look like she was flirting. When Laurie hesitated, Kaatje pointed to several relatively level spots that surrounded her. "Or here, or here, or here."

"Can I stand behind you?" There was a flat surface directly behind Kaatje's seat.

"Sure. But you should probably take your sandals off. The deck can get slippery."

Laurie slipped out of her sandals, then climbed up and stood just to the right of Kaatje. With a big, genuine smile affixed to her mouth, she looked as interested and engaged as it was possible for a human to be. "Did I tell you I've never been sailing?"

"Sure did." Kaatje expertly steered the boat away from the docks, and the wide bay opened up before them. "As soon as we get a few hundred meters out, I can cut the engine and we can really sail."

"Cool. Very cool."

While the front of the boat dipped and rose in the swiftly deepening, quickly darkening blue water, Laurie watched intently, as though studying for a test. When they were clear of the channel, Kaatje stood up and cut the engine, leaving them in silence.

"This is great," Laurie said, just a second before a wave dropped her onto her seat. "Whoa!"

"You've got to stay alert. After a while you'll unconsciously follow the cues the boat gives you." Kaatje hopped onto the top deck and started to unfurl the very large sail. In just a few minutes she had it properly raised, and after securing it she sat back down. "I'd suggest sitting down, or holding on."

"Really?"

Kaatje lowered her dark glasses so that Laurie could see she was serious. "Really. Ready to rock?"

Laurie looked like she was having second thoughts, but she nodded decisively. "Yeah. Totally ready."

Kaatje turned the boat to let the wind fill the sail and catapult them forward. This was when sailing was particularly sweet. With a novice on board, who was about to get a thrill that might make her into a sailing junkie. The first time was the best.

"Whoo!" Laurie giggled while holding onto a couple of pieces of metal that were firmly anchored to the deck. "This is fast!"

"Want me to slow down? I can. Easily." *Don't do it. You'll love it if you give in and let it flow.*

"No. This is fun. I just have to get used to it."

"When you're moving around, the best things to grab are the stays. They're strong enough to take all of your weight." She reached behind herself and grabbed a bunch of very thin stainless steel wires that ran down to the side of the boat. "These hold the mast up and keep it in place. They're the backbone of the boat." She pointed at the back of the boat. "There are stays right there too. Grab them when you need to. They'll never let you down."

"Okay. I think I've got it. You know, the only times I've been on a boat, I've been on a big houseboat cruising down a slow river. That's a lot different than this."

"Ahh. I like that, too. I'm from Amsterdam and we spend a lot of time on boats of all kinds."

"Cool. That's what I'd expect from a flying Dutchwoman."

"Yeah. That's me. I like to go fast."

"I want to learn to. Don't hold back. I like to make myself adapt."

"Are you sure?" Kaatje didn't want to scare her, but they could have a lot of fun if Laurie was as game as she seemed. And there was nothing better than showing a beginner how fantastic sailing was.

"I can take it. Let 'er rip."

"Okay." She moved the wheel a little bit and seconds later one of the hulls was almost airborne.

"Holy crap!" Laurie yelled. "The thing's in the air!"

"That's a hull," Kaatje said calmly. "Come here. Let me show you how to have some fun."

Holding onto anything she could grab, Laurie moved around so she was right next to Kaatje, standing duck-footed with knees bent. It was a real charge to see someone who looked so frightened agree to do whatever she was told.

"Sit on the deck and put your legs over the side."

"You're crazy!"

"No, no, it'll be fun. Really."

Very tentatively Laurie followed instructions. She managed to get one leg up, but a major dip had her sprawled across Kaatje.

"I'll help you," Kaatje said, her voice loud to compete with the cresting waves. She jumped onto the deck while holding the wheel with one hand. Then she grabbed the waistband of Laurie's shorts, holding onto her like a mother cat would a kitten. That stability allowed Laurie to right herself and get her legs over the deck. "Hold onto the lifelines," Kaatje commanded.

"I'm holding on like rigor mortis has already set in."

"You're perfectly safe. The wind is brisk today but it's steady. This is my favorite kind of day—wet and wooly. I'm really glad we came out."

"Me, too. This is a lot more fun than sitting on that ship."

Kaatje didn't comment. There was nothing she could say about cruise ships that was complimentary. She just jumped back up to her seat, pulled her cap a little lower, and kept guiding the boat along the waves.

They skimmed along for a half hour, with Laurie squealing like a baby every few minutes when water washed over her legs or they bottomed out in a deep trough. She seemed giddy with delight, and all of her previous stuffiness was gone. Finally, Kaatje slowed the boat down and they moved along at a very moderate pace. "I didn't ask if you were wearing sunblock. You are, right?"

"On my face."

"Go down below and grab some. It's in a cubby on the starboard side." When Laurie blinked at her, she added, "The right."

"Okay." She went below and came back a moment later. "That's a pretty impressive spread of food you've got down there. Expecting company?"

"Yeah." Kaatje let the sail billow while Laurie carefully applied sunblock to her wet legs. "Want a towel?"

"No, I'm good. I'm drying fast. Who are you expecting?"

"The people who reserved an all-day sail. Six of them."

"Is that why you weren't looking for business?"

"Partly. It's almost impossible to fill the boat with people who didn't sign up with a cruise ship or via my site."

"Isn't it better to have a couple or a single?"

"No, not really. It's often more trouble than it's worth. For one or two I might as well stay in bed."

"You're losing money on me?"

"No. The people who reserved pre-paid."

"And…and you're going to keep their money?" She was sputtering with what looked like indignation.

"Maybe." Now Kaatje was getting annoyed. If some cruise-ship day-tripper thought she could climb aboard and dictate policies…best of luck.

"Maybe what?"

"You ask a lot of questions. Are you planning on going into the business?" This woman was so self-righteous it was comical.

"No," Laurie said as she continued to vigorously rub sunblock onto every exposed part of her arms and legs. "I'm just surprised you'd keep the money, given that they didn't get to sail."

"I don't like to screw people, but I don't appreciate being screwed, either. If they're nice and they have a good excuse, I'll just charge them for my expenses. If they're idiots"—she made a cutting motion across her throat—"their money is now mine."

"Still, they didn't get to sail."

This was getting serious. It was time to lay out the facts. "I should give up six hundred dollars because they changed their minds or they weren't in the mood? How do I recoup that?"

"You could go out on the dock…"

Kaatje knew her voice had grown deep and strong, but there was no reason to sugar coat this. This woman was questioning every tenet of her business…of herself. "That's for those huge party boats where they drag you out to the most crowded spot, let you splash around in the sea for less than an hour, then drag you back…while letting you drink their watered down rum punch that gives rum a bad name. No serious sailors stand on the dock." She could have spit just thinking about being in that class of boat. "That has nothing to do with sailing. Their big, belching diesel engines pollute these waters at an amazing clip. I'd give half my earnings to get those monstrosities out of the water."

"I didn't know…"

"No, but that didn't stop you from having a very strong opinion about me and my work ethic." She leaned over so Laurie could see her eyes behind her dark glasses. "An opinion that couldn't be further from the truth."

"I'm sorry." Laurie put a hand on her shoulder. "That was stupid of me."

"Yeah, it was. This is *my* business and I take it very seriously. I motored over to the dock and waited for an hour. Then I told every guy I knew to keep a lookout for the Harris family. But if one of those punks saw them, they'd tell them they didn't know me. Then they'd lure them onto their boat."

"That's unconscionable!"

Kaatje shrugged. "That's what happens. Those guys get a couple of bucks for every person they deliver. It's dog eat dog."

"You waited a whole hour?" Laurie asked, her voice softening.

"Of course. Then I waited here at the dock for another hour in case they got mixed up and came looking for me. I've also checked my e-mail several times. That's what a professional does."

"You weren't just sleeping. You were waiting."

"In the hot sun. I don't like to turn the air-conditioner on unless I have clients, so I stayed on the trampoline to get a breeze."

"I'm sorry they screwed you."

"It happens fairly often. But I don't let little disappointments like that ruin my day. That's not how I live my life."

"I'm really sorry," Laurie said, pursing her lips while gazing into Kaatje's eyes. "I had no right to judge you."

"That's true." All traces of pique disappeared. Laurie was pretty stiff and very self-righteous, but she was also plucky and really pretty. Plucky and pretty made up for a lot. "I forgive you. And I might even reduce what the no-show Harris family owes me by what I'll charge you. Happy?"

"Very."

She actually looked like she'd be happy to pay more to make up for the no-shows. That was odd, but also strangely attractive.

"It's eleven o'clock," Kaatje announced after they'd skimmed across the waves for a while. "Do you want a snack now, or would you rather wait until after we snorkel?"

Laurie waved her hand in front of her body and made a face. "Oh, we don't have to go snorkeling."

"You don't want to?"

"Well, I've never been…"

"It's easy. And fun."

"I don't want to put you out."

Cocking her head and looking puzzled, Kaatje said, "Why would going snorkeling put me out? It's one of my favorite things to do. But if you'd rather just sail, we can sail."

A tentative grin showed. "It's not hard?"

"Can you swim?"

"Sure."

"Then it's not hard. Let's head over to Pinel Island. It should be free now."

"How is an island free?"

"Oh, the big diesel boats go there, but they leave by eleven. The next shift comes at one. We've got two hours." They set sail again, getting closer and closer to a small island with a white sand beach filled with sun-worshipers.

"It looks crowded."

"Yeah, the beach side can be. There's a ferry that runs until dusk and they have some overpriced restaurants. We'll go to the side where the tourists don't go." She maneuvered the boat to veer away from the crowds. Then they headed for the nearly deserted part without a beach.

When they were sailing, the water had been indigo, but as they neared the island it lightened appreciably until it was now a beautiful, clear turquoise.

"This is a great spot," Kaatje said. "You're gonna love it."

It was time to spit it out, but Laurie was suddenly tongue tied. "Uhm, is it…I mean…should I be…is it dangerous?"

"Dangerous?" Kaatje looked blank. "How?"

Tell the truth. It sounds stupid, but you've got to do it. "I've never been in the ocean. I don't know what's"—she looked over the side of the boat —"down there."

Kaatje leaned back against the lifelines and looked curiously at Laurie. "You've never been in the ocean? Where do you live?"

"Uhm…Los Angeles."

Laughing gently, Kaatje said, "Isn't there an ocean there?"

"Yeah, there is, but nobody goes in the water." It was hard not to sound defensive, but Angelenos didn't go into the water.

"Huh." Kaatje still looked at her with suspicion. "Isn't that where *Baywatch* is?"

"That's a TV show, not real life."

Kaatje kept staring at her.

"Yes," she allowed. "That's where *Baywatch* was filmed. People *do* go in the ocean, but I've only walked along the shore a few times. It's cold and the last time I got tar on my feet."

"Tar? From what?"

"Oil spills, I guess. It's disgusting."

"Well, we don't have tar floating around. And the fish are almost all friendly."

"Almost all?"

"Some things don't like to be touched or poked. But I'll point them out to you."

"Er…I don't know." She looked over the side again. "What about sharks?"

"What about 'em?"

She looked at the aquamarine water cautiously. "Are they…down there?"

Kaatje laughed. "Yeah. They don't do well on land. They're almost always in the water."

"Come on! You're just taunting me."

"Look, I can't guarantee there isn't a shark or two around here, but these aren't the conditions sharks like. If you get bit by one it's usually because you're in shallow water and the billowing sand obscures its vision. It thinks you're food."

"Shallow water?"

"Yeah. That's most common. But out here we're in about twenty feet. They'll only bite you if you're spear fishing and dragging around a bunch of…bleeding fish." She hesitated, then added, "Probably."

"Damn it! Are you confident or not?"

"Entirely. I dive or snorkel or surf nearly every day. I've never known anyone who was attacked. But I don't like to sugarcoat the truth. Strange things can happen."

Smirking, Laurie said, "Is that your spiel for liability purposes?"

"No. I'm an honest person." She took off her glasses and Laurie looked into her eyes. "I'm also prudent. I'd never willingly endanger a person if I wasn't confident.

"Well, it still looks pretty deep." She peeked over the side again, barely able to see the bottom.

"It's up to you. But you're on vacation, right?"

"Right."

"And you've never been in the ocean, right?"

"Right." She started to nod sheepishly. "I know. I should take some risks."

"No, not risks. Just live. Nobody's going to give you back this day if you waste it."

"Fine." Laurie stood up and straightened her shorts. "Oh. I don't have a swimsuit."

"Mmm, are you willing to wear your shorts in the water?"

"Sure. But…" She pulled her shirt away from her neck and looked inside. "I have a nice bra on and I don't want to ruin it."

"I have a rash guard you can wear." Her eyes scanned up and down Laurie's body. "It'll be tight, but that's how it should fit."

"You don't have to remind me that I've put on weight." She reminded herself of that…nearly every day.

"The shirt should fit like skin. I'm just warning you so you don't think it's too small."

"Okay. If you don't mind I'd like to borrow it. I'm a little afraid to ask why I'd get a rash, but…"

"They're mostly for surfing. If you get dumped against rocks or rough sand they can protect you a little. Out here it just lets you use less sunblock."

"I'm all in favor of that."

—⁂—

A few minutes later Laurie emerged from the cabin wearing Kaatje's skin-tight, long-sleeved orange rash guard over her khaki shorts. "Is this really supposed to fit this tightly?" She plucked at it hard to create a few inches of space between it and her body.

"Yeah, it's supposed to be snug. And it'll keep you a little warmer."

"Is the water cold?"

"Not compared to the Pacific. It's probably seventy-eight or seventy-nine." She stood and shucked her shorts, revealing tanned, muscled thighs. Her turquoise shirt was very thin and had a label on one of the breast pockets that claimed it provided SPF 50. "I think I'll leave my shirt on. I hate putting sunblock on my back. I always miss a spot."

"You wear sunblock? With that tan?"

"Yeah, I do. I tan easily, but this sun can burn anyone."

Laurie kept looking into the water, clearly a little anxious. "What do we do now?"

"Now I spend a few minutes telling you about what we'll see. Then I'll explain how your mask and snorkel works. Then, when you're seriously bored, we'll get into the water. How's that?"

"Good. I think." She jumped when a fish leapt out of the water, making a splash. Kaatje politely did not laugh.

———

After all of the warnings, tips and advice, Laurie sat on the top step of a short ladder off the back of the boat. Kaatje was already in the water, smiling and calmly urging Laurie to join her. "Just jump in and get acclimated. Then you can put your mask on."

"Shouldn't I do that now?"

"No, because you might knock it off when you jump in. This way is better. Trust me. I've done this several thousand times with people from four to over eighty."

"Okay." She was holding onto the ladder rails with both hands, and was afraid of looking stupid if Kaatje had to pry her hands off to get her into the water. Trying to remember what it was like when she was a kid learning to dive, she took a breath and jumped, immediately popping up out of the water. "It's warm!"

"It is. But this is a few degrees cooler than it has been. We've had a few cloudy days in a row."

"These fins are great!" Laurie bubbled with excitement as she kicked herself in a circle, no longer fearful.

"They're very helpful. They can let you go much farther and faster than your bare feet can take you. Now, clear your mask like I showed you and put it on."

They both dipped their masks in the water, and put them on. Then Kaatje adjusted the snorkel, making it perfect for Laurie's mouth. "Let's go."

She slid fully under the water and Laurie followed her. But just as Kaatje started to kick, Laurie popped back up to the surface, screaming.

"What's wrong?" Kaatje's worried look was visible even with her mask on.

"There's a whole world down there!"

Kaatje laughed. "I know. And it's fantastic. Come on, let me show you." She reached for Laurie's hand.

Laurie put her hand in Kaatje's slightly larger one, then put her face underwater again. She wanted to talk, to explain how astounded she was, but she stayed under and marveled—marveled at the clarity of the water. the nearness of the fish, their amazing colors and the overpowering feeling that she was no longer in her own world. She'd entered another, hitherto unseen world that vibrantly pulsed with life, and she couldn't have been more amazed if the fish started speaking.

After leading her towards the rocks for a few minutes, Kaatje stopped and popped her head above water. Laurie followed suit and began babbling. "There's a million fish! And they come right up to you like they don't even see you! Is it always like this or is this some really, really special place?"

Kaatje beamed a smile at her. "The snorkeling around St. Maarten isn't great, to be honest. But this is the best spot I've found around here. The reef draws every kind of fish in the area. I thought you'd like it."

"Like it? Like it? I love it!" Was she kidding? "Like" wasn't even in the ballpark. Did everyone know this whole other world existed? Was it like this in LA? If it was, why wasn't everyone snorkeling every weekend? This must be some world-famous place and Kaatje was just jaded.

"I've got my ID pictures here." Kaatje indicated the small, waterproof fish identification charts she had on a coiled band around her wrist. "When we get closer to the rocks we'll be able to stop and stay in one place for a while. I'll point out every species I know."

"Great. Let's go, we're wasting time." Laurie ducked under the gentle waves and started kicking for all she was worth.

—m—

After a while, Kaatje tapped Laurie's shoulder and pointed at her stomach, signaling that it was lunchtime. Laurie hesitated, but nodded. They swam back towards the boat, and when they reached it, she bobbed in the water while taking off her fins. "That was probably the best ten minutes of my life."

"We were out for an hour."

"No way!"

"Yep. A full hour. I bet your stomach knows how long we were out."

"You know, I'm hungrier than I can ever remember being. I'm gonna eat everything that insane Harris family left for me."

———

Laurie didn't fulfill her promise, but she made a good dent in the repast meant for six. "This food is fantastic," she said for the fourth time. "Did you make it?"

"No, no. I buy it from a deli on the French side. They're the best on the island."

"You don't have to provide such a good lunch, do you? You won't ever see most of these people again, right?"

"Right. I get about a ten percent return rate, and that's almost entirely from people who come to the island every year. Very few cruisers come back. The details fade with their memories of the cruise."

"Why do you do it?"

"Do what?"

"Offer such a nice lunch. This had to cost a lot."

"Well," Kaatje sat back against the cushion and said thoughtfully, "I run my business in a way that I'm proud of. I make a lot less than the guys who run the big boats, but that doesn't matter as much to me as feeling fair and honest. Plus, I have to eat the food, too, you know, and I like a nice meal."

"That's cute." Laurie smiled happily, taking another forkful of her shrimp salad. "You seem like a good person. I'm really glad we went sailing today."

"I am too. Sometimes my clients are big pains in the butt. It's always nice when someone appreciates my ocean."

"Oh, I'm more than appreciative. I might even take another vacation before five more years tick away."

"Five years? You haven't had a vacation in five years?" Kaatje's expression showed her astonishment.

"No, I haven't. I've been really, really busy."

Her poker face was back in place when Kaatje mildly said, "I'm glad that vacation brought you to St. Maarten."

—⁓—

Kaatje cleaned the galley while Laurie took a nap on the trampoline. She was fast asleep when Kaatje softly called her name. "Laurie. Laurie."

Blinking slowly, she opened her eyes, then stretched luxuriantly. "Oh, what a nice place to nap."

"I thought you didn't approve of naps." Kaatje's eyes twinkled at her jibe.

"Sometimes you can't fight hard enough to stay awake. This is one of those days." She sat up and tried to straighten her hair, but the salt had rendered it the consistency of straw. "Can we snorkel again?"

"Sure. But only for fifteen or twenty minutes. I like to allow for an hour cushion to get back to port. Let's sail back towards the harbor. There's a good spot that'll let us get back to the dock in fifteen minutes, even if the wind dies."

"Sounds great. Can I sit on the rail again?"

Kaatje smiled broadly. "Absolutely."

—⁓—

Their snorkeling was brief, but Laurie spotted a big sea turtle that entranced her thoroughly. Kaatje almost had to restrain her from following it to points unknown. They got back onto the boat and Kaatje said, "I don't normally offer this, but why don't you go below and take a quick shower. No one likes to be crusted in salt."

"I'd argue, but I'm desperate for clean water. Is it…?"

"Take a left at the table, go down a few stairs and the bathroom's right there."

Laurie went below and took a remarkably fast shower, one just long enough to wash off the salt. Then she put her own clothes back on and stood in the doorway of the cabin, combing her hair with the brush she'd providentially carried in her purse. "I feel fantastic," she said. "Truly fantastic."

"Seeing you comb your hair makes me jealous. I'm gonna at least rinse mine." Kaatje took a liter bottle that she'd stowed in the locker by the captain's chair. "I always bring a bottle of fresh water. The salt can be harsh."

She'd obviously done this many times, bending over the railing to rinse her long, dark hair. "Much better," she declared, throwing her hair back with a sharp snap of her head. She dashed down into the cabin, then came back with a wide comb. "Nice," she purred, combing it until it slipped through without a snag. "I keep thinking I should cut my hair, just to save time, but I've never had it short. I'm not sure I'd like it."

"It's really nice," Laurie said, realizing she'd been staring at her. What was there to stare at? It was just hair! In the distance, massive horns tooted the first ten notes of Teddy Bear's theme song, "Sweet As Honey." Laurie froze. "What's that noise?"

"*The Teddy Bear* is casting off."

"What?" She could feel the blood rush to her head, making her faint. "That means there's like a half hour or something before it leaves, right?"

"No. They blow the horn as they start to back out. Why? Your boat doesn't leave until an hour from now."

Laurie gulped past a massive knot in her throat. "You know how I told you I was on *Kingdom of Denmark*?"

"Yeah."

"I lied."

—⁂—

Laurie had the number for Luxor cruise operations in Miami on her smartphone, but they were too far out to get a signal. She was about to throw it overboard when Kaatje said, "I can usually get a signal, even out here. Use my phone." She took it from a holder by the wheel and tossed it to Laurie.

Laurie was on the verge of hyperventilating, and the boat rocked and dipped as they raced back to the dock, but she managed to thank Kaatje for the kindness.

They were within sight of the bay when Laurie finally got connected to the appropriate person. "No, we wait for no one," a manager said. "No one. Ever."

Laurie slumped down in her seat, utterly defeated.

"Hey, don't feel bad. People miss the boat all of the time."

"You don't understand. I work for Luxor." When Kaatje looked blank, she added, "Teddy Bear's parent company."

"Still, that's a big ship. Who'll know?"

"Everyone," Laurie said miserably. "My boss has the head waiter checking to see if I eat in the dining room. And I made some…enemies on the boat. I'm sure they'll be delighted to find out I'm disorganized enough to miss the damned thing."

Kaatje steered the boat so that the air barely buffeted the slack sail, then sat next to Laurie. "Let's face facts. You did miss it. I can see it moving." Laurie turned and watched as it slowly made its way out of its berth. "It's too late in the day to catch a plane to the next port and no boat could get you there in time. Let's enjoy the rest of the day." She got up and turned the boat into the wind, heading back out into open water without further comment.

"But…!"

"But what? It's late afternoon on a lovely day. You can go sit by yourself in a hotel room, or we can have fun." She stared right at Laurie until Laurie met her gaze. "If you don't let them, circumstances don't have to ruin your day."

"I think they do. You don't understand how much shit I'm gonna get for this."

"Are you gonna get fired?"

Laurie sputtered. "No! Of course not!"

"Then it doesn't matter. You might get chewed out and you might get teased. Neither are fatal."

She said this with such calm, such certitude, that Laurie let herself believe—a little. As soon as she let just the glimmer of belief in, she started to feel better. She relaxed against her cushion and let the wind blowing through her hair soothe her, and after a few minutes she smiled and said, "Can I sit on the rail again?"

—⁓—

. They went much further out this time, cresting over waves like a big fish. Laurie sat next to Kaatje and talked a lot—about her job and the pressure she'd been under, about how she'd been assigned to Osaka the day she started at Luxor, and how it had become the driving force in her life. She told Kaatje about how the earthquake and tsunami had impacted so many of their Japanese colleagues and how sometimes it was hard to remember this was just a theme park that had to be brought in on time— not life or death. She talked about her health scare and about how it drove her crazy to have to take vacation at such a critical time. Kaatje listened attentively and asked an occasional question. It was clear she was interested and engaged, but she didn't talk nearly as much as she listened.

By the time Laurie had given a brief synopsis of her countdown schedule to opening day in Osaka, she was exhausted. She climbed down from the captain's chair and stretched out on the deck and said, "Thinking about how much I have to do makes my heart race. And to not be able to do any of it…" She gently beat her head against the bulkhead.

Kaatje climbed up to the top deck and lowered the main. The breeze and the current moved the boat gently, taking it where it wanted. Kaatje sat at the table in the stern, keeping an eye out while talking to Laurie. "I clearly don't know a thing about business, but the fact remains that you can't do anything right now. Conserve your energy for when you can make a difference."

Laurie sat opposite her and looked at her with a completely puzzled expression. "How do I do that?"

"Well, what do you normally do to relax?"

"I can't afford to relax. I need every bit of energy I have."

"Hmm. Okay, let's talk about your motivations. Why do you work hard? What's the payoff?"

What kind of question was that? "It's my job. I love my job."

"But why?"

A lot of people had asked that question. But it wasn't answerable. You either got it or you didn't. It was clear Kaatje wasn't the type to get it, but it was impolite to ignore the question. "Because it tests me. I like having a really big challenge and working hard to meet it."

"But what's the payoff? Is it the money?"

"I guess. Or it was at first." She sat for a minute really thinking. Most people didn't ask about this part. "I went to grad school to be able to work at the highest levels. Part of my goal was to get rich. Now I make a very good salary, but I don't spend a whole lot." She laughed softly. "I'm too busy." Damn, no wonder talking to strangers sucked. If a person didn't understand the drive to work hard at everything you did, there was no way to explain it.

"Do you want to retire early?"

"God, no. I can't ever see myself retiring. I'd go nuts."

"Power?"

"Not too much. I like having power, of course. Power lets you get things done. Thankfully, I'm not one of those people who likes to have power only to feel important."

"Hmm, not money and not power."

"I'm driven, that's for sure. But I always was. I'm a very hard-working person and working at almost anything gives me satisfaction. I used to practice piano when I was a kid without anyone telling me to. I was gonna be good at it, even though I didn't like it much. And don't get me started on gymnastics. I was really loony about that."

"What about your social life?"

"Mmm, I don't have one at the moment. I broke up with someone about…" she thought for a minute. "We were breaking ground for the hotel. I suppose it's been two years."

"Wow. I wouldn't like it if my girlfriend gauged our time together by her work schedule."

Bingo! The gaydar was working perfectly. She could spot a gay person from fifty yards. "That's how I think. It doesn't mean anything." *It did to Colin, but she doesn't need to know that.*

"I think it would to me."

Urgh. Another sensitive soul. Some people got their feelings hurt too easily. "Then tell me about *your* social life."

"Mine's not in great shape at the moment, either. Did I mention that my first mate went back to school a couple of weeks ago?"

"You didn't say school, but you said your helper left a few weeks ago."

"Well, she was also my girlfriend. We'd been talking about…you know…being serious, but she got a grant to do some postdoctoral work in the South Pacific and she took it." She looked at Laurie with a sad shake of the head. "Without talking to me first."

"Why do you think she did that? Were you not getting along?"

Kaatje shifted a little, looking puzzled. "No, things were good. But I think she wanted more…I don't know…something."

"Money? Power?"

Kaatje flinched, then she seemed to realize Laurie was teasing.

"Maybe that was part of it. A lot of people don't think sailing is a career…whatever that is. Or maybe it was that she couldn't figure out a way to use her degree here."

"What was her degree in?"

"Marine biology."

Laurie pointed to the vivid blue ocean. "Duh."

Laughing, Kaatje said, "We don't have a university with any research capacity. She would have had to get a job at a school in the States and then do field research here for us to have any time together. I don't think that appealed to her." She sighed and looked away, staring at the water for a moment. "I'm not sure."

"How long were you together?"

"Six months. Not very long. Barely long enough to make me think it could be…something more. But I guess we never actually said those words…"

"That's a tough time, that six month assessment period. I've been there a couple of times when it hasn't ended up like I wanted it to."

"Maybe that's because you said, 'Six month assessment period.' That would seal the deal for me. I'd send you packing."

"No, I think it's when I said, 'It's time for your semi-annual performance review.'"

Kaatje gave her a quick look, then smiled when Laurie grinned. "You got me. I believed you."

"That's probably closer to the truth than I'd like to admit, but I never actually said those words."

But if you didn't stop and think about how things were going on a routine basis, how would you know when you were failing to meet expectations? There was nothing wrong with using a business model in your personal life. Results were what mattered—in every area of life… weren't they?

CHAPTER FIVE

AS THEY SKIMMED along, Kaatje pointed out a long, fairly hilly island in the distance. "That's St. Bart's. The beautiful people vacation there."

Laurie blinked a few times. "What? I didn't hear you."

"That's because you're thinking about work."

Busted again. How obvious was it? Maybe Kaatje was some sort of mind-reader. "I can't help it. I know this seems silly, but the worst thing is for me to look spacey. As a woman I can't afford that. Ever. And missing a boat is very, very spacey."

"How long have you worked for Luxor?"

"Six years."

"Wouldn't you think they'd know you by now? I mean…you're not generally spacey, are you?"

"No," she allowed begrudgingly. "But still…"

"How well do you get along with your boss?"

"Really well. We're kind of in tandem."

"Tandem?"

"Yeah. Fernando's a few years older than me and he was my first manager. As he moves up, he takes me with him. He was promoted to executive VP this year, and I should get bumped to senior VP soon. If this escapade hasn't killed my career."

"I don't know much about your situation, but they'd be stupid to hold one scheduling mistake against you. Why don't you call your boss and let him hear what happened from you?"

"I thought I'd call when I got to a hotel."

"I'd let you use my phone, but it's spotty out here too. My satellite internet works though. E-mail him."

"It works? Really?" Try not to drool or to look as excited as you are. She'll just think you're crazier than she already does.

"I've never seen a woman look happier to hear about internet access." She gave her a warm smile and pointed to the cabin. "My computer's under the cushion of the bench by the table. It's not very fast, which means you'll have to be patient...if you can be."

"You're a lifesaver," Laurie said, nearly skipping into the cabin.

———

About ten minutes later Laurie poked her head out. "I don't think I've ever yawned that much in my life. My jaw's getting sore."

"Did you get everything to work?"

"Yeah. I sent a message to him and his secretary and mine. He'll write back soon."

"Is the computer charged?"

"I didn't check. Why?"

"You should bring it out here."

"Really? Won't it get wet?"

"No, we're just using the jib to keep us heading in the right direction. You'll feel better out here."

"I feel fine."

"You think you do, but yawning a lot is the first sign of seasickness. Next comes sleepiness."

"Uh-oh. I can hardly keep my eyes open."

"Bring it out here. Trust me."

Laurie went back inside and disconnected the computer from its power source. Kaatje started putting away the mainsail, the huge bundle of cloth billowing all across the trampoline and the roof of the cabin. "Can I help?" Laurie asked when she stepped back on deck.

"Sure, but only if you put the computer back inside. This can be a wet mess."

Laurie dashed back in and put the computer back in its secure spot. Then she stood on the deck, waiting for instructions. "Hold onto those stays," Kaatje ordered. Laurie reached out and grabbed a stout-looking rope, but Kaatje twitched her fingers, directing her to a bunch of metal strands. "The sheets move. The stays are always there...remember? Now get your balance and help me fold this monster." Laurie pitched in with her full attention, carefully following directions. They quickly had it in order, then Kaatje wrapped some bits of fabric around it to hold it secure.

"All set. Now you can take the computer out onto the trampoline, or anywhere you feel secure."

"Can I sit by you?"

"Of course. I love having company."

"Be right back." Laurie was back in a flash, sharing the bench with Kaatje. She opened the computer and smiled. "My secretary Wendy is always there when I need her. She's going to find Fernando and tell him I need to talk to him."

Kaatje smiled benignly. "It must be reassuring to have someone you can trust."

"Oh, it is. Wendy used to work for the president of our division but she was getting burned out. She thought she'd have less stress working for a senior director, but I think she might regret it sometimes."

"You look unrepentant."

"I guess I am. Wendy could move anywhere, but she's stayed with me for two years. I think she feels a little maternal towards me. She rode in the ambulance with me to the hospital, holding my hand while she kept telling me that having a stroke wasn't that big of a deal." She rolled her eyes. "She can tend towards catastrophe."

"It sounds like she has reason to," Kaatje said, her gaze level and somber. "Fainting from stress doesn't sound like something to ignore."

"It's a low blood pressure issue. Nothing to worry about." People made such a big deal about a little fainting episode. She'd hit the "refresh" button at least a dozen times in the few minutes they'd been chatting and her eyes lit up when she received an e-mail from Fernando. "Here he is," she said. She looked up at Kaatje. "He says, 'You did what?' with about ten exclamation points. That means he thinks it's funny."

"That's good." Kaatje waved her hand. "Go ahead and do your work."

"Okay." Laurie was deep into her back and forth with Fernando, drumming her fingers on the edge of the keyboard while she waited for each reply. She lost track of where she was and looked up in surprise when Kaatje loudly cleared her throat. "Oh, shit! How long have I been e-mailing?"

"About an hour. It'll start to get dark in another hour. We'd better head back."

"I'm sorry. I got involved and…" She was paying for the sail, and didn't owe Kaatje an explanation, but she felt bad for blowing an entire hour. It might be years before she'd be anyplace this pretty again, but she hadn't looked up once. Damned seductive e-mail.

"Were you talking to Fernando the whole time?"

"No. I sent some e-mails to my team in Osaka. Because they're twelve hours ahead they were just getting in."

"At five? In the morning?"

"We have a park opening in a few months. Time's running out." Civilians had no idea how many hours it took to get a new park open. They seemed to think it was as easy as when the circus came to town. "Then I remembered something I needed our ride design guys to take a look at. That reminded me that…"

Kaatje held up a hand. "Got it. One thing leads to another."

"Always. Let me help you with the sail." She closed the computer, put it away and was back in moments, her eyes bright, her mood noticeably improved.

"Fernando was okay with what happened?"

"Oh, yeah. He's a good guy. I think he'll like having something to hold over me and tease me with."

"Will he tell other people?"

"No. And neither will Wendy. As long as those idiots in the cruise line don't know anyone in my division, I should be fine." She wiped her brow dramatically. "I might survive."

"I think you'll be fine. You don't look like the type who's easily defeated."

—⁓—

They were within view of the harbor when Kaatje asked, "Would you like to watch the sunset from out here?"

Laurie scanned the horizon, seeing the big, fluffy clouds that hovered just above the waterline. "Will it be good?"

"Should be really good. These clouds usually make it red and orange and purple."

"Yeah, I'd like to see it. We don't get these kinds of clouds very often in LA."

"Huh?"

"We don't," Laurie said, laughing at Kaatje's amazed expression. "Most of the year we have clear skies or a kind of foggy gloom. Not much in between."

"That's weird." She made a face. "How can you enjoy a sunset without clouds?"

"I don't enjoy many. I rarely get outside while the sun's out. And my office faces East. I get nice sunrises, though."

Kaatje shook her head in a scolding fashion. "You should see those from home."

"One day. When Osaka opens, I'll have more normal hours." She looked out at the fluffy clouds. "This is a heck of a lot better than the view from a hotel."

"Great. I think I'll get my camera. Can you hold the wheel for a few?"

"Me?" Laurie pointed at herself with alarm.

"Yeah. It's easy. Just hold it still." She took Laurie's tentative hand and placed it firmly on the wheel. "It tends to fly around if you don't hold it steady. Just keep it going where we're headed. Be right back." She was gone before Laurie could complain further, but she returned before any decisions had to be made. "No damage," she said, taking the wheel back. She handed a big, complicated-looking camera to Laurie. "Want to take some pictures?"

"I don't think I'd have the first idea of how to. I just use my phone."

"I love photography." Kaatje held out her hand for the camera. "I'll put it on automatic. Then you don't have to think"

"I need more things in my life that do that," Laurie mumbled, putting the viewfinder up to her eye. "Wow, I can see everything."

"I have a wide-angle lens on. That way we can get a nice panorama of the sunset."

"Can I take one of you?"

"You can take dozens."

Laurie aimed at a smiling Kaatje and snapped a dozen frames in a row.

"Can you download these? Then I can send some to myself."

"Sure. Take all you want."

Laurie got into the task, scrambling all around the boat, snapping picture after picture. Kaatje called out to her when she was lying on the deck, pointing up at the mast, "Want a different lens?"

"I don't know. Do I?"

"Yeah. I think you do. Go below and get one that's in a pouch marked 24-225."

"You're the boss."

"Captain," Kaatje called after her. "I'm the captain."

CHAPTER SIX

THE SUN WAS starting to set by the time Laurie had exploited all of the available photographic opportunities. Kaatje then took a few dozen of Laurie: sitting on a cushion, standing on the deck, acting like she was going to jump off the boat and, of course, holding the wheel.

A sense of real melancholy descended on Laurie as she thought about the end of the day. Being with Kaatje had seemed like meeting a new kid in the park when she was young. Someone you clicked with, who thought you were funny. Someone who knew what kinds of games you liked and fit right in without asking a bunch of questions. But in the back of your head you knew you'd never see the kid again. It was fun because you could be anyone you wanted to be, but it was all too brief. And when you got home you had to get back into the "you" that everyone knew.

"Now we can relax and wait for the sun to set," Kaatje said. "I think I'll set the anchor. Want a drink?"

"Sure. What do you have?"

"Name it." Kaatje went to the bow, opened a small door in the deck, took out some sort of device and pressed a button. The anchor shot off the bow and splashed noisily into the water. Yards and yards of chain followed, then Kaatje returned to the captain's chair, turned on the engine and backed up until the anchor caught. She reappeared by leaping onto the deck just inches in front of Laurie, startling her. "What'll it be?"

"How about…vodka and tonic."

"Excellent. I'll have the same. Be right back."

Just minutes later, Kaatje returned and handed Laurie a glass with a flourish. "I pour a lot of rum out here, but I've never developed much of a taste for it. I stick to vodka, beer, and wine."

"I've had a lot of sake the last few years and I don't think I'll ever love it. Vodka's my favorite, but I like beer on a hot summer day." She raised her glass and toasted. "To a great, and surprising day."

"Those are the best kind."

"I probably shouldn't drink, since I have a blazing headache, but what the heck."

"From the sun?"

"No. Stress. I've gotten used to them."

"Want a hand?"

"At what?"

"I know a little acupressure. It helps sometimes."

"Uhm, sure. Couldn't hurt." *Yeah. Sure. Watching the sunset with a pretty, flirtatious lesbian, having a drink or two, letting her work on your muscles. What could be dangerous about that?*

Positioning herself so she could put the tips of her fingers just over Laurie's temples, Kaatje pressed with gentle but constant pressure.

"Mmm, that's…interesting." It felt like having her head in a vise, but the pressure was strangely soothing.

Kaatje let go, then put her thumbs on the back of Laurie's neck and pressed again.

"You know, it feels a little better."

"Give it time. It usually takes a few minutes for the blood vessels to open up and relieve the pain. Let me do a few more."

"No arguments." Laurie sat there placidly while Kaatje applied firm pressure to several spots on her head, then moved down to her neck and shoulders.

"These muscles are as tight as violin strings." Kaatje increased the pressure on the big muscles that ran from Laurie's neck to her spine. Then she started to rub them, digging her thumbs into them until Laurie whimpered. "Just bear with me for a minute," she soothed. "This will help."

Kaatje's confident manner inspired Laurie to let her continue, even though it was painful. As soon as she eased up on the pressure, Laurie turned to her and said, "It's better." She moved her head experimentally, then more vigorously. "It's much better."

"Good. It doesn't always help, but sometimes it can really be of benefit."

"What else can you do?" She took Kaatje's hand in hers and shook it. "Do you have any more talents in those?" *That was a dumb thing to say. There isn't a heck of a lot of difference between a lesbian and a straight guy, and it isn't fair to flirt when nothing can come from it. Gay or straight, nobody likes a tease.*

"Quite a few," Kaatje said, smiling cockily. "But I can improve on one I've already showed you if you want."

"I do. I don't care if it's sailing, mixing drinks or rubbing my muscles. You're expert in all three." *What the heck. A little flirting can't hurt. It's a nice way to stay in practice.*

"Give me your foot."

"My foot? My bare foot?"

"Yeah. Your bare foot." She looked at her curiously. "It's just your foot."

"I'm not crazy about feet. Actually, they gross me out."

"Your own foot grosses you out? How's that possible?"

"I just hate feet. They're always on the ground and they look gross. I don't think I could tolerate having someone touch them." *Great. Now I'm coming off as a workaholic who hates her own feet. Thank God this isn't a date.*

Kaatje nodded, but looked very puzzled. However, she didn't press. She merely said, "Hands, then."

"Oh, no problem. I love having my hands rubbed." Laurie presented her hand and Kaatje rested it on her thigh. She pressed into the meaty part of the thumb, then right into the center of the palm. "That feels fantastic," Laurie purred. "Really good."

As Kaatje worked on each hand, Laurie, limp with pleasure, sank lower onto the deck. Eventually, she was prone, with Kaatje sitting right next to her head. When the massage was over, Laurie tilted her head and looked up at Kaatje like she was drunk, her words slow and sliding together. "Tha' was won'erful." She sat most of the way up, then their eyes locked, and the thought occurred to Laurie that Kaatje's expression was much sexier than it was merely friendly.

As the thought left her mind, Kaatje leaned over, pausing just a second. Laurie could have sat up further or even turned her head and the moment would have passed. It wouldn't even have been too uncomfortable between them, as Kaatje's overture was relatively subtle. But Laurie tilted her chin up, presenting her lips, which Kaatje tenderly touched with her own. *Funny. Not like a guy's lips at all. But it's a little…sisterly.*

The kiss lasted a few seconds, and when Kaatje picked her head up, Laurie was gazing right at her mouth.

"That was nice," Kaatje said slowly, her pupils dilated, the low sun making fire of their pale blue color. "Very nice." She reached out and cradled Laurie's cheek in her hand, and their eyes met for a long time.

That was more intimate than the kiss, and Laurie felt a twinge of sadness that the kiss had been so tepid. It was disappointing. Very disappointing. Having the great unexplored territory of lesbian sex out there had been somehow reassuring. When sex was lackluster or frustrating, it was nice to occasionally think about whether it would be more satisfying to kiss a woman. Now even that fleeting dream was snuffed out. What was it that made so many people risk everything for sex? Was she wired *that* differently?

Dejected, Laurie sat up, and Kaatje shifted her weight, leaning against her for a second. Then she kissed her again. This time there was a sting to it —still soft and sweet, but with a little power lurking around the edges. Laurie's heart skipped a beat when Kaatje opened her mouth slightly and showed a little possessiveness. She could have sunk right through the boat and into the water when Kaatje pressed into her still more forcefully. Now they were getting somewhere. Her mouth responded as if it had its own mind, licking and sucking Kaatje's lip daintily.

Screw it. The damage is done. If you're going to kiss a woman just once in your life, make it count! She removed Kaatje's cap, then released the band that held her dark hair back. Running both hands through the thick tresses, still slightly damp, she tickled along her scalp with her fingertips. When Kaatje shivered and let out a soft moan, Laurie whispered, almost to herself, "That's why men like women with long hair."

"You've never been with a woman with long hair?" Kaatje was busily kissing Laurie's eyelids, then down her cheeks.

"No, never. I like it." She kept playing with Kaatje's hair and scalp, running her fingers down to the base of her neck. "Actually, I love it."

Kaatje threaded her fingers into Laurie's hair, then slowly pulled away to let hanks of it fall to her shoulder. "This doesn't sound very romantic, but your hair is almost the same color as my mother's."

Laurie stopped. Was Kaatje really this clumsy? No one brought up her mom at a moment like this. Was she consciously slowing them down, maybe even reassessing? *Shit, shit, shit. Maybe Kaatje isn't into it.* "I'm not thinking about *my* mom."

"I'm not thinking about her, just about your hair. Is it ash blonde?"

Well, this is clearly over. Might as well talk about hair for a while before she dumps me at the dock. "Yeah, I guess that's a good name for it. What do they call it in Dutch?" Was that right? Was that the language or the people? Damned if she knew. Damned if she'd have to learn since she was done experimenting with the Dutch.

"*Asblond.* Or maybe *peper-en-zout-blond.* Maybe even *donkerblond.* But whatever you call it, it's very pretty. Yours is straighter than my mom's."

A decent lesbian would have had her panties off by now, and Kaatje certainly seemed like a decent lesbian. She must have just changed her mind. Fuck it all.

Kaatje put her hand over her mouth. "No more talk of mothers. Promise." Her eyes twinkled with playfulness. "But your eyes are very much the same blue as my father's."

There was probably more bite to Laurie's comment than she'd intended, but her feelings were hurt. "You might want to talk to a professional about your attachment to your parents."

"No, no, I'm not overly attached. My mom's a psychologist. I'm perfectly sane." She grinned again, remaining close enough that Laurie could count her long, dark lashes. She moved just an inch and placed another soft, sister-like kiss upon Laurie. "Having fun?"

"Occasionally." God only knew what Kaatje was up to, but this was a golden opportunity, and she wasn't going to waste it. If Kaatje couldn't make a move—she would. She slipped her hand into Kaatje's hair again, then slowly expanded her territory to include her neck and shoulders, encouraged by sensual sighs. "Your muscles are very pliable." While Kaatje's eyes were closed, Laurie started kissing her chin, her cheeks, atop each delicate eyebrow.

"Sailing is a great stress reliever." Kaatje kissed her back, pressing harder into her as the kiss grew in intensity. "So's this."

"I'd almost forgotten."

Kaatje pulled away and gazed into her eyes questioningly. "How long has it been?"

"Two years."

"That was a serious relationship, right?"

"Right. Very serious. With Colin. No one since."

"Two years is a very long time." Kaatje ran the tip of a finger across Laurie's cheek, then along an eyebrow, then caressed the shell of her ear. "Don't you miss it?"

"Right now I do. I miss it more right this second than I have in two years."

"Why do you think that is?"

Such an odd question. Such an odd way of interacting. Start, then grind to a stop. But now it was reasonably clear Kaatje was into it, and having her go slowly was strangely nice. Each step lasted longer, and those first steps were awfully fun. "It feels wonderful to be touched again."

"I'd love to touch you," Kaatje whispered. "We could go lie on the trampoline and watch the sunset."

"Can you carry me? I'm limp."

"I could, but I'd spill my drink." She grinned widely and stood, holding a hand out. When Laurie took it, she was pulled to her feet without helping a bit.

"You're strong!"

"I know." Kaatje showed that cocky grin again, then she took Laurie's drink and scrambled catlike onto the upper deck. When Laurie joined her, Kaatje handed her both drinks and said, "Don't go away." She returned a few minutes later with her camera, now equipped with the lens she'd originally had on it, a soft blanket and a tray with cheese and fruit and bread. She put the tray onto a spot on the upper deck that must have been made for it, then spread the blanket down on the trampoline. Lastly, she wrapped the strap of her camera around a line that allowed it to swing freely without hitting anything.

"You've done this before."

"Once or twice." Kaatje sat down and patted the surface next to her. "Join me."

Laurie put the drinks on the tray, then gingerly sat down. Their bodies immediately rolled together, and feeling Kaatje's warm body suddenly press into hers made things move too fast—like it was a given that they were going to have sex. She wasn't sure she could go through with it. "I'm kinda nervous."

"You don't need to be. I won't push you, and if you change your mind…it's okay." She smiled reassuringly, then stroked along Laurie's cheek. "No pressure. Promise."

That was better. They'd just play around a little. And if everything was perfect… "Okay." She took in and let out a deep breath. "It's just…you know. The first time you're close to someone…"

"Sex can be scary, but it doesn't have to be. It's just the two of us." Her eyes gazed out at the turquoise water that surrounded them. "And a lot of fish." She chuckled and Laurie joined her, laughing nervously. "You're single…I'm single…you're pretty…I love pretty women…isn't that enough?" She was just inches from Laurie's face, and her smile was calm and reassuring.

"You're pretty, too." She stroked Kaatje's face, gazing wide-eyed at her as she did. "You're very pretty. Such nice cheekbones. Well defined. And such a good nose." She touched it with the tip of her finger. "Strong but not big. It matches your profile perfectly."

"Sounds like you've been studying me for a while."

Was that true? Sure. But didn't everyone pay attention to detail? "I guess I have."

Kaatje took her hand and kissed the fingers, one at a time. "There's nothing wrong with that. I've been looking at you every second. When you came out of the galley in my shirt, I almost whistled. But I thought that would be unprofessional."

She'd been had. But it was awfully nice to have someone notice her. "Should it have fit that tightly?"

Kaatje held up two fingers, spaced an inch apart. "Maybe it was a little tighter than it should have been. But I'm the last person to complain. You rocked that shirt. And I could draw a picture of how your butt looked when you were in the water. I almost plowed into you."

"Really?" When was the last time that had happened? When had a guy told her he was really into her? No, not her. Colin was into *her*. But he didn't compliment her body once she gained a little weight. It was like he withheld any comments until she got back down to the waif-like size he liked. "I don't get many compliments any more. I don't go out much, and no one at work would notice if I shaved my eyebrows off."

"I would," Kaatje said seriously. "And I wouldn't advise it."

"Give me another kiss." Laurie smiled as Kaatje responded immediately and they rolled into one another, one body pressed fully against the other. "Nice," she murmured when Kaatje broke the kiss. "Let's do that again." The timing was strange, but kinda nice. She'd never had to tell a guy to keep going, but sometimes that testosterone-driven push made her feel like she was losing control. This felt much safer, and safe was good with a stranger.

Now that she'd been given a command, Kaatje snapped to it, kissing Laurie every way possible. How long had it been since someone had immediately responded to a suggestion? "Good?" Kaatje asked after a while.

"Very good. Kiss me any way you want." Slowly, quickly, tenderly then forcefully the kisses rained down. Every pace and pressure; making Laurie's heart beat quicker, then slowly. "Very nice," she murmured. "You're a very, very good kisser."

"I could almost live on kisses." Kaatje looked over Laurie's shoulder and said, "Prime sunset picture time. Want some?"

Laurie paused just a second to decide. "Yeah." Why not take a photo break? That was no weirder than the start and stop pace they'd been keeping. "I'd love a picture that I can look back on and think about today."

Kaatje sat up and got her camera ready. She took shot after shot, getting up on her knees at one point and balancing herself on the bouncing, flexing surface.

Laurie watched her, looking at the muscles in her legs as she knelt on the trampoline. They were remarkably taut and lean, like a long-distance runner's. They were fantastic legs. Not soft and pillowy like her own, but really appealing. They probably felt great when they were wrapped around you.

Kaatje turned the camera around and focused carefully on Laurie. Then she lay next to her and held the camera out at arm's length. "This will take a few tries," she predicted. It did, and they didn't get a decent picture the first fifteen times. But Kaatje finally came up with one she was happy with. "How about one like this?" she asked, leaning in for a kiss.

"How do I know that won't wind up on the Internet?" Boy, that sounded far too suspicious. She'd been listening to too many people in Human Resources, always badgering them about keeping their anonymity whenever possible.

"Uhm, I guess you don't." She turned the camera around again and took a few more shots of the deepening sunset while making appreciative sounds.

Laurie touched her shoulder while the camera was still raised to Kaatje's eye. "Did that hurt your feelings?"

"What?" She turned and faced her. "About the Internet?"

"Yeah."

"No. You're right. You don't know me. It's best to be careful." She put the camera by her side and lay back down. Then she extended her arm and Laurie put her head on it and nestled against her body. "The light's beautiful on your face and hair. Your skin's glowing with a color that's perfect and I'd love to shoot it. I'll give you the memory card if you'll send me anything good from it."

"You don't have to do that. Go right ahead and shoot."

Kaatje did, her entire demeanor shifting from the half-smirk she often wore to pure concentration. She didn't speak, focusing fully on her subject and her camera. Laurie noted that she fussed with the complicated-looking controls, but she never stopped shooting, managing to get off at least fifty shots before the smirk was back and she said, "Light's gone. Now we're going to have to think of something else to do."

"There's still a lot of light."

"Yeah, but the good stuff's gone. It only lasts for a minute or two. What's the English word? Effervescent?"

"Evanescent, I think. You mean fleeting, right?"

"That's good enough. And much easier to spell. Fleeting."

"I had to pull that one out of thin air. I'm sure I've never used it."

"I don't want to stress your brain any more." She tucked the camera into the folds of the blanket. "I don't like to let condensation build up on it."

"You know what else is evanescent?"

Kaatje shook her head.

"Our time together. I'm going to have to fly to St. Thomas tomorrow, and I don't want to regret anything."

Kaatje kissed her gently, lingering for just a moment. "Like what?"

"Like not having sex. I'd look back on this with regret if we didn't."

Kaatje smiled brightly, the setting sun coloring her features a burnished gold. "I'd regret it, too." She leaned in and kissed Laurie with a renewed vigor that raised goose bumps on Laurie's arms and legs in seconds.

"Wow," Laurie murmured, smiling contentedly. "This is gonna be great."

—◊◊◊—

Kaatje broke the mood one more time, getting up to put her camera away. But she brought a pillow, which lifted Laurie's head just enough to make the vague ache in her neck vanish. "I'm certain you've done this before," she teased again.

"I've done a lot of things more than once. But I appreciate each time." Her dark blue eyes looked sincere and totally earnest. Laurie had to kiss them, placing delicate caresses on each salty lid.

"Now comes the hard part. Getting our clothes off." They bumped and pushed and tumbled over each other as they tried to undress. Finally, Kaatje said, "We'd better go one at a time. We'll kill each other the other way."

This was almost like being at the gym. Just two women taking off their clothes. No big deal. They each shimmied out of their clothes in a very unromantic, workmanlike way. But Laurie forgot all about how they got there when she wrapped her arms around Kaatje and clutched her warm body against her own. The air had cooled them, rendering parts of her skin chilly. But Kaatje's breasts and belly were warm as toast, delighting Laurie's body in a way that was completely new and exciting. "Ooh, you feel fantastic."

"You do too. Your body's just what I love about women. Soft, smooth curves." She ran her warm hands all over Laurie's skin, a completely satisfied smile on her face. "I'm almost dizzy."

"I've let myself go. I weigh a lot more…" She was cut off by Kaatje's fingers pressed against her lips.

"Let me enjoy your body. It's fantastic."

Damn, this was scary! Her breasts were bigger than they should have been and she had some extra flab on her belly. Her thighs weren't in such great shape either, but she hadn't expected anyone to be looking at them this closely.

Feeling unattractive made it hard to let a stranger touch her this intimately. But seeing the pleasure on Kaatje's face made things easier. Still, it was too frightening to merely lie there. She distracted herself by touching Kaatje simultaneously, gingerly feeling across her back, her shoulders, her ass. It was like sailing uncharted waters, but she got her sea legs faster than she would have predicted. She explored Kaatje carefully, letting the feel of skin transfix her. It was soft and smooth, yet stretched tightly across those long, firm muscles—a unique and tantalizing experience. There was something completely compelling about it and she got bolder with her roaming, probing the muscles deeply with her fingers while she kissed and accepted kisses in unceasing succession.

The sun had fully set when Laurie looked up at the still blue sky. Eyes bright with desire, Kaatje hovered over her. "Tell me what you like."

Flustered, Laurie just looked at her for a few seconds. *Is this an interview? I don't know the right answer! I'll probably screw it up if I guess. Why can't she just do what lesbians are supposed to do?* "Uhm, I like… everything." *Was that a dumb enough answer?*

Kaatje kissed her firmly, then pulled away. "Let me know if you think of anything. Meanwhile…" She scooted down her body, stopping to tenderly suckle her breasts, which were soon heaving with desire.

"Oh, that's wonderful," Laurie moaned. "Gently. Just like that." Had anyone ever touched her so tenderly? Finally someone who knew her breasts had nerves. She put her hands into Kaatje's hair, sliding through it as Kaatje continued to caress her. "That's so nice. I'd never get tired of this."

"Neither would I," Kaatje promised, her mouth filled with pink, flushed skin.

They stroked one another for a long while, until Laurie was squirming under Kaatje's touches and kisses. Kaatje looked up at her as she moved down, settling between her legs. "My favorite part," she said, her grin almost a leer.

Laurie felt herself grow tense again and she consciously tried to relax her muscles. But Kaatje was very gentle with her, slowly exploring every part; touching her thighs, then her lips with a single finger. After a few minutes of slow, determined caresses, Laurie let her legs drift open, but she was almost shocked by the first soft kiss Kaatje placed right on her skin. There was something shockingly intimate about it and she tightened up again.

It took a while, but Kaatje's feather-light kisses and gentle touches eventually allowed her to relax into the experience. She felt her hips start to lead her body into Kaatje. The sensations intensified, starting at her feet and traveling up her body to lodge in her clit. Kaatje's dark head never lifted. Laurie stared at the long strands of her hair and caressed and smoothed them as Kaatje made her body sing.

Laurie felt her legs rise involuntarily, until her feet were planted on Kaatje's broad shoulders. Laurie could feel with her whole body how much Kaatje was enjoying her—how much pleasure she was giving by receiving pleasure—and it made her head spin. They barely knew each other, but they were making love. There was no doubt in her mind. They were making love.

As that thought hit her, Kaatje slipped one of her fingers into Laurie, making her squirm and thrust against her. Kaatje immediately added another, then another, filling Laurie tightly. That pushed her over. She started to spasm against those fingers, shivering against the incessantly divine feel of Kaatje's tongue against her pussy. All at once she couldn't take another second. She pushed at her shoulders, while simultaneously trying to pull her into her body. She knew she was fighting against what she most desired, but she was too overstimulated and needed a few moments to let her body recover.

Kaatje met her eyes, grinning like the Cheshire cat. "Can I do that again? Now?"

"Really?" Didn't Kaatje know she'd climaxed? Was it rude to tell her?

"Yeah. Right now. Can I?"

"Uhm…" Kaatje *had* to know she'd had an orgasm, but she clearly wanted to keep going. Colin used to get so excited watching her climax that he'd be inside, thrusting away before she could catch her breath. But Kaatje clearly didn't operate that way. Laurie swallowed her suspicions and nodded before Kaatje could change her mind. "I'd love it." Having a lover focus on her this completely was beyond fantastic. But Kaatje must've been unique. If lesbians were generally this good at sex, there wouldn't be a heterosexual woman left.

This time Kaatje was even more methodical. She was gentler and slower, too. She'd obviously paid rapt attention in the past few minutes, learning how to please Laurie's body. In just moments she'd learned things that Laurie didn't know about herself, which was more than a little hard to admit. But she never would have guessed how fingers stroking just inside her opening made her want to squirm right off the boat. And when Kaatje added an achingly gentle kiss on her sensitized flesh—there were no words for how delicious it felt. And how did Kaatje know to devilishly tease with her clit, stilling those knowing fingers until Laurie almost lost her mind and demanded to be fucked. Then Kaatje pumped into her, using her powerful forearm to push and relax, push and relax until Laurie grabbed at her shoulders and pulled her in, mewing out another sweet orgasm. Still, Kaatje wasn't sated. *Kaatje*! And she wasn't being touched anywhere! Immediately, she nuzzled gently but tenaciously until another orgasm rolled over Laurie's body. This one wasn't as thunderous. It was more a wave of pleasure that pulsed through her, enveloping her in sweet sensation.

Finally, Laurie couldn't bear another caress, no matter how delightful. She grasped at Kaatje's shoulders. "Come hold me."

Smiling a very satisfied grin, Kaatje climbed up and tightly held her now-chilled body. "You're freezing."

"No, I'm not. I'm fine."

Nonetheless, Kaatje gathered up as much of the blanket as she could and draped it over both of them.

"That was remarkable. Fantastic. Wonderful. Add some other adjectives that I'm too drained to think of."

"I hope you enjoyed it as much as I did. That will make me happy."

"Be happy. Be very happy." Laurie kissed her again, then cuddled into her embrace, their bodies warming each other by contact.

"Is there a better way to end a great day?"

"No. I'm certain of that. If there were…well, people would be doing that other thing to excess."

"Don't let two years go by again. It's not good for you. We need touch."

"We need good touch. Touch from hands like these." She held Kaatje's hand up, kissed it gently and looked at it in the swiftly darkening sky. "Just like these."

—⁓—

They lay there in the dark night, watching the sky as a few stars first appeared. "This is what life's all about," Kaatje said softly. "Being close to someone you like, giving each other pleasure, and enjoying our beautiful universe."

Laurie didn't respond verbally. She started to let her mind take that statement in, but thoughts of Osaka started to destroy her serenity. *This was crazy!* The last thing she should be thinking of was work. Kaatje was right.

Every sane person knew that people meant more than jobs. And as soon as the park was open she was going to concentrate on having more fun. Today had taught her something precious. She had to take time out for herself. Luxor couldn't own one hundred percent of her heart and her mind. She had to keep something in reserve to share with other beings not of the genus *Ursus*.

She burrowed into Kaatje's embrace, nuzzled into her neck and kissed her skin. It was time to reciprocate. Inexperience was no excuse. Her hand tentatively started to roam, stopping at a small, firm breast to cup and hold it. Kaatje kissed her several times, each time holding the caress a little longer, like she was encouraging her.

Laurie continued to explore, touching Kaatje with a light hand. She brushed her fingers across her arms, her chest, her belly and thighs; trying to get a feel for Kaatje's responsiveness. Kaatje's chest was exposed and Laurie bent her head to take a nipple into her mouth, rolling it around with her tongue. She made a few small sounds as she continued to focus on the breast, finally lifting her head to see how she was doing. "Is this okay?"

"Yeah, it's great." Kaatje wrapped her arm around Laurie and hugged her. "Do you…" She used the dim light of the cabin to look into her eyes. "Do you want me to tell you what I like?"

"Yes," Laurie said while Kaatje was still enunciating the last word.

"I'd love to feel your tongue on me, but I'm too salty for that to be fun for you. You've really got me excited, so we can keep it simple." She took Laurie's hand, then reached for her index and middle fingers, placing them on her clit. She smiled, letting out a soft groan when Laurie's fingers settled against her. Then she moved them, guiding them as though they were her own. Laurie was up on one elbow, carefully watching Kaatje's face as she touched her. Occasionally, Kaatje would lean forward and catch a kiss, which Laurie tenderly gave. "Your fingers feel fantastic," Kaatje murmured. "Nice and soft and gentle."

"I think I know what you like," Laurie said. "Can I explore a little?"

"Yeah. That'd be great." Kaatje opened her legs wider and laced her hands behind her head, staring up at the sky while Laurie stroked her just the way she'd been shown. "I'm very happy," Kaatje said after a while. "This is perfect."

"I like this," Laurie murmured, kissing Kaatje's neck and the hollow of her throat. "I like touching you."

"Can you…?" Kaatje took Laurie's hand and guided her to slide inside. "Yeah, that's the way." She took over stroking herself while Laurie carefully watched Kaatje's face for every reaction. "A little slower…yeah…perfect. I'm close," Kaatje whispered. "Really close."

Laurie leaned over and kissed her, probing her mouth as she probed her pussy; trying to discover every spot that could give Kaatje pleasure. Kaatje's fingers sped up, moving over her clit like a blur, but Laurie kept stroking her slowly, just the way Kaatje had guided her.

"Slower," she whispered, her body as taut as a wire. "Nice and slow." Then she started to jerk and shiver, moaning softly as she began to relax and release some of the tension that had built up in her body. Laurie's fingers were still inside, her gaze trained on Kaatje's face as her body pulsed gently around her fingers. Finally, Kaatje grasped her hand and withdrew it, placing it on her chest where Laurie could feel her rapidly beating heart.

Kaatje put her arms around Laurie's neck and pulled her into a long, luxurious kiss. "Did you like your first time?" The question was nonchalant, and Laurie took a moment to let it register.

"Oh, God, was it that obvious?" She buried her head in the crook of Kaatje's neck.

"No, not at all." Kaatje cupped her cheek and forced her to raise her head. "I'm really happy that you chose me to be your first."

Smiling, Laurie said, "I think you chose me. I never would have had the nerve to kiss you." She kissed her quickly, glad she could do it without reserve. "When did you know?"

"It wasn't any one thing. It was the sum of a bunch of little clues. I'm glad I wasn't wrong," she said, chuckling. "Can you imagine how insulting that would have been if you'd had sex with women hundreds of times?" She laughed harder, the sound carrying across the dark, calm water.

"How did you know?" Laurie asked again. "Tell me. I must have seemed like I didn't have a clue."

"No, not true. You seemed like someone who knew how to make love. Just not in this variety. Like when I asked you what you liked. You acted like no one had ever asked you that before." She smiled impishly. "That sounds like someone who's only been with men."

Laurie gently slapped her cheek. "I hate to admit it, but you're right. Most men don't ask for a lot of guidance. They know what they want and they try to get it. Then, if they're good guys, they'll do their best to please you. But they're not all good guys."

"Neither are women. Good women, I mean. But most of us know you have to give and take. I've never been with a woman who didn't try her best to give me an orgasm."

"Some didn't succeed?" Laurie looked at her expectantly.

"More than a couple." She took Laurie's hand and kissed it again. "You're very talented. I think you should try this again."

"Okay," Laurie said gamely, putting her hand down to reach for Kaatje again.

Laughing, Kaatje pulled her hand away. "I meant with another woman."

"Oh." Laurie sat up and gazed at her, concerned. "Don't you want me to touch you any more?"

"I'd love for you to do that. But first, I need to eat. Aren't you hungry?"

"I'm starving. I assumed you ate only once a day."

"Let's go to the cabin and polish off the remains of our lunch." She picked up the tray she'd brought out earlier. "Soggy bread won't satisfy me."

They moved along the dark deck, Kaatje quickly and Laurie slowly and carefully. Kaatje was standing on the lower level, holding her hand out to steady Laurie when she jumped down. Without warning, a pressure settled around Laurie's sternum and she wanted to jump into the dark water and swim to shore. Seeing Kaatje standing there looking at her was suddenly too…intimate. Moving from the gorgeous open seas into the interior of the boat somehow broke the spell and she didn't want to go.

"Are you okay?"

She managed to nod, but that was it. Seconds passed, then she got out, "Bathroom?"

"Stomach upset?"

"No. Fine. Just need the bathroom."

"You go in and I'll pick up our stuff."

Laurie slipped past her, almost lunged into the bathroom, and locked the door before dropping weak-kneed onto the toilet. She was stark naked and had just had sex…lesbian sex…with a complete stranger. Add in the fact that she'd missed her boat, and it made for a day more dramatic and traumatic than she'd ever had. Of all of the terms ever used to describe her, "madcap" had never made the list. But today had been madcap.

She sat there for a few minutes, head in her hands. It was too much to process. Too many things were flying around to even start to organize and assess them. Maybe tomorrow, safely back on the cruise ship, there would be time to sift through this crazy day and make some sense of it. As for now, Kaatje was in the galley and it was time to go out there and act like a spur-of-the-moment kinda woman. There was no need to admit that missing the boat was weighing much heavier on her mind than having sex was.

She opened the door, went upstairs and spied her clothes lying on the banquette of the galley table. Kaatje was only wearing her shirt. That gave some indication of where they each were on the comfort scale. Laurie would have put on a snowsuit if she'd had one. Anything to cover up. "Tell me about this boat," she said, trying to get on safe conversational grounds. "I don't know the terms for anything." She slipped across the cabin and jumped into her clothes as quickly as she could.

"Okay. We were up on the trampoline, then we walked along the deck and jumped into the cockpit. Now we're in the cabin. The galley specifically."

"It's bigger than it looks. Does this seating thing and table area turn into a bed? You could live here if it did."

"No, it doesn't. But you can easily live here. I do."

"Where do you sleep?"

"There's a berth on either side of the bathroom."

"I don't know how I missed that. I'm usually pretty aware." Getting away for another few seconds seemed like a really good idea. "I'll go take a peek."

She stepped down and saw a narrow hallway with doors to the right and left. "I have my choice," Kaatje said, standing right behind her. It was hard to get any privacy on a boat. But smelling Kaatje's salty skin was strangely nice. Even though she was right there, she didn't seem to be infringing too much on Laurie's space.

Kaatje opened the door to the left, revealing a double bed that rested atop low cabinets in a room so narrow one would have to jump onto the bed to get in it.

"This is cute," Laurie said. "It's like a den."

"Yeah, kinda." They moved out and Kaatje opened the other door. "This is my berth."

This one held what Laurie guessed was a queen-sized bed with shelves on the wall at the head for magazines and books, and lamps shooting a warm light onto the pillows. A few framed photographs of sunsets and sunrises and sailboats were on the walls.

"These are your photographs, aren't they?"

"Yeah. When I take a shot I like I have it blown up to ten by twelve. Then I switch these out to keep things interesting."

"It's nice," Laurie said, sliding her arm around Kaatje's waist and giving her a squeeze. Why had she done that? A second ago she was considering jumping to her death. There was something calming about Kaatje. Almost like she was a big Valium. "I could easily see living here, even with the tiny bath."

"It is small for an apartment, but kinda big for a boat. Still, it's a turn-off for a lot of people. And I have to share it, when I have a full boat, but, other than that, I couldn't ask for more."

"Where are we?" She made a circle over her head. "I can't get my bearings."

"We're in the hull." At Laurie's blank look she added, "The part that stays in the water. The forty-seven foot long thing that looks like a canoe?"

"Oh, I thought they looked like kayaks. What's in the other one?"

"Two more berths and one small bath. I use one berth as my office, but I can turn it back into a regular berth in ten minutes. In high season I try to fill the boat and take people out for as long as they want to go. That's where I make most of my money."

They started to walk back up to the galley. "How many do you take?"

"I can only take six. That's all I'm legally allowed with the kind of license I have. One time I had a woman and five kids. That was a rockin' two days. I earned my two thousand dollars that trip."

"Wow, that's a good chunk of change."

Kaatje was standing in front of the half-sized refrigerator, pulling out white containers. "A thousand minimum US per day for an overnight. I'm on duty every minute. That doesn't seem like a lot to me."

"No, I guess not," she said thoughtfully. "What will you do next?"

"For…?" She started to dish out the contents of the containers onto colorful plates.

"For you. For your business plan. More boats? Bigger boats?"

"No." Kaatje finished what she was doing and brought the plates over to the table where Laurie was sitting. "What would you like to drink?"

"Just water.'

'Sparkling or flat?"

"Uhm…sparkling. You're a very good hostess."

"Practice, practice." She handed Laurie a glass and carried her own back to the table. "My business plan is to have good weather and customers with available balances on their credit cards." She smiled quickly, with Laurie noting that this was her perfunctory smile, the one she used to show the topic was finished.

But Laurie was too tenacious to let a facial gesture put her off. "But you're very young. You can't be satisfied with where you are in life."

"I can't?" She took a bite of shrimp-laced pasta, her perfunctory smile absent. "You must be mistaken, because I am."

"But you could have much more."

"More what?" She chewed, barely looking at Laurie as she reloaded her fork.

"More business. More money. You could really make a good buck if you expanded."

"Then what?" She took another bite, still with no eye contact.

"Then you'd be able to do more. You could…retire early."

Now their eyes met. "Retire from what?"

"From having to take people out. You could do what you want."

"This *is* what I want. I like taking people out."

"But it's human nature to want to improve, to keep striving."

"Not this human. I'm happy. Doing more would make me unhappy." She got up and took a baguette from the counter, rapping it on the counter to test it. "A little limp, but not too bad." She cut a few slices, raised an eyebrow at Laurie, then brought her bread back to the table. She poured a little olive oil and vinegar from cruets on the table onto a corner of her plate and dipped the bread, then took a small bite with each bit of pasta. "I love bread. I'm always looking for good bread near my harbor."

"Come on," Laurie said, trying to engage Kaatje in the discussion. "Talk to me."

"I am talking, I just don't have anything else to say. I'm happy. I don't want more. I do what I love for six or seven months, then I take a month or two off and go to the Netherlands to see my family and friends. I don't know how to improve on that life."

"I didn't realize you had family in…Europe." She was embarrassed to admit she wasn't sure what term to use, recalling some confusion in her mind about the difference between Holland and Amsterdam and the Netherlands. Or was that Denmark? All of those countries were scrunched up in that little corner of Europe.

Now it was Kaatje's turn to look blank. "I said I was Dutch."

"I said I was half Norwegian, but I don't have family in Norway…that I know of."

"Oh, I didn't make myself clear. I'm Dutch. From Amsterdam. I've only been here around ten years now."

"Ahh. I thought your accent was…I don't know…Caribbean or something."

"Mmm. It gets to be a little Caribbean after I've been here for a few months. My friends in Holland have told me that."

"Why did you come here? How did you even know about the island?"

"My father got transferred here when I was just entering university. I wasn't…well, I assume I would have done well, but I didn't have any idea what I wanted to do in life. It made sense to come along. My parents are still here, but they'll probably go back home to retire. I'll stay." She patted the wall behind her. "This is my home."

"What does your dad do?"

"He's a banker. He manages the Royal Dutch Antilles branches in the Caribbean. It's not a good name since the Antilles doesn't exist any more. Our side of the island is an independent country now, as I assume you've heard."

Laurie nodded even though she had no idea what an Antille was or why it didn't exist. "I guess I'm surprised you…the bank has a branch here."

"The island is still a part of the Kingdom of the Netherlands," Kaatje said slowly. "Is that what you're confused about? The news media didn't cover the constitutional change very well?"

Trying not to look completely dull witted was not easy. Kaatje was speaking gibberish, but she seemed to think whatever she was talking about was common knowledge. There was one morsel that might be exploited. "You said *your* side of the island. What did you mean by that?" *An intelligent question. Hurrah!*

But Kaatje looked even more puzzled. "The island is half Dutch and half French. Did you not know *that?*" She emphasized "that," as though the dullest of the dull would know at least that much.

"Uhm, no. I had no idea." They'd barely covered geography in school. No one in America knew anything about this stuff. And what did *half* French mean? Which half?

"Didn't they give you something on the ship to tell you where you were going?"

"Yeah, I guess they did. I didn't bother reading much of it. I guess I should have, huh?"

"Only if you're interested." She resumed eating. "Americans can get away without knowing much about the world. The alpha dog doesn't have to know about the pack, but the pack better understand the alpha."

"I guess I'm more interested in business than…geography." That wasn't the right word, but what was? Not politics, not sociology. Who the hell knew?

"There's room in the world for all kinds of interests. I have no interest in business, but I know a lot about…geography. I travel whenever I can."

"We could start a business teaching people about geography. We'd make a killing."

Slowly chewing, Kaatje nodded politely with no interest showing in her cool blue eyes.

It wasn't going to be easy, but she had to be able to show she wasn't a dunce. "Is this island like the US Virgin Islands are to America?" Thank God she'd read that part in the book that was in her cabin.

"Kinda. Everyone here is a Dutch citizen and we can travel back and forth without restriction."

"Really? You're all citizens?"

"Sure. But more people come here from Holland than go the other way. Most of our professional class is Dutch, but the island is much more Caribbean than Dutch. The French side is a different matter. Many West Indians speak French and a lot of French retire here."

Okay, there is no way to understand this without looking even more stupid. Might as well get it over with. "The French side? Side of what?"

"Of the island. Half of the island is Dutch. Half is French." She was speaking so slowly she must have thought Laurie was hard of hearing…or thinking. "They drew a line across the middle of the island—well, not quite the middle, the French side is bigger—and each country took half."

"Recently?"

"No," Kaatje said, clearly trying to stifle a laugh. "Not recently. In the seventeenth century. Legend has it they were going to war over the island, but the generals met in a tavern, had a few drinks and decided to just draw a line."

"That's interesting. I wish I had more time to explore."

"Are you going back to work as soon as you get home?"

"Yeah. After four more days of punishment on that stinkin' boat." She rested her head on her hand, looking glum.

"Why don't you do what you want?" Kaatje said this remarkably softly, as if she were afraid of being dismissed.

"I want to go back to work now. That's what I *really* want. But Fernando won't let me."

"Second choice?"

"Oh, I don't know. It'd be nice to poke around and see what's on the islands, but it wouldn't be that much fun going alone."

Again, Kaatje nodded, her eyes heading back to her plate. She finished her meal in silence, still methodically eating in a neat pattern. When she was finished she got up and picked up their plates and set about washing the dishes. Laurie sat at the table, gazing out at the dark sea that surrounded her. Kaatje was ticked off about something, and Laurie was pretty sure it wasn't geography. She was hard to read when she got quiet, but she'd closed down even more when talk of work came up. Maybe a woman didn't want to rock your world and then have you say your fondest wish was to go make some phone calls about a theme park.

Once finished, Kaatje stood by the table. "What now? I can take you back to the tender dock or…whatever you want."

"Really?"

"Sure."

"Do you have any plans?"

"No."

"Would you like company?"

Now Kaatje's real smile was back. "I'd love company."

"Then I'd like to stay here."

"Great. We could stay overnight at anchor, but I should move further out just to be safe. Or we could go back to my mooring."

"Your mooring is…?"

"Where I dock my boat."

"It doesn't matter to me. If we have to move, I suppose we should just do it once, right? The mooring sounds most efficient."

"Great. We'll go over there in a bit. In the morning I'll take you to my parents' house and you can use your phone and their computer."

"Damn it, I don't have my laptop. I feel like I've been robbed." She sighed heavily, then looked back up at Kaatje. *Stay focused and stop thinking about work. You'll be back in civilization tomorrow.* "That's very generous of you. Do you have to work in the morning?"

"Yeah. I've got people coming at ten, and I have to get lunch made. I'll probably have to take you up to my parents' at about eight. Is that okay?"

"Sure. Can I get a cab to the airport from there?"

"Yeah. No problem." She grinned, then held out her hand, lifting Laurie to her feet. "Let me take a shower and you can pick up where you left off."

Trying to hide her trepidation, Laurie enthusiastically said, "Great!"

———

They both showered, separately, since there was barely room for a solo adult in the tiny enclosure. When Laurie was finished she found Kaatje outside, an extension cord leading to the blow dryer she held. She was naked and seemed completely unconcerned with modesty as she stretched her arm behind her head to finish drying her hair. Laurie stood in the doorway, wrapped in just a towel. "Hi." *Time to pay the piper. Can't let a woman go down on you like a pro and beg off just because you're chicken.*

"Come on over here." When Laurie stepped outside to stand next to her, Kaatje wrapped an arm around her and pointed to the town's glittering lights that created a soft blip of interest in an otherwise dark void. "Look."

"It's remarkably beautiful."

"So are you." She put her lips to Laurie's neck and delicately kissed all across her skin. "I'm glad you decided to stay."

Laurie rested her hands on Kaatje's arm, then leaned into her embrace. "I am too. You probably can't tell this, but I'm a little nervous."

"You're kidding," Kaatje said, flatly. "Who would ever have guessed?"

"I know you can tell. That's why I can talk about it."

Kaatje kissed the top of her ear, then made her way down her neck, resting for a moment on her collarbone. "Don't worry. I have no expectations. We don't have to have sex again. I just like you and want you here as long as you can stay."

"You do?" She tried to turn to see Kaatje's eyes, but she was held tightly by that strong arm. "You're not just being polite?"

"No. I really do like you and I'm very happy you're staying with me. I always sleep well when someone shares my bed. It's soothing."

"It usually takes me a while to get used to sleeping with someone."

"Then you should stay longer."

What a perfect thing to say! She didn't come on too strong, but she's not afraid to show her feelings. Those are awfully nice traits.

———

They went into the bedroom, where Kaatje opened small windows on either side of the bed. Laurie smiled when a cool breeze wafted across the room. "I love to sleep with the windows open." She stood as far from Kaatje as she could, hoping to delay the inevitable move to the bed.

"Let me hang up your towel." Kaatje took it and went to put it into the bathroom. Laurie quickly slipped into bed and covered herself with the sheet, not nearly as unconcerned with her nakedness as Kaatje was.

A few seconds later Kaatje reappeared and she got under the covers as well. "Nice, isn't it?" She put her hands behind her head and took several deep breaths. "The air is saltier out here, even though we're just a few hundred yards from the bay."

"Are we going back to the mooring soon?"

"Yeah, but there's no rush. I like being alone out here."

"Me too."

They were quiet for a minute, then Kaatje said, "Tell me, how did a girl like you wind up in a Dutchwoman's bed?"

Laurie giggled despite her nerves. "I have no idea. I guess the Dutchwoman's just too charming to resist."

"That's not very likely. I think you might have had an…inkling you might like being with a woman, and you let yourself go with the feeling."

"I've said no to that question every time someone asks. But I was probably fooling myself."

Kaatje shifted quickly and sat up enough to lean on an arm. She looked almost incredulous. "People have asked?"

"Yeah. Quite a few."

"No one has ever asked me if I'm possibly straight. Well, not since I've been an adult."

"Really? I wonder why people ask me?"

"Strangers? People on the street?"

Laurie elbowed her. "Of course not. But my mom and my sister and my boss have all asked. Actually, Colin asked. Several times." She looked at Kaatje. "That's odd, isn't it?"

"Seems a little…different. I'm not sure what I'd think if a girlfriend asked me if I were straight."

"When you say it that way it sounds silly."

"It doesn't really matter. Maybe they've just asked because you're not married or serious about anyone."

"Yeah, maybe. But that doesn't explain Colin." Nothing explained Colin. That was probably worth thinking about. Some time. Later.

A few seconds passed, and when Laurie didn't elaborate, Kaatje said, "You didn't seem surprised when I told you about my girlfriend leaving me. Did you guess I was gay?"

"Yeah, I thought you were. I work with a lot of gay people, and I can usually tell. My friends tell me I'm one of the few straight women who can almost always pick out lesbians."

"Maybe that's why people ask about your sexuality. Maybe they think it takes one to know one." Kaatje grinned, looking so pretty Laurie had pull her close to kiss her seriously.

Their kisses, growing in intensity and fire, continued until their bodies were entwined. "I like this very, very much," Laurie breathed, her voice heavy with lust. "No wonder men are sex crazed." She kissed her again. "We should have sex again, don't you think?"

With a very seductive grin, Kaatje nodded. "Fantastic idea."

"I'll do my best to give you an orgasm or two, then we can conk out."

"I've got a few things to do before I can sleep, but I've never refused an orgasm." Her bright eyes were twinkling, and she looked happy, relaxed and expectant.

"Let me see how involved in this lesbian sex-exploration program I can get."

"That's a good idea." Kaatje stroked her hair as Laurie started to move down her body. "This is one of my favorite views. The top of a woman's head. Better than a perfect sunset."

Kaatje was obviously trying to lighten the mood by making a joke, but it didn't cut the tension. Laurie was as nervous as she'd been the first time she'd had sex, and she knew it was blatantly obvious.

She had fourteen years of experience, but she felt like a raw rookie, unsure of how or where to move, what or when to do it. She tried to still her racing heart and concentrate on what Kaatje had done to her, but she was terrified she'd put her mouth on her and gag or pull away. The first time she'd given oral sex to a boy, she'd held her nose under the covers, sure the taste would make her sick. But she reminded herself that she got over that response and eventually became pretty good at giving head. She had to admit she'd never, ever liked it, and was fairly sure this would be more of the same. Bodily fluids and odors weren't her thing, but you had to be fair. If you loved getting, you had to give in return.

Kaatje had gone down on her with enthusiasm and what seemed like real pleasure. She pushed on, kissing her way down Kaatje's lean, muscular body, without a sheet to cover her if she were inept. She stopped at her abdomen, amazed at the tight muscles she found there. In a way, it reminded her of her first boyfriend's body. He'd been a swimmer and she'd loved to tease his hard belly with kisses, always taking her time to get to where he wanted her to go.

But with Kaatje, a few inches below the muscle was a woman's belly, soft and smooth, with none of the wiry hair most men had. Kaatje encouraged her, stroking her head, keeping a hand on her shoulder. She didn't push or urge her on. She just touched her, letting her know she wasn't alone.

As Laurie got closer to her target she could detect the first hint of a scent. It was strangely pleasant—clean and just a little musky. Intrigued, she kept kissing her way further down, now lingering on the remarkably soft skin at the very tops of her thighs. She started to get into it, spurred on by the way Kaatje moved under her, twitching and shivering when Laurie kissed a particularly sensitive spot.

Without thinking, she opened her with her thumbs and delicately touched her pink folds, amazed at their complexity. Kaatje was unable to stay still. She moved her hips around, blindly searching for Laurie's mouth. Instinctively, Laurie touched her with just the tip of her tongue, amazed at the incredible softness of her skin. *It's just skin*, she reminded herself. *I can do this.* Emboldened, she ran her tongue from bottom to top, ending at the bright pink nub of Kaatje's clit. The reaction was immediate and intense. Kaatje's entire body shivered roughly, blatantly showing her need. Laurie had to slake that need, had to show Kaatje that she could adapt. She would be good at this. Steeling herself, she dove in, plunging her tongue right into the small opening that flicked open and nearly closed.

Kaatje grabbed at her shoulders, holding her close while she groaned in pleasure.

Laurie was smiling, proud of her nerve and overwhelmingly pleased at her own reaction. None of the off-color jokes she'd heard over the years were true. There was nothing off-putting about the experience. In fact, she began to feel a heady burst of power when she saw how much control she had over Kaatje's pleasure. She played with her, keeping one hand on her belly to be better able to feel her twitch and quiver. She ran her tongue over Kaatje's hot skin, trying to make her groan, make her gasp, make her shiver with need. It was remarkably easy. Kaatje was very responsive and couldn't seem to stop herself from making near-constant vocalizations. It was like being guided where to pet a cat based on her purring.

Laurie slipped a finger inside and moaned her own sweet pleasure at the sensation. This was the warmest, smoothest, slickest part of a woman she could imagine. She could have grasped Kaatje's very heart with her hand, and it made her feel incredibly close to her. In awe of how tender and intimate this was, she chided herself for ever thinking that she'd been close to other lovers. This was a whole new level of connection, and she was elated by it. *I can be close! Colin was wrong, wrong, wrong!*

Buffeted by her feelings, she lost track of Kaatje. But she was brought back to their connection when Kaatje rasped out, "Slow your hand down.

Just barely keep it moving." She followed instructions, but moved her mouth faster and let her tongue flitter across Kaatje's clit, just as she'd seen her touch herself. It was hard keeping her hand and mouth moving at vastly different paces, but she managed. Her desire to please Kaatje was incredibly strong, and she would have done nearly anything to make her happy.

With a strong thrust of her hips, Kaatje moaned through gritted teeth, "Fast. Harder. Don't be afraid. Let me have it."

Laurie pressed into her, moving her tongue as fast as it was capable of going. Then she pursed her lips around Kaatje's clit and shook her head back and forth until she heard her cry out and felt her body gently push against her mouth, demanding just a little more pressure. Laurie gave it to her, nuzzling her mouth into Kaatje until she finally put her hands on her head and, whimpering softly, pushed her away.

Laurie watched her pussy twitch, her cunt opening and closing rapidly. Completely changed from its initial tint, the pink skin had turned a dark rose. Tentatively, she blew on it, making Kaatje laugh weakly. "No more. I need a minute."

"I have a stopwatch. Fifty-five more seconds…"

"Come up here. I want to see you."

"All right, but I want to come back down here as soon as I can."

Smiling sweetly, Kaatje spent a moment gazing at Laurie questioningly. "Are you good?"

"Very good. I enjoyed the heck out of that." She lay back and gazed up at the ceiling, unable to stop smiling. "Either you're the sexiest person alive or I'm definitely bisexual."

"Maybe both." Kaatje chuckled when Laurie met her gaze. "Well, don't rule out a strong possibility."

Laurie gave her a kiss, lingering on her soft, full lips. "You're right. You're the sexiest person alive." She lay back and mused, "I can't tell you how much your body turns me on. It's hard to describe, but the things that men most love...well, they aren't my favorite things. They're more like things I have to put up with or tolerate to get to the things I like."

"Like feet?" Kaatje asked, straight faced.

"Yeah, exactly like feet." She reached down and tweaked one of Kaatje's nipples and felt it harden under her touch. "I think you could take a little more now."

Kaatje put her hands on Laurie's shoulders and held her still. "In a minute. You've fantasized about women. Yes?"

"Uhm...not really. Not much." She shrugged, embarrassed.

"But my body turned you on. I assume you mean more than men's bodies did."

"Yeah. I think that's true. It was softer and smoother and the whole thing was...gentler. I won't wake up with bruises where we banged into each other."

"But were you turned on by men's bodies? Their big shoulders and things like that?"

"Uhm...sure. I guess. I...I've never seriously considered what I like about men."

"And you've also never seriously considered you might be a lesbian."

Her eyes were full of questions Laurie was sure she was too kind to ask. "Not really. I can't explain it..." *Please don't make me keep talking about this.*

Kaatje's intent expression turned gentle and she placed a long, slow kiss on Laurie's lips. "It's not important." After another soft, lingering kiss she added, "I'm really glad we've had today."

It was hard not to cry at that empathic gaze. Partially to distance herself, she slid down her body again, keeping her eyes on Kaatje's, which soon were suffused with desire. "I am too. And I'm gonna stay down here until I learn how to do this right."

Kaatje laughed softly. "You know how I said you should be less obsessive? Forget that. Compulsivity is a virtue."

CHAPTER SEVEN

THE SUN WAS just coming up when Laurie placed a few soft kisses on Kaatje's bare back. Awake for almost an hour, she had taken a shower and brushed her teeth while she waited for Kaatje to wake. Now she was going over the astounding events of the previous day.

There was no way to explain this to anyone and have it make sense. The most vexing element was the fact that making love to Kaatje wasn't a surprise, even though she could honestly swear she'd never had overtly sexual thoughts about a woman. The embarrassing part, the part she wouldn't even tell her sister, was that she'd never had many overtly sexual thoughts about anyone. Her sex drive had always been mild, and had always been more passive than active. The men she'd been with wanted a lot of sex and she'd gone along, and she'd gotten a pretty good return on her investment. If a guy had been a good lover, she'd always been able to respond. Colin was good—probably very good. But Kaatje had given her more pleasure in a hour than Colin had in a month. There was something there. Something she couldn't name or even think about in a concrete way. But after Osaka opened, she was going to spend a good, long time figuring it out. It was foolish to assume anything from one night. Perhaps Kaatje was some lesbian superwoman, and she'd never have as good a time with another woman.

The funny part was thinking about her mom. While she wasn't the only person who'd chided her about the uncharted depths of her personality, she'd been the first. Her mom believed a person needed a great deal of introspection to live a fulfilled life, but Laurie had effectively proven her wrong. Introspection was fine if that worked for you, but you didn't need to be like that to be happy. She'd gotten along great letting things happen and only thinking about them on an as-needed basis. She wasn't going to change now. She'd had a great time having sex with a woman, and she hoped to do it again if the opportunity arose. That was enough time spent on the subject until the park opened.

She turned on her side to regard her bedmate. Kaatje seemed like the introspective type. But she obviously had a hedonistic streak that was very appealing. How wonderful must it be to let the tide and the wind be your main guides. No meetings, no committees, no chain of command. You saw a woman you found attractive, you took her out for a sail, and you made a play for her. On a weekday! That kind of freedom boggled the mind.

Kaatje lay there with the morning sun painting golden stripes across her shoulder and back. She looked peaceful, with not a furrow or a wrinkle on her tanned skin. Like she didn't have a care in the world. *That* was something to envy. A stress-free life would bore her to death, but the thought of Kaatje's independence was something she could learn to love. If only she were the owner and sole operator of Luxor, she'd be perfectly happy. All she needed was a few billion in seed money and she could easily have that. *Ack! Enough about Luxor!*

She reached out and touched the part of Kaatje's back that the sun was warming. Her skin was ridiculously attractive. Soft as a child's, but nothing else about her was child-like. She was a woman. A beautiful, sexy, warm woman who might like to rock the bed once more before they had to leave for the airport.

Thinking of the airport made Laurie's stomach clench. As though the thought of flying frightened her. But that wasn't true at all. Leaving Kaatje was upsetting her, but that made no sense. She could easily come back and visit her after the park opened. It would be time for another vacation, and this time she would go without Fernando's help.

It was getting late. She touched Kaatje a little more firmly. Kaatje mumbled a small complaint, then shot up, staring at Laurie as though she were an intruder. "I was about to scream!"

"I'm sorry." Laurie sat up too, then wrapped her arms around Kaatje and hugged her. "I didn't mean to startle you."

Kaatje sat up taller and swiped the hair from her face, settling it over her shoulder. "I guess I'm used to being alone." She reached for her watch on the shelf by her head. "What time is it?"

"Six thirty. Is that too early for me to wake you?"

She blinked a few times, then rubbed her eyes with the backs of her hands. "How long have you been up?"

"A while."

Kaatje leaned over and kissed her tenderly. "You should have woken me the minute your eyes opened." She laughed almost to herself, hopped out of bed and started to leave the room. "Don't go away."

A few minutes later, she was back, now clean and happy-looking. "We've got an hour to blow. Let's make good use of it." She jumped onto the bed and grasped Laurie in her arms, wrestling playfully until she had her pinned. "That didn't take long. You don't put up much of a fight."

"I love to win, but I'd rather not waste time. I haven't had sex in two years. Every minute counts."

—m—

"I want to taste you again," Kaatje grumbled an hour later as they got out of bed. "Not that I have any right to complain…"

"You know what you're doing. I'm just learning." Laurie grinned at her and leaned over to grab the duvet to help neaten up the bed. "I've never had sex that was that…easy."

"Easy? That's a funny word for sex."

"Maybe it's not the right one, but it was great to be able to talk and have you tell me what you liked. I've never had a guy do that."

Kaatje looked adorably confused. "They just let you guess?"

"No…well, yes, but that's mostly because they're in charge."

"Hmm…I don't think I'd like that."

"I don't mind that part, but the men I've been with have been pretty serious about the whole thing."

"Sex is too important to be too serious about it. It's got to be fun too."

"Colin was a screenwriter. He saw the drama in everything."

"I like movies, but only comedies." Her eyes radiated playfulness when she grinned.

"I like your attitude. I'm not going to have sex with another person who isn't into having fun."

Kaatje intercepted her as she started for the main part of the cabin. How could simply being held feel this fantastic? But they had to go! There wasn't time for getting all mushy.

"You can always come back to St. Maarten."

"I'll do that. After Osaka opens I'm going to finally take some planned vacation time. And next time it'll be where *I* want to go." She gave Kaatje a sweet, lingering kiss. "My next cruise will be on a much smaller boat with a much prettier captain."

Smiling at her, Kaatje looked like she was going to say something, then stopped. She finally said, "If you're serious, I'd love to take you sailing. We could see five or six islands in a week."

"Could you afford the time?"

"Yes, of course. High season is November through April, but other than that I can easily take a week…or a month. I don't have to inform any Teddy Bears of my whereabouts." She grinned slyly.

"Don't remind me. We'd better get going. I want to be at the airport to try to get on that noon flight to St. Thomas, or I'm screwed again."

———

They went out onto the deck and Kaatje started down the ladder at the back of the boat. "Where are we going?" Laurie asked, seeing nothing but pale turquoise water surrounding them.

"We're swimming to shore." Kaatje looked completely serious, and Laurie almost believed her until she heard her feet hit something that didn't splash. She leaned over and saw Kaatje standing in a small, gray inflatable boat.

"Where did you hide that?"

"Here at my mooring."

Laurie went to the stairs and let Kaatje help her into the boat. "I thought your mooring was at the big, concrete thing."

"No, that's where I pick up some of my clients. I dock here in Simpson Bay." She pulled a cord roughly, with her whole body getting into the movement. The engine roared to life and she sat down and started to guide the boat, while pointing at the dozens of sailboats surrounding them. "Doesn't this look different?"

"Uhm, I wasn't paying much attention, but I guess it does. Did we come back here last night?"

"Yeah. You were asleep, but we definitely did."

She reached over and patted Kaatje's leg. "Sorry about that. I should have helped you."

"Not much to do. I just had to grab the mooring ball. I've learned to do it alone."

"I slept through that? You must have been walking around right over my head."

"I take that as a compliment."

"You should. I've never conked out like that with…someone new." She was going to say "a stranger," but realized how cold that would have sounded.

They reached the pier and Kaatje expertly tied up the dinghy, then helped Laurie out.

"Do you have a car here?"

"No. I ride a bike. It's right over here."

They approached a decent-sized motorcycle chained to a scrubby tree. "I only have one helmet, and you will wear it," Kaatje said, presenting it.

"No, it's more important that the driver be safe."

Kaatje pressed it into her hands. "If we go down, it won't help you to have me protected at that point. Come on, take it."

Laurie hesitated, then accepted. She could tell that Kaatje would insist, and she didn't think she could win an argument with her—at this point.

They got on and Kaatje started the engine. The loud rumble surprised Laurie. "This sounds fast."

"It's got to have some power. We've got a hill to climb." They took off and almost immediately started to climb. Kaatje didn't drive very fast, nor did she take any risks, but the road was not very wide and they were treacherously close to the edge of an increasingly high cliff. It reminded Laurie of going up Topanga or Coldwater Canyon in LA, but she'd always been in her car then.

They climbed for almost five minutes, finally pulling up to a modern home firmly anchored to a large bare spot on the scrubby green hill. "Wow!" Laurie jumped off and stood with her hands on her hips, looking down at the lovely bay. "This is a million dollar view. Actually, it's a ten million dollar view in LA."

"It is nice, isn't it?" Kaatje stood next to her and put an arm around her shoulders. She looked happy, almost serene as she joined Laurie in taking in the view. "People here seem to prefer being by the water. Hillside property is less expensive."

"In LA both are expensive, and everything in between is more reasonable. But this view is better than anything I've ever seen in Malibu."

"I love my island."

"I thought tropical islands would be more green. Like with bananas and monkeys and rain forests."

"They can be. Actually there's a huge number of monkeys on St. Kitts, and there's a rain forest on Saba, but this is a dry volcanic island. Not much arable soil, and almost no fresh water."

"Speaking of soil, this house isn't attached to much of it. But it's very cool. I love the green roof and trim." Laurie looked at it carefully, noting that it was probably made of poured concrete.

"It's modular. All pre-made at a factory and shipped here. It's very green—figuratively."

"Green is good. We're spending millions trying to be more green, and it really looks good to the public. Our ROI…" She slapped her hand over her mouth. "Sorry. I'm getting back in work mode since I'm leaving."

"When did you get out of work mode?" Placing a gentle kiss on her lips, Kaatje showed a smile as she pulled away. She knocked briefly on the leaf green door and entered. "I'm home," she called out.

"Kaatje?" a woman's voice answered.

Kaatje responded in Dutch, or Antille, or some other tongue that Laurie didn't understand. She spoke several sentences, and Laurie guessed she was telling her mother she had someone with her, since she heard her name mentioned at the end.

A lovely woman walked into the living room. She was as pretty as Kaatje, but a bit shorter and more overtly feminine. She was dressed in bright green slacks and a green and pink print blouse accented with tasteful gold jewelry that set off her dark blonde hair. "Hello," she said to Laurie in an accent stronger than Kaatje's.

"This is Laurie, Mammie. She missed her boat yesterday and I told her you'd let her use your computer to get her travel plans settled."

"Oh, how terrible. You must have been very upset." She extended her hand. "I'm Antonia. You're welcome to stay as long as you like. Theo will be leaving soon and I never use the computer."

"Is Papa still home?" Kaatje asked.

"Yes. He should be leaving any minute. You know he likes to be early."

Laurie heard a man's deep voice asking a question. He spoke Dutch as well, and Antonia answered him, also mentioning Laurie's name. A handsome, fiftyish man came into the room. He was dressed in a steel-gray suit and he wore pewter-colored, steel eyeglasses. His thick hair was graying, but the dark swath across the top of his head looked just the color of Kaatje's. "Hello. My wife says you're visiting a bit longer than you'd like."

"That's true. I'm Laurie Nielsen." They shook hands, his grip firm to the point of discomfort.

"Theo Hoogeboom. If there's anything I can do to help, don't hesitate to let me know. I have some contacts that might be able to smooth things out for you."

"Thank you, Mr. Hoogeboom."

Theo's stern expression morphed into a grin. He turned and removed his glasses, which he then cleaned. When Laurie heard a snicker, she turned to see Antonia and Kaatje both unsuccessfully trying to hide their laughter.

"What did I do?"

Kaatje composed herself. "Nothing. It's just that the way you pronounced our name sounded funny."

"Hoogeboom?"

All three laughed again. "It's Hoogeboom," Kaatje said, saying it just like Laurie had.

"That's what I said. Isn't it?"

"No. The way you said it sounds like 'hug a tree.'"

"But…"

"It sounds rather nice," Theo said. "Now, let me know if I can help you make a flight."

"I don't care how I get there, but I have to get to St. Thomas by five."

"Hmm." He gave her a doubtful glance. "There's a daily flight, but it's usually full. We could use two flights a day, but the facts don't always win the argument here."

Laurie saw Kaatje roll her eyes at this comment, but she didn't say anything.

Theo turned to his daughter and gave her a very formal kiss on the cheek, then said a few sentences in Dutch. Kaatje shrugged, looking a bit adolescent, then said, in English, "I'm sure Mammie will give Laurie your number if she needs anything. Thanks for the offer."

Theo extended his hand again and shook Laurie's with an almost military formality. "I hope you've enjoyed your time here, Miss Nielsen, and that your trip home is without trouble."

"Thank you. I appreciate your offer to help."

"My pleasure. Kaatje." He nodded at her, kissed his wife on the cheek and left, leaving all three women in silence until the door closed.

Kaatje crossed the room and dropped onto a modern, white love seat. "Do you have any breakfast left over, Mammie?"

"For you, my dear one, I always have food." She went into the kitchen with Laurie and Kaatje following.

"I just have a few minutes," Kaatje said. "I've got clients at ten and I have to order lunch."

"Do that from here," Antonia said. "They'll take your order on the phone, won't they?"

"Maybe."

Kaatje took her phone from her pocket and dialed a number, waiting just a second to begin speaking in a language that sounded different. How it was different, Laurie couldn't say. It just sounded softer somehow. She gestured with her free hand when she spoke, and Laurie watched her, smiling at the animated way she explained what she needed. Antonia interrupted her rapt interest by asking, "What can I make you for breakfast, Laurie? We have fruit and yoghurt and cereal and toast…"

"I'm very worried about getting to St. Thomas. Would you mind if I used your computer? I'm too nervous to be hungry."

"Coffee?"

Laurie smiled. "I'd love some." She waited for Antonia to pour her a cup, then they walked to a small room set up as an office and Laurie headed for the computer. "I know what to do now."

"Great. I'll leave you to it."

A few minutes later Kaatje came into the room and gently touched the back of Laurie's neck while she worked. "What have you got?"

"Nothing yet. The noon flight is sold out and the only other way to get there is to go to St. Kitts, then Anguilla, then Antigua, then St. Thomas. If everything goes right I'd probably make it, but…" She looked up and made a face. "I'm not counting on that."

"Bite?"

Kaatje held out a piece of toast that Laurie bit into. She almost spit it out, composing herself to ask, "What's on the toast?"

"*Anijshagel.* Anise flavor. You don't like it?"

"I'm not used to anise for breakfast. It just caught me by surprise." She twisted Kaatje's hand to see white tubular shapes covering the bread. "Interesting."

"Do you like sweet things? I can bring you some toast with *appelstroop* on it. My mom makes it herself."

"Apple...what?"

"Like apple syrup. I'll bring you some." She started to leave, but Laurie caught her by the hem of her shorts.

"Stay with me as long as you can."

"I actually have to leave." She leaned down and kissed her, holding the contact for a few long seconds. "I've had a great time with you, and I'd love to see you again."

"I would too." She patted Kaatje on the butt, one of her favorite parts of her body. "Go to work now and have a nice day."

"Send me an e-mail or call me, okay? I'll worry about you until I know you're set." She took a pen and paper and quickly wrote her phone number and e-mail address. Another quick kiss and she was on her way, with Laurie looking after her as she walked down the hall, her long, lean, tanned legs taking her away all too quickly.

———

Antonia brought in two pieces of toast a short while later. "Kaatje said you might like my *appelstroop*. Don't worry if you don't. I won't take offense."

"Oh, that's very nice of you, Mrs. Hooge—"

"Antonia, please. Now, what can I do to help?"

Frustrated, Laurie leaned back in the chair. "I can't decide what to do. The flight I need is full and the other one stops three places before it gets to St. Thomas. If I don't make my boat, I'll have to stay until Saturday, then go to Miami and try to find my luggage."

"Would that be a bad outcome?" she asked benignly.

Laurie blinked at her, stopping for the first time to consider her plans. Her focus had been only on following through on her original schedule. She hadn't given a moment's thought to alternatives. "I guess not. Actually…" she trailed off, not sure what else to say.

"Kaatje likes you a lot. I can tell."

Laurie felt her cheeks color. "I like her, too." It was very odd talking to the mother of the first woman she'd ever slept with about her feelings, but Antonia was just the kind of person she liked. Subtle, polite, and not too inquisitive. "I guess I could…" She wracked her brain, trying to figure out a way to get her luggage. "My luggage will get to me eventually. I could stay until Sunday and go directly to LA."

"Are you trying to get to the boat to meet friends? Family?"

"No, it's an enforced vacation."

At Antonia's puzzled look, she spent a few minutes explaining the whole situation. When her spiel ended, Antonia said, "If I were your boss, I'd want you to stay here and relax. But you have to do what makes sense for your situation. If you want to go to the airport, I'll gladly take you."

Laurie bit her lip, considering the possibilities. She hated to have her plans change abruptly, even when she didn't like the plans in question. But they'd changed in a major way when she missed the boat. No matter what she did now, that mistake had been made. "I'm not sure Kaatje would want me just hanging around. She has to work."

Antonia smiled, looking a little sly. "She wants you to stay. And if she's busy you could stay here at the house while she's working. You could use our computer or just relax."

Laurie's eyes lit up. Fernando had blocked her access to the cruise ship's computer, but he couldn't stop her from using her personal e-mail account to keep in touch with her staff. Getting in a couple of days work in advance of her return made her salivate. "That's very tempting."

"Do what you need to do, but take my advice about one thing."

"What's that?"

"Tell Kaatje that you chose to stay. If she thinks you stayed only because you couldn't get the flight, she'll…well, she's a very proud woman."

"Thanks for the advice." Laurie took a big bite of the toast. "Delicious! Could I use your phone to call her?"

"Of course. Her number is right there on that button. Just press it." She closed the door as she left the room.

Laurie punched the button, and in a few seconds heard Kaatje's clear, lilting voice. "Met Kaatje."

"Hi, it's Laurie. What did you just say?"

"I just answered the phone."

"But you said something besides your name."

"Oh, I said 'with.' Shorthand for 'you're speaking with Kaatje.'"

"That's cute."

"I wasn't trying to be cute. I thought you were my mom and I went back to Dutch. How is it going?"

"Good. Hey…I was thinking…why am I rushing to get back on that dumb boat?"

Kaatje's laugh rumbled through the line. "Why, indeed?"

"If I hung out for a couple of days, would you have time to see me?"

"Of course. You could sail with me. As a matter of fact, my mother could bring you down to the dock right now. I'm still waiting for my clients."

"Hmm…" Laurie thought of all of the things she could do with an internet connection. "I've got a lot of calls to make. Maybe I'll ask your mom to take me to a hotel."

"Fine."

Not another word. That wasn't good with Kaatje. She was garrulous when she was happy, stoic when not. Recalling what Antonia said, she tried a different tactic. "What would you like for me to do?"

She didn't wait a beat. Her voice had no inflection at all when she spoke. "Whatever you want."

Kaatje's lack of affect might have fooled a woman into thinking she didn't care. But Laurie had heard that flat tone enough times now to know it meant she not only cared, her feelings would be hurt if one answered the wrong way. "What I'd really like is to get some things settled and then spend as much time with you as possible."

"Then you should stay with me." Now there was an affect. It was an undeniably happy one.

"Do you want me to?"

"Yes. Of course. Why would I ask if I didn't want that?"

Laurie realized that Kaatje was not going to be the type of woman to give her thoughts away without a certain amount of work. But she was certain the work could be very rewarding.

―⁓―

Antonia and Laurie set off for Philipsburg on a short shopping spree. When they returned home, Laurie used their bath to take a shower, shave her legs and put on the new clothes she'd bought. Antonia insisted on washing her dirty things, and Laurie gave in, finding Antonia as hard to refuse as her daughter.

Since Kaatje was out on a full-day sail, Laurie could hook up to the Hoogebooms' computer and scratch her itch for getting some work done. Thank God Fernando didn't control the entire Internet.

Since it was midnight in Osaka and no one was in that office, she had to limit herself to communicating with her staff in Los Angeles. It was seven a.m. at her office, and she was pleased to receive a reply to her first e-mail in moments. She'd trained her staff well. They might drop dead of a heart attack at thirty-five, but no one could say they didn't work for every dime they earned.

Antonia went out some time in the early afternoon, after Laurie refused her generous offer of lunch. No longer having to respond to the occasional polite question, she kicked things into high gear. Her phone was working, the internet connection was fast, and she was able to get updates from everyone on her senior staff.

An e-mail came in from Hiroshi in Japan, and she bristled with excitement now that she was finally able to talk to the people with their fingers on the pulse of Osaka. But Kaatje came in just minutes later. She leaned against the door frame, then said, "I hope you didn't sit in this room all day."

"No, I got up." Laurie stood and started to approach her, but then got shy and stopped mid-room. Now feeling awkward and unsure, she shrugged her shoulders and smiled. "I was just sending a few e-mails."

Kaatje clearly wasn't feeling shy. She closed the distance between them and put her arms around Laurie, holding her possessively. "Did you miss me?"

It would have been unspeakably rude for Laurie to admit the thought of Kaatje had barely crossed her mind. Resorting to her usual tactic with a lover, she said what she knew should have been her answer. "Of course. I've been waiting for you to come get me."

"Good." Kaatje put her hands on her shoulders and held her at arm's length. "How are you feeling?"

Laurie wracked her brain to recall why she might be feeling unwell, then it hit her. "Good!" She said this with far too much enthusiasm and Kaatje noticed it.

"Second thoughts?"

Laurie stood there, transfixed by Kaatje's kind eyes, bluer than the ocean she loved. "No. Not one." This was true. She'd not had a second to have a personal thought. But now that she did her stomach flipped and she was lost, adrift, even while gazing into those lovely eyes. She nuzzled her face into Kaatje's neck, unwilling to let her see the doubt, the uncertainty that she knew the perceptive woman would discover.

"That's surprising." Kaatje pulled back and scanned Laurie's face as carefully as an MRI. "I came out when I was a girl and it took a while for me to adjust." She gently touched Laurie's chin, tilting her head as she continued to look at her. "Are you sure?"

Laurie couldn't stand to have her look at her with such empathy. "No," she said, breaking into tears, something she did so rarely she hardly knew how to react. "I don't think I came out. I just…I don't know." Wiping at her eyes quickly and roughly, she felt her hands pulled away, replaced by a nicely ironed blue handkerchief that Kaatje used to dab gently around her reddening eyes.

"Let's go have dinner and talk."

—⁓—

Kaatje wanted to treat Laurie to dinner at a restaurant, but Laurie prevailed when she insisted she'd like to go back to the boat. They didn't bother to stop for food as Kaatje said she had a good supply of leftovers from lunch.

Kaatje stood at the counter in her galley, carefully filling two plates with various cold salads while she companionably told Laurie about her day. They sat down at the banquette and Laurie found herself wolfing the food down, remembering just how hungry she was after skipping lunch.

"Do you cook at home?" Kaatje asked.

Laurie's mouth was full. She shook her head, chewing quickly. "No, not much at all." She wiped her mouth with her napkin. "I can cook, a little, but I haven't used the oven in my new condo."

"How long have you been there?"

"Mmm." She squinted her eyes, as if she could see a mental calendar better that way. "A year and a half? Two years? Maybe a little more?"

"You don't cook," Kaatje said, giving her a quick grin.

"After I broke up with my boyfriend…" She trailed off, then made a face. "That's such a stupid term for someone you lived with. Anyway, after Colin and I broke up, I let a lot of things go to pot." She pinched the flesh around her waist. "I've gained twenty pounds in two years, and it's just from eating the wrong things."

"Twenty pounds? You must have been like a stick."

"Not really. Everyone in LA is thin."

Looking doubtful, Kaatje said, "Maybe you exaggerate?"

"Not much. Luxor wants us to be lean and mean. Not one person above me is overweight. They think it's a sign of lack of control. For me—they're right."

"What do you eat?"

"A lot of junk." She tried to hide her disgust with herself, finding that unattractive in others, but it was difficult. "I have good intentions. I eat a healthy lunch and think I'll stop for sashimi or a salad on the way home. But then I get involved in something and wind up eating pizza that someone orders in or, even worse, eating a couple of candy bars and having a couple of Cokes to keep me alert. I know I should drink Diet Coke, but I can't stand the taste, and sometimes a Coke is the only pleasure I get all day."

"It wouldn't take long to gain weight eating that way. Were you… depressed after you broke up with Colin?"

"Not really." Her reply was so offhanded it made her wince. "I was sad, of course, but not depressed."

"Who made the choice?"

"To break up?"

Kaatje nodded.

"He did. After six months of arguing about this and that, he said he wasn't happy. He moved out the next week when I was in Osaka." She took another bite and chewed for a few seconds, hoping Kaatje would change the subject. But when she was met with those inquisitive eyes, she added a little more. "He was pretty needy."

"How do you mean—needy?"

"He wanted to spend more time together." She let out a sigh. "I tried. I really did. Colin liked to have dinner together, and I made a huge effort to get home and cook. It was usually just a big salad or something simple, but I tried." She deftly transitioned back to the previous topic. "After he moved out, I didn't have to rush home, and I started my candy bar and pizza nonsense."

"I don't think anyone recommends candy for a balanced meal." Kaatje gave Laurie an impish grin that didn't show a bit of judgment on her part.

"Even worse," Laurie said, popping a cherry tomato into her mouth, "I stopped exercising. Colin was a runner, and he dragged me with him on weekends. Once he was gone it was all too easy to go to work."

"It sounds like you need a supervisor." She adopted a stern tone. "Laurie, we're not going to be able to keep you on if you don't eat some vegetables and go out for a walk."

Smiling, Laurie said, "You might not believe this, but I'm…I was… very athletic."

"Why wouldn't I believe it?" She reached over and pinched the same area Laurie had. "You can call this flab, but this is what makes you look womanly. You're not overweight." Her eyes lingered on Laurie's body for a moment. "You have a beautiful shape. Such nice, shapely curves." Kaatje's voice had taken on a husky, sexy timbre, but when she looked up and their eyes met, Laurie almost cried again.

"Sorry," she said, shaking her head roughly. "I'm not usually very emotional. I must be getting my period."

Kaatje reached over and took Laurie's hand, holding it tenderly. "Maybe you're upset. I would be if I were you. This has caught you by surprise."

Head nodding quickly, Laurie said, "I guess I am." She took a long breath. "It just seems silly."

"Silly? What about this is silly?"

"I'm almost thirty-two years old. I should have had my sexuality figured out when I was fifteen. How old were you?"

"You can't compare yourself to other people. And thirty-two isn't old. Lots of people, women especially, come out when they're adults."

Laurie shook her head. "I'm not coming out. Everyone says sexuality is fluid. I'm just being a little...fluid," she added weakly, looking unhappy with her choice of words.

"I'm only using 'coming out' as a term for people who discover a new part of their sexuality. Like my father's sister. She fell in love with a woman when she was a grandmother."

"Really? A grandmother?"

"Yes. Absolutely. She fell in love with a woman at work. Things were very...tense, I guess you'd say, with her children, but that only lasted a year or two. They were mostly upset that she divorced their father, I think. She seems very happy now, and my uncle remarried and he seems good too."

"Wow. That must have been hard for your cousins. Not to mention your uncle."

Kaatje shrugged, seemingly unconcerned. "I think everyone deserves to be happy and fulfilled. It's awful to disappoint the people you love, but sometimes you have to." She took Laurie's hand in her own and turned it over to run her finger down the lines on her palm. "Will you upset the people who love you if you tell them you're...you've had sex with a woman?"

Laurie thought about the question for quite a while. "Not much, I don't think. I told you yesterday that my mom has asked me if I might be a lesbian. She made a point of telling me it would be just fine with her if I am."

"That's encouraging. Maybe she sensed something."

"Yeah. Maybe. My sister has asked me a dozen times. I'm not sure how she'll take it." The truth of that statement made her stomach flip, and she couldn't back away from it fast enough. "If it turns out that I think this is something I want to do again...you know. I won't tell anyone now. It's too...new."

"Yeah, I know," Kaatje said, still looking at Laurie with calm equanimity. "You don't *ever* have to tell anyone." Her mouth quirked into a grin. "You have vacation immunity."

Laurie smiled back. "Immunity, huh?"

"Absolutely. You can go home and forget all about it. Just tell yourself you had Caribbean fever."

Laurie scooted over until she was pressed up against Kaatje's side. Looking at her smooth skin, burnished by the sun, she was unable to resist the urge to kiss her soft cheek. "I don't remember ever being as attracted to anyone as I am to you."

Kaatje gave her an almost lecherous look. "You make my pulse race. I thought about your body so many times today I could barely keep up a conversation."

"Really?" A flash of doubt hit her in the chest.

"Really. When you were grousing at me yesterday morning, I thought, 'I don't like getting chewed out, but having a beautiful woman do it makes it tolerable.'"

"You're teasing." Laurie playfully slapped at her tan leg.

"No, I'm not. You're a great-looking woman. I don't want to seem shallow, but if you hadn't been as pretty as you are, I never would have offered to take you out."

"Ack!"

"Well, it's true. You were pretty grouchy, not to mention judgmental. The only positive aspect I could see were these." She ran her hands ostentatiously along Laurie's curves.

"That's a funny compliment, but I kinda like it."

Kaatje tilted her head and moved a little closer. "Can I kiss you again?"

"Yeah." Laurie was surprised to hear the desire in her voice. "I want you to."

Moving forward, Kaatje captured Laurie's lips in a long, tender kiss. Their lips merged as though they were made for each other, soft, yielding and welcoming. They continued to kiss and gently touch each other until Laurie whispered, "Let's go to bed."

"Let's," Kaatje echoed, smiling like a happy fox.

They lay together in a tangle of sheets, a cool, light wind drying the perspiration from their bodies. Feeling drained, Laurie could easily have fallen asleep, even though it was barely dark. But Kaatje seemed alert and energized, so Laurie forced herself to sit up and try to get a second wind. She stretched and stuck her hands up in the air, then shook them briskly. After taking in a few deep breaths, the lethargy started to ebb. She looked down at Kaatje, who was gazing at her with ill-disguised desire.

"You are remarkably beautiful," Kaatje said softly. "If I had to tell someone about my ideal woman, I'd describe you."

Laurie tweaked her nose playfully. "You can't be serious."

"I am." Kaatje's voice was calm and thoughtful, and her expression was earnest. "Why would I say that if I didn't mean it?"

Laurie thought about the question for a moment and couldn't think of a good answer. "Well, I didn't know I had an ideal type of woman, but if I had, she'd look like you ."

Since Laurie was sitting up, resting against the wall, Kaatje was able to scoot around and lay her head in her lap. "Why don't you do something fun like play with my hair?"

Laughing gently at the way she'd phrased the request, Laurie did as she was asked, taking strands of hair and idly arranging them. "I've never played with a woman's hair. I like it."

"Let's explore your psyche for a while." Kaatje said this with the same tone she'd used for having Laurie play with her hair.

"I'm not much for that kind of thing."

"Okay. That's fine. But you'll indulge me and answer a few questions, won't you?"

"I guess it can't hurt."

"Good enough." Kaatje was looking up at her, a playful grin quirking up her lips. "Why do you think people have asked if you might be a lesbian?"

Laurie rolled her eyes. "Because my mom and my sister love to be in my business."

Kaatje's hair rubbed against Laurie's thighs when she nodded. "You might want to think about that for a while. That's not the first question most people ask if they're curious about your life."

"Maybe they're really lesbians and they're projecting their hidden desires onto me." She giggled and gently picked Kaatje's head up and placed it back down on the bed. "I'm going to get something to drink. Want anything?"

"No, thanks."

When Laurie returned, Kaatje was lying right where she'd left her. Laurie lay down and sipped at a glass of water. "It's awfully nice out here."

"Yeah, it is."

A long silence descended upon them and Laurie could feel a flash of anger start to bubble up. By her silence, Kaatje was forcing her to talk about something she had no interest in, not to mention something that was none of Kaatje's business. "I don't know why my family asks questions, or why Colin or Fernando asked me. How can I know what they're thinking? Do I have to tell them all I slept with a woman just to get more feedback on things that aren't their business?"

Kaatje looked at her for quite a few seconds. Her eyes blinked slowly, then she sat up and said, "I didn't mean to pry. We don't have to talk about it."

A frustrated sigh made Laurie's lips flap. "No, I'm being a jerk. I don't like to talk about feelings. I ignore them whenever humanly possible."

"Isn't that hard to do?"

"Not if you practice hard enough." She noticed that her plastic smile wasn't returned. "Okay." She took in and let out a big breath. "My sister has been on me since I was in high school, asking why I never seemed to care whether I had a boyfriend or not. She's two years older, and always tried to see my world through her eyes. I always thought she was being overdramatic: Will a guy call? Does he like me as much as I like him? What will I do if he breaks up with me? Stuff like that."

A small frown settled between Kaatje's brows. "That seems common to me. I thought the world revolved around whether my girlfriend would call me when I first came...when I started having sex."

"I've never been like that. I like having a boyfriend, but they're a lot of work too. Being single is underrated."

"What's the best part of being single?"

"Easy one," Laurie said, smiling. "Being able to do what you want when you want to. Not having to think about the other person before you commit to anything."

"What's the worst part?"

Laurie's smile faded slowly. "Holidays."

"Holidays?"

"Yeah. When I take a few days off and visit my family in Cincinnati."

"I don't know that place."

"It's in Ohio. A little east of the center of the country. My parents and my sister and brother-in-law all live near there. And sometimes, like at Christmas, I see how my sister and my mom have something I've never had."

"And that's...?"

"It's hard to describe." She took a minute, thinking of what quality her mother and sister shared. "I suppose it's love." She fleetingly met Kaatje's gaze. "I can tell they're both happy to have someone to share things with. For them, the good things about a relationship seem to outnumber the bad ones."

"That should be true for every relationship." Kaatje stroked Laurie's leg, making her skin pebble.

"It hasn't been for me." Laurie's voice was very quiet. "I've never been in love. I know that now."

"Now?" Kaatje's eyebrows shot up. "You've just now realized that?"

Laurie nodded. "Just now. I was going through the motions, but I didn't love Colin, or Ben, or Jeremy. They told me they loved me, and I replied like I thought I should."

"How did you…what makes you know this now?"

Laurie slid down until she was right in front of Kaatje. Looking into her eyes, she said, "I wasn't connected. I've just met you and I feel like we've really shared something." Tears came to her eyes and she wiped the annoying distraction away. "You made me feel more than I ever felt with Colin and I knew him for years. We had sex hundreds of time." Her tears continued and her voice shook. "Was he as absent as I was? How could he not have known I was barely there?" She cried harder, sobbing as Kaatje took her into her arms.

"Shh, don't cry. It'll be all right."

"I know," Laurie sobbed. "I'm going to make it right. I know what I've been missing, and I won't ever settle for less. I'm going to find love. It can be with a man or a woman, but it's going to be love."

―――

It was still early when Laurie came back to bed for the second time. She stood in front of Kaatje and deliberately ran a brush through her hair, removing all of the tangles their thrashing around had created. "Have you ever slept with a virgin? I mean a woman like me?"

"Probably."

"You don't know?" Laurie paused, brush in mid-air.

"I assume the first girl I had sex with was a virgin, but I didn't specifically ask her."

"Why not?"

Smiling slyly, Kaatje said, "Why should I have? I thought we'd discovered something new."

Sitting down next to her, Laurie said, "That's cute to think of. How old were you?"

"Fourteen."

"Mmm, that's pretty young. I was sixteen when I started fooling around. Almost eighteen when I had real sex."

"Real sex means intercourse?"

Laurie nodded. "Yeah."

"Mmm, then I haven't had real sex yet. I hope I like it."

Laurie almost fell for her innocent smile. "Lesbian sex is real. It's just...I don't know." She blushed, the color racing to her cheeks. "That's how my friends and I referred to it when we were in high school. Sex meant intercourse."

"I suppose many people feel that way. But all of the categories seem unnecessary to me. To me sex is sharing your body with another person you're attracted to. Giving and getting pleasure doesn't have to be complicated."

Laurie moved so she could reach Kaatje's head. She started gently untangling her hair and brushing it. "Do you like this?" she asked unnecessarily, given Kaatje's purring.

"Very much." She shifted to lie on her belly, allowing Laurie access to the back of her head.

"Have you had sex with a lot of people?" There was a moment of silence, then she said, "I can't believe I asked you that!" Patting Kaatje's back, she added, "Don't answer."

A muted laugh rose up from the bed. "I wasn't going to. I'll talk about relationships I've had, but not my sex life. No good can come from that."

"That's probably a good practice. I'm sorry I asked, but...I'm very interested in you." She put the brush aside and started to run her hands down Kaatje's back, feeling the muscles under the thin layer of flesh. "Everything about you is fascinating."

Kaatje turned her head but her eyes couldn't reach Laurie. She lay back down and said, "Do you have a crush on me?"

"Yes." Laurie bent over and kissed along Kaatje's spine, making her giggle. "I have a very big crush on you."

They slept together, cuddling against one another while a cool ocean breeze blew through the cabin. The bed was smaller than Laurie was used to, but she didn't need an extra inch. Kaatje wasn't like most of the men she'd slept with, who seemed to take up massive amounts of space. In fact,

Laurie realized she was encroaching on Kaatje's half of the bed and started to move away. But Kaatje's arm ensnared her and held her in place. Then Kaatje rolled onto her side and nuzzled against Laurie's neck. "Stay close," she murmured.

Now enveloped by her body, Laurie pushed back against Kaatje. A deep sigh left her lips and she felt herself drift towards sleep, not one thing on her mind save for the decadent feeling of Kaatje's warmth pressing into her.

———

Laurie woke when the sun hit the sheet that covered her. She was alone, but a delightful scent tickled her nose. As she got up, she pulled the sheet from its moorings and wrapped it around her body. She padded down the short hall to the galley where the smell of pancakes drew her towards a naked Kaatje.

"This is something I could get used to," Laurie said, looking longingly at Kaatje's firm ass and square shoulders. "The pancakes look good too."

Kaatje turned and smiled broadly. "I know Americans like pancakes. I thought I'd surprise you. These look like American pancakes, don't they?"

"What other kind are there?"

"Dutch. Ours are thin and we eat them for dinner. I changed some proportions, so this is an experiment."

"Your American instincts are perfect." She stood next to her and felt an unexpected thrill when Kaatje kissed the top of her head. Impulsively, Laurie wrapped her arms around Kaatje, hugging her tightly. "I'm very happy to be here. With you."

Kaatje switched the spatula to her right hand and draped the left around Laurie. "I'm happy you're here." She kissed her again, letting her lips stay right on Laurie's head for a minute. "I have to work at noon. Want to stay with me or go to my parents'?"

She said this offhandedly, and Laurie could have believed Kaatje didn't have an opinion. But Kaatje's body gained tension as the seconds ticked by. The desire to work was almost overpowering. Almost. But she looked

Kaatje in the eye and let her heart speak. "I have to leave Sunday. I want to stay with you until then."

In a flash, the tense muscles in Kaatje's body relaxed. "That's how I would have voted." She dropped another kiss onto her head and focused on cooking their breakfast.

Laurie stood there for a few seconds, shocked into immobility by her decision. She was intentionally giving up a day's work—a day that would save her more than a day when she was back in the office, what with meetings and other time wasters. And she was doing it only to spend the day with Kaatje. On a boat. Sailing. What a difference a day made!

After their afternoon sail, they set off on Kaatje's bike. There were many people crowding the street, with most of them heading for the bars and clubs along Mako. But Kaatje went a bit further, away from the casinos and clubs, pulling over when they'd passed every commercial-looking enterprise. Dilapidated homes lined the street, and mangy brown dogs ambled along, looking like it had been quite a while since they'd had a good meal. "It looks like all of the action is by the casinos," Laurie observed, trying to be diplomatic. She never would have stopped at a place like this by herself, and she wasn't sure she wanted to be there with Kaatje.

"Yeah. That's where you go if you want to get laid." Kaatje quirked a grin. "That's what I'm told."

Laurie reached for her hand, then stopped herself. Kaatje must have seen or sensed her furtive move, for she nonchalantly took Laurie's hand in hers as they walked.

"Is it okay to hold hands?" Laurie asked.

"Okay with me? Yeah. I'm the one who took your hand."

Laurie squeezed her hand hard. "You know what I mean. I've never had to think about things like this, but my gay friends are always careful if they don't know the neighborhood."

"I know the neighborhood." They walked past a scramble of parked cars and Kaatje nodded towards the entry. "Here we are."

Laurie looked at the sign that read, "No Jerks" on a wooden post that seemed to demarcate the entrance. The place was open-air, with just a roof to make it a building. They passed four or five grills that held something delicious smelling. The crowd was ethnically mixed, with about three quarters of the patrons West Indian and the rest whites.

When they walked up to the bar, the bartender, a middle-aged West Indian man nodded to Kaatje. "Here's my friend," he said as he leaned over the pick-up area to offer a hug.

"Good to see you, Winston. This is my friend Laurie. Laurie, Winston."

"Nice meeting you." Winston smiled warmly. "What can I get you ladies?"

"Carib for me," Kaatje said. "Laurie?"

"Is that a beer?"

"Yes," Winston replied. "We have beer, soft drinks and Planter's Punch."

"I'll have the same as Kaatje."

"Sit down at a table and have something to eat," Winston said.

"What's fresh tonight?" Kaatje asked.

"Coffer fish, red snapper and lobster."

Kaatje looked at Laurie and said, "Do you like lobster?"

"Sure. I like almost everything."

"Great. Let's have lobster and red snapper. And…" She narrowed her eyes, clearly thinking. "Macaroni and cheese, peas and rice, coleslaw and more peas and rice."

"You know what's good," Winston said, chuckling as he wrote the order down.

Kaatje pressed her hand against the small of Laurie's back and led her to a table. They sat, then Laurie looked around, finally asking, "How do they close up at night?"

"They don't. Winston's rigged up a way to lock up the liquor and he has a refrigerator over there that's got a huge chain around it." She shrugged. "People don't tamper with his stuff very often."

"I can't imagine having a place in LA with no walls."

"There are a lot of open-air places here. We call them lo-los. There are more of them on the French side, but I like this one."

Laurie looked at the low-keyed crowd and saw that many of the people seemed to know each other. Kaatje returned several waves and a few greetings, but when their food and drinks were delivered, she focused on them and Laurie. "Ooh, this is good," Laurie said, biting into the remarkably sweet bit of lobster that Kaatje held up before her.

"Spiny lobster. You probably haven't had it before."

"I don't think I have, but there's a really good lobster in Japan that I like. It costs an arm and a leg though."

"This was twelve bucks," Kaatje said. "Including the side dishes."

"Fantastic." Laurie looked around again, getting a sense of the place. "I like it here. No tourists."

"Just one," Kaatje said, looking a little sad.

It hurt the pit of her stomach to think of leaving. Laurie tried to get back to happier topics. "You've said you don't go out much. Isn't there much to do?"

"There's enough to do, but I don't like to go through my money too quickly. It's much cheaper to stay on the boat and eat leftovers. Plus, I like to read a book and relax after being with the public all day. That works for me here."

"Are you different in…Holland?" She'd heard Kaatje refer to it that way, but she was going to have to do some research on the different ways to refer to Kaatje's home country.

"Yeah. Night and day. You'll have to visit to see."

"I've never really been to Europe. I just changed planes in Iceland once."

"Well, you saw most of it," Kaatje teased.

"I'd like to come." *I would? I've never had the slightest inkling of an interest in Europe.*

"I'd love to have you. I usually stay at my parents' home, but I sneak off for quick trips to various places. I'm a good tour guide."

"Maybe I should start reading travel guides."

"What *do* you like to read, if not travel guides?"

"I'm not much of a reader. For pleasure, that is. I have to read a lot of things to keep up in my industry."

"Sounds like fun."

"You're a bad liar. What about you? What holds your interest after a long day's sail?"

"It depends on my mood. I like a good lesbian romance—"

Laurie almost spit her drink out. "Lesbian romance? Is there such a thing?"

"Yeah. Of course there is. There are millions of straight romance books. Why shouldn't lesbians have them?"

Laurie stopped to think about that for a moment. "I guess that makes sense. I don't think I've ever seen them though. Is there a big, blonde, arrogant looking woman on the cover with a smaller woman clutching at her?"

"Not usually." Her grin was wry. "I read e-books. Cheaper and more environmentally friendly. And I don't *just* read romances. I like technical books about sailing and travel. And I read about politics and social issues when I'm in the Netherlands. I like to go to used bookstores and pick up a suitcase full."

Laurie took her hand, which had been playing with a pepper shaker. "Did you think I was making fun of you for reading romances?"

"Yeah. A little bit." Her eyes were slightly hooded, but Laurie couldn't tell if it was from embarrassment or pique.

"I didn't mean to." She squeezed Kaatje's hand. "I'm sorry."

Kaatje looked into her eyes. "It's okay. It's just that I get lonely when I'm single. I was made to be in a relationship."

"Ooh," Laurie cooed. "I bet you do get lonely." Her heart hurt from thinking about Kaatje sitting on her boat all alone.

"It's reassuring to read a story about women falling in love and being happy. It makes me feel like I'm part of that community, even though the lesbian community here could fit in a bus."

"Maybe I should read one. Although I probably wouldn't feel like part of the community. I'm sure there aren't any thirty-one-year-old straight women in them."

Kaatje chuckled long and hard. "If it weren't for straight women, there'd be no lesbian romances."

Most of the other patrons had finished eating, but no one seemed in a hurry to leave. Children ran around, a dog or two tried to cadge a few morsels and the vibe could not have been more relaxed. Laurie had another beer while quizzing Kaatje about her family in Amsterdam.

"Yes, I'm the baby of the family. Daniël is six years older and Margriet is just fifteen months younger than he is. I think I was a surprise."

"Maybe Margriet was too. Having kids that close together must be agony."

"Hey, maybe Daniël was too. My parents might have had three surprises."

"You're a nice surprise. Tell me about your niece and nephew."

"With pleasure." She took out her phone and turned it in Laurie's direction. "This gorgeous child is Roos, Daniël's daughter. She's seven and probably the smartest child in the world."

Smiling up at her, Laurie said, "You're clearly impartial."

Clicking through, she stopped at a picture of a small boy. "And this is Thijs, Margriet's baby. He's going to be four by the time I visit. He's equally adorable, and a very rough and tumble little guy. He's going to be a sailor, just like his Tante Kaatje." She lingered on his picture, looking at him with such fondness that Laurie could have choked up.

"They're lucky kids to have you. Do you want to have kids?"

"I do, but I won't." Her head shook forcefully. "I don't want to have to have a real job, and it would be impossible to raise a baby and work on the boat."

"What if you had a partner who wanted to have one?"

"Not a partner." Again, she shook her head. "A wife. I'd only have a baby with a woman I was married to. That's the way to make sure the baby has two parents obligated to care for him."

"Can you get married here?"

"Not yet, but I can in The Netherlands. And St. Maarten recognizes all Dutch marriages. I just need a woman."

"You're lucky. My gay friends will have to wait a long time for the US to allow gay marriage."

"Again, I don't know a lot about it, but from the little I know, the US isn't very much like The Netherlands."

"When will you visit your home again?"

"I have to go to a wedding in January, so I'll stay there for at least a couple of weeks."

"Sounds expensive."

"Not too. My brother-in-law works for KLM. If I give him a few months notice, he gets me a great fare. But even if I had to dig into my savings, I'd go. Stefanie is a dear friend, and I put friendship above finances." She shrugged. "You have to keep your priorities straight."

Sure you did. But flying to Holland for a wedding and missing weeks of work sounded like something people wanted to do—but couldn't. Somehow Kaatje didn't play by the rules other people seemed to accept without question.

"But you said you go to Holland to escape hurricane season. When's that?"

"I like to take the boat down island in July. If I pay someone to do my maintenance, I can take off right then."

"When do you have to come back to work?"

Kaatje's smile was a little haughty. "I can come back whenever I want." She stuck her arms straight up and inhaled deeply. "Freedom."

While her hands were out, Laurie took advantage of the bit of skin exposed by her shirt riding up and tickled her.

"Okay, okay. I'll give you a serious answer. Depending on the forecast, I could work until September, but I'm usually tired by July. Then I start up again in November. "

That was probably the strangest sentence Laurie had ever heard. Kaatje had a job that was as close to a vacation as any job in the world. And she needed months to recover from it? Maybe she had one of those chronic fatigue diseases. That was the only possible explanation for an otherwise healthy young woman to need months of rest after sailing.

"You're really tired? Like exhausted?"

"Well, not exhausted, but I need time in Holland to recharge. Seeing my family for a couple of months is like a tonic."

"I'm sure it is, but who can afford that?"

"I can." Kaatje looked smug again, and Laurie had an irresistible urge to wipe the smirk from her face.

"But that's why you can't afford to go out very often. If you worked more you'd have the freedom to do whatever you wanted in your free time."

"Which I'd have less of." She put her hand over Laurie's and gazed into her eyes. "I don't love money nearly as much as I love my family. My life is good because I see them for a long time every year. Having more money wouldn't make up for missing Roos' and Thijs' childhoods."

"I feel the same about my nieces." Damn, that was an effective argument, but there were probably ten people in the whole world who could manage it. Still, loving your family was an awesome attribute. She took Kaatje's hand and leaned over to speak softly. "It's nice to find someone who feels that way. Most of the people I know left home and only go back when they can't avoid it."

"I love it here, and I plan on staying. But if I had to choose between staying here or seeing my family, I'd be back in The Netherlands in a heartbeat."

"I guess I'd do the same, but The Netherlands sounds a lot more exciting than Cincinnati."

"I don't know Cincinnati, but Amsterdam can be a lot of fun. It's the opposite of St. Maarten."

"Uhm…do you have…is there anyone special…" *Stay out of her business! She's already told you she doesn't want to talk about her sex life.*

"Do I have a girlfriend?" At Laurie's weak nod, Kaatje said, "If I did, I wouldn't be with you right now. I don't cheat." That was awfully good to hear. It was dreadful to meet someone you were attracted to and find out they didn't keep their promises.

"I don't either. Of course, that's not saying much since I was never much into sex…until now."

"Don't start cheating." Kaatje leaned over and kissed her gently. "Sex is never worth the damage you cause."

"I won't." It was like Kaatje was a much older, wiser woman, giving her tips on how to live. It was adorable, and once again made Laurie feel like she could tear up. "I bet you could get married in ten minutes if you wanted to."

"Not true. I love the way I live, but it's hard to find a woman who wants to join me."

"Why? I'd think women would be jumping right onto your boat."

"Not really. Most people like to have one place to live. I had a girlfriend who thought she could live with a long-distance relationship, but she gave up after two years." She sighed, looking a little sad. "I don't make enough money to fully support a partner, and no one I've met has a job that will let her come to St. Maarten for months at a time. It's a problem."

"Why couldn't she live here full time?"

Kaatje's smile was slow to form, and when it did it was playful. "That was my question. But she couldn't find a job here that would have let her go to The Netherlands for a few months."

"And she probably thought you should give up the Caribbean for her."

"Very perceptive. That was almost a quote. But I couldn't imagine giving up my home."

"You'll find someone. You're too adorable to be alone for long." Of course, if Kaatje worked more she could afford to support a girlfriend, but she clearly didn't want to hear that argument again.

———

Back on the boat, Kaatje grabbed a bottle of wine and a thick blanket and Laurie carried two glasses up to the trampoline. They were on the mooring, but the boats around them were all empty, giving them complete privacy. The night was warm with a slight breeze, not even enough to ruffle their hair. Muted sounds abounded: hardware on the boats creaking and clanking, plus the soft lapping of water against hulls. The air smelled lightly of salt and some vaguely perfumed flower.

Kaatje sat down first and rolled the blanket up to provide a backrest. Then Laurie sat down in front of her and leaned against her body. "This is the most comfortable I've ever been," Laurie said after a few minutes of perfect silence.

Kaatje poured a few ounces of wine in each glass, then slipped the bottle into a holder at the base of the mast. She clinked her glass against Laurie's. "I have no complaints." She kissed the crown of Laurie's head. "Well, I guess I have one." Gently playing with Laurie's hair, she said, "I wish you didn't have to leave soon."

Laurie sighed. "You have no idea how much I want to stay. I'm having the time of my life."

"I like you." Kaatje kissed down the side of her head, bending as much as she could to reach Laurie's neck. "I like you a lot."

"I like you too. And I feel like I could get more comfortable with this new 'sleeping with women' idea if I could work at it." When she turned to look up at Kaatje their eyes met and lingered. "You're the most beautiful person I've ever kissed."

Kaatje made an outraged face. "I hope so!"

Laurie smiled at her for a long moment. "You're really very pretty. And soft and huggable. Do all lesbians like to touch as much as you do?"

"I haven't slept with all of them yet. I can't be sure."

Patting her leg, Laurie said, "Let me know when you reach your goal."

"I know you were kidding, but my goal isn't to sleep with a lot of women. I'm ready to settle down. I used my twenties to explore. Now I'm ready to marry."

"Have you been in love before?"

"Love is hard to define. But I've never made a commitment to a woman."

"No one?"

"Not a permanent one. As I said earlier, I've had preliminary discussions about moving here or there but that's all. I need to find someone who's willing to compromise so we can both be happy."

"I'm like that too. I want to be with someone who wants to hang in there and work on a relationship."

"Have you had that?"

Laurie was contemplative for a surprisingly long time. "You know, this sounds awful, but I had it with Colin."

"Why is that awful?"

"Because I didn't do the same for him."

"Oh." Kaatje hugged her tenderly. "Does that make you feel bad?"

"Yeah, it really does. He put a lot of effort into making things work and I just glided along. That really sucked."

"All you can do is learn from past mistakes. Just try not to make them again."

"I'm really going to try," Laurie said, determination filling her voice. "I won't be in another relationship where I'm not fully invested."

"It's scary, isn't it?"

"Very. But I'm not going to let that stop me."

A breeze blew the wind direction signal above their heads in a circle. Kaatje wrapped her arms around Laurie and cuddled her tightly. They didn't say another word until they'd finished their wine and Kaatje patted Laurie's leg to signal it was time to go in.

———

They'd been very close and tender with each other while on deck, but entering the cabin seemed to break the spell. Laurie was close to tears as she headed for the bathroom. Her gratitude towards Kaatje for showing her another way to express herself was massive. The desire to stay right in St. Maarten, sailing, talking, making love, and sleeping in the open air pulled at her fiercely. But the magic dust was almost gone. Soon she'd be going home and her feet would have to be on the speeding treadmill as soon as she arrived.

She stood in the small bathroom, brushing her teeth, thinking about how she'd start to tackle her backed-up work. Her mind lingered on such a myriad of details that when she exited into the narrow hallway she didn't feel Kaatje come up behind her. But when one strong arm encircled her waist and Kaatje's warm mouth attached itself to her neck, all thoughts of work vanished.

All she could think of, imagine, and feel was that they were going to have sex again. Soon. Her body was flooded with images of Kaatje's body, her strength, her softness, her beauty. Her own body started to move involuntarily, pressing up hard against Kaatje's, their hips swaying together in a slow, sensual cadence.

Laurie could feel her nipples harden without being touched, could feel her pussy tingle deliciously and her gut tighten with need. She'd never had such a lightning-fast physical reaction to another person, and she couldn't wait to get Kaatje into bed.

But Kaatje wasn't in such a hurry. Her hands rose and started to massage Laurie's breasts, holding and squeezing them while Laurie pushed against her, whimpering from the sensation.

Laurie started to move, but Kaatje held her still, capturing her body in a tender, yet forceful, embrace. It was unnerving. Laurie wanted to fill her hands with Kaatje's body, kiss her beautiful lips. But she was compelled to stay right where she was, with nothing to do except experience her own body while Kaatje leisurely explored it.

Those determined hands slowly unbuttoned her shirt, then one slipped into her shorts, skimming past her panties to cup her sex and gently squeeze. Laurie purred with pleasure as Kaatje's hands moved up and down her body, pinching, grasping and delving into any place that caught her interest.

Laurie shifted her weight from foot to foot, itching to move to the bed, but Kaatje maintained her infuriatingly delightful hold, finally pushing Laurie's shorts to the floor and sneaking inside her panties to probe her pussy. "Oh, God," Laurie groaned. "I can't stand up any more."

"Yes, you can," Kaatje whispered hotly, right into her ear. She slipped into her, biting Laurie's neck as her fingers slid in easily. "I've got you," she said, holding on even tighter. "Just relax and let me take over."

Laurie did her best, consciously relaxing her muscles. But she couldn't stop shifting her hips and thrusting against Kaatje's hand. Those fingers knew her better than anyone ever had, dipping and swirling to touch every part of her. Then, just as she felt she might come, Kaatje slipped out and held her hips while biting her neck again. "Not yet," she whispered as Laurie moaned her disappointment. "Soon, but not yet." Then she swept Laurie off her feet and carried her into the cabin, laying her on the bed as she stood over her, removing her own clothes with deliberate speed. She grinned down at her, so beautiful that Laurie almost burst into tears at her lovely face. "I want to remember tonight," Kaatje said, her voice a little rough. "Let's go slowly."

Laurie found herself nodding, even as she wondered what about the last ten minutes had been slow.

CHAPTER EIGHT

THEY LAY TOGETHER in the gently rocking boat, each of them nearly exhausted from their lovemaking. Kaatje was almost asleep when something hit Laurie and she had to share it. "I think I know why sex wasn't a bigger issue for me."

"Hmm?" Kaatje absently patted Laurie's shoulder, then sat up enough to rest her weight on her forearm.

Laurie looked at her briefly, then put her hand gently on Kaatje's cheek. "Did I wake you up? Go back to sleep. I was just thinking aloud."

"No, no. I'm awake. What about sex?"

Laurie smiled at her, seeing the fatigue in her eyes. "It's nothing important. Go to sleep." She kissed her lips, smiling when she pulled away. "That's another difference." Grimacing, she acted as though she were zipping her lips closed.

Kaatje sat up taller and pulled Laurie to her chest as she leaned against the wall. Now she sounded awake when she said, "Difference in what?"

"I used to hate it when I could taste myself on a guy's lips. I always felt kinda sorry for him." She pointed at her vulva. "Having to go down there."

Kaatje didn't reply, but her chest bounced up and down when she laughed.

"But it's nice," she said, turning to see Kaatje's eyes. "It's really sexy to have my mouth on you and feel how it turns you on." She shivered roughly. "Just thinking about it makes me want to do it again."

"It wasn't like that with men?"

"No, not for me. I was up for just about anything, but oral sex always seemed kinda demeaning." She turned again, meeting Kaatje's interested gaze. "I can't figure out why."

"I can't guess. But I bet it'll come to you."

"Yeah." She nodded slowly. "I was thinking about sex in general when I woke you up." She patted Kaatje's muscular thigh. "You're a bad liar."

"But I'm polite. That makes up for the lying."

Squeezing Kaatje's leg, she continued. "My boyfriends weren't jerks by any means, but sex was always about intercourse. That was the main event. They focused on me long enough to get me ready to do the deed."

"Maybe you haven't met the right guy." Kaatje hugged her again, kissing her head repeatedly. "Not that I want you to go back to men. I think you're a pretty good fit right here."

Laurie reached behind herself to pat as high up on Kaatje's thigh as she could reach. "I like fitting right there." Nestling back into the embrace, she added, "Maybe I wasn't good in bed and that made my boyfriends kinda focus on themselves. Does that make sense?"

"Yeah, I guess. You can't have good sex if you're not both into it and each other."

"Yeah. That's the point. I wasn't into them."

"In case you're wondering," Kaatje said softly, "you're very good in bed."

"I guess I *was* wondering…at least a little bit. But given that you're an admitted liar, I don't know if I should believe you."

"No lies," Kaatje said, her voice sounding sleepy again. "I'm into you, and I didn't have any doubts you were into me." She kissed Laurie one last time, pausing to gaze into her eyes for a few seconds. It looked as though she were going to speak again, but her blue eyes closed and she lay down and snuggled into Laurie's arms.

⚊⚊

They spent the next day cruising around the island, while Kaatje leisurely taught Laurie about the parts of the boat, some elementary lessons about how to sail, and some more in-depth instruction about how to drop and retrieve the anchor. After Laurie had worked on properly dropping the anchor for a long time, Kaatje said they might as well use their position to go snorkeling.

The cove they were in was deserted—not another boat in sight. Kaatje ducked into her cabin and returned with a wetsuit and a rash guard. She handed Laurie the wetsuit. "I think this will fit you."

Laurie looked down at the relatively thin suit, then back at Kaatje questioningly.

"It'll be a little colder in this spot given the way the current's moving. Plus, you won't have to put sunblock on."

Laurie shrugged and started to doff her clothing. Once she was naked, Kaatje helped her struggle into the too small suit. Getting it zipped was tricky, but once Laurie was encased, Kaatje stood back and gave her a long, assessing gaze. "Damn, you're a great looking woman." Her eyes glowed with desire. "And as soon as we're done looking at fish we're gonna move out there"—she pointed at the unending vista—"and I'm gonna chew that right off of you."

Laurie beamed a smile at her. "I can't tell you how good that sounds."

After they chased fish around the ocean and each other around the boat, Kaatje sat in her captain's chair, wearing a bikini that showed off her body to such effect that Laurie had trouble focusing on anything else. "What's this?" Kaatje asked, slapping her hand against a gleaming stainless part.

"A winch."

"Right. This?" She reached behind her head.

"The…wait…I know this." Laurie bit her lip, thinking. "The vang?"

"No. Try again."

"Darn it, it was one of the first things you taught me."

"Want a hint?"

"Sure."

"It's what I wish you could do."

Frowning, Laurie thought, quietly saying, "What you wish I could…"
Her face lit in a sad smile. "Stay. I wish I could too. I really do."

To thank them for their hospitality, Laurie offered to take Kaatje and
her parents out for a nice dinner. Kaatje wasn't crazy about the idea, but she
admitted her parents would appreciate it, and she called with the proposal.
After speaking for a few minutes, in Dutch, she hung up. "Bad news."

"They can't make it?"

"No," Kaatje said, pouting. "They can."

Laurie didn't have any clothes to wear to a nice restaurant, so she
convinced Kaatje to take her shopping. Kaatje swore she hated shopping
for clothes, but she was very helpful, looking Laurie over and suggesting
different colors and styles she thought would suit her. It took an hour, but
they were successful.

When they reached the Hoogebooms', neither Theo nor Antonia were
home yet, and they went into Kaatje's room to change.

"Do you stay here often?"

"Never. My mother calls this my room, but it's really the guest room."

"Never? Not ever?"

"Well, I lived here when we first moved to the island, but I haven't
slept here in a long time."

"Do you just like being independent or…?"

"I live on my boat. It's my home. Why would I sleep somewhere else?"

There was clearly more to it than that, but it didn't seem that Kaatje
was in the mood to expound.

"What did you do when you first came to the island?"

"Oh, it was a hard road," Kaatje said, frowning.

It was hard to decide how much veracity to put into Kaatje's
pronouncements about work. She wouldn't last a week at Luxor, and that
was being generous.

"I worked on a series of boats, doing all kinds of scut work. It took me five years to get to where I felt confident owning my own boat, then another two until I'd saved enough to make a down payment and qualify for a loan. But I'm glad I took my time. I made most of my mistakes on other guys' boats."

Laurie grinned at the dry way she put things, then started to remove the tags from her dress.

"My mom likes you," Kaatje said, making Laurie do a double-take.

"Where'd that come from?"

"I was just thinking about when I brought you here that first morning."

"How do you know she likes me? Have you talked to her? You haven't had a spare minute." She tried to waggle her eyebrows, but was largely unsuccessful.

"No, I haven't spoken with her. But she made you breakfast, and that's not like her."

Puzzled, Laurie looked at her blankly.

"I think this is a cultural difference. It's one of the things West Indians will never understand."

"Dutch people don't eat breakfast?"

"No, we do, but we have to know you to welcome you into our homes. Did you think my dad was very friendly?"

"Uhm…" She looked around the room, acting interested in the books on the shelves over the desk. "Did you ask me a question?"

"Right. He might have seemed distant, but that's pretty common. My mom has loosened up since we've been here, but my dad thinks it's peculiar to have strangers over for more than coffee."

"Interesting. If I told my mom I had a friend passing through Ohio she'd tell me to have you stop by and spend the night if you were gonna be within a hundred miles."

"That's not very common in Holland. We take it slow. First we have coffee, then you have us to your place for coffee. Then we'd have you over for dinner if those coffee dates went well."

"My mom has the mailman come in for cocoa when it's really cold out. For all she knows, he's a serial killer."

"That's not the Dutch way. At least that's not how my parents are. I'm more like a West Indian. I offered you a place to stay when I'd only known you for a couple of hours." She wore an angelically innocent expression that had Laurie giggling.

"Yeah, but I had to take my pants off first."

"Only for your comfort. You were comfortable, weren't you?"

Laurie sat down next to her and kissed her firmly. "Remarkably."

⁓

Theo drove them to a restaurant on the French side of the island. Other than many French language signs, it didn't look much different to Laurie. After they passed a large swath of undeveloped land, they went along a stretch of road lined by houses held together with nothing but hope. The brown dogs were everywhere and most of the residents were on the street corner or on their ramshackle porches. Men congregated in cliques, and everyone was holding a beer. The women and small children sat on kitchen chairs or sofas left in the yards. It was as poor a neighborhood as Laurie had ever seen—making the least advantaged parts of LA look prosperous.

She wanted to ask about the stunning poverty, but she didn't know how to frame the question. Maybe this was common in the Caribbean. But if so, why? And why didn't anyone do anything about it?

The neighborhoods slowly improved, and they passed two and three story apartment buildings and tidier single-family homes. They were close to the ocean, but only caught brief glimpses of it between buildings. Laurie was still thinking about the island when Theo squealed to a halt next to a parking place on a very narrow street. Antonia and Kaatje exclaimed something in Dutch. Evidently, finding the spot was some sort of accomplishment.

The restaurant was open-air, but it was a big step up from the lo-lo, with white tablecloths, a French speaking maitre d', and an upscale crowd. After they were settled at a nice table overlooking the ocean, the Francophone server left to get their drinks. "It's very nice of you to take us to dinner," Antonia said. "But it's not necessary. We only let you use our computer for a few hours."

"You saved me a huge phone bill," Laurie insisted. "International roaming costs an arm and a leg."

"We were surprised to see you're still visiting," Theo said, looking at Laurie with eyes that reminded her of Kaatje's." I thought you were in a hurry to get to St. Thomas."

"I was." Laurie couldn't help but spare a fond glance at Kaatje. "But Kaatje is such a good hostess, I couldn't make myself go."

"What was the situation? You were on a ship?"

"Yes." The server brought their drinks and Laurie took a sip. "I was on a cruise and missed the boat because I...told Kaatje the wrong time."

Frowning, Theo said, "That wasn't very wise. What about your traveling companions?"

"I didn't have any." At his puzzled look she said, "I work for the company that owns the boat. My boss sent me on a cruise to get me out of the office for a while."

Theo looked at Kaatje and said something in Dutch.

"No," Kaatje said, chuckling. "You understood her correctly. Laurie doesn't like to take vacations."

"I don't either," Theo said, still looking stern. "You leave for a week and you worry about the office while you're gone, then you have to do twice as much work when you get back."

"Exactly!" Laurie sensed a kindred soul.

"Theo likes to go into work on holidays," Antonia said, raising an eyebrow at him. "He says that's the best day to catch up."

"I'm with you on that. Even the cleaning crew doesn't come in on holidays."

"We have altogether too many holidays on this island. Everyone who's done anything to merit an entry in the history books has a holiday named for him. It's ridiculous. Do you have any idea how many lost man-hours we suffer from each of these so-called holidays?"

"I can imagine," Laurie said, while Kaatje and her mother exchanged weary looks.

"Tell me more about your job. You must have an important position if your company sends you on a cruise."

"She's very important," Kaatje said, smiling at Laurie. "I'm surprised they're still in business after having her gone for just a few days."

"What is your title?" Theo persisted.

"I'm a vice president," Laurie said, "but they throw titles around instead of money."

"But you're going to be promoted," Kaatje prompted.

"Yes, I should be promoted to senior VP in a month or two."

"How old are you?" Theo asked.

"I'm thirty-one."

He pushed his steel-framed glasses up on his nose and nodded solemnly. "That's remarkable for such a young woman. I'd like it if Kaatje got her first steady job by the time she was your age."

"How old are you?" Laurie asked, having never thought to bring it up.

"Twenty-eight. Well, twenty-eight in May."

"I thought you were at least my age," Laurie said, then she backtracked quickly. "Not that you look older than you are, but…"

"I've always looked older than I am."

"Tell us about your job," Theo said, ignoring all of the cross talk. "What division are you in?"

Laurie reluctantly pulled her attention away from Kaatje and said, "I'm in Theme Parks and Hotels. Ever since I started I've been working on our new park set to open in Osaka in June."

132

Again Theo sat back in his chair, looking very surprised. "The earthquake hasn't scrapped your plans?"

"No. It set us back a bit, but the government wants us to proceed with the original date. They think it will be a sign that Japan's open for business."

"Hmm," Theo said, narrowing his eyes. "I'm not familiar with Osaka. Is that where you're located?"

"No. I'm in Los Angeles, but I go to Osaka every other month."

"I didn't know that," Kaatje said, frowning. "Every other month?"

"Yeah, that's how it works out."

"But that kind of travel is awfully tiring. You haven't been exposed to any radiation, have you?"

"Travel is sitting in a chair," Theo said, scowling at his daughter and completely ignoring the question of radiation exposure. "It's a good time to catch up on things without interruption." His stern gaze landed on Laurie. "Do you agree?"

She did. Intensely. The thought of having cell-phone service in the air made her break out in a rash. It would just force her to take calls when she could be getting real work done. But she didn't care for his manner, and she ignored the question to get back to the original thread. "On the months I don't go to Japan, my boss does. Ideally, one of us would be there full time, but we need to be in LA to deal with the corporate side of the company." She made a face. "Accounting, finance, personnel, government regulations. All the fun stuff."

" You're the second in command for the whole project?"

"Yes, for the operations side of it, that is. Other divisions are responsible for construction and ride design and a million other things."

"But won't you have to relocate there when the park opens?"

"Oh, no. I didn't make myself clear. I'm in project management. My division does all of the planning and implementation for new parks and the remodeling and expansion of old ones. Once the park is operational the permanent staff takes over. I'll have to be there for a month before and a few months after, but then I'll move on to the next project." *Maybe in a Florida location that's awfully close to the Caribbean…*

"Will that be out of the country again?"

That snapped her out of her daydream. "It's impossible to know. I've worked on this project since the day I started with Luxor. If everything goes well, I might get to choose my next assignment. If not—I might be swabbing the decks of a cruise ship."

Evidently, Theo didn't share his daughter's wry sense of humor. He kept probing, ignoring Laurie's mild joke. "That's a very, very important job. I can't imagine what kind of compensation package a senior vice president at a major US corporation would receive." He sat up even straighter, as though his comment had surprised himself. "Not that I'd ever ask such a rude question, of course."

Laurie could tell he really wanted to know, and she offered up a tidbit. "Luxor is a little on the cheap side, to be honest. But they award a *lot* of restricted stock to senior VPs, reasoning that we'll fight to increase profits if our compensation is tied very closely to the bottom line."

He nodded, looking at her with undisguised admiration. "Maybe you can convince my daughter that working for a corporation can help secure her future."

"I love my work," Laurie said, looking at Kaatje, "but I don't think Kaatje would care for it. I'd be better off if I could copy some of her views."

"My daughter has, as we say, 'gone native.' I don't think her work ideas would help you advance."

His attitude irked her and she found herself showing off, something she rarely did. "There are only two people above me in Theme Parks Operations, and they're both fairly young. I probably won't have an opportunity to move up for quite a few years. I'd be fine if I slowed down a little to enjoy life. To be honest, I don't have time to spend what I earn now."

"That's a problem Kaatje will never have," Theo said, his tone fairly neutral.

"And one I will never want," Kaatje said, looking at her father with an unblinking stare.

They were back on the boat by eleven and Kaatje stopped Laurie when she started to unzip her dress. "Leave it on for a little while," she said, seductively. "You look really sexy in it."

"I do?" She blinked fetchingly. "My foreign lover helped me pick it out." Laughing, she said, "That sounds funny."

"It does." Kaatje sat down at the table in the galley. "You're the foreign one. I'm a local."

"True." Laurie wedged herself onto Kaatje's lap. She put her arms around her neck and said, "I hope dinner wasn't too tedious for you."

"Tedious? Why would it be tedious? I had a good time."

"I just thought you might have been bored hearing me talk about my job."

"Not at all. If you didn't have an important job we would have talked about whatever's on my dad's mind these days, and it probably would have been politics. You saved the day." She grasped Laurie by the shoulders and looked at her carefully. "You're safe in Osaka, right?"

"Yes, we didn't go to Japan for a couple of months after the earthquake, and Luxor gave us radiation detectors to wear on our belts. None of them ever went off."

"Maybe they were broken!"

"They were fine. They take very good care of us in many ways. Safety is always important."

"Risking your life to help others is one thing, but for a job…"

This wasn't where Laurie wanted the conversation to go. She'd been lectured about her commitment to the project far too many times, and having Kaatje do it made her skin itch. "I was surprised to learn that your mother has a job. I had the notion she stayed at home."

"She doesn't work a lot. Probably no more than twenty hours a week." She smiled devilishly. "My dad probably wants her to have two jobs. He never has enough savings. Or insurance."

"Insurance?"

Kaatje slapped herself on the forehead. "I'm embarrassed to admit this, but when we were young he bought divorce insurance. He was afraid child support would bankrupt him."

"You can get divorce insurance?"

"You can get insurance on anything you can name in The Netherlands. We're probably the most heavily insured nation on earth, and that's all because of people like my dad. And if someone doesn't have insurance and then suffers a loss? Good luck getting any sympathy."

"That's really different from what I'm used to. I've got a lot of life insurance, and the company pays for my car and health insurance, but most people buy the legal minimum. We're a nation of optimists."

"Or fools, if you asked my dad."

They had sex that night, as they had every day. But this time part of Kaatje wasn't available. Laurie wasn't sure what it was, but something was missing. A fragile wall had gone up, leaving Laurie feeling sadder than she already did. She was leaving in the morning, but Kaatje was already gone.

They were near the St. Maarten airport at eight fifteen the next morning, sitting at an open-air café, having breakfast while planes puttered over their heads. "This is a fun place," Laurie said as yet another small prop plane settled onto the runway right behind them. "The planes look like little toys as they go over."

"Some of them do." Kaatje turned, shielding her eyes from the sun as she scanned the skies. "Some don't."

Kaatje had been a miserly with her words, leaving Laurie to carry the load of their conversation. It was impossible to know if Kaatje was withdrawing because she was sad, or if she'd shut down because their time together was over. The flight was in a little more than an hour and she took the last bite of her spinach omelet and looked pointedly at her watch. Kaatje probably knew when the proper time was to leave, but she didn't look like she was in any hurry to take charge.

"Right." Kaatje got up and took her wallet out of her shorts.

"I've got it," Laurie said at Kaatje's raised eyebrow. "To thank you for the ride."

Kaatje jammed her wallet back into her shorts and walked out of the restaurant, where Laurie found her a few minutes later, astride her motorcycle. Somewhat tentatively, Laurie got on and they took off, reaching the airport in fewer than five minutes.

Since she had only the clothes she'd arrived with, and the few things she'd purchased, her baggage consisted of a plastic bag from the clothing store Kaatje had taken her to. She got off the bike and stood on the curb, not sure how to say goodbye.

Kaatje cut the engine, and sat there, looking at Laurie expectantly.

Surprisingly, Laurie felt her eyes well up with tears and, when Kaatje's arms encircled her, she started to cry harder. "I don't want to leave," she sniffed.

"Then don't." Kaatje's voice was firm and sure.

"But I have to." She looked towards the building, watching taxis stop to let out passengers. "My job…" She shook her head slightly. "It's too important to leave…Osaka means…" She caught herself when she almost said "everything." That didn't seem true any longer. But it meant an awful lot, far too much to abandon it.

Kaatje's gaze was level, unflinching. "Okay." She reached over and gave Laurie a quick hug. "Come back when you finish with Osaka." She gazed at Laurie for a few moments, looking like she was about to cry. "I'll…miss you." She turned the key and the engine caught. One more soft kiss and she started to roll away, with Laurie watching her until her eyes were so filled with tears she couldn't focus.

It took a remarkably long time to get through security. Every person going to the US was there at the same time, and the place was woefully understaffed. Standing in line, her gut roiling with tension over the possibility of missing yet another connection, Laurie tried to think of Kaatje and mentally borrow some of her calm.

Kaatje. What in the hell had gone on for the past week? It was one thing to have sex with a gorgeous native on a Caribbean island, but quite another to be sick at the thought of leaving her. But she did feel sick. Sick to the core. The thought of waking up in her sterile condo, with air conditioning blowing over her instead of salty sea air, was enough to make her run out of the airport and hail a cab. But she'd worked six long years to bring Osaka online and it would take a hell of a lot more than a sexy woman with a beautiful smile to make her throw that overboard. When Osaka was running, she'd get back to her life. If things went perfectly, she'd be able to see Kaatje within a year. But there were months of hard work ahead, and dreaming about something that couldn't happen wasn't doing her a damn bit of good.

CHAPTER NINE

KAATJE WAS JUST pouring her first cup of coffee the next morning when her cell phone rang. "Do you miss me yet?"

"You know, I really do."

The sound of Kaatje's voice almost transported Laurie back to vacation mentality, but she was at work now and couldn't linger in the fantasy. "I really don't like where we left things. This doesn't feel finished…to me at least."

"I don't want it to be either. But I don't know what to do."

It sounded stupid now that she was going to say it aloud, but it was the only answer she'd come up with when her thoughts kept returning to Kaatje. "Why don't we talk to each other…a lot. Then we could continue to get to know each other."

"Talk to me, huh? Yeah, I guess that's okay." Kaatje paused. "Of course that's okay. I'd like that."

"I need to hear your voice." *Wow! Where did that come from? We barely know each other.* "But…I don't want you to have a big phone bill. Do you ever use Skype?"

"Yeah, I have."

"I did some research when I was waiting for my connection in Miami, and it looks like Skype is the best solution for people in our situation. I don't have an account yet, but I'll get one tonight when I have some free time."

"It's nine in the morning here, Laurie. Doesn't that mean it's five in the morning in LA?"

"Something like that." She changed the subject deftly. "You'll be glad to know that the cruise-line folks did a great job of packing up all my things and having them waiting for me at the airport in Miami. The bags were right where they said they'd be."

Kaatje laughed softly. "They probably figured out that you were a big deal."

"That might have had something to do with it," she agreed, chuckling evilly. "There was a nice hand-written note from the woman who complained about me interfering with the cruise line. If it was possible to grovel in print, she did it."

"Are you going to…" She trailed off, then started again. "She probably had somebody slap her hand for making a big-wig angry."

"I've had it happen to me more than once. But Fernando was right. I was meddling where I didn't belong. I dashed off an e-mail to the head of cruise operations commending her for getting my stuff back to me. That should get her out of any hot water she might be in."

"I miss you more right now."

Damn! Kaatje is putting it right out there! Is that a lesbian trait, or is she just very open? "Uhm…why's that?"

"Because you did something nice. I have a tough time with people who use their positions to cause trouble for the little guy. I'm glad you don't do that."

Oh-oh. Might as well knock the stars out of her eyes right now. No sense in setting up false expectations. "To be honest, I'm not afraid to use anything at my disposal to cause trouble for people who deserve it. If I see someone on campus behaving in a way that makes the company look bad, I'll call them out. But I don't go any higher than that unless somebody begs for it."

"You sound very feisty. I'm trying to envision your expression. I can't manage it."

"God knows I can be feisty. Especially at work."

"Who have you batted around? Co-workers?"

Why is she asking such pointed questions? They're impossible to dodge. "Well, yeah, that's happened. I got a couple of women in the cafeteria fired."

"The cafeteria? Did you catch them spitting into food?"

"No, but it was almost as bad." She heard her own voice and realized she sounded shrill. Not as shrill as she had the day it had happened, but still... "I took some of my staff from Osaka up there for a working breakfast and one of my team members asked for something that one of the workers thought was odd. I think it was fish or something."

"For breakfast?"

"Yeah, but that's not the point. The woman made fun of his accent and told a coworker that she couldn't understand him, but it sounded like he wanted fish and that was just stupid."

"That's pretty insensitive."

"At the very least! I intervened and got him something acceptable. After breakfast I went back and gave both of the women a quick talk on cultural sensitivity."

"I have a feeling it didn't go very well. Am I right?"

"It went very poorly. I'm sure I had a bit of an attitude, but all things considered, I was very mild. Let's just say they questioned my authority to speak to them. One of them used some pretty profane language and that does not *ever* fly at Luxor. I marched back into the kitchen and found the person in charge. I had to write the whole thing up and talk to Human Resources and waste hours of my time, but they were both fired—as they should have been."

"Was getting them fired the only option?" Kaatje asked quietly.

Oh, Lord. It was nearly impossible to explain the Luxor dynamic to outsiders. You had to live it to truly get it. "In my view, yes. I didn't ask for them to be fired, but that's what their boss chose to do, and I thought it was the right move."

"Maybe they were having a bad day. You might have come across stronger than you think you did."

"That's possible. But you don't make fun of team members. That's nonnegotiable. For anyone at any level of the company. And even if you're having a bad day, you don't curse at team members in a public area. I'm sure their jobs are difficult, but we need people who have some resilience. You don't screw with the brand."

"Okay. It's your brand. I've gotta get going now. This boat won't sail itself. If you get Skype set up, call me tonight when you get home. It doesn't matter how late."

"Okay, I will. Happy sailing. And Kaatje?"

"Yeah?"

It was hard to step back and try to connect with her feelings, but she tried to inject a little of the tenderness she felt about Kaatje when she'd let herself think about her that morning. "Don't train any new first mates. That's my job."

Laurie was able to find a way to call by eleven, Kaatje's usual bedtime. She had her phone set up properly and was already at home, even though it was only seven o'clock, an impossibly early hour for being only a few months from opening. They talked for a long time and the emotional connection between them was much better than it had been in the morning. After an hour they were both exhausted and agreed to go to bed.

Laurie remembered one last thing. "Hey, I stopped and got some sashimi on the way home. No fat, no simple carbohydrates, no sugar. And I left work by six thirty."

"After getting in at five."

"It was three, but who's counting?" She giggled tiredly. "Sleep well. I'll call you soon." She hung up and stared at her phone. She knew she'd call the next day. Getting home on time to talk to Kaatje had motivated her to fly around the office like a dervish. Now she just had to perform the same feat the next day, and the day after that...

Chapter Ten

TALKING EVERY DAY was a dream that Laurie had fully intended to realize, but her reality was far removed from the dream. She had to find a different way to connect with Kaatje or risk losing her. She'd tried to stop briefly to call her during the day, but the few such conversations they'd managed hadn't gone well at all. They were stilted, and Laurie found herself constantly distracted. She also tried, but she simply could not manage, to get home by seven. The solution came to her during a meeting she should have been paying more attention to. That night, right before tumbling into bed, she wrote a long e-mail to Kaatje. It wasn't much, but it helped her vent some of the tension that built up throughout the day, and it made her see how many of the things that had seemed important were pretty trivial.

Kaatje responded by calling and leaving a message when she woke up. It was short, just a minute or two, but it was enough to keep her in Laurie's heart, right where she'd discovered she needed her. Amazing. It was simply amazing.

About a week after she returned home, Laurie caught Kaatje on the boat on Saturday night. She was calm, relaxed and loquacious, having spent the day with a taciturn group of businessmen whom even rum hadn't made chatty.

"You know what I was thinking about today?" Laurie asked.

"Numbers. You were thinking about how to make numbers dance before your very eyes."

Laughing, Laurie said, "That's not far from right. But I was also thinking about you. Actually, I was wondering if you're getting as much out of this…this getting to know each other…as I am." That was a sentence that might go down in the ineloquent hall of fame. Talking about touchy subjects was never going to come easily.

"Let's see," Kaatje said slowly. "I'm getting to know someone who I'm remarkably attracted to. What are you getting?"

"Well, that's what I'm getting too, but if you did a focus group on which of us is the better catch, there's no contest."

"Braggart."

"No! You're the one!" *That was dumb. Kaatje was clearly teasing. Learning to lighten up was going to be a full time job. But where to find another hour, much less forty a week?*

"Laurie, I'm very, very interested in you. From my perspective, your only fault is that you work too hard. When you relax you're playful and fun, not to mention really smart and clever and hardworking. It might not seem like it, but I admire people with determination, and you've got more than anyone I've ever met."

"Why wouldn't it seem like that's something you'd admire?"

"Because I'm lackadaisical."

"That's not the right word. You follow your loves. Just because you don't put in eighty-hour weeks doesn't mean you don't care."

"Yeah, I know, but I seem like a sloth to most people."

She seemed like a sloth to her father. Everyone else was just jealous. "Not to me. It's hard to be a gracious host to a bunch of strangers tromping all over your home. We train people for years in how to manage visitors, but you just picked it up on your own. That's a skill."

"Maybe. More likely that's just my personality. But we're talking about me again. I wasn't finished with telling you what I get from our…whatever you called it."

"I called it something dumb. I can't even remember what."

"Whatever it is, I get the hope that I've met someone I can learn to care for. Someone I can trust. Someone who makes my knees quiver when she looks at me. I don't think I've ever had all of those things at once, and

I

I'm going to keep learning about you until all of your horrible faults start showing up."

Laurie found it hard to wipe the smile off her face. "Keep looking. I know they're in there somewhere."

———

About a month after returning to LA, Laurie drove over Laurel Canyon to Sunset Boulevard. There was no way to justify taking a whole day off to get ready for her coworkers' wedding, but that didn't stop her from trying. Luxor wanted their executives to look good as well as be good. Getting her hair trimmed was just part of polishing the brand. And having good-looking nails was required. People looked at your hands when you signed contracts, didn't they? A good manicure was good business. Being able to accomplish multiple tasks with a minimum of effort showed resourcefulness. Buying a new dress after finishing at the salon was just good business sense.

The wedding was in Burbank, a quick drive from her home, and she was planning on sitting with some of her oldest friends from Luxor. At different points in her career, Laurie had worked with both grooms, Steve and Ray. But Steve had moved from Theme Parks to Corporate and she didn't see him nearly as much as before. They were the kinds of guys she'd loved to have spent more time with, but all she managed for the last couple of years was a quick lunch with one or the other when they ran into each other in the cafeteria.

The ceremony was being held at a country club, and the grooms set it up so they would say their vows on a small, round stage in the middle of a very large room. That gave everyone a good view, and allowed the guests to sit at their tables and have a drink during the service. That was just what Laurie would have expected of them. They both loved to have fun, and neither was a stickler for formality.

As she sat at the table, looking around at her friends, she realized that all, except one, were gay or lesbian. That struck her, and she sat up straighter and looked around at the other tables. She knew people at nearly every one, and saw that most of them were segregated by sexual orientation. Fernando and the other higher ranking people all sat together. There were two lesbians in his group, but both of those women outranked him. Title must have trumped orientation. Otherwise, the straights sat with the straights and the gays with the gays. These were not prejudiced people. They probably just felt more comfortable with people like themselves. An entire table of their black colleagues confirmed this in her mind…until she saw Eric, a black gay man sitting with other gay men, all white. It seemed that people aligned themselves with the group they most identified with. The senior VPs probably felt more like executives than gay or straight people.

She studied her table again. Nine other people—one woman who, to Laurie's knowledge, had never had a relationship with man or woman, three lesbian couples and one gay couple. What did that say about her? She could have made plans with any number of other people. Fernando had explicitly asked her to sit at his table. But she hadn't wanted to. She felt more comfortable socializing with this group than any other.

The ceremony started with the band playing "A Taste of Honey," Teddy Bear's theme song, but after a few bars it segued into "Here Comes the Bride." Everyone laughed, since that was just what one would have expected from Ray and Steve. But when each man entered the room from opposite sides, accompanied by parents and siblings, the room grew quiet. Astonishingly, Laurie felt tears spring to her eyes. She hadn't even brought a pack of tissues, never considering that the ceremony would make her tear up. A friend seated next to her discreetly handed her a tissue, whispering, "Knock it off or I'll lose it too."

That broke the tension and Laurie smothered a laugh. "I'll behave."

But when the grooms met on the dais, she had to bite both of her lips and then escalate to fingernails digging into her palm to keep from bawling. Ray and Steve looked incredibly happy. She didn't think she'd ever seen two people who looked more excited about committing their lives to one another. Then Kaatje's image flashed in her mind and thoughts of the two of them having a similar ceremony washed over her before a fist lodged in her stomach. Whether it was Kaatje or not, she could no longer ignore the fact that she belonged on that dais with a woman. Only a woman.

The next morning Laurie woke with a hangover. The two glasses of wine, plus a little champagne, were well within her capacity. But spending the entire evening thinking about her sexual orientation? That was definitely out of the ordinary, and her body and mind had rebelled in this foreign territory.

She got up and went to make coffee, something she rarely did since it was much easier to stop at Starbucks on her way to work. Rummaging through her cabinets, she found an unopened can of coffee, then saw that it was dated two years ago. Colin probably bought it.

She started to cry. *Colin was a great guy. A guy any thoroughly straight woman would have loved to have had.* But she'd treated him like he was another project to manage. Given him the minimum amount of time to achieve the maximum output. It shamed her to think how little she'd given. She was tempted to call him, but wasn't at all ready to discuss her feelings, and rather doubted that Colin would be interested, at this late date, to hear them.

Instead of making coffee, she went to her computer and started to make a list. Evidence for lesbian versus evidence for straight. Hours passed. By the time her headache was so bad she couldn't ignore it any more, she took a shower, got dressed, got in her car and drove around, foraging for food and drink. Her headset was in her ear, as it almost always was, and she pressed a button on her phone. Moments later her mother answered.

"Hi, Mom. Guess what?"

It was nine o'clock in the evening in St. Maarten when Laurie called Kaatje. "Hi," she said, not sure of where to start. "I took the day off today."

"Really? I'm surprised, but happy. Did you do something fun or did you party too much last night?"

"Not really. I had a tougher time than I do at work, but I figured something out."

"What?"

"I'm gay."

There was a significant pause. "You're gay…and you figured that out since I talked to you yesterday morning?" The suspicion in Kaatje's voice was more than slightly evident.

"Well, I started thinking about it last night at the wedding."

"Oh, well, that's entirely different. A day and a half is ample time for that."

"Don't tease me," Laurie said, slightly stung. "That's more time than I've put into thinking about my life in years."

"Laurie." Kaatje's voice took on that warm, soothing tone that made Laurie's heart melt. No one had ever said her name with such care. "I'm very glad you're thinking about this, but you can't make up your mind about such a big topic in a few hours."

"Yes, I can. I'm a doer, not a thinker. I've obviously had this percolating in the back of my head for a long while, and I sat down today and laid out the facts."

The spurt of sound made it obvious Kaatje was suppressing a laugh, but, to her credit, she did not guffaw. "Tell me the facts."

Laurie rustled the sheets of paper she'd printed out. "It's a long list. But on the straight side there's only one item. 'Usually enjoyed sex with men.' That seems a little lean, doesn't it?"

"Yeah, unless the gay side said, 'Usually enjoyed sex with Kaatje.'"

"I'm sending you the document right now. I'll call you back in a half hour." She hit Send and went into the kitchen to finish her salad.

A half hour later, Kaatje answered on the first ring and started to speak without even bothering with a greeting. "I don't mean to be unkind, but how did you ignore these clues?"

"I didn't let myself or didn't want to think about them. I've been too busy to have a personal life." That sounded like whining, but that's how she felt. Like a kid who'd been called on the carpet for neglecting her homework.

"I know, but all of the crushes you had on other little girls. That didn't even make you think you might be gay?"

"Not really. When boys started trying to steal kisses, I figured that's what the next step was. I honestly didn't stop to think if that was what I wanted."

"Do you think you've always been like this?"

"Gay? Or something else?"

"Uhm…uninterested in thinking about your needs."

"That's a polite way to put it. Yeah, I suppose I have. I broke a bone in my foot when I was in a gymnastics meet. I didn't say a word and kept going until my coach caught me trying to borrow a shoe from an older girl with bigger feet. My own shoe would have burst if I could have even gotten my swollen foot into it."

Kaatje laughed softly, but her laugh didn't have its usual gaiety. "I'm surprised I didn't see you in the Olympics."

"Oh, you would have. But my parents made me quit when I was fourteen. I've never been that mad at two people. I barely spoke to my mom for months."

"Why'd they made you quit?"

"Because I developed an eating disorder and hadn't gotten my period yet, even though the doctor said I should have."

"Laurie, Laurie, Laurie."

"They were right, of course. I'd probably have osteoporosis by now if I'd stuck with it. I had to limit myself to about six hundred calories a day to keep from growing."

Kaatje's tone was incredulous. "You intentionally tried to keep yourself from growing?"

"I *had* to. If you start to develop, you screw up your center of gravity. Breasts and hips don't work in gymnastics." Of course it sounded stupid to an outsider, but inside gymnastics you realized that was one of the sacrifices you had to make. It was all about the team, and the team always won over the individual.

"Okay. Let's get off this dismal topic and talk about today. How do you feel?"

"Fine. Good, actually. I called my mom and told her and she's going to tell my dad and my sister."

"You called your mom already?"

"Sure. I'm not going to change my mind. I might as well get the process started."

"This isn't the same as building a roller coaster. It takes time, and you'll have second thoughts. Everyone does."

"No way," she said, chuckling. "I've thought about it, made my analysis and disseminated the information to the interested parties." She waited a second, met by stone cold silence. "I was kidding, Kaatje…partially."

"It's the partial part that has me worried. I don't want this to come back and slap you in the face. Why don't you take it slow?"

"No, that's not me. I'm a lesbian. I've always been one, I just didn't stop to smell the…" She chuckled evilly. "That probably isn't the best analogy. But I am one, and that's a major item I can cross off my to do list for my personal life."

"This isn't how I'd handle this, but I think I know you well enough to know I can't change your mind."

"Not me. I'm still considering going back into competitive gymnastics. My mom can't keep a close watch over me out here in LA."

"I wish I was sure you were kidding."

"I'm obviously kidding. Do you know how many hours a day you have to work to be competitive in gymnastics? Teddy Bear would never allow it." She hung up with the sound of Kaatje's lovely laugh caressing her ear.

CHAPTER ELEVEN

A WEEK LATER, Kaatje was back in Holland for her friend's wedding when Laurie called late on a Saturday afternoon. "Hi," she said, unable to keep the excitement from her voice. "How would you like to meet me in Madrid?"

"Madrid?" There was a slight pause. "You know Madrid's not in The Netherlands, right?"

"Very funny. I've been studying a map of Europe, and I know right where it is. You know Madrid's where our European theme park is, and I've cleverly managed to convince Fernando that I could learn some things from the people there—since that was the last park to go on-line."

"Clever. That's a fantastic idea. When do you want me?"

She felt a lump form in her throat. "Right now."

"But will we be able to spend time together? I know your schedule in LA. I'd like more than a few hours while you're asleep."

"Well…" She could feel herself deflate. "I need four days in Madrid. I'll add a vacation day and we can have a long weekend. We can tour Madrid together for three whole days. Fernando will think I've lost my mind, but he'll let me do it."

"How about this? You do your work, then come to Amsterdam. If you want to know me better"—her voice lowered to a sexy register—"and I think you do, this is the place to do it."

Two weeks later, after having spent three days grilling her fellow operations-staff team members about everything from weather problems to security issues, Laurie was ready to leave Teddy Bear Europe. She'd kept the poor people so late into the evenings that she was finished a full day before she'd planned, and she guessed each of them would call in sick the next day. She was on her phone on the way to the airport, finagling an earlier flight to Schiphol. "Kaatje," she said into her earpiece when she'd arranged everything. "Change in plans. I'll be there by six tonight."

"Really? Then I'd better get rid of these other women and get dressed. I'll be waiting."

———

Because neither Kaatje nor her parents owned a car, Laurie took a cab from the airport. The Hoogeboom house was on a neat, well-scrubbed, narrow street, not far from the historic center of town. The tall black building with sharp, white trim had five floors, with three windows on each of the first four floors and one small window on the top floor. She was pondering why each floor was distinctly smaller than the one below it, when Kaatje poked her head out of the window on the fifth floor. "Come on up!" she called out, smiling a ten-thousand-watt smile.

Laurie's one suitcase wasn't hard to carry up the stairs. The stairs, though, were another matter. They definitely were built for someone with feet shorter than hers, and each flight curved strangely, taking up much less space than US staircases. Kaatje bounded down to meet her on the second floor. She tossed the suitcase behind her, then grasped Laurie in her arms like a treasured doll. "It's so fantastic to see you," she whispered in her ear.

"Kiss me," Laurie murmured. "I've missed your kisses so much."

They exchanged many, finally stopping when the second-floor resident excused himself as if he'd done something wrong when he had to wedge his way past them.

Kaatje picked up the suitcase and took Laurie's hand. They climbed to the third floor, where they stepped into a space different from any Laurie had ever been in. She would have wasted a minute looking around if not for the pink, full lips located conveniently close to her own. They fell into each other's arms. Laurie was not even aware that she still wore her heavy coat, scarf, and gloves. It wasn't until she thought she'd faint from Kaatje's fervid kisses that she realized she was ridiculously overdressed.

"Can I take off my coat?"

"If you insist." Kaatje grinned at her while helping her out of her coat. "You know," she said, taking her in her arms again, "as long as we're at it, why not keep going?" Her eyes gleamed devilishly when her fingers played at the buttons on Laurie's blouse.

"I've been working since dawn," Laurie said. "How about taking a shower with me?"

"We can do something like that."

It wasn't that she was tired, even though she was. Being in Kaatje's other home was very disconcerting. She even looked different, with her hair hanging loose against her shoulders, and her skin a shade or two lighter than it was in the summer. It would take a few minutes to reconnect with her. Minutes that Laurie needed to be clothed.

Kaatje took her hand and led her up an open set of stairs strangely located right in the modern living room. On the fourth floor a pair of bedrooms, bracketed a modern bath, all white, with sparkling tile and angular fixtures. The room was big, with a free-standing shower in one corner and an ultra-modern tub with a wide, flat lip.

Kaatje put her arms around Laurie again and kissed her gently. "Indulge me?"

"In anything."

"I'd love to bathe you. I've been fantasizing about it."

"I'll never take another shower if it would make you happy." That was true. In just the time it took to walk up the stairs, she was ready to reveal every part of herself.

After starting the bath, Kaatje slowly undressed her, an expression of intent interest on her face. After she lent a hand to help Laurie step into the tub, she sat on the side and lathered up a cloth. She washed her tenderly, tsking when her hands slid over the curves that had diminished since they'd been together. "Eat more candy," she grumbled, a grin poking through her scowl.

"You should encourage me to be thin. I feel better when my clothes aren't tight."

"I feel worse. Doesn't that count for something?" After she finished her task she helped Laurie to her feet and beautiful blue eyes glided over Laurie from head to toe. She wrapped her in a big, white towel and continued to gaze at her longingly. "You're clean. I'm clean. Got any ideas?"

"Just one." They were connecting perfectly now, as though it were just a few days since they'd seen each other. When she looked into Kaatje's eyes Laurie saw concern, kindness, avid interest and that spark of eroticism that could emerge on a moment's notice. It was out now, and Laurie took her by the hand and started to walk to the closest bedroom, but Kaatje cleared her throat and pointed at the open staircase. "Got it."

They climbed to the fifth floor, where the ceilings were a little low, but a big skylight let in the grey light of twilight. The room was tiny, just big enough for a carved, blond-wood bed with small tables on each side that held thin, modern lamps. Kaatje flipped one on, and the room looked golden and cozy. Taking her time, Laurie began to methodically undress Kaatje. Her hair was a little longer, not held back in a ponytail, and her tan had faded, but the biggest change was Kaatje's clothing. Laurie had only seen her in shorts and swimwear, and having her all covered up in a heavy wool sweater and jeans was odd. But once she got her down to her underwear everything was perfect. "I've missed these," she murmured, placing a kiss on a nipple hardening through the soft fabric of her bra.

Kaatje reached down and opened the front closure, releasing her breasts to Laurie's care. "They're yours now. Do whatever you'd like to them. They've been lonely."

Laurie tumbled her to the bed, where they rolled around for a moment or two, relishing the feel of their bodies contacting again. After peeling off Kaatje's panties, Laurie sated herself on getting reacquainted with Kaatje's delightfully soft skin. It had lost much of its golden glow, but tan or not,

Kaatje was a beauty. A true beauty. And Laurie would have been content to stay right where they were until she had to leave in a very short three days.

———

They sat up in bed, eating everything Kaatje could rustle up from the refrigerator. "I don't know what kind of hold you have over me," Laurie said, "but I've never been more focused on sex in my life."

"Tell me about that."

"I just did. I think about you and I start thinking about having sex with you. I hardly ever think of you with clothes on," she admitted, chuckling.

"Does that make you think about…oh, I don't know…being gay?" She stared at Laurie with comically wide eyes.

"I'm done with that. I barely have time to squeeze in a few minutes of fantasizing about doing it with you before I fall asleep every night."

"Interesting." Kaatje got up and started to gather their empty plates and containers. She didn't say a word as she busied herself for quite a few minutes.

"I said something wrong."

Silently, Kaatje looked up at her.

"Come back to bed." Laurie patted the surface. "Please?"

She didn't rush to comply, but Kaatje finally meandered over. "Yeah?"

"I still don't think you understand how busy I am." Kaatje rolled her eyes but Laurie continued. "I mean it. I have to squeeze about twenty-four hours of work into an eighteen-hour day. The only time I have to reflect is when I force myself to shut off the pile driver that's slamming around inside my head and focus on you. I lie in bed and write you a note, then try as hard as I can to keep those other thoughts out. You just don't know how hard that is." She looked like one cross look would make her break down, so Kaatje took her in her arms and cooed gently.

"I hate that you let yourself be this consumed by work. It's not good for you, Moppie, it's really not."

Letting out a sigh, Laurie raised her head. "Moppie?"

Kaatje's tan had faded, and no longer provided cover for her blushing cheeks. She nodded. "I hadn't planned on that coming out." She hated being such an open book, but she'd never been able to hide her thoughts or her feelings.

"What's it mean?"

"It's a pet name. Like 'honey' or 'sweetie.'"

"I like it. Moppie," she repeated, trying it out.

"Would my Moppie like to get dressed and take a walk around? I have an awful lot to show you."

"Sure. Maybe we can get dessert."

Kaatje touched the tip of her nose. "You get two. I have to put those curves back on you."

—⁓—

They walked through Kaatje's neighborhood, with Laurie stopping every other minute to remark on a house or a church. "How old are these buildings? They look like nothing I've ever seen."

"Seventeenth century or a little later, for many of them. There are lots of sixteenth-century buildings a few streets from here. But when we get to the more commercial streets you'll see some new, very modern buildings. It's a nice mix."

"This couldn't be more different from LA if it were on Venus."

"I haven't been to LA."

"But you've been to the US."

"Yes. New York, Philadelphia, Washington, and Boston just to do the tourist thing. Florida quite a few times to buy things. And a few friends and I went to the Grand Canyon to do a long river rafting trip. That was fantastic. Have you ever been there?"

"No, I've never been anywhere near it. Did you camp?"

"Yeah. It was a week-long trip. Pretty exciting stuff. We don't have anything like that in Europe. Different animals, plants, everything. You should go."

"Eh…I'm not one for camping. I'm not crazy about plants or animals either," she admitted, slightly embarrassed.

"Maybe you haven't been camping with the right people."

"I'm lying. I might love camping. I've never been."

Kaatje put an arm around her shoulders and squeezed her. "I think you might be a little tentative to try new things. I don't know where I get that idea…"

"Maybe a little." They were now on a street teeming with life. People filled the sidewalk and filed in and out of restaurants and shops. "Let's go to a coffee shop or a café and find a snack."

"Do you want coffee, food, alcohol or marijuana?"

"Marijuana? Why would I want that?"

"That's what the coffee shops sell. A coffee house has coffee. And a café has alcohol. All of them usually have food."

Laurie pulled her to a stop. "You can buy marijuana? Legally?"

Laughing, Kaatje said, "You might be the first person to come here and not know you can buy marijuana. It's not legal, but we don't enforce the law prohibiting it."

"Did this just happen? I haven't been reading the news since I've been so busy…"

"Since before I was born." Kaatje looked like she was going to laugh, but was polite enough not to.

"I've gotta get out more," Laurie mumbled. "I just want something sweet. Is there a special place for that?"

"I can make you happy."

⁓

They were soon seated at a small coffee house, with Laurie thoughtfully chewing on a bite of Kaatje's pie. "Apples and raisins?" She took another tiny bite. "I'm not a big raisin fan, but that's really good. I prefer my *krumulvlie* though."

"*Kruimelvlaai*," Kaatje gently corrected. "We're going to have to spend some time getting your mouth around Dutch."

With sparkling eyes, Laurie said, "You set yourself up for that one. You know you're the only thing Dutch I want to attach my mouth to. But this *krummel*...stuff is fantastic. Although who would refuse crumbled butter and sugar is beyond me."

"Have another piece, or two."

"You're not going to put the five pounds I just lost back on me that easily. Only one two-thousand calorie piece of pie a day. Unless we go to a coffee shop and get baked. Then I have no control."

"Do you want to go?"

"No. I haven't smoked since I was in college. Do you do it often?"

"Not often, but if I'm out with friends we'll go and smoke a bit. You can order many different kinds. It's a nice way to relax or get in the mood before a concert."

"Different kinds? Really?"

"Really. Different kinds of marijuana and light and dark hash." She chuckled. "Your eyes say 'yes,' but your mouth says 'no.'"

Laurie took her hand. "It's kinda late, and it's obvious I don't need any help getting into the mood with you."

"Mood?" Kaatje looked positively innocent. "Do you want to have sex again?"

Laurie started to tug her along, but she was headed the wrong way. "And again and again and again. Let's go!"

The next morning, Kaatje woke at her normal time. The sun was up, but the sky was gray and seemed close enough to touch. The difference in the weather between St. Maarten and Holland was enormous. Besides the temperature, the skies in St. Maarten rarely made her feel claustrophobic, but the low cloud cover in Holland sometimes did.

Even the weak, gray light didn't dim Laurie's beauty. Kaatje lay on her side and gazed at her for a while. It took only a few seconds for a knot of emotion to form in her chest. The perky, lively woman she'd started to fall for in St. Maarten now looked tired, and her pretty skin didn't have the glow it did in the Caribbean. Even in this light, she could see the dark circles under her eyes. But that outsized work ethic had led them to this point, so it wasn't all bad. If only there were a way to convince her to take better care of herself, but she wasn't the kind of woman who took her responsibilities casually. The good thing about that was that she'd be a very devoted lover. There was no doubt about that.

Doing her best to stealthily creep out of bed, Kaatje went downstairs to make breakfast. In just minutes, Laurie shuffled up behind her and leaned heavily against her body. "I feel like I've been drugged. Did you take me to a coffee shop when I wasn't looking?"

Reaching behind, Kaatje patted her. "No. I'm afraid you're just a normal human being, trying to figure out what time it is. You're body thinks it's"—she looked at her watch—"one in the morning."

"That's about what it feels like. When I don't have a million alligators biting at me, I actually notice how tired I am."

"Go back to bed. We don't have to do anything today."

"What did you plan?"

I should say nothing, but… "Well, I thought we'd go to the Amsterdam Historical Museum and spend a few hours, then take a bike ride around town, have dinner, then we can stroll over to Het Concertgebow. Koninklijk Concertgebouworkest is performing Brahms tonight, and everyone loves Brahms."

"I have no idea what that last part was, but if you planned it, I want to do it. I'm off to plunge my head into a bucket of cold water to wake up." With that, she headed straight upstairs to the shower, emitting a shriek of pain when she turned the cold on full blast.

Kaatje sat at the table, eating while she waited for Laurie to join her. It really would be better for Laurie to sleep all weekend, but that defeated the purpose of the visit. Kaatje had been mulling over their options, and one was to have Laurie find a job in Holland. Giving up the boat would be a blow, but losing Laurie would be worse. Since Laurie had never been to

Europe, or anywhere else for that matter, her adaptability to Kaatje's home was critical.

—⁓—

That evening they leaned into one another high up in the concert hall while they waited for the performance to begin. "You won't believe this, but I've never been to a classical music thing."

"No," Kaatje whispered, feigning disbelief. "Well, even if you've been many times, this hall is special. A lot of people believe it's the most acoustically perfect hall in the world. Even up here, we'll be able to hear every note."

"I hope I like it. I know you love music."

"You will," Kaatje said, oozing confidence. "Everyone loves Brahms."

As the music began, Kaatje's confidence began to falter. Laurie wasn't sitting particularly still. It seemed like she was struggling to focus, and that wasn't a good sign. Laurie's foot was tapping nervously, something she did much of the time. It was like she had an internal metronome that beat faster than anyone else's—definitely faster than Kaatje's.

Trying to reassure herself, Kaatje calmly considered that Laurie didn't have to enjoy symphonic music. If she got a job in Holland, there would be many, many nights when she didn't come home before ten o'clock. That would leave lots of time to indulge in her favorite pursuits—alone or with friends. Laurie didn't have to like everything she did for them to get along perfectly well.

Dividing her time between listening and worrying, she lost track of Laurie's reactions. Then, she glimpsed Laurie's eyes flutter to a close and a sated smile settle on her lips. It was the satisfied expression she sometimes had after she climaxed. Thrilled to the core, Kaatje leaned over to kiss her head and murmur, "I think you like it."

—⁓—

They strolled home, walking down sidewalks that were as crowded as any Laurie had encountered in Japan. There was a liveliness about the city that gave it a charge she'd never felt in LA. "I'm an idiot for never having traveled."

"You're not an idiot, and you have traveled. Just not for fun. Until now."

"I feel like such a dunce. You know so much about music and art and history. You speak two languages…"

"Uhm…three," Kaatje interrupted. "Four if you count the German I learned the summer I spent volunteering on an organic farm in Schleswig-Holstein." She shrugged when Laurie scowled. "Just being honest. I don't want you to be surprised if we go to France and I start speaking *la belle langue*."

"How'd you learn French? Did you live there?"

"No. I'm good with languages. I took French in school and I'd forgotten much of what I'd learned, but I met a woman on the French side of the island. She was a French national living on St. Maarten for a year and she helped me…practice." She graced Laurie with a lascivious grin.

"I still can't understand how you can afford to take so much time off and travel. I can't imagine anyone I know being able to take the summer off to volunteer to work on a farm."

Kaatje gave her a gentle smile. "Well, I was still in school, and I didn't volunteer because of my good heart. I got food and lodging for my efforts, and I got to travel around on my days off. I'd catch a ride when the farmers had to go to various cities. I don't go first class, Laurie. I don't even go second class if third class is available."

"Still…you're all cultured. You pick up a new language as easily as you do a new woman. I just work."

"You can always change that. Life is about choices."

"Yeah, yeah," she said dejectedly. "Tell that to the demonic Teddy Bear."

—⁂—

They got into bed as soon as they got home. It was still early, only eleven, and Laurie had been able to battle her jet lag to a draw. Instead of ravishing each other they slowed down and made love in such a leisurely fashion that it felt like they had years to play with each other.

Laurie started at the top, giving Kaatje a sexy head rub, then meticulously working her way down her body. Neither of them gave voice to it, but it seemed as if she were imprinting the images of Kaatje's entire body onto her brain to sustain herself for the months they'd be apart.

It took a very long time to go all the way down, kissing, caressing and teasing all the while. She was almost in a trance of concentration when Kaatje tapped her on the shoulder. "That's my foot," she said conversationally.

Laurie looked up at her, then shifted her eyes down. Kaatje's smallest toe was in her mouth, and she was sucking on it like it was a life-giving nipple. Her mouth opened and the toe dropped out. Then she looked at Kaatje helplessly. "First vaginas, now feet. Don't ever doubt how much I'm into you."

"I don't." Her expression was tender and very sweet. "Is it okay I didn't mention it until you were on the last toe?"

Laurie felt the other foot, noting the entire appendage was slightly damp. She shook her head and went back to business, taking a nibble out of a giggling Kaatje's instep.

—⁂—

They spent the next day with Kaatje's immediate family. Her brother Daniël owned a power boat, and they languidly motored up and down the canals, with everyone in the family calling out interesting buildings and monuments. Kaatje and Laurie sat beside one another, with little Thijs on Kaatje's lap. After precocious, seven-year-old Roos impressed one and all with her English skills, Laurie leaned over and said, "I used to think my nieces were bright. They're dullards compared to yours."

Kaatje turned to see her teasing expression. "I'll have to meet yours before I can offer an opinion."

Laurie sighed and snuggled up against her, only mildly tempted to knock Thijs off so she'd have Kaatje all to herself. "That would be great. We'll have to get on that. Grace and Lily would love you."

Kaatje frowned for a moment. "Funny names," she said, with such a straight face Laurie couldn't tell if she was teasing or not.

———

That night they had dinner with some of Kaatje's closest friends. All of them spoke English to a greater or lesser degree, but Kaatje was always ready to jump in with a quick translation. They all had regular, year-round jobs, but the way they talked about vacations they'd taken together made Laurie ask, "How much time off do you all get?"

They each answered in turn. "Five weeks."

"I get five, but I buy two weeks extra."

"I can take a sabbatical every other year for up to three months."

"Damn." Laurie shook her head. "I practically had to have a heart attack to take two weeks off, and I'm still getting teased about it. My staff still calls me 'the slacker' just to torture me."

"They say Americans love to work," said Marieke, a woman Laurie suspected was a former lover. "Is that right?" She looked at Kaatje for confirmation.

"This American certainly does," she agreed, bumping her shoulder against Laurie's.

———

They decided to go to a jazz club, and the majority wanted to stop for a quick buzz on the way. Kaatje held back and whispered, "Are you okay with getting high?"

"Sure. I probably won't, but it's fine with me if we stop. It'll enhance my tourist credentials."

Kaatje's friend Elodie seemed to be the expert, and she decided on a light hash that she decreed was perfect for jazz. A nice, mellow high without too many visual effects. They shared a few bowls, with Kaatje passing it along after Laurie declined. But on the second round Laurie took a tentative drag and Kaatje followed right behind her. It had been at least ten years, but the familiar buzz slammed into her like a freight train. If this was a mellow high, she was awfully glad they hadn't gone for a intense one. At that moment, Laurie remembered why she'd stopped smoking. She had two chronic side effects from drugs. Fits of the giggles mixed with lust, which, surprisingly, most guys hadn't found attractive. She reasoned the lust was good, but the giggles made them suspicious. They walked down the street after they'd polished off three bowls, with Laurie hanging back to avoid embarrassing Kaatje with her unstoppable giggling. "I'm really sorry," she whispered loudly, "but this always happens to me."

"Don't worry," Kaatje said, her voice as slow as poured honey. "Just have fun. Enjoy yourself."

The club was crowded, but they were able to find several tables they could squeeze together. They jammed them against the back wall and somehow managed to slide into seats. After they ordered drinks, a four piece ensemble came onto the low stage and started to play. To Laurie's ears each instrument was alone, then inextricably mixed with the others, then alone again. The melodies were pure, and yet so intricate that it was like listening to a flock of songbirds of every variety. She was lost in the music, her eyes closed, head resting against the wall. After a long time, Kaatje leaned over and whispered, "You can't do that to me," and carefully removed Laurie's hand from her very upper thigh. "I'm not going to have an orgasm in front of my friends."

"Oh, shit!" Her volume was definitely too loud for the venue, and a dozen people turned in her direction. "I'm sorry," she whispered, blushing furiously. "I didn't even realize."

"This is my leg," Kaatje said, taking Laurie's hand and sliding it from knee to mid-thigh. "This is my *kruis*." Now she pressed her fingers firmly between her legs. "Don't touch that part until we're home, okay?" Her smile was playful and indulgent and made Laurie melt.

"I can't promise that," she whispered back, wishing they could time travel right back to bed.

—⁓—

Laurie had her hand everyplace she could respectfully get it on the walk from the tram. She'd behaved herself beautifully while traveling, and she thought she deserved a break. By the time they climbed to the third floor, she was working the buttons on Kaatje's blouse and things got rougher as they entered the apartment. She'd never felt so ravenous, and found herself taking control in a way that seemed strangely natural. Kaatje just looked at her with her half-lidded eyes and let herself be led upstairs.

Kaatje was half undressed, her slacks hanging off one foot, blouse and bra missing. Laurie's fingers had burrowed under her panties and were caressing every spot she could reach. With a thump, she pushed Kaatje to the bed and stood over her, quickly whipping off her own clothing and throwing it over her head as she did. "I'm going to latch onto your kris and never let it go," she growled.

Kaatje couldn't help but laugh. "My kris? I'd rather you played with my *kruis*." She took her hand and pressed it into herself. Feel how wet my *poesje* gets when you show me how hungry you are for me."

"Sexy talk only!" She tried to look fierce, but it didn't translate that way. Kaatje held out her hands and pulled her onto her body, nuzzling her face into her neck.

"That *was* sexy talk."

"*Poseje* is sexy?" She pulled her head up and looked at Kaatje suspiciously. "Really?"

"Make love to me," Kaatje whispered, her eyes filled with desire. "Make it last for months."

Laurie gazed at her for a long time. She was lost. Kaatje was the person…the woman she'd been looking for. She desperately wanted to be as gay as possible with the lovely woman who lay under her, hungry for love.

It had been easy to tease when they'd been clothed, but when Kaatje looked at her with those soulful eyes, it was impossible. What they shared was so much more than sex. It was hard to think of the right words, but sex was just the vehicle they used to get to the important part. This had to be love—it had to be. It was love and desire and need and passion and security and danger. And they communicated each of those tender feelings by sharing their bodies.

It was such a different experience from what she'd had before, and one she'd never be able to effectively communicate to Kaatje. She'd been searching for this love—this passion—for half of her life. And there was no way she was going to let it go. She ran her hands down Kaatje's arms, marveling at the wonders of her body. Every sweet sensation was hers for the taking—and she never, ever wanted the night to end.

———

Kaatje woke the next morning to hear Laurie on her cell phone, obviously speaking to an airline.

"No, I want the last flight out of Amsterdam. There has to be one later than two o'clock in the afternoon."

Kaatje got out of bed and walked over to her. "Don't do it," she said quietly. "You're on the best flight."

"But I have to leave in an hour," she said, tension locked into her face.

Taking the phone from her, Kaatje said into it, "Thank you," and hung up. "Laurie," she said soothingly, "flights to the US leave early. You're on the only nonstop KLM has. I don't want you to leave either, but three or four hours together isn't worth your having to sit in some airport waiting for a connection."

"Minneapolis. Two and a half hours."

"Come on now," she took her hand and led her back to bed. "Lie with me for a while." Laurie sprawled over her body like a rag doll. "This is hard," Kaatje said needlessly.

"I…we haven't talked about the future. How…how can we stay in touch?"

Kaatje stiffened, her body feeling like it had turned to stone. "Stay in touch? That's what you want? You'll see me the next time you're in Europe?" The rigidity vanished, replaced by strong, fluid hands that lifted

Laurie and placed her on her back. Kaatje sat up, flinging her hair from her eyes, the sheet tenting over her knees as she leaned heavily on them. "That's all this is?"

Laurie shot up and tried to put an arm around her, but Kaatje squirmed away.

"No! Don't…I didn't mean that literally. I just don't know where we go from here."

Kaatje stared at her. It was impossible to tell if she was angry, or frightened or frustrated. "What do you want?"

"If you were in the US, I'd want you to move in with me. If I were here I'd want to live with you." She stroked her arm, relieved that Kaatje did not shirk from her touch. "I'm really, really into you." That was beyond lame. But this wasn't the time to talk about the future. There were too many balls in the air to add another one to the juggling act.

"But you're *not* here and I'm *not* in the US."

"No, but that isn't a surprise, is it? We knew we'd have to figure something out."

Kaatje jumped out of bed and started pacing. "What can we figure out? You've been a lesbian for a matter of days. I can't commit myself to a woman who's married to her job, who isn't sure of her sexuality, who has no interest in my way of life. This is crazy!"

Laurie slipped out of bed and approached her tentatively, as though she were a feral animal. When she got close enough she grasped Kaatje by the waist and held onto her. "I *am* sure of my sexuality. And being together is not crazy. Once Osaka's open I can stop and think. I'll take some time off. We can focus on us."

"Two weeks?" Her tone was cold.

"No, more than that. I promise I can get enough time off to let us spend a long time together. We can travel anywhere you want, or you can come to LA or I'll go to St. Maarten. We can make this work if we really want to." She shook Kaatje gently. "I want it to. Do you?"

Her expression softened inch by inch. Finally, she closed her eyes and sighed. "I do." They held each other for a minute or two, bridging the emotional gap that had unexpectedly opened up. Then Kaatje led the way back to bed. She sat down and Laurie did the same, looking at her expectantly. "I want to make sure of something."

"Okay."

"Is our distance the only thing we have to fix? I don't want to get into this and find out you can't be with me because I'm not successful enough or I don't make enough money."

"That kind of thing has never crossed my mind—" Laurie began, but Kaatje interrupted.

"I want to be clear." Kaatje's eyes burned with an intensity that was a little frightening. "I'm ready…I'm anxious to move forward. Are you?"

Shit! She wasn't ready for this discussion. But she had to get it out now. Right now. "There's one thing you have to try to change."

Kaatje's expression immediately softened and turned open, almost earnest, like a student listening to a favorite teacher. "What is it?"

"It feels like you punish me with silence when you're angry, and that's hard for me to take."

Kaatje flopped onto the bed and stared into space for a few moments.

"You're doing it now," Laurie said. "You might not mean to…but you're doing it."

Kaatje patted the space beside her. "Lie with me for a minute."

Laurie did, waiting patiently. Just having brought it up made the minutes she waited seem less like punishment and more like a pause in their conversation. Kind of like rebooting a computer.

Finally, Kaatje spoke. "When I was young, I was encouraged to have any type of feeling towards my parents and my siblings. It was perfectly fine to be angry or even hateful. I could wish that I could drown my sister in the canal, but I wasn't allowed to express those feelings aloud because they were hurtful. They were valid, and I wouldn't be punished for having them, but they were mine alone."

That sounded kinda healthy. Was she complaining about that? It was hard to tell when she seemed this thoughtful and gentle.

"I had a bad temper when I was young. I was prone to yell and throw a fit, but that wasn't allowed. I had to learn to control myself to avoid being punished, and the only way I could do it was to shut up." She looked at Laurie, her eyes almost begging for empathy. "It's still the only way I know to avoid snapping off some rude comment I'll regret."

The look in her eyes was so fragile—it was unforgettable. She was laying herself right out there without any protection. That was such a loving act. "I understand," Laurie managed, choking back tears. "We'll figure it out. We can figure anything out." She kissed her lovely lips gently. "We're invincible together." *Please, please let that be true. Nothing has ever been more important. Nothing.*

———

They took public transportation to the airport. But Kaatje didn't point out all of the sights they passed. She didn't say a word. She just clutched Laurie's hand until it hurt. When they got to the security line, Kaatje had to say goodbye. They kissed as platonically as they could, since neither liked to show her feelings too much in public. Then Kaatje whispered in her ear, "Do you still have a crush on me?"

Tears sprang to Laurie's eyes, and all she could do was nod, decisively, and blow a kiss. Then she watched Kaatje lope through the airport, knowing she was crying and needed to find a quiet place to be alone. All alone.

Chapter Twelve

SOMEHOW LAURIE HAD to make up for the time she'd spent in Europe. Even though only one day had been vacation, it was still seven days out of the office, counting the weekend—and no one did her work when she was gone.

The only way through her backlog of e-mails and reports was to skip meals and work even later. After sleeping on her office sofa for a week, she woke to find Wendy, her admin, standing over her. "I know it won't help much, but I found a food service that will make deliveries here to the office. Here's your breakfast. I have your lunch and dinner in the refrigerator."

"Aww, you don't have to do that." Laurie sat up and tried to work out the crick in her neck. "But I'm going to gobble this down before I head over to the gym to shower. Is anyone else here?"

"Of course not. You've got a half hour before Aaron will be here, and he's always the first in—after you, of course."

"You're the best, Wendy. Use my credit card to pay for this. And keep it coming," she said, smiling as a very pleased-looking admin walked out of the office. "This will save me twenty minutes a day." It was amazing and a little depressing to admit how much that meant.

———

Kaatje called just a few weeks after their meeting in Amsterdam. "Hey, I was thinking I needed a break. What's LA like?"

"Now?"

"Yeah, now would be good."

"It's fantastic! Really the best time of the year."

"Sounds pretty good. Do you want me to come?"

"Yes! Yes, yes, yes, yes and more yes!"

"Are you sure? I can't really tell." Kaatje's soft chuckle made Laurie feel absolutely giddy.

"You know how much I'd love to have you visit. But…can you afford the ticket?"

"I can pay my own way," she said briskly. "I'm not hinting for charity."

Damn, Kaatje had thin skin. "I know you'd never do that." She tried to make her voice low and gentle. "But you've told me you try to live pretty simply and an extra trip to LA probably isn't in your budget."

"It wasn't, but I can get a ticket for under a thousand dollars, taxes included. I can manage it."

"I'm going to offer something, and I don't want you to say 'no' until I finish. Okay?"

"No." Kaatje giggled, making Laurie smile at her playfulness.

"I've been going to Japan five or six times a year for six years, and I only use my frequent flier miles to go to Cincinnati a couple of times a year. I have enough miles to go to Saturn. Let me use some of them to buy you a ticket. Then you can use your money to do things here in LA, when I'm at work. Which I will be most of the time. You know that, right?"

"I do."

"Well? Will you let me use some miles before my airline goes out of business or merges with someone and I lose them all?"

"Sure."

That was ridiculously easy! She had thin skin, but you never knew where it was thinnest. "How long can you stay?"

"You know I don't have much of a schedule. I've been farming out requests I've gotten for sails to other boats. I can keep doing that as long as I want."

"Damn that sounds nice," Laurie sighed. "I can't imagine having that kind of freedom."

"Maybe I can help you imagine it."

Nothing sounded more appealing. Having Kaatje in LA would make the next months bearable. "You know how busy I'll be though, right? It's really bad."

"Yeah, I think I've got a good idea. I'll just have to make coming home something you won't want to delay."

"If you're here when I come home, I might let the whole project slide. It doesn't matter if the damned park opens on time, right?" She felt giddy enough to make a joke about something that terrorized her almost every night. Having Kaatje beside her might even make the nightmares stop. That was asking for a lot, but it couldn't hurt to hope. Funny how you could go from disapproval of your girlfriend's work habits to joy at her decision to drop everything just weeks after visiting her in The Netherlands. Double standards came in very handy at times.

—⁂—

Kaatje arrived at eight the following Thursday night. As soon as she was through customs, she called Laurie's cell phone. "Well, your immigration service believes I'm just here for a visit, and I'm finally walking on US soil."

"Fantastic! After you get your luggage you'll see a guy holding up a sign with your last name on it. That's your car."

"My car?"

"Yeah. By the time you get to my place, I'll be home." She paused for a second. "You didn't think I'd actually be at the airport, did you?"

"Well, yeah, that's what I thought."

"Oh, Kaatje, I'm sorry I didn't make that clear. But nobody in LA actually goes to the airport. I would have had to leave here at five to get there."

There was a perceptible lag, then Kaatje said, "Okay. I'll look for my car."

"He has my address, and I've already paid him and given him a tip. You just relax and let him bring you to me."

"All right. I'll practice my kissing."

"Not on him!"

"No, just on the back of my hand. See you soon."

———

Laurie was standing in the doorway when the elevator door opened. Kaatje looked fantastic. Tired, but fantastic. Her dark hair was loose and curled softly around her shoulders. It looked darker and more lush than normal against a white cotton sweater that clung to her body like a hug. And her legs looked a mile long in snug jeans and navy blue boat shoes. She was truly a sight for sore eyes. "Get in here this minute."

Kaatje grinned and started jogging, reaching Laurie in two seconds, despite the big backpack thumping against her. "Good enough?"

She wrapped her arms around her, feeling the solidity of her body like an anchor in a storm-tossed sea. "I've never had a better sensation than this. I can't tell you how much I've missed you."

"Me too. Can we go inside? I've been practicing that kissing stuff and…"

Giggling, Laurie pulled her inside and threw her arms around her neck. They kissed as though it had been ages since they'd seen each other. "I missed you so much." Laurie rubbed her face against Kaatje's shoulder, purposefully inhaling her scent and feeling lighter yet more grounded when she detected the familiar notes.

"I'm glad I'm here."

"No gladder than I am." She pulled away and looked down at the floor. "Is that all you brought?"

Kaatje gazed down at her backpack. "That's how I travel. I can manage with this for months. You don't want to have much to carry when you're staying at hostels."

A hostel was some sort of hotel, but why it had a different name must have something to do with Europe. Or something else.

Kaatje's eyes roamed around the apartment. "This is a very nice place." Chuckling softly, she added, "It doesn't look lived in. How long have you been here?"

"A while. I'll get around to personalizing it after Osaka. I hired someone to decorate it, but it's not much like me."

"Show me around." Kaatje took Laurie's hand and started to walk, even though Laurie couldn't imagine why she was interested in the place.

"Well, we're in the living room. I sit on the couch to work and it's good for unscheduled naps."

"Does that mean when you pass out from exhaustion? I know you disapprove of scheduled naps."

"Something like that. But I also fall asleep there the second I turn the TV on."

Kaatje walked over to the set and appraised it. "Big and thin. Like a supermodel. You really don't watch it?"

"I haven't turned it on this year. TV was Colin's thing. He told me what to buy and he got it installed. Then he left."

"Do you have a picture of him?"

Laurie blinked. "Of *him*?"

"Or of the two of you. I'm interested."

It felt darned odd to be searching for a picture of her ex, but Kaatje seemed like she needed it to get acclimated. Going through a basket of photos, programs, invitations and flyers she was someday going to put into binders or throw out, Laurie pulled one out triumphantly. "Got one! This is from the time he had a short film make it to Sundance." She handed the photo to Kaatje and watched her face as her focused gaze took it in. "That's in Utah, in the mountains. It was colder than heck that year." She and Colin were standing outside the theater where the movie was to be shown. His long dark hair was almost covered by a faux-fur trapper hat and they both had on layers of down and fleece. Their cheeks were tinted pink, and they both looked very happy.

Kaatje finally handed the photo back, without commenting.

"You look...something," Laurie said. "I'm not sure what."

Standing there for a moment, Kaatje put her arm around Laurie and turned to gaze out the floor-to-ceiling windows. "You have a wonderful view." They stood together looking out at the white lights that dotted the hillside. "What are we looking at?"

"The line of moving lights is the Sepulveda Pass. It's the road that cuts through the mountains between LA and The Valley."

"The dark part is a mountain?"

"Yes, technically. But it's not very tall. There must be a rule prohibiting people from building on it, because a hill like that would never stop a developer."

They moved over to the other window wall and looked out at the wide valley with tiny lights blanketing it.

"Mmm. This is a big city. It seems like it goes on forever."

"And this is just a tiny portion. It's not adorable and compact the way Amsterdam is."

"Being spread out has its charms. The density of Amsterdam can wear on you."

"I suppose." She snuggled against her side. "Did it upset you to look at that picture?"

Shrugging, Kaatje finally said, "A little. I'm not usually jealous, and I have no right to be anyway, but yeah, it bothered me."

Laurie turned, and looked into Kaatje's face. "Tell me why."

Kaatje delayed by fussing with Laurie's hair, tucking some strands behind her ear. "Uhm, I was thinking of how happy you looked. Then I thought of how you said you were just acting the whole time. It makes me wonder…"

"If I'm acting with you," she said softly. She gripped Kaatje's shoulders and tried to make her voice clear and decisive. "Not ever. Not even once. I'm done with that. I will never put on an act with a lover again. It's not fair to either of us. And I *cared* for Colin. I truly did. I honestly didn't know that what I felt wasn't love."

Kaatje nodded solemnly. "Okay. I just…I'm not sure of what's…you know…going on with us."

"We're moving forward, just like we talked about in Amsterdam. Aren't we?"

Still tenderly but idly fussing with strands of hair, Kaatje nodded again. "Yeah, I guess that's what we're doing." She swallowed noticeably. "Are we…exclusive?"

Startled, Laurie jerked a bit. "Yes! At least *I* am." She put her hands on Kaatje's shoulders and squeezed. "Did you meet someone?"

Laughing gently, Kaatje shook her head. "Of course not. But I'm screwing around with my income pretty severely by turning away jobs. I don't mind, but I want to make sure you're considering the future."

Laurie threw her arms around her and squeezed until Kaatje winced from pain. "I think about the future every chance I get. If I didn't think we could work this out I'd never, ever spend this much time with you." She pulled away and showed a teasing smile. "I wish I were kidding, but I'm not. This has come at a really bad time for me, but I can't walk away. I thought I could…" She shook her head, still smiling. "By the time I left St. Maarten, I was already trying to figure out how to get back to you."

"Okay. That's all I need for now. I just don't want to be chasing a dream that can't come true."

"You're not," Laurie said firmly. "Neither of us is. Still want the tour?"

"Yeah." With Kaatje not budging an inch, Laurie took charge and tugged her along. "This sparkling clean room is the kitchen. I've used the plates and glasses…sparingly…but neither the oven nor the range has been touched."

"Until tomorrow. I'll make you a good breakfast."

"No, no. I've got a breakfast meeting at seven. And you're going to be in bed, getting over your jet lag."

"Then dinner. I'll make something nice."

"You'll have to go to the grocery store. My cupboards are bare." She opened the door to a big cabinet next to the refrigerator, showing only a few bottles of liquor, wine, and salad dressing.

"Give me directions."

She put her arms around Kaatje's neck and grinned seductively. "Take me down the hall, open the bathroom door, remove this silly business suit I have on and get into the shower with me." She gave her a fleeting kiss. "Good directions?"

Kaatje took her hand and started to lead her. "Fantastic."

The next day Laurie chose to wear a skirt with a pocket. She wanted to be able to keep her cell phone at hand, and knew she'd leave it behind, as she often did, if it was in her jacket. The phone vibrated at eleven, and it took her a second to figure out why her skirt was humming. She stepped out of a routine meeting to take the call. "Hi. What's up?"

"I finally am. How's your day?"

"Oh, you know. I can't talk for long. Need anything?" *Dear God, don't need anything.*

"No. I just wanted to see how you were."

"I'm great. I'll be home early. Don't go to the store. We're going down to see Teddy Bear tonight."

"Hurrah."

Kaatje needed to work on her false enthusiasm. That lame effort wouldn't have fooled either Teddy or his cousin Brownie, and Brownie was a real dope.

Laurie threw the door open and bustled into the house just after four. "Kaatje? Are you ready?"

"Yeah. I've never had my lover's secretary call me to tell me what to wear to an amusement park, but I'm learning to roll with the punches."

"Wendy makes a lot of calls for me. I wanted to make sure you brought a sweater, and I knew I'd never have time to call."

"How'd you get off early?" She seemed a little wary.

"Well, the good news is that I'm going to get to show you off tonight. We're having a big dinner at the park. All of the big names will be there.

Then…" *How to break this to her?* "We get to go someplace new and exciting next Wednesday."

Kaatje's eyes narrowed. She was never going to be an easy one to fool. "Where's that?"

"Osaka."

"Osaka?" Her eyes narrowed dangerously. "Did you know about this before I decided to come here?"

"No, I swear I didn't. I thought I could put it off for a month, but a few big problems cropped up. I might be able to come home in a week…if everything goes well." She put her arms around Kaatje's waist and held her. "I'm sorry. I really am. But Japan's very cool. I know you'll like poking around."

"No, I don't think I will. I'll stay here and wait for you to come back."

Laurie's enthusiasm collapsed along with her knees and she dropped onto a handy chair. "I can't guarantee I'll be back in a week."

Kaatje dropped down beside her and they shared unhappy looks. "I don't want to go to Japan if you'll be working the whole time."

"But I told you how busy I'd be. You said you understood."

"I do. But I understood that we'd be in Los Angeles."

Didn't I tell her how volatile the schedule was? How could she have not known? "Uhm, I thought I told you I'd have to go to Osaka at least two or three times, and then for the month before we open. I just assumed…"

Kaatje stood up and smoothed the creases in her slacks. "You said we had to leave the minute you got home. Can we talk about this in the car?"

Laurie stood up and started for her bedroom. "I've gotta change. Business casual tonight."

A few minutes later they were in the back seat of a big, grey sedan. "Do you own a car?" Kaatje asked quietly.

Laughing, Laurie said, "Yeah. Well, they lease one for me. A nice Japanese one, of course. But I tend to order a car service if I have to go a long distance. I can work if someone's driving me."

Kaatje blew a breath out of pursed lips. "I don't think I really knew how hard you work. I thought it would be like my dad—really, really busy during the day…"

"It was like that for the first few years. But it's ramped up every year since. These last six months have been torturous." She leaned against Kaatje, desperately hoping it wasn't all too much for her. "But it'll be much, much better after the park opens. I promise that."

"But that's not until June."

"Yeah. June the first. A day that will live in infamy or accolades."

"You go on to Japan. I'll hang out here for a few days and see how I like LA."

"Really?"

"Well, if we have a future, that might mean we live in LA…right?"

Laurie's eyes lit up. "You'd do that?"

"I'd consider it." She looked very serious and it was clear she was choosing her words carefully. "I'm willing to give a lot to make a relationship work. I just have to know…"

"That I'm willing to give too."

"Something along those lines. Yes. I don't like to be made a fool of. I'm careful with love, and I don't mind going slowly, but things have to be fair."

"I understand. I really do."

"I'll wait for a week. Then I'll go to St. Maarten and scrounge up some business if you can't come back."

"No, no, please don't go. I promise you'll have fun in Japan. We'll have an extra week together if you come. Isn't that worth something?" How quickly one could be made to grovel. She wanted to grab onto Kaatje's leg and not let go no matter how much she kicked.

Kaatje reached out with those strong, sure hands and cupped her face. Just that simple touch made her stomach stop churning. But the words were not calming. "I don't want to see Japan alone. I want to see you."

"But you've come all this way!"

"I know. But you can't help what you have to do, and neither can I."

Yes, she could. Kaatje had nothing planned. She could easily go to Japan. She just didn't want to. Unable to think of a response, Laurie put her head on Kaatje's shoulder and nestled up against her, ignoring the slightly shocked look on their driver's face reflected in the rear view mirror.

———

Later that night, on the way home, Laurie dropped off to sleep at least five times. Finally, she felt Kaatje scoot over to the far corner and tug on her until she was lying across the seat, head cradled in Kaatje's lap. A gentle hand played with her hair, and she struggled mightily to remain sentient. "Everybody liked you."

Chuckling, Kaatje said, "Everyone was very nice. I've got to say, it amazed me how open you've been with your co-workers. All I've heard are horror stories about how antagonistic people in the US are about lesbians."

"Not at Luxor. The president of Theme Parks is a lesbian. If not for gay people there would be no Bear."

"Do I have to blame gay people for taking you away?"

She blinked up at her, caught by her simple, classic beauty. "You can come with me. I have a ticket for you. Business class."

Kaatje smiled that patient, knowing smile, but shook her head. "I don't mind traveling alone, but it would trouble me to be wandering around all day while you're just a few miles away working. And I don't want to be one of those people who whines because you're busy. I think that could be bad for us."

"I really wish you could see the park. I'm…proud of it."

"I'll come for the opening."

Laurie shot up, feeling the blood rush from her head. "You will?"

"Of course I will. I've been checking on fares. If I sell some blood I think I can swing it." Her teasing smile was like a hug.

"Oh, Kaatje." She leaned against her. "That would mean so much to me."

"You've worked on this for years. You'd do the same for me."

"Yeah, I would, but still…" She put her mind on overdrive, trying to think of an angle to keep her in LA for a while. "How about this? Have your sister come to LA. She could bring your niece and nephew. You could go to the parks…VIP treatment…stay at the best hotel…and you'd have someone to kick around LA with. I'd gladly…gratefully pay for everything, including air fare. Then you can just change the date on the ticket I bought for you and use it to come to Japan."

"You can't just change dates. They have all sorts of restrictions."

"When you buy an unrestricted business class seat you can."

"How much did that cost?" She looked like her eyebrows were going to land in her hairline.

"A lot. Courtesy of Teddy Bear. We get to bring our partner on one trip a year. And if an assignment lasts more than a month you can have your partner come visit every month." She leaned over and kissed Kaatje on the cheek. "You don't mind being my partner do you?"

Tears shone in Kaatje's beautiful eyes. "No, I like it." She kissed her, then let their heads touch for a moment. "I'll think about it."

"Great. Now put your arm right here and I'll take a cat nap." Kaatje put her arm across Laurie's chest and held her tightly for the seconds it took her to fall asleep.

CHAPTER THIRTEEN

As ALWAYS, LAURIE woke before dawn, her heartbeat thudding wildly in her ears. What time was it? What day? Was she late? But a warm body was pressed up against her and a massive sense of relief flowed through her like a sedative. Kaatje was there. She wrapped her arms around her and nestled against her body, tenderly nuzzling her face against Kaatje's back. It took a few minutes to convince herself, but she eventually relaxed and enjoyed the sensation of having Kaatje in her bed. The cool breeze from the air conditioner wafted across her back, while Kaatje's warmth seeped into her chest and her thighs. Nothing could have felt better.

———

Hours passed before they were both awake at the same time. When Laurie finally pried her eyes open, Kaatje was lying on her side, blue eyes blinking alertly.

"Hi. Been up long?"

"No, not very. I was just enjoying this bed." Kaatje rolled onto her back and stuck an arm and a leg out. "It's big."

"Yeah, it is. The room's really big, and my old bed looked silly in here." Laurie sat up and brushed her hair from her face. "The room looks pretty sparse, doesn't it?"

"It's not sparse as much as not personalized. It looks like one of those apartments you see in a design magazine. No clutter."

"I don't like clutter, so you'll never see that." She lay back down and stretched out lazily. "I'm not the ideal home owner. I don't get a lot of pleasure out of owning, but it looks better."

Kaatje looked at her questioningly. "Looks better?"

"Yeah. Colin and I shared a cute house in Hollywood, but it was a rental. After I was made VP, Fernando suggested that I'd better put down some roots."

"Interesting. Do they tell you what to wear? How to cut your hair?" She filled a hand with Laurie's hair and let it spill from her fingers.

"Not technically." She slipped out of bed and went into the bath, leaving the door open. Splashing cool water onto her face made her brain start firing faster, and she ran her toothbrush under the water, then applied paste. "They want their executives to live in a local neighborhood and be part of the community. They'd prefer it if we were on the right side of the hill too."

"The hill?"

"The Santa Monica mountains. The road I showed you last night. Hollywood's on the wrong side."

Kaatje gave her a suspicious look.

No civilian had ever been able to understand the Luxor ethos. Maybe that was why every third person was married to a team member. "I've been able to slide along, but after Osaka I'm going to have to find a charity or a community organization and start donating my time."

Kaatje sat up and stared at her. "They really *do* tell you what to do."

Laurie started to brush her teeth. Speaking through a mouth of foam, she said, "Every big company does that. If I got arrested for a DUI or had the cops come to break up a fight with my boyfriend, I'd probably get fired."

Kaatje's eyes popped open. "You'd better not have a fight with your boyfriend!"

Laurie rinsed her mouth and walked back to the bed, falling onto Kaatje's body, laughing when Kaatje started to wrestle with her. "I had to say boyfriend just as an example—'cause I'll never fight with my girlfriend."

After a quick but satisfying bout of lovemaking they got ready to go to Laurie's office so she could get organized and work at home for the rest of the day. She was trying to think of something to do that would give Kaatje a sense of LA, without taking too much time out of her schedule.

"Hey, I know what we'll do. When I first moved here, Fernando told me to start in downtown and follow Sunset Boulevard all the way to the end. That's an easy way to see how the neighborhoods change."

"I'd love to see anything you want to show me."

"Great. Then we can stop at the grocery store and get some things." She paused and grinned slyly. "I can use the GPS on my car to find one."

When they reached her floor, the big "Theme Parks" logo was splashed across both doors, along with a picture of a happy Teddy Bear in front of his Bee Hive. "Here's where all the magic happens," Kaatje said, smirking.

Laurie used the card she had attached to a coiled cord tethered to her belt loop to open the door. Once inside, they went past masses of cubicles, many with a person inside, working away. Moving down an aisle of cubes, they passed a big glass door. "That's Carolyn Smith's office. She's the president of the parks." She leaned close to Kaatje's ear and added, "Big dyke."

Kaatje snorted as they continued down the row of offices. "Oh, there's Fernando. Your office must be close."

"Yep. Right here." Laurie patted her office door, displaying just her name in modest typeface.

"No title? I'd expect something like 'Her Royal Highness.'"

"Nope. We don't do that." She smiled sweetly. "We're all just team members."

They walked in and Kaatje turned her head slowly, taking in the big desk, two monitors, full-length sofa, round table with four chairs, and coat rack. Then she walked to the wall of windows. Before them was a beautifully manicured, garden-like setting with other buildings set around the perimeter of the square. "The other team members sit in boxes," Kaatje said, a teasing smile on her face. "This belongs to a princess."

"It is pretty nice." Laurie once again felt the thrill of accomplishment as she took the time to really notice her surroundings. "Carolyn's is just like this, but she has another wall of windows and two sofas. We call her the queen bee behind her back."

"Is it worth the climb to have more windows and another place to collapse?"

"I have no idea." She stood there for a second, trying to imagine how she could possibly work harder. "I don't notice the perks much. What I've always wanted was to be promoted to have one less person to report to. Fewer is much, much better, even though the bosses are more demanding the higher you go."

Kaatje wandered around while Laurie got some reports ready. Poking her nose back into the office, Kaatje said, "Is this the Aaron you talk about?"

Laurie walked out and patted the name "Aaron Rosenberg" on the office next door. "That's my boy. He's in Osaka right now. It's tougher for him than it was for me. When I had his job I was still able to have a social life. Not so for him."

"When did you get this job?"

"It's been a couple of years."

"Two?"

"Yeah, right around then."

Kaatje stood there, her eyes scanning the floor in front of them. Quietly, she said, "Isn't that when you and Colin broke up?"

"No, I don't think so. I know we were together when I was promoted." She thought for a few seconds, trying to get the dates straight in her mind. They definitely went out to celebrate her promotion. She recalled sitting at a great restaurant in Marina del Rey, then extemporaneously checking into a five-star hotel on the beach with a smuggled bottle of champagne and a box of condoms from a liquor store. And Colin did all of the legwork in finding the condo. Did they really break up that close to her promotion? She remembered how pleased he was to be able to pick out the Lexus they leased for her, but it must have been shortly after that when his complaints about how little time she was home escalated into fights. "I…I guess it was. It all seems like a blur."

Kaatje put her arm around her and held her close. She gently kissed the top of her head. "I bet it was a blur. And it still is."

⸻

They stopped at a grocery store on the way home. As always, Laurie was chattering away as they got in line, and after a wait of just a few seconds, she scanned the various lines and said, "This is so poorly set up."

Kaatje was standing there, looking perfectly happy. She blinked and followed Laurie's gaze. "What is?"

"This system." Laurie pointed to the middle cashier. "The single line should start there. It should run down the wide freezer aisle and loop back on the housewares aisle, since that's not a high traffic area."

"Why does it matter? There are only four or five people in each line."

Laurie stared at her, wondering what kind of perspective led one to believe five people wasn't excessive. "It's Saturday afternoon. That has to be one of the busiest times of the week. Every register should be open. Supervisors and managers should man a register. When each cashier has a separate line the customers are punished when they get a slow cashier. A single line is the only way." She shook her head, wondering why everyone didn't put their full efforts into their job. There was no job too small to do it poorly.

Kaatje slung an arm around her shoulders and pulled her in for a hug. She was smiling when she said, "Do you do this all the time?"

"What?"

"Think of ways to improve every situation you encounter?"

Laurie pulled away and looked at her. "Of course. Everyone does."

Letting out a soft laugh, Kaatje assured her. "No, they don't. I promise you, they don't."

That made no sense at all. Why bother getting out of bed in the morning if you weren't going to do your best?

———

Laurie spent the day working at her laptop, the time flying by with Kaatje beside her. They were out by the pool, and she stopped for a while to get a drink. When she sat down again she said, "I should work from home more often. It's really nice out here."

"Yeah, it is. Why don't you?"

"Oh, it's a lot of trouble to make sure I have everything I need. It's a huge drag to get involved in something and find you're missing some report that's not on the system. I usually just go in and stay until I'm finished."

"Which you never are." Kaatje reached over and tugged on her earlobe. "You've got awfully cute ears." She lay back against her chaise and her eyes drifted upwards. "Do people live on those hills? I didn't see a lot of lights up there last night."

"I have no idea. I think that's a different set of mountains. But we could drive over that way later."

"I'd rather go down Sunset Boulevard. I want to see the neighborhoods change."

Laurie looked at her watch. "Let's go at four. Then we can get to Santa Monica in time to see the sunset."

"Sounds great. I'll tell you when it's four."

Grinning, Laurie said, "I just bet you will."

———

At five thirty they sat on a bench in Santa Monica in a park overlooking the ocean. Kaatje had brought a bottle of wine and some plastic cups, and they sipped a nice rosé while the sky turned a fantastic shade of pink, then burst into a vivid orange that covered the horizon. "This is the life," Laurie said, sighing in pleasure. "We don't get many sunsets like this. LA must know you're here and want to impress you."

"It's not too hard to relax, is it?" Kaatje teased.

Laurie nuzzled against her warm body. "Not when I'm with you. Actually," she said, "I have a heck of a time concentrating when you're here. I took more breaks today than I normally do in a week."

Kaatje started to laugh, then caught herself. "Are you serious? You touched me a few times and told me I looked cute in my swimsuit, but other than going to the bathroom or getting a drink you didn't flinch."

"Oh, I normally put my head down and don't pick it up until I'm ready to wet my pants. I was all over the place today."

"Laurie," she said, earnestly, "that's no way to live. I know this is important to you, but you're not in the emergency room trying to save people's lives."

"I know, I know." She let her head settle on Kaatje's shoulder, feeling her heartbeat slow down when they touched. "I just get involved. I don't know how else to be."

"You've got to try. Your life will be over before you know it if you don't learn how to nourish your soul."

"I'll just try to copy you. You're a very good teacher."

"But I can't keep an eye on you when you're at work."

"Maybe I'll let Wendy take an easier job and hire you. My life would be perfect if I could walk out of my office and see your pretty face smiling at me."

Kaatje blew out a short burst of air. "Only one of us could be happy if I was sitting in front of your office, and it wouldn't be me."

Kaatje hadn't hidden her disdain for corporate life. It was hard to imagine leaving Luxor, but it didn't look like there was another way. Kaatje would just have to get used to having a vice president in charge of something-or-other on *The Flying Dutchwoman*.

Chapter Fourteen

LAURIE WAS AT work by five thirty on Monday. They'd agreed that Kaatje would take her to work and then have the use of the car, but when Laurie woke without the alarm, she couldn't bear to rouse Kaatje. She looked serene, lying in the big bed with the covers pulled up to her chin, so Laurie called a cab and snuck out of the apartment without a sound.

She had a million things to finish before she left for Osaka, and just two days to finish them. Normally, she would have been able to focus with pinpoint precision, but her mind strayed to Kaatje a dozen times before lunch. What was she doing right now? Was she still in bed? Would she remember how to use the coffee maker? If she went out, was the GPS easy enough to use?

It was a struggle all day to keep her eye on the ball, and by the time she got home at seven thirty, the day seemed much longer than usual.

But Kaatje was there, smiling at her when she walked in, the scent of something tasty coming from the never-before-used kitchen. "There's heat coming out of that room," Laurie teased, pointing at the kitchen. "Call the fire department!"

Kaatje went to her and enveloped her in a hug. "Welcome home, honey bear."

Laurie kissed her, nearly swooning with pleasure when Kaatje's arms encircled her. There was something so primally fulfilling about merely having her close that she spent a moment puzzling over why she'd never felt this way before. At the time, she'd been certain she'd loved at least two of her boyfriends, but this sensation was entirely new—and it struck her heart like a dagger to know she would only be able to enjoy it for two more days.

—⁂—

Kaatje had spent the day in Marina del Rey, on a busman's holiday. She'd checked out the harbor, poked around the moored boats, and enjoyed a long session on a rented kayak. Laurie could tell that she was tired, but Kaatje insisted on cleaning the kitchen while Laurie took a bath.

Relaxing in the cloud of bubbles, Laurie reflected on how wonderful it was to have such a generous woman sharing her home. Kaatje was neat, quiet, and thoughtful. She was also beautiful, sexy, and fantastic in bed, and Laurie spent the rest of her bath thinking of ways to exploit that talent.

After emerging from the bath, Laurie dried off, brushed her teeth and went to find Kaatje and pull her into bed. To her surprise, Kaatje was lying on the bed, fully clothed. When Laurie sat next to her she was greeted with a lazy smile and half-lidded eyes.

"Tired," Kaatje said before curling her body around Laurie's and making some soft, contented murmurings. "Still jet-lagged."

"You can't sleep with your clothes on." Laurie briskly rubbed her hand across Kaatje's back. "Come on. Get up and get ready for bed."

Kaatje allowed herself to be drawn into a sitting position, then she got up and went into the bath. Laurie turned down the bed, and got in, waiting just a minute for Kaatje to join her.

Kaatje almost fell onto the cushy surface of the bed. "Nice," she said, still wearing that contented half smile. "I like having such a big bed."

Laurie scooted over until they were side by side. Her arm slid behind Kaatje's neck, then Kaatje turned and faced her. Laurie felt a thrill run up her spine when Kaatje's warm breasts touched her own, but when Kaatje offered a single kiss before closing her eyes and sighing lazily, disappointment replaced the thrill.

She'd been thinking of Kaatje all day. Not purely in a sexual way, but that had been the undercurrent. Having Kaatje in her arms and feeling her soft skin and womanly curves made that undercurrent morph into a stronger drive. One that hadn't often concerned her up until that moment.

That struck her. She'd been having sex since she was eighteen years old, but she could have counted on one hand the times she'd made an overture. It had always seemed like the man she was sleeping with made the first move, and she was more likely to fend him off than encourage him. Up until tonight, having sex with Kaatje before they fell asleep had been a given. Neither of them had to make an overture. What was the right thing to do? Kaatje was obviously tired. But they only had two nights together before Osaka, and losing one seemed awfully wasteful.

Kaatje's face was peaceful, almost serene. Her eyes moved under her lids, and her body twitched as she fell into a light sleep. Laurie debated her next move. She had to show her interest, but she had to be subtle. She'd had far too many erect penises wake her from a sound sleep to be heavy-handed about it.

She placed her hand on Kaatje's hip, gently moving it down to the thigh, relishing the feel of her skin. When Kaatje showed no response she expanded the territory, moving around to the small of her back, carefully watching her face for a flicker of interest. Nothing.

At that point, the pleasure of touching Kaatje began to outweigh the demands of her libido. Having Kaatje in her bed was as important as having sex. It was the closeness that Laurie had been missing in her life, and having Kaatje near made those years of emotional isolation fade from her memory. Without conscious thought, her hand moved down to Kaatje's ass and was filled with the warm flesh. Kaatje had a truly fantastic ass and Laurie found herself smiling when she palmed it. Being able to play, unnoticed, while Kaatje slept was an entirely new sensation, and she let her hand move up to stroke her muscular back.

Laurie laughed to herself when she thought of the times she'd tried to play with a boyfriend's body. She'd never rubbed a back, no matter how briefly, that she wasn't on her own back moments later. Men's fuses were remarkably short in her experience, and she'd never been able to just explore without having the exploration turn into intercourse. But this was fun as well as soothing.

Kaatje let out a sigh and slid her leg up until it settled on Laurie's thigh. Their bodies were entangled, pressing against each other from shoulder to toes, and Laurie felt a wave of tenderness envelop her. She moved her lips to delicately touch Kaatje's forehead, then along her cheek. Kaatje let out another soft mew and draped her arm around Laurie's waist. Laurie snuggled even tighter against her and let their foreheads touch. They couldn't be closer together, and that fact made her pulse start to beat more slowly, until it synced with Kaatje's. Moments later, they were both asleep, Laurie's heart as full as it would have been from the best lovemaking.

―――

Laurie came home at the ungodly hour of three o'clock on Tuesday afternoon, surprising Kaatje, who was out by the pool. She threaded her hand into her hair and said, "You love any kind of water, don't you?"

"I almost screamed," Kaatje said, fanning herself. "You're the last person I expected to see."

"Ha. Ha." Laurie sat on the next chaise and took her hand. "I surprised the heck out of Andrea, I'll admit to that. But I couldn't leave without doing anything with you. We have to go see a little bit of LA."

"We saw a little bit the other day."

"One drive down Sunset Boulevard isn't going to cut it. I've…actually, Wendy…arranged for something nice for us. Let's get changed and head out."

―――

By four o'clock they were parking at the base of what looked like a fairly green, carefully planted hill. "What's the Getty Center?" Kaatje asked.

"It's a museum with some of the best views in LA."

"Aren't the best views supposed to be inside, where the art is?"

"Not in LA. We're an outside people."

———

Kaatje spent a long time photographing the lovely buildings, the beautifully planted hillside, and the manicured gardens that surrounded the place. Then they stood in the most private spot they could find and kissed as the sun went down. The wind came over the pass and Kaatje started rubbing Laurie's back. "Keep doing that," Laurie said. "It's freezing."

"This is the oddest weather. I never imagined a place where you can sit by the pool in the afternoon, then freeze less than a minute after the sun sets. This is very much beyond my experience."

"Let's get a bite to eat and then go home and warm up the fun way." She took Kaatje's hand and they started for the train that would take them back to their car. "Actually, dinner's optional."

"That's what I think too. You're mandatory."

———

They lay in bed, cuddling and kissing, taking a short time out before they got back to the business at hand. "You know," Laurie said, taking a moment to kiss a wet path down Kaatje's chest then rest her head on her abdomen, "when we had that little fight in Holland, one of the things you kinda threw out there was that you weren't sure I was confident about my sexuality."

Kaatje had been drawing her fingers up and down Laurie's spine, but she stopped abruptly. "Uhm, well, I'd have to say you're not showing any signs of confusion." She let out a giggle.

"You probably won't believe this, but whenever I have a few spare seconds I try to think about my orientation."

"I believe that. I just don't believe you have many spare seconds."

"True. But I have been thinking about it. I'm amazed I didn't figure this out sooner, especially when I think of the differences in how I feel."

Kaatje sat up, taking Laurie with her. She scooted around until Laurie's head was on her shoulder. "That's better. I like to be able to see your face when you talk."

"That's one difference right there. I didn't like to hang out in bed with men, but I could live here with you."

"Why didn't you like to be in bed?"

Laurie rolled her eyes. "Because they wanted to have sex all of the time. If I was feeling lazy and wanted to sleep in, eventually they'd wake me up and want to have sex. Guys love sex the minute they wake up, if you let 'em."

Kaatje laughed softly, her chest bouncing up and down when she did. "I find this hard to reconcile. You're *so* sexual."

"Only with you," Laurie said. "I know I'm a lot older, but when I compare my first time with a guy and the first time with you—they're not the same act at all."

"You said you were…eighteen?"

"When I had intercourse. Yeah. After I graduated from high school."

"What was the guy's name?"

"Jeremy. We'd been going out for about a year, and he was ready to lose it." She laughed, thinking about how much he'd begged, pleaded and cajoled her. "Before I left for college I figured I might as well get it over with. I knew him, and I trusted him, so he seemed like a good candidate for sex."

"Did you hire him?" The look Kaatje was giving her was more than perplexed. She looked positively dumbfounded.

"No, but I have to admit I was really dispassionate about it. I made the decision, and prepared. I went on the pill, waited two months to make sure it was working, then bought condoms and lube and arranged to go to my sister's apartment to do it. She happily complied, since she'd been bugging me about it for two years."

"Sounds like a project rather than a loving act."

"That's about right. We'd been doing everything but intercourse, and he'd gotten pretty good at giving me orgasms, but it always felt kinda mechanical. I had to fantasize about something else to distract myself enough to let go."

Very quietly, Kaatje asked, "Do you have to do that with me?"

"Never." Laurie slipped her hand behind Kaatje's head and pulled it down so she could meet her lips. "I'm right there with you. Every time."

"It's okay if you do. Everybody's different."

"No. I look at you while you touch me and I just fall over the edge. There's a surprising dearth of thought involved." She laughed and kissed the pert breast so close to her mouth.

"How did it go with Jeremy?"

"I didn't care for it," Laurie said dryly. "Actually, I hated it. He was a big guy. He was a swimmer, but he did the butterfly and his chest and arms were huge. He was gentle and tried his best, but when he finished he collapsed on me and I came this close to screaming for help." She held her thumb and forefinger a hairsbreadth apart.

"Why then? I'd think having him enter you would be the hard part."

"I wasn't crazy about that, but having this big, sweaty, heavy body on me freaked me out. I realized I couldn't have moved him no matter what and that almost made me have a panic attack."

"Oh, that breaks my heart. You weren't ready to have sex, Moppie."

"No, that wasn't it. I felt like a frog on the dissection table in biology class. Like he could do whatever he wanted to me, and I couldn't stop him. I never, *ever* liked that feeling, and to let someone penetrate me always makes me feel vulnerable like that."

"I penetrate you," Kaatje whispered, kissing the top of Laurie's head. "Do you ever feel too vulnerable?"

"No, no." Kaatje wasn't getting the point. She'd never been with a man and she didn't have the right frame of reference. "We share." She looked into her eyes, but could only see confusion. "You're pleasing me when you touch me. You're focused on me. Then I focus on you. That's not what it was like for me with men. It seemed like they mostly wanted to get off, frequently. They'd do what I liked, but I could always tell they'd prefer for me to just let them go at me. Nothing made Ben, my college boyfriend, happier than when I let him do me really fast before his first class. He walked around like he owned the world when that happened."

"Okay," Kaatje said. "I hate to speak up for men, since I have no real knowledge, but some of them have to enjoy pleasing women as much as I do. There have to be good lovers out there."

"Mine were goodish," Laurie insisted. "I talked to lots of other girls, and most of them weren't even getting orgasms from their boyfriends."

"But you were kids then. It takes a while to mature and grow into a good lover." Kaatje sat up straighter, and Laurie could tell she had something important to say. There was something about the way she settled herself before saying something that tipped her hand. "How about this? You just said sex with me was sharing and pleasing each other, right?"

"Definitely. It's about us, not about you."

"But for there to be an us, there has to be a you too."

"Nothing." Laurie leaned back so Kaatje could see her smile. "None of that registered."

"If I could feel that you weren't into me, or weren't into really having something special, I might let you get me off and then turn off the lights."

"You would?" *No way! Kaatje was the most considerate lover ever!*

"Well, honestly, no. I wouldn't be with a woman who wasn't into me. But if I loved you, and thought you loved me, and thought I was giving you good sex…"

"You're saying I fooled them?"

"Maybe. Or maybe they wanted to believe you were into it. I'd try to convince myself you were into me, even if you weren't."

That earned her a long, lusty kiss that had them prone in seconds. "Please be into me," Kaatje cried out.

"I left work at two thirty today. That's more than I did for Colin in years." She took in a breath, then nodded. "You're right. I probably chose guys who weren't very perceptive. They were easily fooled into thinking I was satisfied, so they didn't try harder to share with me."

"I might be wrong, but if I was into a guy, I'd like to exhaust him and have him collapse on me. I'd like to feel I was the one who had that power over him. I think it could be fun to have something that fit right inside me that my partner could feel at the same time."

Laurie grasped her and kissed her hard. "You're so naive. Those darn things are never hard when you want them to be. You've gotta have all the luck in the world to be turned on just the right amount so he can get inside and put you over the edge before he explodes. It's like alchemy. Everyone says they can do it, but it's rare."

"Alchemy's more than rare," Kaatje said, chuckling. "I'm going to have to ask my mom or my sister about this. I need some real straight women to confirm or deny your biased report."

"I guess that means you believe I'm a lesbian, right?"

"There's not a chance that you're straight, so we'll put you in the lesbian camp until you prove you don't belong here."

The next morning, the alarm sounded at the diabolically early hour of five. Laurie desperately wanted to shut it off and spend the day wrapped in Kaatje's embrace, but she had to get to work and get a few things organized before her nine o'clock flight to Osaka. She sat up and blinked in the dim light, seeing Kaatje's blue eyes looking up at her. The sadness in them broke her heart, and she slid down until they were in each other's arms. "I don't want to leave."

"I know. But you have to. Maybe you can get finished quickly and come home."

"I'll do everything in my power. I promise." She placed soft kisses all around Kaatje's face, trying to memorize the planes of her lovely face with her lips.

Kaatje sighed and slipped out of bed, walking over to Laurie's side to take her hand. She answered Laurie's puzzled look by saying, "I'm going to drive you to work after I shower with you." Laurie stood and they held each other for a minute or two. "I've never had a better time than when we're in the shower and my hands roam all over your body."

"See? LA isn't that bad. We have big showers."

"LA is good because of you," Kaatje said, smiling sadly.

―――

At around nine thirty Laurie called, reaching Kaatje at the pool. "Hi. Guess what?"

"You're coming home?"

"No, I'm not that lucky. But I did get promoted. I'm a senior vice president. A friend and I were both elevated. We started together and we're rising together. Kinda cool."

"Oh, Laurie. Today? When you're leaving?"

"Yeah. The timing sucks, doesn't it?"

"It sure does. This is a very big day."

"I know." She let out a heavy sigh. "I'd love to celebrate with you, but I'm stuck on this plane, which is, as always, delayed."

"You won't get to have any celebration at all. That's awful."

"Maybe the flight attendants will share a glass of champagne with me." She laughed wryly. "Pitiful."

―――

They'd talked until the flight attendant raised her eyebrow, which was almost a rebuke from the always-courteous attendants in first class on Far East Airlines. It had cost a ton of miles for the upgrade, but Laurie felt she deserved at least one treat in celebration of her promotion. Being able to lie down on the long flight was a luxury she should have mentioned to Kaatje, but she hadn't. Everything that wasn't mission critical slipped right out of her head.

Kaatje. It was unfair on so many levels to have to leave her. It had cost her a lot of bookings to make the trip to LA, and it was all a waste. All they could hope for was that she'd be able to get a feel for LA and decide if she could live there, if it came to that.

If it came to that. Ha! Kaatje could stay forever, and then some. There couldn't be a more perfect partner. She had all of the obvious things—looks, brains, independence, and good morals. But it was the less obvious things that made her a gem.

Her calmness and certainty were tremendously appealing. Kaatje was a woman who would always be a source of good, prudent advice. Just being near her was mildly sedating, and for someone who was always a little wired up, it was a welcome balm. But she was also playful and funny. That was such a great combination. *And, unlike Colin, she took me at my word. She didn't have to be in my head to believe me. Most women would be quizzing me constantly about whether I was sure I was gay. Not Kaatje. She has the confidence in herself to let me live my life without her supervision.* That was fantastically attractive—even a turn on. Independent women were hot, and the fact that Kaatje hadn't complained about being left in LA showed just how self-sufficient she was. She was the real deal, and keeping her happy had to go on the top of every priority list. Teddy Bear could suck it or deal with it.

Laurie worked unceasingly until the flight attendant finally caught her attention. "Would you like to have lunch?" she asked.

"Oh, no, thanks. I'll take a soda, but that's all."

She slid out of her seat and stood up to stretch. Then she went to stand in the relatively generous space by the rest rooms. Luxor had made them all watch a movie about deep vein thrombosis, and she tried to stand up at least fifteen minutes every hour or two to avoid getting a blood clot.

As soon as her eyes weren't glued to her laptop, she thought about Kaatje, wondering, as usual, what she was doing. It struck her that she was concentrating better on the plane than she'd been able to at home. Having Kaatje around was both a joy and a curse. She'd never in her life had such a hard time staying focused as she had in the last few days. How did people have children and pets and every other kind of distraction while committed to a high-pressure job? Wouldn't it make things harder on all involved? But nothing was better than getting home at the end of a stressful day and seeing Kaatje's face beam like the sun breaking through the clouds. But how was it possible to work as though nothing else mattered when something…some*one* else…did?

CHAPTER FIFTEEN

IT TOOK A few days, but they figured out a way to talk when both of them were awake. Laurie called one night, sounding a little slap-happy. "I had to go to Tokyo today. Yet another pointless meeting with another mid-level government factotum."

"You sound…happy," Kaatje mused. "Are you?"

"No, I'm really, really tired. I think I'm at that laugh-at-anything point. But I did have an interesting train ride. Have you ever used a traditional Japanese toilet?"

"No," Kaatje said, laughing softly. "I've never been to Japan."

"Right. That was a dumb way to ask the question. Well, they have squat toilets—"

"Oh, I used one of those in France. They still use them in Japan? I thought everything would be ultramodern."

"You'll find out in a couple of months. I'll take you to see all kinds of toilets." She started to laugh, knowing she sounded manic. "Uhm, they have very elaborate toilets that do everything you can think of, but they also have the traditional style in a lot of public places. Anyway, I had to go —and go fast. The modern one was in use, and the only one available was the traditional style. I went for it, even though I hadn't used one before. I truly didn't have a choice."

"I sense humiliation coming."

"Almost. But I learned a valuable lesson. Never wear slacks when you might have to use a squat toilet." She waited just a second and burst into a laugh. "I came so close to ruining a perfectly good suit it wasn't funny. But it is now."

"That's horrible!"

"It was. It really was. I managed to pull one leg out of my slacks but the other one got stuck. I was moments from disaster. And if I hadn't held onto the little rail they thoughtfully installed for the uninitiated I might have been thrown from the train."

"The one I used it France took every bit of concentration I had. I can't imagine using one on a train."

"It was a sight to behold. I could have done it without a second thought if I'd stayed in gymnastics, but my poor thighs aren't used to that kind of move any more."

"I have a mental picture I'll try to get rid of. It doesn't fit with your polished business image."

"Don't remind me. I was itching to tell someone, but I'd never reveal something like that at work. I knew you'd appreciate it."

"I do." Kaatje voice took on a more reflective tone. "And I appreciate that you chose me to confide in."

"You're the only one. Things have more meaning for me after I share them with you. That's pretty cool, isn't it."

"It's very cool. But if you're giggling like this over toilet humor, it's time for bed. No arguments."

"But I want to talk to you. You're the best part of my day."

"You're the best part of mine too. But I'm the one person in your life who cares for you more than the deadline. That means I'll give up some of our time to make sure you get your rest. Go to bed. Right now."

"Can I kiss you goodnight?"

"Yes," Kaatje said, chuckling. "But quickly."

"Smooch. G'night."

"Sleep well. And call me if you have a second before work. I don't care when it is."

"I will. 'Night."

"Goodnight, my Moppie."

A week passed, with Laurie sleeping so little she was starting to have hallucinations. But everyone was doing exactly the same, and she couldn't be the one who fell by the wayside. She'd started to think of the opening like D-Day, but instead of the beaches of Normandy, she had to co-ordinate the movement of men and machinery from all over the globe to a plot of land outside Osaka. Lives were in the balance, or so it seemed.

It was three in the morning and she was ready to lie down on the sofa in her office. Checking her watch, she saw that it was midmorning in LA, and she took the opportunity to call Kaatje. "How's life in LA?"

"I'm not very good with the international timeline, but I think it's really, really late in Osaka. Why are you still up?"

"We had a big meeting with our HR people in LA. We knew it would be a long one, since we had to get them to sign off on all of our employment practices and procedures. We decided to do it when *they* were fresh." She laughed, but it was weak-sounding even to her own ears. "We thought they'd go easier on us if they didn't have to stay really late."

"Did it work?"

Laurie yawned. "I'm not sure. We got close to finishing, but there are just enough questions unresolved that I'll have the damn numbers marching around in my head while I'm trying to sleep."

"Are you back at your hotel or still in the office?"

No sense in lying. She could always tell. "I'm at the office. I'm going to sleep right here. That'll let me catch an extra hour."

"Laurie." That was Kaatje's motherly voice. It was pretty precious.

"I know it's bad, but I honestly can sleep longer this way. That's my goal."

"Is there a place you can shower?"

"Yeah. They have a big executive lounge with showers and a soaking tub. I'll go up there before my first meeting. Luckily, I brought a couple of suits and blouses and underwear to the office. I knew I'd be stuck here at least once."

"I'd love to talk to you, but you need to get to bed. Now turn off the lights and hit that sofa. Bye-bye."

Before Laurie could reply the line went dead. She locked her door, took off everything but her underwear, and lay down on the chilly leather sofa. It was tough, but she had begun to get better at turning off her mind and sleeping whenever she got the chance. She was almost out when she sat bold upright, grabbed the phone, and called home once again. "I can't believe I didn't ask how your trip to the park was!" She did not have to admit she'd forgotten Margriet and the kids were in LA. Kaatje didn't have to know everything.

Kaatje laughed gently. "It was great. The kids loved it and Margriet was very impressed by how well we were treated. I think she'll expect the same thing if she ever goes to your park in Spain."

"If I send her a pass, which I will, they'll treat her just as well."

"We had a great time, Laurie, but it would have been massively better if you were with us."

"I know. I ache from wanting you."

"I ache from knowing how tired you are. Bye-bye."

Laurie hung up and gazed at the phone for another moment. Knowing she could call Kaatje whenever she needed a lift was better than she would have ever imagined. She'd clearly never been in love because no one had ever made her feel as good as Kaatje could—just by hanging up on her. And as soon as they had a few minutes alone she was going to tell her just what she meant to her. Whenever that would be.

—∞—

After a few hours sleep, Laurie called again. "Hi," she said, trying to get the cobwebs out. "I wanted to talk a little more before I had to go slay dragons."

"I'm glad you called. We're down at your lovely pool. For some reason, we're the only ones here. If we had this kind of weather in The Netherlands at this time of year, you'd have to wait in line to get in."

"If you had it all the time, you'd hardly notice it. Now talk to me. Tell me how you're feeling."

"I feel good. But I have to make some plans. Any chance of your coming back to LA?"

"Slim and slimmer. I'm going to have someone come by and pack up the rest of my suits and send them over. Is that okay?"

"I can do that for you. It's no trouble."

"Okay, if you don't mind. Just put them into a suitcase and I'll have someone come get it and ship it. Throw any blouses from the dry cleaners in there too."

"Shoes? Underwear?"

"No, I'm good. I can buy extra underwear, and I brought all of my favorite shoes. Since I'm not coming home…"

"Yeah. Well, I'll go to St. Maarten and try to scrounge up some business. Maybe some of my friends will throw a few jobs back at me for the ones I've given them."

"Are you sure? You could come over here any time. Even if it's just for a weekend."

"Can you take a weekend off?"

Laurie could almost feel the hope drain out of her body. "Not a chance. If I broke a leg, they'd have a mobile unit come in and set it."

"Look," Kaatje said. She'd obviously moved away from Margriet and the kids because the phone made some funny noises, then she started to speak louder. "I'd sail solo to Japan if my being there would help you. Will it?"

"Yes and no. Yes because I feel immeasurably better when I'm with you, but no because I'm only crashing in my hotel room for a few hours a night. I'd feel guilty about ignoring you."

"I don't want that, and I know you don't either. I'll get on-line and try to get a ticket to St. Maarten. Then I guess I'll come back here and use the ticket you got for me to go to Osaka."

"That's too much flying. I'll call Wendy and have her rebook you. When do you want to go to St. Maarten?"

"No, no, I can pay for the ticket."

"Don't waste your money. You've lost enough cooling your heels in LA. I'll have my secretary handle it for you. Actually, can you call Wendy? I won't have a free moment. Just tell her what you want and she'll take care of it."

"Okay." She let out a soft sigh that hit Laurie right in the heart. "I wish I could see you. The Caribbean seems very far away from Japan."

"It is. I was really looking forward to having you here."

"And I'd be there if it made sense."

Laurie thought of the coming day and how many things she had to accomplish. "Having you here to sleep with would sure be nice. Lovemaking energizes me."

"We'll just have to wait a while. Would you rather have me come to Osaka before the opening or stay for a while after? I was planning on staying a week."

"After—if it's an either/or choice. My family is coming a week before. When you're here I want to focus on you."

"And Teddy Bear."

"Don't remind me. I've gotta go see to that furry beast right now."

CHAPTER SIXTEEN

MARCH SLID INTO April in such a seamless way that Laurie didn't notice. Her mother's birthday was in early May, and when Wendy called to remind her of the date, she almost accused her of intentionally screwing with her. More than one team member made statements that smacked of paranoia.

She'd had one weekend off since St. Maarten. That was during her brief trip to The Netherlands, and even that involved a twelve-hour flight and a good bit of jet lag. But everyone else was in the same boat. Short tempers, people bursting into tears for no reason, a fistfight or two, and colds that lingered for months were all part of the deal.

The only thing that made the whole enterprise endurable was Kaatje. Surprisingly, being in Japan made it easier to connect with her emotionally. Japan was thirteen hours ahead, and Laurie could call before she left the hotel for work, or sometimes catch Kaatje around lunchtime in St. Maarten. That was the best. Kaatje was letting her guests relax after lunch, and Laurie was in bed, trying to wind down.

Having those conversations made her appreciate everything about Kaatje. She was consistently kind and gentle, and her playfulness always made Laurie laugh, even after a horrible day. Just a few minutes of loving conversation let her clear her mind and get four or five hours of sleep. She wasn't sure what Kaatje was getting out of this lunacy, but without her, Laurie was sure she'd be on long-term disability with Jim Haden, the ride-design guy who'd snapped and had to be dragged off the property, kicking and screaming. Everyone felt bad for him, but feeling bad wasn't going to get the Honey Bear Log Jam working properly.

Whether or not the rides were working, Kaatje was coming in a few weeks. Knowing that kept Laurie going. If the whole park failed, at least Kaatje would be there to watch her career go down in flames. That would make it all okay.

It was obvious that the team members wouldn't have a moment to spare during opening week, and Teddy Bear had generously offered all of the senior vice presidents a Japanese/English-speaking member of the park's hospitality staff to accompany their families around. Laurie asked her assistant, Michiko, to arrange for the friendliest, least formal member of the group for her family. That didn't help with the guilt feelings, but nothing could be done about that. Having had to skip Christmas in Cincinnati was still a sore subject, so ignoring her family in Osaka could just be added to the "things to make amends for" list.

There would be a three day overlap of the Nielsens' and Kaatje's visits, and she knew Kaatje would adapt very well to hanging out with her family. Even if Kaatje hadn't been open and friendly, Laurie's mom was affable enough for two.

It had been such a given that everyone would be there for her when the park opened, but she'd never thought about her not being there for them. As the date drew near, it was obvious she wouldn't have a second to spare for her family. Everyone she knew was in the same position, and all of them were stressed about it.

She and Fernando were sitting in a windowless office at two in the morning four nights before opening. "My parents and my sister and her family have been here for two days and I haven't seen my nieces yet," she grumbled.

"Same for me," he said, his thin face so haggard that he looked ten years older. "Marisol showed the kids my suits and my shaving kit to prove to them I was here."

"Ouch." She was tempted to say more, but it was one thing to not be around when your nieces were visiting and quite another when it was your own children. He'd been in Osaka for a month, and it had to leave a mark to be gone for that long.

He leaned back in his chair, and his shirt tightened against his ribs, which she could have counted. When he was stressed, he couldn't eat, a reaction she would have liked to have had. "But we'll get to spend a load of time together in just five days."

As soon as the park opened he was going to take a week off to show the kids the park in detail, then spend a couple of days at home. Her jealousy was intense enough that she would have tried to pass herself off as him, if he weren't much taller and thinner than she was. She dropped her head and rested it on the table. Her neck muscles were so rigid they'd started to burn, but she couldn't do a thing about it. "I never thought it would be like this. Did you?" she asked. She was about to cry, but it'd be a cold day in hell before she'd show that kind of emotion at work.

"Like what?"

"I used to dream of how much fun it would be to have my nieces here for opening day. I had this image of holding their hands and skipping merrily down Bear Boulevard. It didn't occur to me that we'd be locked up in makeshift offices, working until three or four in the morning."

"I guess it didn't occur to me either, but I never thought about skipping down the street." He laughed, but it sounded so weak she felt sorry for him. "I'm too macho to skip." He reached over and gave her a firm clap on the back. "The kids will have fun whether you're there or not. They're very adaptable."

She sat up and tried to loosen her neck muscles, even though she knew it was futile. She was sure Fernando was partially right. The kids would still have fun. But she wasn't as sure as he was about their adaptability. One day they'd look back on photos from the trip and recall that dad was working most of the time, and that couldn't be good.

―――

Kaatje arrived on "Open Minus Two," the ridiculous way that Laurie now kept time. After moving heaven and earth, and promising to let

Fernando leave early the next night, Laurie got back to the room at two in the morning. Poor Kaatje had spent forty-one hours getting to Japan. She was now lying on top of the made bed, fully clothed. Although she was sound asleep, she wasn't in any of her usual sleep positions. Actually, it looked like someone had pushed her onto the bed after she'd passed out.

Remarkably disappointed at not having her smiling face greet her, Laurie quietly moved around the room, taking off her clothes and going to brush her teeth. Kaatje hadn't moved, so Laurie went to the closet and took out a blanket. She lay next to Kaatje, who still didn't budge, covered them both with the blanket and tried to touch her just enough to sate her need. She settled on holding her hand, which was limp in her grasp. But having her there made everything seem right, and she fell asleep even more quickly than usual.

———

When the five a.m. alarm shocked Laurie awake, she sat bolt upright in bed. Her heart raced and she wasn't sure where she was for a few seconds. But a light was on and she looked across the room to see Kaatje, still dressed, sitting in a chair, waving at her.

"You look miserable." Laurie slipped out of bed and went to sit on her lap.

"You look exhausted."

They hugged for a long time, neither speaking. Talking couldn't add a thing that being in each other's arms didn't already say.

Laurie finally sat up. "I've gotta get going. Can you go back to bed?"

"I've been up since three. I'm beat, but I can't keep my eyes closed."

"I know the feeling. Try to stay up if you can. Have breakfast. It'll help." She went into the bathroom, took a shower and brushed her teeth. When she came back, she held Kaatje's face in her hands and kissed her a dozen times. "My mom will keep you busy if you let her."

"I will." Kaatje stood and they hugged tenderly. "I had fun with your family last night. We all missed you."

"I'm sorry I couldn't at least introduce you all. Was everyone nice to you?"

"Very nice. Your mom acted like I was a member of the family who she'd just seen a week ago. She was fabulous."

"That's her. She's been an angel, trooping everyone around to keep them busy."

"When I get some rest, I'll meet up with them. I love being led around."

"Then the Nielsen women are just the ticket." She kissed her one more time. "I miss you already." She sighed. "Tomorrow's the big day. I wish I could say I'll be home tonight, but I'm taking another suit and blouse just in case. I might have to bathe in the Pirate's Lagoon."

"I wish I could go with you, but I'm looking forward to spending time with your family."

"They've got you for two more days. Then you're all mine." She stood in the doorway, looking at Kaatje longingly. "I've been fantasizing about how it would be when you got here. I had all of these dreams of jumping into your arms and making love for hours." She let her head rest upon the door for just a second. "I promise this is the crappiest reunion we'll ever have. We've got nowhere to go but up."

June the first, nine o'clock in the morning, and every important person in Osaka as well as in the national government of Japan was seated on a massive dais in front of the entrance gate. Since the park was the biggest project to open in Japan since the earthquake, the opening had garnered extensive international attention, adding to the pressure. But there was nothing to do at that moment but reflect while the speeches droned on.

Laurie had stood on this very spot over six years ago, fresh from completing her MBA. She and Fernando had been in Osaka for some meetings with the governor of the Osaka prefecture, and she was going to stay on for a few months to co-ordinate a mass of details with the site managers and transportation planners. She'd been terrified. It was her first time out of the country, and she didn't speak a word of Japanese. Now, here she was, six years and what seemed like a billion miles in travel later, knowing her parents, her sister and brother-in-law, her nieces, and most important, Kaatje were all here together. She couldn't find any of them in the crowd. In fact, she was fairly sure she wouldn't be able to catch up with them until she was back at the hotel. But knowing they were there made the whole, ridiculous journey seem like it had been worth it. Now, if the gates opened properly, the food wasn't toxic, and the rides didn't kill anyone, it was all downhill.

—⁓—

The park closed at eleven, and everyone responsible for a department or division met at 11:05 in a well-disguised conference room not far from Teddy Bear's Bee Hive. They picked apart every minor problem that had occurred until the Chairman of the Board of Luxor appeared and personally thanked each of them. When he stopped in front of her, he leaned in and said, "We have big plans for you, Laurie. I know it's too soon to talk about your next assignment, but your work here has guaranteed you a ticket to do whatever interests you." Then he shook her hand while patting her firmly on the back, like a coach would to a player.

Unlike someone heading out to put a hit on a wide receiver, she felt nothing but relief. Having the chairman know her name and praise her should have been a highlight of her career. But standing there, watching him speak to the next person in line, she was hit with a bolt of insight. She'd finished a huge, soul-draining project. It was a major accomplishment, but it was over. She'd given all of her time, energy and attention just for this day—but it felt completely hollow. It sounded stupid to even consider this important in the scheme of life. She knew now that she should have figured this out long ago. But the truth was that neither Luxor nor Teddy Bear could ever give her what mattered. Kaatje mattered, and she couldn't leave the room fast enough to get back to what was truly important.

—⁓—

It was twelve thirty when she slipped her card key into the lock of her suite. As she knew she'd be, Kaatje was wide awake and ran to the door before it was completely open. "Best sight I've had all day," Laurie sighed as the heavy door thudded behind her.

"Seeing the president of Japan on that big roller coaster wasn't better?"

Laughing tiredly, Laurie shook her head. "Nope. You win." She almost fell into Kaatje's arms and they hugged tenderly for several sweet minutes. Nothing was better than holding someone you loved. It was an injection of a wonder drug. Everything was fine now that she was where she belonged.

"I'm proud of you," Kaatje whispered. "If there were more people like you, the world would run like a Swiss clock."

"Maybe. And a lot more people would die of exhaustion." Kicking off her shoes, she started for the bedroom, but Kaatje stopped her and tightly held her in her arms for a minute. "Don't toss off a funny comment. I'm very proud of you, and I want you to take that in."

Laurie stood there for a bit, letting the words reach her emotions. "I do," she whispered, then suddenly felt tears come to her eyes.

"And the thing I'm most in awe of is that you did it while staying remarkably, actually ridiculously, good humored." She put her hands on Laurie's arms and held her a foot away, gazing at her. "I can't imagine working as hard as you have, but if I'd had to—everyone would have known I wasn't happy about it. That was never true for you."

"Thanks." It was hard to swallow around the knot in her throat, but she nodded and smiled.

"I hope you're at least half as proud of yourself as I am."

"It will take me a while to be able to reflect. Right now I just want to get into that bed."

Kaatje put an arm around her shoulders and they moved across the room. "You can sleep until noon, then I'll get you a big American breakfast."

She can't be serious. How can she not know? "I've got to be at the park at seven. Everything we couldn't get finished for the opening has to get done now." She turned and put her hands on Kaatje's shoulders, seeing the disappointment in her eyes. "I'm sorry. I assumed you'd know…"

"I should have. I knew you'd only just been able to get your 'no go' list done. There must be a thousand other things you have to see to."

Laurie unzipped her skirt, then turned to catch a glimpse of the bed, looking at it like it was her lord and savior. "I wish it were only a thousand. I'd be a very happy woman." She fought through the torpor to focus. Her hands settled around Kaatje's waist and she gazed into her eyes, seeing how open they were to anything she might say. "I've been crazy to work this hard for this long. Meeting you has been the best thing that's ever happened to me. I'll never let work rule my life again."

Kaatje's smile was so lovely that Laurie forced herself to ignore the rest of the truth. Finishing the job after coming to this realization was not going to be easy.

—⁓—

Finally, two days later, on Sunday morning, Laurie stayed in bed until noon. She and Kaatje ordered room service, and stayed in bed after they ate, talking and kissing and cuddling. Laurie was still a long way from rested, but she could imagine a time when she'd get there.

"What are our plans?" Kaatje asked. "When can you go back home?"

"Mmm, probably three months. If everything…" She stopped, knowing she'd screwed up again. "I'm sure I told you that."

"I'm sure you didn't." Kaatje slipped out of bed, heading for the bathroom.

Laurie sat there, stunned at her own inability to communicate with her lover as well as she did with ride designers. There was a loud *bang* in the bathroom, and she guessed it was Kaatje hitting something hard.

She jumped out of bed and went to lean against the door. "Kaatje?"

"Not now," she said, her voice tight.

"I'm sorry. Really, I am. I was *sure* I told you the shake-out would take a while. I have to turn everything over to Hiroshi. That's six years of—"

The door opened and Kaatje walked out, cheeks pink. "I know. I know. Six years. I've heard that a thousand times. Everything revolves around the fact that you've given a fucking stuffed animal six years of your life!" She grabbed a shirt and a pair of jeans and stormed out into the hallway, stark naked. Laurie stared after her, too stunned to follow. Tears started to flow and she mentally kicked herself savagely for screwing everything up this badly.

She knew, she was one hundred percent certain she'd told Kaatje the shake-out would take a while. But she was equally sure she hadn't ever sat down with her to go over the timeline. She'd expected these dates to just be obvious to her, and that was utterly ridiculous.

Kaatje had never, ever cursed like that. Actually, she'd never come close to raising her voice. Laurie had no idea how to approach her. Maybe letting her have time alone would help, but it could just as easily make her feel abandoned. Why wasn't there a clear, easily understood manual for how to handle a relationship?

She headed for the bathroom, acknowledging that it hardly mattered. She'd be too busy to read it. She got into the shower and afterwards got dressed as quickly as she could. Kaatje had been roaming around the area, and she might have been oriented, but Laurie had seen nothing but the front entrance of the hotel where she got into and out of cars. Still, she had to go looking for her even if it was a waste of time. When she opened the door she almost tripped over her. Kaatje was sitting right next to the door, her legs splayed out in front of her. "I don't have any money. Or shoes," she said miserably.

Laurie reached down and helped pull her to her feet. "Want to go inside or go for a walk?"

"Inside." They went back in. Kaatje was deflated. Her affect was glum and her voice soft. "It makes sense that you still have work to do. You don't just open the door and walk away. I didn't think to ask." She finally met Laurie's eyes and said, "I'm sorry for getting angry."

"It's okay." She petted her cheek, trying to maintain eye contact. "I won't have to work nearly as hard as I have been. And there are dozens of places to see that would keep you busy all day."

Her answer was obvious before she said a word. Kaatje often didn't say everything that was on her mind, but sometimes her expression did. "No. I can't stay here for three months. Besides going broke, I need my quiet time. The ocean nurtures me." She looked into Laurie's eyes as if begging for understanding. "That's who I am. Amsterdam wires me up, St. Maarten calms me down. Osaka has wired me up pretty fast, but not in a good way. I don't have friends or family or any of the homey things that sustain me."

"Could you stay just for a while?" If there was a chance, she'd gladly beg.

Kaatje took her hand and gazed into her eyes for a few minutes. There was no way this was going to be a good talk. Kaatje looked like she was going to lower the boom, and no one could have blamed her.

Laurie started shaking like a dry leaf in a strong wind. Kaatje's voice was soft, but determined. "I'll go back to work. I'd much rather be with you, but I'd go crazy being alone in a country where I don't know anyone and can't speak the language."

"Cherry blossoms?" That was not the home run she was trying to think of, but it was all that came to mind. "Osaka's kinda like Amsterdam. There are rivers everywhere, and when the cherry blossoms bloom there would be amazing pictures you could take."

Kaatje looked like she was trying to figure out a way to say "yes." Her eyes twitched just a millimeter from left to right. "Don't they bloom in the spring?"

"Isn't it spring?"

"No, Moppie. It's June."

"Right, I knew that. I know! Someone was talking about the Tenjin Matsuri Festival. It's a very big deal. I'm not sure what it is, but they said they have great fireworks. It sounded like it'd be great to shoot."

Kaatje looked contemplative. "If it's in a couple of weeks, I should be able to stay busy. But that's about my limit."

"But what about the future? What will happen when I'm free?"

"Then we have to make some decisions." That was not a news flash, but Kaatje didn't add a word. It was like she was tossing a grenade at Laurie.

"Did you like LA at all?"

"I could live there. I went down to Huntington Beach and got to surf waves that were better than any I'd ever ridden. And if I could run my business out of Marina del Rey, I'd be content to just see you at night. You're worth an awful lot of sacrifice, Laurie." She held her by the shoulders. "I hope you know that."

"But," she said, her lip quivering.

"But I did a lot of research when I was there, and it looks like it would be impossible for me to get permission to live and work in America. Unless I read things incorrectly, the only way we can be together is if you move to Holland or St. Maarten."

Stunning. She was willing to give up what she loved and live in Holland full time. Who wouldn't love this woman? Kaatje fixed her with those beautiful blue eyes. She desperately wanted to say she'd throw everything away to go sail on Kaatje's boat. But that wasn't true. It might be true next week, or next month, but making a decision like that right now was beyond impossible. For Kaatje to even ask that meant she still didn't understand the true meaning of exhausted. "I want to say I'll drop everything and go. But I need a few months to decompress and think. I'm not sure what day it is, other than open plus five." She slapped the side of her head with her open hand. "Who talks like that?"

"You do." Kaatje kissed the top of her head. "You've been thoroughly indoctrinated."

"That's for sure. I can't make any decisions until I've gotten some sleep. I honestly don't feel like myself any more, Kaatje. Do you understand?"

"I do. You've been sleep deprived for months. That screws you up."

"It does. I'm screwed up. But once I rest, we can figure this out. There's a way through this that will make us both happy."

Looking heartsick, Kaatje leveled her gaze and said, "What if we can't?"

"We will. I just opened a multi-billion dollar theme park on a different continent. Practically by myself. We can figure this out too." Her exhaustion might have made her promise or say anything.

Kaatje took her hand and led her to the bed. After undressing, she held her close under the fluffy duvet. "Let's sleep a little right now. Just close your eyes and listen to my heart beat."

Laurie heard three beats. Then nothing.

CHAPTER SEVENTEEN

LATER THAT EVENING they had a fantastic dinner and managed to find a sake they both enjoyed. They were sitting there, digesting their meal when Laurie asked, "How would you like to go to work with me tomorrow?"

"How do I do that?"

"If you want to, I'd like to have you with me for a day. I could show you the park close-up. I think you'd enjoy it."

Kaatje smiled warmly, showing her teeth. "I'd love to be with you for a whole day. Won't your bosses think it's a little funny?"

"They all went back to LA today. I'm in charge until I pack up and head home." She picked up both arms and held them over her head for a moment. "I'm king of the forest. Bears live in the forest, right?"

The alarm buzzed loudly, waking them at six. Laurie lay there for a moment, trying to get her bearings. It was Monday, and Kaatje was coming to work with her. With a surprising amount of energy, she leaned over and kissed Kaatje's still face. "Wake up, sleepyhead."

Kaatje let out a grunt of acknowledgment and Laurie went to start the shower. When she was blow drying her hair, Kaatje stumbled into the bathroom and wrapped her arms around Laurie's bare body. Laurie stroked her back and kissed her sleepy face. "Too tired? You can come over later if you want."

"No, I can do it. It just seems really, really early." She went into the shower and stood there with the hot water hitting her right in her upturned face.

Kaatje wasn't as fast as she should have been and they got to the park later than Laurie planned. Laurie flashed her pass, then spent some time getting Kaatje set up with an all-access visitor's pass. It was almost seven, but there was no way she was going to be late. Especially when she was bringing her girlfriend. As they walked down the deserted main street, she started to pick up the pace and by the time they reached the Bee Hive, they were practically at a jog. Laurie took a quick look at her watch as they walked into the conference room. Seven on the dot.

Five people had obviously just arrived. They were all opening up their laptops and had been chatting companionably. But all conversation stopped when Laurie entered. It wasn't a sense of power that filled her when that happened. It was a sign of respect, and she liked that more than she would have admitted. "Good morning, everyone. This is my…" She didn't know how to introduce Kaatje. There were many terms, but none of them were perfect. Especially for her staff. She took the easy way out and ignored using a title. "This is Kaatje Hoogeboom. She's going to shadow us today. Kaatje, this is Hiroshi Oh, the manager of the park, Toshi Yakamoto, his assistant, Tim Holmes, head ride engineer, Reiko Ishii, head of food and beverage, Seiji Okada, head of security, Kunio Miura, head of maintenance, and Eichi Maeda, head of entertainment." The door opened and two Americans entered, both looking nervous. "Glad you could join us," Laurie said, with a smile that bordered on sarcastic.

"No excuses," the man said, holding up a hand as he scampered to put his laptop on the table and power it up.

"This is the late Aaron Rosenberg and Andrea Fields. Aaron's my lieutenant and Andrea is Aaron's lieutenant." She put her hand on Kaatje's shoulder. "You both met Kaatje in LA. She's going to shadow us today. Everybody ready?"

Everyone made some sort of affirmative response and Laurie launched into her agenda. She went to a huge white board with writing covering two thirds of it and put a marker on the blank section. "Let's make our list of action items. I assume everyone agrees that the queues at security are much too long. We've got to reduce that waiting time today." Her eyes scanned every person. "No excuses."

She wrote "security line" on the board and put a big number one next to it. Going down the list, she moved through the items already on the board, erasing some and transferring the others onto the new list—with different numbers next to them.

When the list was finished she looked out at the group and said, "If your initials are next to an item, I'll want a status report when I get to the attraction. I want that from you, not a subordinate." She lowered her voice to make sure everyone was paying attention. "I will not accept any excuses for not knowing the status." Every head nodded, including Kaatje's, which almost made Laurie spit.

It was quarter of eight when someone knocked and entered. A young Japanese woman pushed a cart into the room. "Michiko, good to see you. Okay. Let's get some food and get going." Everyone went to the cart and started to pour coffee or tea into paper cups. Laurie scanned the repast, looking past the miso soup and pickles and grabbing a bagel.

After everyone had something Laurie said, "Michiko, will you copy everything from the whiteboards onto your tablet? Then we'll get rolling. We're going to go through the park, starting at the hotel." Turning to address the group, she added, "I assume you'll all be ready to meet when we get to your area. Don't keep us waiting, okay? We've got a lot of ground to cover." She pointed a finger at Aaron. "Stick with me today. Andrea, you follow Hiroshi. Everybody clear?"

Seven heads nodded. "Okay. We're off!"

———

They went outside and got into a four-seat golf cart. "Will you drive?" Laurie asked Aaron. He and Michiko got in the front, and Laurie and Kaatje hopped into the back. "Head to the main hotel. They got a few complaints about hot water."

"You're like the king," Kaatje whispered into Laurie's ear when the electric cart took off.

"I *am* the king. Until we turn this place over to Hiroshi, I'm in charge."

"I don't think anyone doubts that." Kaatje's grin was playful, and Laurie got a distinct thrill from seeing her job through Kaatje's eyes.

As they arrived at the hotel, Laurie jumped out while the cart was still moving. The lobby was filled with guests, most of them hovering around the concierge desks. Laurie stopped for a second, saying to Michiko, "Make a note to have someone clock how long it takes to speak to a concierge. Fifteen minutes is the max we should ever allow."

"Right," she said, tapping the note onto her tablet computer.

They found the head of the hotel, the chief engineer, and the chief plumber waiting for them. Only the hotel manager spoke enough English to conduct complex business, but all were able to speak well enough to be understood. After a few minutes of introductions and bows, they all trooped down to the boiler room. "Ever been in a plant this complex?" Laurie asked Kaatje.

"Not hardly." She stood there for a moment, her eyes scanning across the myriad of pipes, gauges and tanks. "And I've been on a Dutch naval ship."

"Ask them if they're sure there's enough hot water," Laurie told Michiko.

Michiko and the staff spoke back and forth for a minute, then she reported they had the biggest hot water boiler of any of the hotels. They were certain there was enough for a sellout, with ten percent excess just in case.

"Aaron? Ideas?"

"Temperature in the tanks?"

Again Michiko asked and listened to a long explanation. Walking away from the group. Laurie took out her phone, made a call, and paced up and down a catwalk as she talked. Michiko spoke loudly, "Temperature is at the maximum allowed per regulation."

Snapping her cell phone closed, Laurie walked back to the group. "Let's go to a room."

They went in a service elevator to an empty room. The whole crowd entered a bathroom and Laurie turned on the tap. In just seconds, it warmed up to its max. "Not hot enough," she said. "Make it hotter."

The plumber removed the shiny chrome trim from the wall and adjusted the mixer on the valve by moving it up just a millimeter at a time. When Laurie was satisfied she said, "Why wasn't it at this temperature to start with?"

The hotel manager said, "We have to make sure no one can scald themselves. I think the way we had it was correct."

"Not for me. Maybe it's a cultural issue. Michiko, ask the engineer if this temperature is safe. If he's one hundred percent sure it is, we'll make the change."

While Michiko relayed the message, Laurie asked Aaron, "How would you implement the change?"

His eyes narrowed as he thought. "How many maintenance workers do we have?"

The manager started to answer just as Michiko's walkie-talkie went off. She stepped out of the bathroom, speaking in Japanese, leaving the hotel manager to answer. "We have six on duty during the daylight," he said in his precise English.

The engineer spoke and Michiko ducked back in to translate. "He says it's safe, but only just."

"How many complaints were reported?" Aaron asked.

"Ten," Michiko replied.

"It looks like it will take at least twenty minutes to change each control valve. To do three hundred rooms will take…a hundred hours. That's a big investment of man-hours. I'd change them as complaints came in, then start changing them as each room opens up. I'd keep one worker doing it full time, and have the others do rooms as they have time. No overtime for this. I don't think it's serious enough."

Laurie looked at him sharply. "Anything else?"

He stared at her for just a moment. "Yeah. I'd offer something to the guests who complain." He caught the attention of the hotel manager. "What's an inexpensive perk?"

"A photo with Teddy Bear? A free movie?"

"Good. I'd offer either of those things, and have one phone operator take all complaints about water temperature. He or she can make sure the guest gets the perk they want and that the dedicated maintenance worker gets the call." He looked directly at Laurie, waiting for her verdict.

She winked at him as she started out of the room. "Make it happen."

―⚊⚊―

They got onto a passenger elevator to go to the lobby. "Was that a test?" Kaatje asked.

"Of Aaron? Yeah. I want him to start taking over. I think he's ready."

"He seems it. But he looks pretty young."

Laurie bumped her with her shoulder. "He's your age. Old enough to sleep with—old enough to make decisions."

―⚊⚊―

At 11:40 they stood at the Jungle Safari ride, seven sets of eyes trained on people entering and exiting the boats. "The engineer says the boats are performing exactly like they did during testing," Michiko related.

"That might be, but the line snaking all the way to Tokyo is a big, big problem." Laurie stared at the families slowly boarding the eight passenger boats. She clicked her stopwatch, then clicked it again. "Kunio, what was the clock during testing?"

Michiko asked the question, her walkie-talkie squawking in Japanese the whole time. Laurie continued to time each group as they got on.

"Ten seconds," Michiko related.

"It's taking between fifteen and twenty," Laurie said. "That's unacceptable."

Kaatje cleared her throat and asked, "Uhm, is there a difference in how long it takes families with kids?"

Laurie shot her a look, then started timing again. After a few minutes she said, "Yes. With small kids it's taking twenty seconds. With bigger kids, eight to ten."

"The kids have to step down too far," Kaatje said. "They look tentative."

Laurie moved to where Kaatje was standing, now able to see how many of the kids looked frightened. "How young were the kids in our testing?"

A few bouts of translation gave the answer, "All ages. Ten seconds was the average."

"Is there a tide?" Kaatje asked, wrinkling her nose. "Or is this all fake."

Laurie gave her a sharp look. "It's all *engineered*. Everything is static." She whirled and glared at the engineer. "It *is* the same, right? Everything is exactly the same as it was during testing?"

Michiko translated her question and the engineer scrambled to the edge of the walkway and stuck his tape measure into the water. He was pale when he returned. He spoke, looking like he wished the ground would open up and swallow him. Michiko gave him a stern look when she translated, "The water is three inches lower than it was during testing."

Laurie didn't say a word. She just glared at the man, turned and headed back to the golf cart with Kaatje scampering after her.

Laurie jumped into the cart, mumbling, "When a visitor can guess the problem long before the experts, you're fucked." Hearing how harsh that sounded, she consciously put a smile on and kissed Kaatje on the cheek. "Thanks. You saved me untold thousands of dollars. Figuring out the problem in something like that is the hard part."

"Does ten extra seconds make that big a difference?"

"Yep. A one hundred percent increase in loading screws everything up. Makes people mad too. You can't afford that." The more she spoke the madder she felt. "The engineer thinks I can't understand him, but I heard him admit he didn't test water levels yesterday. He didn't think it was necessary." She looked like she was going to get out of the cart and strangle him. "And I'm going to have to slap Michiko around for not translating that. But I'll do that in private." She was still fuming when Aaron and Michiko joined them. "Idiot," she growled. "How can you call yourself an engineer and not test that conditions are identical. Does he know why it's low?"

Aaron shook his head. "Probably a leak. We're going to waste a lot of water until they can find it and seal it."

"Make sure the company that built the lagoon is involved in the troubleshooting. We're not eating that cost."

"Already did," Aaron said, looking pleased with himself.

Michiko tentatively spoke up. "The engineer didn't test the water levels before opening."

"Why didn't you say that then?" Laurie asked, peevishly.

"He would lose all respect," she said quietly. "His mistake was very bad."

"Right, right. I'm sorry for snapping." Michiko nodded and she and Aaron spoke quietly while they started up.

Laurie whispered, "One of my biggest faults is not being culturally sensitive enough. I've gotta work on that. Calling somebody out in front of other people is really harsh."

"It's best not to do that in St. Maarten either. You're not wasting your time in working on that."

―――

Lunch was steamed anpan with Teddy Bear's head imprinted in the dough and an apple ice block, a frozen fruit ice with the same imprint. Everything was obtained by Michiko, who jumped out of the cart as they passed a snack stand and caught up with them at the next attraction. Still trying to down their lunch, they stopped at a ride where a number of children had fallen getting out of the car the day before. When the very contrite supervisor went into an elaborate explanation of his view of the situation, Laurie interrupted to ask, "What's the height requirement? That sign looks wrong."

They had to wait for Michiko's translation again, and Laurie took the delay to make a phone call, knocking another one off her list which was now down to twenty. "Thirty-six inches," Michiko announced.

Laurie met Kaatje's gaze.

"No way," Kaatje said.

Laurie took the tape measure off the ride engineer's belt and headed over to the sign. It stood at thirty-nine inches. She tossed the tape measure back at him, growling, "Fix it, and check every other sign in the park. Send me a memo by the end of the day telling me you personally guarantee that every sign is at the stated height." Then they were off again to sort out the next small but significant problem.

———

"I think you were being culturally insensitive," Kaatje said quietly. "I can't imagine it's a good idea to yank things off people's belts and then throw them back at them."

"I know." Laurie dropped her head into her hands. "I'm just so short-tempered. These problems seem ridiculously simple to me, but I have to consider they're working just as hard and doing things I don't ever see."

"By the way, you've never told me you understood Japanese. How much do you speak?"

"Just enough to understand numbers and their context perfectly. That's all I care about," she said, grinning unrepentantly.

———

They were on their way back to the conference room when Aaron said, "I don't like the length of the lines at these food carts. None of the other ones were this long."

Laurie looked up from furiously scribbling notes. "I haven't been paying attention. How long were the others?"

"Half this length."

"Michiko, get Kunio and an engineer over here ASAP." They got out and watched people order. Laurie had her stopwatch out, timing how long it took for a gyoza to be delivered. When the manager and the engineer arrived, they spent twenty minutes going over every possible permutation in the gyoza ordering and delivery process. They had the entire thing timed to a variance of fifteen seconds, but the actual process was taking considerably longer. "What else could it be?" Laurie asked. She paced around the cart, her eyes like an eagle's spotting a mouse from fifty yards. "The staff is doing it right, the cash register is working, the grill is working, the food is at the proper temperature…" She crossed her arms, staring blankly.

Kaatje said, "Ask the workers."

Laurie signaled Michiko. "Ask them if they have any ideas why the line is this long."

She returned in a minute. "They say the grill they trained on cooked the food faster."

Aaron took over, asking the engineer, "What affects cooking speed?"

Michiko started to translate, but Aaron said, "Just tell him to troubleshoot it. I don't need to hear what he's going to do."

They all stood there, with Laurie making another two phone calls while they waited. Finally Michiko had an answer. "The grill is only operating at a hundred and ten volts. They are supposed to be at two hundred and twenty volts."

Laurie sighed and said, "Report by the end of the day. How many carts are affected, when they'll be fixed, who's responsible for the error, and who will pay for it if it wasn't our fault."

They were close by, so they walked ahead to the conference room while Michiko and Aaron gave Laurie's instructions to the staff.

"Do you go at this rate every day?" Kaatje asked. "You haven't even been to the bathroom."

Laurie's eyes lit up and she took off running, turning to call over her shoulder. "Thanks for reminding me!"

———

From five until six, the core staff met to eat a bite and discuss strategy for the next day. Everyone had his or her laptop out and each took notes as things popped up. There wasn't one word of chit-chat. At six on the dot, Laurie looked at her watch and said, "That's all the time we have for fun. Let's get started on our status reports. All hands in the conference room."

They started to walk from the private dining area to the Bee Hive. Kaatje said, "All hands means what?"

"Every division manager. The same group we met with this morning."

"What kind of reports do you have to do?"

Laurie put her hand to her neck, acting like she was strangling herself. "The bane of my existence. Without the reports I could have left at five."

"It sucks," Aaron chimed in. "Worst part of the job—by far."

"What's in the reports?" Kaatje asked.

"I have to update LA on everything from attendance and hotel occupancy to overtime, injury reports, and more and more and more."

"Every day?"

"Every day," Aaron agreed. "The only good part of it is that no one is at the office in LA when we send the reports. If they were there, it would take twice as long because they'd have a million questions."

"Small favors," Laurie said, smiling tiredly.

———

The managers were grilled over the most minor of costs, expenses and problems. After an hour they were released and Laurie, Aaron, Andrea, Hiroshi and Toshi worked at their laptops for another hour. Then Laurie took all of their reports and went over each item, asking question after question. Finally, at eight thirty, she sent the entire batch of reports to the proper people at headquarters and slammed her laptop closed. She sat back in a chair and let her body relax for the first time all day. "Well, that was fun. Who wants to do it again tomorrow?"

———

As they were walking out of the building, Laurie asked, "Michiko, will you make a note that my niece's birthday is next Wednesday? I've got to send something tomorrow or it'll never get there."

"Which niece?"

"The younger one."

"I'll have a selection of gifts for you to choose from. Clothes or books or games?"

"She likes books, but she's still into toys. Might as well go with that. She'd love something Japanese."

"It won't be a problem."

"Thanks." Laurie patted her on the back. "You've saved my life more times than I can count. And thanks for reminding me that I come on too strong with the staff sometimes. I'll try to be more sensitive."

"I'm just doing my job." The young woman waved goodbye and veered off to an employee parking lot. The three of them kept going, walking through throngs of people enjoying the new park.

"How long will you be in Osaka?" Aaron asked Kaatje.

"I have one more week. Then it's back to St. Maarten."

He looked at her with longing in his eyes. "I was there once. What a fantastic place to live."

"I love it," she agreed. "But I'm afraid it will take me a while to get back into the slower pace."

"It is rocking tonight," Laurie said. "Thank God. It's nice to walk through the place and see people having fun, isn't it?"

Aaron chimed in. "Yeah. It reminds you there's an end product."

"Besides taking all of the cash these people have in their pockets?"

"Now, now," Aaron teased, "Check your cynicism at the gate. You make Teddy Bear cry when you say things like that."

⁓⁓⁓

They walked into their hotel room and Kaatje fell, face first onto the sofa. "I don't know how you do it," she moaned into the fabric. Laurie sat on the edge of the cushion, chuckling. Kaatje rolled over and faced her. "I mean it. How do you run around like that? You were nonstop. And you're going to do it tomorrow and the day after and…"

"I know. It's been like that for over two years. It's not a good way to live, but I don't work harder than any of my peers. Or my subordinates, for that matter."

"It's beyond me." Kaatje lay there, the look on her face slightly troubling to Laurie. It wasn't like Kaatje was praising her work ethic. More like she was questioning her sanity.

CHAPTER EIGHTEEN

AS THE WEEK wore on Laurie was able to knock off a little earlier every day. The problems started being more routine, and she started handing more and more of them off to Hiroshi. The daily status reports were still her responsibility, but she moved the deadline up to three o'clock, letting her have a little room to breathe. By Friday she was home by six and she was starting to feel less like a robot and more like herself.

She and Kaatje lay in bed that night, Kaatje holding her against her chest. "I can't tell you how happy my father would be to have you as his daughter."

Laurie laughed while she patted Kaatje's encircling arm. "My own father is pretty proud of me. That's enough." She turned and placed a soft kiss on Kaatje's cheek. "Your father loves you. He just worries about you. He's obviously a guy who values security, and you don't have a whole lot of that."

"Yeah, you're right. And if I wanted to make him happy I always could. I choose not to."

"No, you aren't someone who does things for or against other people. You've found what makes you happy. You don't do what you do to annoy him."

"True. But if you moved to St. Maarten to be with me, he could focus on you. Then both he and I would be happy...forever."

Laurie slipped out of her grasp and turned to face her. That last word was the kicker. That wasn't what you said when you wanted someone to come hang out and see how things went. "Are you serious?"

Kaatje's expression was hard to read, but her eyes burned with intensity. "Completely. I love you, Laurie, and I want to be together for the rest of our lives."

"You love me?" It was like this was the first time she'd ever heard the words. They were brand new, made just for her.

Kaatje didn't respond with words. She just extended her arms and Laurie fell into them. They kissed, tenderly, for a long while. Then Laurie lifted her head and said, "I love you too. I think I fell in love with you the first time we made love." Tears filled her eyes and she didn't bother to wipe them away. "I love you. I really love you."

"Come to St. Maarten," Kaatje whispered earnestly. "Don't kill yourself working this hard. Life is made for us to enjoy."

"It is," Laurie said, having never heard more sage words. "Life is made for sharing with you. If I could remake myself, I'd be just like you. You know how to live."

"I know how to make *myself* happy, Moppie. You have to find your own way."

"No," she teased. "I want to be centered just like you are. You're content and peaceful. That's sooo appealing."

"Well, I like your energy. Maybe it's the way we're different that attracts us."

"No. It's your body, your mind, your gentleness, your concern for other people, your tranquility. That's what attracts me." She grasped her firmly and kissed her until her lips were tired. "If I work as hard as I can I think I can learn to be like you."

Laughing, Kaatje said, "I don't think you can work your butt off to be tranquil. I think you're who you are. You just have to learn to be a little... okay, a lot more moderate."

"I'm gonna take a first step," she said, eyes blazing with determination. She jumped out of bed, found her cell phone, and punched in a number, grinning at Kaatje's puzzled expression.

"Aaron? Laurie. Can you handle the park this weekend? Kaatje's going home on Monday and I want to spend some time with her." She nodded, then said, "Fantastic. Call me if anyone dies…and it's our fault. Other than that, see you Monday. And pick a couple of days next week to relax. Have Andrea do the same. We're out of the woods, and we have to scale back before we drop dead."

Because Kaatje's flight was late in the afternoon on Monday, they had most of the day together. But instead of sightseeing, they made plans to spend their last day together in bed. Laurie woke before dawn; the habit was too ingrained to stop. Looking at Kaatje's still face, illuminated only by the cold, unnatural light from the park, Laurie's heart clenched with emotion. Meeting Kaatje was the best thing that had ever happened to her. There was no competition. Even if she was eventually made the CEO of Luxor, being loved by Kaatje was the thing that she wanted to be known for.

It was impossible to refrain from touching her, but it was very early, and Kaatje had almost two full days of travel ahead of her. Laurie tried to satisfy her desperate need while letting her lover get a little more sleep. She let her fingertips caress her cheek, just barely contacting the soft skin. As always, Kaatje's body was cool in the air conditioned chill. Laurie relished the sensation, letting her hand linger for a few seconds to warm her. Kaatje nuzzled against her hand, then let out a heavy sigh. Somehow that sigh encapsulated what was in Laurie's heart. She wasn't good at forming her feelings into words, but the sigh spoke for her, and she felt tears spring to her eyes. If there were any reasonable way she could have left with her, she would have jumped at the chance. But she had to honor her commitment —to her employer and her co-workers. She'd worked too hard to be remembered as the woman who walked away before the job was finished. But looking down at Kaatje made that commitment waver. Just a few pleas from Kaatje would have done the trick. But part of what she loved about her was her own work ethic. Kaatje understood. She knew that you had to make short-term sacrifices for long-term gains. It's just that this sacrifice was cutting out a piece of her heart, and it hurt more than she could have guessed.

———

Kaatje chose to take a cab to the airport and to go alone. That might have hurt, coming from another person, but Kaatje needed her space. When they parted she was always nearly silent, and her being alone was probably best.

Laurie stood next to her, trying to find a quiet place in the lobby of the hotel to say their final goodbyes. "I put riding to the airport with you on my schedule," Laurie said once again.

"I know. But you can get a few hours work in if you don't go. Every hour of work you finish means you can come to St. Maarten an hour earlier."

"I'm not sure that's true, but if it is I'll work around the clock." She leaned against Kaatje, wishing they had just a few more hours to hold each other.

"Don't work any harder," Kaatje teased, carefully arranging a few fly-away strands of Laurie's hair. "You'll be a mass of tangled nerve fibers."

"I shouldn't have told Aaron you were leaving. They'll all be watching me now that they know I don't have my moderating influence."

Kaatje tilted her head and placed several soft kisses on Laurie's head. "I love you. Please try to take care of yourself for me."

"I will. And don't get sunburned or let any of those ropes bite you."

"Sheets."

"Definitely don't let the sheets bite you." Laurie looked into her eyes and saw the mixture of love and sadness she felt in her own heart. "Take care of yourself for me."

Kaatje nodded, tears in her eyes. They hugged, fiercely and briefly, then Kaatje pulled away and quickly strode toward the door, turning one last time to meet Laurie's eyes.

Then she was gone.

CHAPTER NINETEEN

BY THE END of the first week they'd moved away from talking about work. There were a million things Laurie could have told Kaatje, but none of them seemed to matter. They were just niggling details about a job she was less and less engaged with. Hearing Kaatje's voice was what got her through each day, and the last thing she wanted was to rehash the minutia that kept them apart.

"Guess what Fernando brought up today?"

"I have no idea. But I bet it was good since you sound pretty happy."

"Good guess. He brought up the idea of my taking a leave of absence. Cool, huh?"

Kaatje was silent for a few beats. "Is that possible?"

"Apparently it is. He did a little investigating before he mentioned it. He knows I'm not locked into this stuff like I was before, and I think he wanted to catch me before I could quit."

"Would you do that?" Kaatje's voice had a tentative quality to it.

"Yeah. I think I have to."

"Because you want to live in St. Maarten?"

Letting out a breath, Laurie told the unvarnished truth. This was too important to hide anything. Besides, Kaatje could always tell if she kept even a sliver of doubt inside. "If I could have anything, I'd take a less demanding job with Luxor that I could do in forty or fifty hours a week. We'd live together and you'd run your business out of Marina del Rey. But I talked to people in our legal department who work with immigration and they're certain you'd never be able to get a work permit. You could live with me half the year and spend the rest of the year with your family, but you couldn't work, and I need you all year—not just part. I think I've got to quit and move to St. Maarten."

"That's a very, very, very big decision."

"Yes, but it was a very big decision on your part to offer to live in Holland." Laurie waited for Kaatje to toss that selfless act off.

"Yes, it was. But I love Holland almost as much as I love St. Maarten. The same isn't true for you."

"Not yet. But it was like a paradise. I'm sure I'll come to love it."

"You'd have a better chance of working at a decent job in Amsterdam."

"Don't most people there speak Dutch?" Laurie teased.

"Yes, but American companies have major offices there. You could learn enough Dutch to get by."

"Maybe. But as long as I'm going to leave my job why not move to St. Maarten? Then one of us has her dream."

"This is life changing, Moppie, and as different as night from day. Are you sure?"

Even though she couldn't see her, Laurie could picture her expression. It was both guarded and hopeful, just like her voice.

"So was deciding I was a lesbian. I made this decision the same way. Add up the plusses and minuses, and go with the longer list."

"Once again, that's not how I'd do it. I can't have you come here and then decide you don't like it. That would destroy me, Laurie. I mean that."

She said those words with such feeling and certainty that they almost took Laurie's breath away. "I don't backslide on decisions. Besides, it's not like St. Maarten isn't a fantastic place to live. And I really want to travel with you. Being with you has no downsides, Kaatje. I promise."

"Okay. But keep thinking about it. Don't do anything rash."

"I won't. I've been trying to decide when I should resign. I don't want to hang around long once I've done it, but I want to make sure they don't spend a lot of time finding a new job for me. If I can have a leave, I might as well take it. There's no sense in losing my benefits until I have to."

"Does that mean you'd take the leave just to keep your benefits?"

Kaatje was clearly suspicious. But of what? "You don't think I'm playing around do you?"

"No, that never crossed my mind. I'm just surprised you'd take a leave if you were sure you were going to quit."

"I'm certain we're going to be together. But I'm also certain we haven't figured out the timing. I've got to sell my apartment and do all kinds of things to get permission to live in St. Maarten. This will just give us more time. Trust me."

"I do. You know I do."

Laurie tried to hear the confidence in Kaatje's voice. But it was entirely absent. She couldn't blame her. Up until now Teddy Bear had always won her allegiance. But that was in the past. Now Kaatje was number one and would always be first in her heart.

—⁓—

Kaatje called a few days later to report, "Hey, your mom followed through and sent me some pictures of you when you were younger."

"She did? I didn't know you'd asked her."

"If I asked you, I knew my request would go at the bottom of one of those white boards you have. I tried to go around the bureaucracy."

"Clever. What did you get?"

"Quite a few shots of you when you were a baby, then a big bunch of pictures from your gymnastics days. Boy, you must have been good."

"I wouldn't have worked that hard if I wasn't any good," Laurie teased. "I would have tried something else."

"You were a beautiful girl. Really striking. And you were the prettiest girl in your high school class. But..." She hesitated just long enough to make Laurie anxious.

"What?"

"Uhm, you don't plan on losing a *lot* of weight, do you? I mean..."

"What are you getting at?"

"Just…I don't know how not to sound shallow, so I'll spit it out. I'm really turned on by your body just the way it is. I'd hate for you to be skinny like you used to be."

Laurie spit out a laugh. "I thought you were teasing. Do you really prefer me chubby?"

"You're not chubby. You look like a woman, and I'm really attracted to women. I'd still love you if you weighed what you did in high school, but you're much, much sexier now."

"You're not just yanking my chain? You really mean that?"

"Of course. All you have to do is get undressed and I'm ready for action. That's all because of your fantastic body."

"Hmm, you know, that's pretty accurate. You look at me like you want to devour me." She laughed, amazed at what she was hearing. "You're the world's most perfect girlfriend. Not many women want to stop you from going on a diet."

"You do what you want. Just don't lose weight for me. I like you with some padding. Some nice, soft padding on the sexiest body I've ever felt." She sighed heavily. "Come down here so I can feel it again. I miss you."

"I miss you too. And as soon as we hang up I'm going to do yet another status report, letting LA know how many items we've crossed off our list. I'm a few steps closer to St. Maarten, and the world's most perfect lover."

———

At the end of their first month apart, Laurie called with a status update. "We're way ahead of schedule. Aaron keeps hinting that I can go back to LA if I need to. I think he thinks they'll be able to slow down if I'm gone."

"You've been working as hard as you did before the park opened. Are you sure that's a good idea?"

"Yep. As soon as I'm done, I'm gone. And having Hiroshi take over is good for everyone. Then he can run the place like he wants to, without having me interfering constantly."

"Have you given any thought to what you want to do when you get here?"

"Hey, was it a coincidence that you said that right after I mentioned interfering?"

"What do you mean?"

"Are you worried I'll start bossing you around like I do Hiroshi?"

Kaatje barked out a quick laugh. "I'm not as easy to push around as Hiroshi is. I only saw him in action one day, but he seemed quite a few rungs beneath you in the aggression department."

"I think he's just respectful. He'll be fine when he's in charge. And, no, I haven't thought about what we'll do in St. Maarten. I assumed it'd be like it was when I was there. Take people sailing. Make love. Have dinner. Make love. Were your plans different?"

"Nope." Kaatje laughed easily. "We're in agreement. But I'm the captain on this ship."

"As long as I can be first mate, I'll be happy."

———

Six weeks after Kaatje left Osaka, Laurie called with news. "Well, I just spent an hour on the phone with Fernando, and I think we're in good shape. Corporate will grant me a three-month leave of absence, and Fernando thinks I could extend it for a month or two more if I needed to."

"Fantastic! What does that mean?"

"That means that I can leave with no guilt. They might kick around some ideas for my next assignment, but they won't make any firm plans without my agreeing. This is the absolute perfect way to work up to my resignation. No one gets hurt."

"That's great. If you're happy, I'm happy."

"I'm very happy. Fernando's being fantastic about this. You wouldn't believe it."

"I think he really cares about you."

245

"Yeah, he does. I think he's a little jealous too. If he didn't have a big house and a couple of kids in private school, he'd like to cut back too. But he's decided to hang in until he's fifty, then retire early."

"Do you think he will?"

She thought for a moment, considering all of the variables. "He will if he's topped out. But he's too aggressive to quit if there's another promotion in his future."

"How about you? I'm sure there are a few promotions in your future. Will it bother you to walk away?"

"You sound pretty doubtful, my friend," Laurie teased. "You'd think I was a workaholic or something."

"If work were alcohol you would need a liver transplant. Be honest with me. Are you having second thoughts?"

"I can't wait to get out of this madness." She had a mental image of Kaatje lying on the trampoline between the hulls, completely naked, looking up at her with lust in her eyes. "The only thing I want is you. I'm going to make a reservation for two weeks from today. I might not be able to leave that soon, but having the reservation will give me a goal to work for. And if Aaron knows he can get rid of me in two weeks, he'll break his neck to hustle me out. Andrea, too, for that matter." She chuckled evilly. "You're the one who should have second thoughts. I've got a whole staff who can't wait to get rid of me."

―――

On August fifteenth, Laurie fidgeted in her seat, peering out the window of the aircraft, wishing the ground crew would move faster. They finally got the staircase aligned and the door swooshed open. The other first-class passengers started to stand, but Laurie leapt to her feet and dove for the door, making the flight attendant laugh. "You must really be looking forward to your vacation," she said.

"Much better than that. I'm moving here to be with the most fantastic woman I've ever met."

"Well, good for you!"

She grinned so happily she knew she must look like a madwoman. But she didn't care one bit. Mere months ago she was a workaholic who only looked forward to spending a random holiday in Cincinnati with her nieces. Now she was announcing her sexual orientation to strangers before deplaning to begin her new life—on a sailboat of all things. Real life was stranger than fiction.

—⁓—

Kaatje was planted just past the exit at customs. As Laurie walked out the door she jumped into Kaatje's arms, holding onto her as tightly as her jet-lagged body would allow. Actually being in Kaatje's embrace drained all of the nervous energy from her, and she could have fallen asleep right there at the airport. But when Kaatje murmured several times in her ear, "I love you," one more burst of energy—along with her appetite—hit her.

"I love you too. But before I drag you to bed I've gotta get some food. I slept through three meals."

Kaatje took her hand and clasped it to her chest. "We'll have a late breakfast, then go take the boat out. I want to set anchor, lie in the sun and sleep all day." She grinned and the expression was so beautiful that Laurie wanted to kiss her. Deciding she had no reason to censor herself, she pulled Kaatje to a stop and tenderly pressed their lips together.

"Just because I can," she proclaimed giddily.

—⁓—

Laurie had stopped in LA for one night to relieve herself of her business suits and heels, and load up with her laptop, all of her shorts, T-shirts, swimsuits, and a few more formal items for having dinner with the Hoogebooms. Because of the luggage, Kaatje had borrowed her mother's car, which they drove to the popular restaurant/bar at Maho Beach, just next to the airport.

Strangely, it was like they'd just met. Laurie was as nervous as she'd be on a first date with someone she was very, very interested in. The facts didn't support the feeling. But this was a new chapter in their lives. The biggest, maybe the ultimate chapter. And there was nothing more important than having a happy ending with Kaatje. They ordered and sat there on the terrace under the Caribbean blue sky, seemingly at a loss for conversation. Kaatje broke the tension by moving to sit next to Laurie. Putting her arm around her shoulders, she let their heads rest against one another. "You're wired pretty tightly today. I think you need a few days to get some rest. Do you want to stay at my parents' until you get your sea legs?"

Seeing the concern in her eyes and hearing how empathic she was made Laurie fall in love all over again. She tilted her chin and gave Kaatje a kiss she normally wouldn't have considered in public. But she was exhausted and nervous and delighted all at once, and she let her guard all the way down.

Kaatje responded at once, returning the kiss, making Laurie's pulse race with desire. Blood hammered in her ears and the ground actually seemed to shake. As they broke apart the sensation continued and Laurie slowly opened her eyes to gawp at a full-sized commercial jet flying directly over their heads. The noise was bone-rattling and she blinked, staring at a smirking Kaatje. "Gets a little loud," she shouted, cupping her hands around her mouth.

"Wise guy!" Laurie shouted back. "Let's grab our food and get out of here before I go deaf!"

"That was the show for the day." The noise abated as the jet landed and squealed down the runway. "We only get two 747s a day." She put her hands over Laurie's ears. "I'll protect you."

Laurie playfully slapped at her. "I honestly thought my ears were ringing because of kissing you."

Kaatje gave her a love-filled smile. "Mine were." She leaned close and gifted Laurie with another earth-shaking kiss, this one without any help from outside forces.

CHAPTER TWENTY

LAURIE WASN'T SURE what time it was, and it took her a few hazy moments to remember she was on the boat with Kaatje. Her internal clock was completely screwed up, but she ignored her fatigue and the four times she'd woken during the night. What mattered was that they were together, and she was starting her new job—permanent first mate to Captain Hoogeboom.

—m—

By the time Kaatje woke, Laurie was finished with breakfast and was sitting in the captain's chair, tossing bits of bread to the gulls. Kaatje went up behind her and wrapped her in a hug. "This is a scene I'd like to wake up to for the next forty or fifty years."

Laurie tilted her head back and gave Kaatje an upside-down kiss. "I'd rather wake up next to you. I bet it takes me a week to sync up to this time zone."

"They say it takes a day for every zone you jump."

"I hope they're wrong because I jumped thirteen zones. I used to power through jet lag, but that's not working now."

"Your body tells you what it needs, and you might as well listen to it." Kaatje hugged her tightly. "Just take it slow and ease into the sweet life."

"It'd be sweet no matter where we were. Being with you is the key."

—m—

Just before Kaatje left to get their guests for the day, she handed Laurie a bag and stood there, hands behind her back, looking expectant.

"What's this?"

"Something for your first day."

Laurie peeked inside, then pulled out a sky blue sailing shirt, just like the ones Kaatje wore. But this one was special, bearing the logo of *The Flying Dutchwoman* on one sleeve and her name embroidered over the breast. "Kaatje, this is fantastic!"

"I got one for myself too. I thought we should look more official." She dashed into the galley, emerging with her shirt. She slipped into it and started to button it.

"Mine doesn't have my title," Laurie said, pouting playfully. "Yours says 'Captain.'"

Kaatje delivered a quick kiss, then climbed down the ladder to her dinghy. "'Mrs. Captain' would have looked dumb. And 'Lesbian In Training' would have been too revealing." She started the motor and cast off, still talking. "Once you learn how to sail, I'll officially promote you to first mate. But you've got to earn it!" she called out as the little boat zipped to the shore.

—〜〜—

Laurie knew there was trouble before Kaatje even got back to the boat. She could see the expression on her face when she was still around twenty-five feet away, and something about it didn't look quite right.

The dinghy was filled with five young women, and by the time they pulled up, Laurie could see they were in their early twenties, perhaps recent college graduates celebrating the end of school. Kaatje was acting cooler than normal, or maybe she was just being more professional, but she didn't show any of the easy warmth that usually flowed from her.

Kaatje jumped onto the boat and quickly helped each of the women off the dinghy. She stood there for a second, looking a little odd, then said, "This is Mandy, Lisa M., Brittany, Lisa P., and Kim."

"Hi, I'm Laurie."

"Laurie's my new first mate," Kaatje continued. "She's only been aboard for a short time, but she has a lot of experience in making people feel at home. Just ask her for anything you want, and she'll do her best."

That's why she looked uncomfortable. They hadn't even discussed what her duties were going to be. She would have fired anyone in Osaka who'd been so casual about a new job, but she was pretty sure she had a lock on this one.

Mandy appeared to be the type who was pampered and doted on her whole life by relatively wealthy parents. And her friends seemed like more of the same. They spent a good five minutes making sure their designer handbags, sandals and sunglasses stayed dry. But then they complained because the sun was too bright. Kaatje wasn't able to insure no salt spray would hit them, and reluctantly, they put on their expensive glasses—which probably gave them less protection than the five dollar ones from the Venice Boardwalk.

They paid almost no attention to Kaatje during her brief, but important safety lecture. All of the girls had been on sailboats before, but none of them seemed to have much of an idea of what one did on a boat to stay out of the way of the captain. It seems that one or the other of the girls was always standing right where she shouldn't have been standing for Kaatje to get them out of the harbor safely. Each of them seemed very fond of her own voice and pretty uninterested in hearing anyone else's.

They'd only been off the buoy for fifteen minutes when Laurie's head started to hurt. They were vapid. They weren't biologically dumb; they were happily, willingly dumb, and that was hard to take. Kaatje smiled and chatted, but she was not her usual self, something that Laurie was secretly glad for. It would've been more than a little upsetting to have Kaatje flirting with these airhead girls.

It was fairly early in the day, just about ten thirty when Mandy decided it was time to start drinking. Kaatje called out to Laurie and asked her to make Planter's Punch for their guests. Laurie went below and mixed up a batch, having learned the recipe from Kaatje on her previous visit. However, she used less rum than was called for and decided she would only add more if one of the girls demanded it. Luckily, none of them seemed to be connoisseurs of Planter's Punch and they happily quaffed the light-alcohol beverages. To Laurie's dismay, even using a little rum was dangerous when your guests wanted their glasses refilled every fifteen minutes. She began to understand why parents worried about binge drinking, because these girls had obviously learned how to binge with the best of them.

By the time they got out to the best snorkeling spot an hour and a half had passed. Kaatje set the anchor herself, having not properly worked out the details with Laurie, and when she signaled to Laurie she said, "I don't think we can let them go snorkeling. I don't see how we can keep an eye on all of them since they don't seem like the sorts to follow directions."

"I agree, but how do we stop them? It's part of the deal."

"The deal's off. I'm the captain, and I'm responsible for their safety. I'm not afraid to make them mad. I'd rather have a mad customer than a dead one. But let's see what they want to do."

Determinedly, she walked up to the trampoline where the girls were sunbathing and said, "Snorkeling doesn't look great today. The water's been turbulent and visibility is limited. If you really want to go we'll need to go in pairs. Laurie and I will each take one of you, and then we'll take the next two out."

The girls exchanged unhappy looks, then Mandy said, "We don't need to snorkel. Can we jump in and swim?"

"Sure. Just stay close enough for Laurie and me to keep an eye on you."

"Are there sharks around here?" Lisa P. asked.

Stunningly, Kaatje nodded slowly. "Yeah, we have our share. That's why you need to stay close. I have a bat I can use if I need to. Just yell really loudly if you see a dorsal fin."

"No thanks," Mandy declared. "We'll stay on the boat. Can we hook up an iPod or something?"

"Yeah, sure. I have a stereo system. More drinks?"

"Can we take off our suits?" Mandy asked.

"Absolutely. I'll be right back."

When Kaatje walked back to the cabin, Laurie said, "Was that really the best idea? More drinks?"

"I'd rather have them drunk on the deck than drunk in the water. It's not always easy to come back with the same number of people you left with."

"Especially with the sharks," Laurie said quietly. "Where did that come from?"

"I'm just glad they didn't ask to see the bat." Kaatje chuckled and climbed up to sit in the pilot's seat. Even at anchor, she clearly wasn't off duty, as she gazed across the nearly empty horizon then turned her head to the left and started again.

Laurie got busy and served another round of drinks, studiously avoiding looking at the girls' now-bare breasts. She tried to coax them into having lunch, but too much rum and too much hot sun had robbed them all of their appetites. Laurie came back to the cockpit and said, "We don't have to buy dinner for a couple of days. I don't think they're going to eat a bite."

"Cool. I bought some really good lobster salad." She smacked her lips. "I could have a little right now if someone wanted to get me some." Pointing to the horizon, she added, "I'm working."

"I can see that." Laurie gave her a quick kiss and went to rustle up lunch.

———

They had a pretty nice afternoon, all things considered. The girls slept on the trampoline and worked on their tans and they seemed fairly happy with that setup. Their music was loud and mundane, but it was nice to know they weren't getting into trouble.

About two hours before they were scheduled to be back in dock, Laurie went up and told them that they were going to pull the anchor up and start to sail again. Everything seemed fine until they were about a half hour away. Laurie hadn't heard the sound in quite a while, but there was no way to disguise the awful, grating noise of someone vomiting. And as soon as she heard one person do it, another one started. She looked at Kaatje, who just shook her head. "Let them get it out of their system. When they ruin the trampoline, they'll come back here. Go downstairs and grab a bucket, then fill it up with seawater, because once they start throwing up back here it'll get really slick."

Feeling a little green herself, Laurie complied, bringing up the bucket and filling it by standing on the transom. Unfortunately, as Kaatje predicted, the girls did contaminate the trampoline, then came back to the aft, where they were, and continued to be sick. Kaatje took pity on them. She dropped the sails and turned on the motor. That made the ride a little less bouncy, then she spent a few minutes trying to convince them that there was a way to get over their nausea by staring at the horizon or focusing on something stable. That didn't seem to help much, but eventually they were back at the buoy. After returning the women to the dock Kaatje pulled up in the dingy. She looked up at Laurie and said, "We'd better take the boat over to the pier to wash her."

"Really?" Laurie deadpanned

Kaatje climbed aboard, her usual snarky smile back in place. "My prediction was correct. I'm glad I got them to pay ahead of time because I didn't get one cent for a tip."

"Not a cent?"

"Nope. Usually people leave something for the first mate even if they stiff me, but you obviously didn't impress our first guests."

"I'm glad we got through our first day, but if every day is like this, it's going to have to become a non-alcoholic party boat. I was really close to hanging over the rail when they started to vomit." She cast a disgusted glance down at her feet. "I'm still close."

Kaatje started up the motor. Laurie cast them off and they drove around the tip of the island to a public dock. It took a while to clean the boat properly, and having Kaatje playfully hit her with the water from the hose every once in a while was very welcome.

As Laurie carefully dried the brightwork, she asked, "How would you rate today's sail?"

"In terms of what?"

"I don't know. Just in general. Like on a scale of one to ten."

She looked thoughtful for a minute. "Probably a seven."

That couldn't be true! They were thrown up on! "A seven? Like if ten was the best?"

"Yeah," Kaatje said, seemingly seriously. "They didn't complain about anything, and it's nice when I don't have to go snorkeling."

"But you love snorkeling."

"Yeah, but only when people appreciate it. I don't think the girls were nature lovers. I would have had to supervise them like babies." She grinned. "Do you disagree?"

"No, they would have been several handfuls. But if they were sevens what kind of creature would rate a one?"

Without a flicker of humor, Kaatje said, "I hope you never meet a one, or a two for that matter."

A cold chill settled around Laurie despite the heat. Those girls could not have been sevens. Kaatje was teasing. She had to be.

CHAPTER TWENTY-ONE

A FEW DAYS later Kaatje arranged to have her parents come for a sunset sail. They'd gone to the store to buy wine and snacks, and Laurie busied herself arranging the food while Kaatje cleaned up from their previous guests.

When everything was shipshape, Kaatje called her father and gave him their estimated time of arrival. To Laurie's surprise, they motored over to the dock rather than going to get them in the dinghy. "It's kinda cool being able to drive over to pick your parents up," Laurie commented.

"My father can catch a line and help me touch and go. He's a good sailor. It'd be nice if I could do this for my paying guests, but I'd be in dry dock every other week handling the repairs."

The Hoogebooms were right on the dock, looking more casual than the last time Laurie saw them. Theo wore khaki shorts and a short-sleeved Madras plaid shirt, making him look ten years younger. And Antonia looked lovely in a simple print sundress. As they approached, Laurie mused over how much they looked like a couple. There was something about them that made them fit together, and she wondered if she and Kaatje would someday be the same.

Antonia boarded quickly, vaguely ignoring Theo's instructions and following Kaatje's quieter ones. Kaatje winked at her mother when she passed by, then held a hand out to her father who jumped aboard like a cat, quick and sure-footed as Kaatje was. With barely a second's pause they motored away from the dock.

Antonia offered Laurie a hug. "We're very happy to have you back."

Theo's greeting seemed sincere, but more formal. "Very good to see you again. Kaatje's told us all about your big success."

Laurie poured wine for all, while Kaatje guided them out of the harbor. "It was more successful than I had any right to expect. But I'm very, very glad that part of my life is over." She held up her glass and tapped it against Kaatje's. "To my second act."

———

They sailed out into open water, skimming along small waves in the steady breeze. It was a picture-perfect night, with a few clouds in the west serving as stunning backdrops to the setting sun.

Antonia said, "Kaatje showed us hundreds of photos from the park, but I admit to being jealous of her. I'd love to see it for myself one day."

"Show them the DVD," Kaatje said, urging Laurie towards the galley. "Her staff gave her a wonderful going-away gift. She makes it sound like they were glad to get rid of her, but you can see how much they love her by this." She looked over at Laurie with a proud smile.

Laurie sat between Theo and Antonia, opened her laptop and inserted the DVD. Even though she'd watched it five or six times already, Kaatje dropped the sails and came over to perch on the railing behind her parents. "It's really cool," she said, exchanging a bright smile with Laurie.

The disk started by showing a close-up of the Bee Hive, then it pulled away at a very fast clip to provide an aerial view of the entire park. "They used some canned footage," Laurie said. "They didn't hire a helicopter to shoot this just for me."

"They would have," Kaatje said, still grinning at her.

As they took the viewer around the park, Laurie's staff commented on the role she'd played in bringing each attraction to fruition. There were a lot of inside jokes, and a few shots obviously taken from security cameras, one which showed Laurie kicking a stalled car on a ride, then falling onto her butt from the impact.

"Could I convince you I did that just for a joke?" she chuckled.

The disk was fairly short, just ten minutes, but it gave the viewer the very clear message that Laurie was held in high esteem by the people she worked with the closest. At the end of it she felt tears come to her eyes, and she wiped them away, embarrassed to show how it had gotten to her.

"It must feel a little like a death in the family," Antonia said.

"It would feel like being released from prison for me," Kaatje said. "But that's not how Laurie feels about leaving." She put her arm around her and hugged her tightly.

"No, it didn't feel like prison until the very end when I wanted to leave to be with Kaatje. You're right, Antonia, it was like being in a big family."

"And now you have to ride out those feelings of loss."

"I don't think of it like that," Laurie said. "That part of my life is over. I'm going to be too busy to think about Teddy Bear and his friends. I have to learn to be a sailor, or I'll never get promoted to first mate."

"If you were to go back, what would you do next?" Theo asked.

"She's not going back, Dad," Kaatje said, somewhat testily.

"But you haven't resigned, right?" Theo asked.

"No, not technically. I'm on a leave."

"Couldn't they offer something you'd consider?"

"That would be a very tall order. The chances are slim. I assume I'll resign when my leave is over."

"But what might you do…if you went back?"

What would be a job worth taking? That was a tough one, especially since Luxor would have to figure out a way to get Kaatje legal status. But where there was a will… "I've been in project management since I started, and there isn't much left for me there. I'd probably want to get some experience in park management. If you want to get to executive VP you've got to show your versatility."

"How many executive VPs do they have?"

"Not many. Fifteen or sixteen."

"Were you aiming for that?"

Laurie laughed. "I was aiming to be CEO."

Looking a little surprised, Theo said, "Did you have a chance?"

She leaned back, stretching while gazing up at the darkening sky. It was hard to answer that without sounding like a blowhard, but an honest question deserved an honest answer. "I had a good chance. I was the third youngest senior VP, which means I'd have time to get there. If you're made SVP when you're forty, you can run out of years. Another thing in my favor is that they try very hard to promote women. The president of my division is a woman, and she's on the short list of people who could take the next step. But she's fifteen years older than I am, and she might time out. If I made president of a division by the time I was forty-five, there isn't a reason in the world I couldn't keep going. At that point, timing has a lot to do with it. And keeping yourself in the business news as much as possible, of course. The market has to believe in you." She sat there for a second and let herself consider what it would be like to run a huge, international company like Luxor. It made a thrill chase down her spine, but when she caught Kaatje's gaze, the pleasure of that thought disappeared. Kaatje would never be happy being the spouse of the CEO. That was an eighteen-hour-a-day job, with tons of international travel, and it didn't matter that the pay was in the millions. Those six free hours a day didn't allow for a happy family, and that's what she wanted from life.

—⁂—

After taking Theo and Antonia back to the dock, they moored, and Kaatje started to clean up. Laurie wanted to help, but a wave of fatigue hit her and she sat down, hoping it would pass quickly. She was still waking up every hour or two, and not getting a full-night's rest. Her body believed it was ten in the morning, and no matter how much she wanted to sleep at night, her internal clock was sure it was daytime and that she'd pulled an all-nighter.

"Tired?" Kaatje asked, giving her a look.

"Very." Feeling like she could fall asleep in seconds, she stretched out on the banquette. "But when I get into bed, I lay there for hours. The only time I'm sure I could sleep is the middle of the day, when we have guests."

Kaatje walked over and sat next to her and started to play with her hair. "Can I help?"

"No, you've been very thoughtful. I have to just let it run its course. My body doesn't understand why it's not running around like mad, and why we're up at night and asleep during the day."

"Regrets?" she asked very, very quietly.

That not only woke Laurie, it propelled her into a sitting position. "No! I've never been happier in my life." She held onto Kaatje, burrowing into her body. "Don't ever think anything like that."

Kaatje gently stroked her back, murmuring into her ear. "Sorry. It hit me when you had such a ready…and complex answer for my father. It made me wonder if maybe…"

"Kaatje, pay no attention to that. That's how corporate people entertain themselves." She pulled back and said, "Have you ever seen male dogs walk down the street?"

"Uhm…yeah."

"Notice how they try to mark higher and higher to let other dogs think they're big?"

Kaatje smiled. "Yeah, I know what you mean."

"That's what corporate people do. We boast about how big we are and try to show everyone else how high we can pee. It's just a game. It means nothing."

"Are you sure? If you really need to stay in the corporate world we might be able to figure something out."

"I'm absolutely sure. It wouldn't be good for us, and us is all that counts now."

Kaatje put her hands on Laurie's shoulders and gazed into her eyes for a long time. "This is a very, very big change for you, Moppie. It would be a smaller change for me to move to Florida or LA than it is for you to be here. Make sure you're comfortable with this before we get too invested."

"I'm happy here. Being on this boat with you is a life most people couldn't even dream of. It's like being on vacation every day of the year.

Who wouldn't want that?" She tickled under her chin with a finger, and joined in when Kaatje broke into a fit of the giggles. For scant seconds and with a great deal of sympathy, she thought of Aaron and Andrea and Hiroshi and Toshi and Michiko just getting to work in Osaka. *Poor fools. They'd kill to be able to trade with me.*

―――――

The next two weeks gave Laurie nothing but positive feedback on her decision to be first mate of *The Flying Dutchwoman*. Their days were perfection, with clear skies, moderate wind, and happy customers. It was as if Luxor had engineered the experience, and that perfection was assured.

It took the two full weeks, but Laurie was finally on Kaatje's schedule. After work they relaxed on the boat, or went back out on the ocean for a little snorkeling. Now that Laurie was well rested and alert, Kaatje began teaching her to scuba dive, and she was ready to buy her own gear.

It was a warm afternoon, warmer than it had been in weeks, and after Kaatje took their guests back to the dock, she gazed up at Laurie from the dinghy. "You look like you want to jump in," Laurie said.

Kaatje lobbed the painter up at her. "I do. And I'm going to."

"Hey, why don't we go to the beach? We haven't been since I've been back."

"Sure. Do you have your suit on?"

Laurie pulled her shirt up, showing her bright red suit. "Hang on. I'll grab your book and a couple of towels."

"I'm hanging."

Soon they were on Kaatje's bike, driving across the island to her favorite beach. Most of the tourists had gone back to their hotels, and they were almost alone on the wide cove of calm, aquamarine water on the French side. Kaatje laid their towels out and plopped down, smiling up at Laurie. "I'm happy."

"I thought you wanted to go into the water."

"I did. But I'm perfectly content now. You go in for me."

Laurie ruffled her hair, then playfully pulled on an earlobe. "You're constantly inconstant."

"That's what keeps you interested."

Bending over, Laurie kissed her head. "Among other things." Waving, she ran for the water and submerged herself as soon as it was deep enough. Then she lay on her back and kicked until her legs were tired. The water was still shallow, but the color changed dramatically just ten yards further out, turning a dark indigo. She'd learned that meant deep water, so she stayed where she was, watching for fish.

She squealed in delight when a tilefish skimmed right across her foot. The water was now shallow enough to walk, and she slogged through it looking for more, when she spotted a pair of starfish. They looked completely inert, letting the current move them where it would. It struck her that she was doing basically the same thing, and she suddenly needed to share that with Kaatje.

Because she had been working on her fitness by swimming for at least a half hour every day, she was able to return quickly. Nonetheless, she was winded when she tramped out of the surf and stood, dripping, over Kaatje. "Guess what I am?"

"A big drip?"

"Funny girl." She sat next to her, and spent a moment just gazing at her. Kaatje was pretty in every light, but she was never lovelier than when she was outdoors with the late afternoon sun burnishing her face. Her dark hair shone brilliantly in the light, and her eyes held flecks of gold and many shades of blue, making tiny mosaics of them.

"So what are you?"

Now that she had to state her musings, they sounded funny. But she spit it out anyway. "I'm like a starfish."

Kaatje leaned back and narrowed her eyes. "A starfish, huh? I think I need a little more explanation."

Laurie reached over, took, and squeezed her hand. "I was looking at a pair of starfish and thought about how they just float along. That's how I feel. Like I don't have a schedule, or a boss, or a to-do list. I just let you and the ocean guide me." She knew she was grinning like a kid, but she didn't have to act like an adult with Kaatje.

Kaatje put a hand on her cheek and looked at her tenderly. "Does that make you happy?"

"Don't I look happy?"

Kaatje grinned and nodded. "Yeah. You look very happy."

"I've honestly never been happier in my life. If you'd told me a year ago that the biggest accomplishment of the year would be that I'd fall in love and move to the Caribbean, I would have told you you were mad. But I've fallen in love with a woman, and an island, and an ocean."

"Don't forget the *Dutchwoman*," Kaatje teased.

"And a boat. But the woman's at the top of the list."

"You're at the top of my list too." Kaatje slipped an arm around Laurie's shoulders and pulled her close. Her lips were warm and dry and felt fantastic when they touched Laurie's.

"Let's go home and make love," Laurie breathed.

"You read my mind."

CHAPTER TWENTY-TWO

THE PERFECT WEATHER was finally exhausted. Laurie woke, gazed out the window, and lay back down. A few minutes later Kaatje lifted her head, looked outside, then started to get up.

"It's not even dawn," Laurie yawned.

"It's eight thirty."

"No." Then with less certitude, "Really?"

"Yeah. It's really gray. It'll probably start to rain soon."

Laurie got up and went to the galley, staring out at the gray, gloomy day. "What do we do when it rains?"

"Get wet."

Laurie turned and saw Kaatje's smirk. "I know we'll get wet. But what do we *do*?"

"Whatever we want. Read, go shopping, go hang out at my mom's."

"What can we do on the boat?"

Kaatje walked over to her and wrapped her arms around Laurie's waist. "We can make love."

"All day?"

"I could manage." She leaned over and nibbled on Laurie's neck. "Are you tired of me already?"

"No, of course not, but what if it rains for *two* days?"

"What happened to being like a starfish? Letting the wind and the weather carry you?"

She tried not to show the anxiety she felt. "I'm good with that. But...I don't know where they're gonna carry me."

Kaatje playfully patted her bare butt. "That's the fun of being carried."

Being carried. Suddenly the thought of being carried along without direction wasn't very appealing. A starfish didn't look like it had a brain, and if it did it wasn't a big one. Sailing was wonderful, and having guests was unpredictable and often more fun than she'd imagined. But sitting on a boat while it rained was going to take some getting used to. How did you get used to doing nothing? More important, why would you want to?

—⁓—

They spent a long time making breakfast, something they didn't normally have time for. Laurie was beginning to like Kaatje's favorite Dutch breakfast dishes, and to pay her back she cleaned the galley.

By the time they'd finished, it was raining. It wasn't a downpour by any means, but it was August, peak of the hurricane season, and they were relying on last minute reservations to fill out their week. Kaatje was reading, and she had some of her favorite CDs in the stereo. Laurie poked around in Kaatje's small library, finding nothing that caught her interest. Eventually, she got out her laptop and found a project that pulled her back into her favorite level of concentration—deep.

—⁓—

Around six o'clock, Kaatje walked up behind Laurie and tickled her neck. Then she leaned over and put her lips against Laurie's ear. "Want some dinner?"

Flinching, Laurie turned and stared at her in surprise. "It's dinner time?"

"Pretty close. We should go into town, since we didn't go outside today."

"Okay. That'd be fun. Just let me finish one last thing."

Kaatje stayed standing behind her. "What are you doing?"

Laurie finished the note and started to shut her laptop down. "Writing thank-you notes. Seemed like a good day for it."

"Thank-you notes?"

"Yeah." She stood and picked up her laptop to return it to its secure spot in their cabin. "I sent out a mass e-mail after the park opened, but it wasn't personalized. A personal note is the least I can do for all of the people who helped."

"How many do you have to write?"

Laurie's eyes shifted skyward. "I wrote around sixty today. I probably have another twenty to do."

"Damn, that's a remarkable number. Are you writing to every person who cooked a hot dog?"

"No. Just the ones I know by name." She patted Kaatje indulgently. "Wouldn't be very personal if I didn't know them. I'm trying to mention something they did to help us succeed." She slapped the side of her head with her hand. "It's really taxing my memory."

"I couldn't have been more wrong. I assumed you were goofing off all day. Playing a video game or something."

Laurie laughed. "I've never played a video game. I've never had time."

"Now you do. We'll find some teenager to teach you how to while away the hours, accomplishing nothing."

"Not a good idea. I'd be obsessed with the game and work like a lunatic to master it. That wouldn't be a bit of fun."

Kaatje turned quickly and planted her hands against the wall, trapping Laurie between them. She pressed their bodies together, then kissed her. "We've got to find something for you to do—besides make love. Thank God you haven't tried to be competitive with that."

Laurie put her hands on Kaatje's waist, then let them ride up a few inches to tickle her. Kaatje dropped her hands to protect herself, and started to back down the narrow hallway. "I'm keeping track of how many orgasms we each have," Laurie called out. "I'm winning!"

⁓

The next morning had them making and enjoying another leisurely breakfast. Laurie started to look about for something to do when Kaatje's phone rang. Laurie heard her engage in a long conversation about sailing. To her surprise, Kaatje told the caller that she couldn't accommodate him that day, but that she'd be glad to take him the next. When she hung up, Laurie was staring at her. "Why'd you refuse a client?"

Kaatje shrugged her shoulders in a gesture that either meant, "I'm not sure," or "I don't want to tell you." Either definition was irritating on the best of days, but when she was antsy, the gesture was particularly irksome.

"Kaatje," she said, trying with all of her might not to betray her anger, "Come on. Tell me why you refused."

Kaatje stuck her arms in the air and yawned loudly. Then she moved her shoulders around for a moment or two. "I could tell they'd be pains in the butt."

"How does that enter into the equation? You can't only work with people you like."

That sly smirk was back in force. "Yes, I can. I've done pretty well avoiding difficult people, and I'm not going to change my style…now."

She meant "for you." It was clear as day she was drawing a line in the sand and declaring that she was still the captain. Fine. It was Kaatje's boat and her business. She paid for everything and took all of the risk. It wasn't fair to expect her to share the decisions when she bore the hazards. But there was still a strong temptation to grab something heavy and bean her with it. "I don't mean to second guess you. I'm just trying to understand."

Kaatje leaned back in the chair and nodded. "Okay. Here's how I think. This guy had four and a half hours. He wanted a four-hour sail. That alone is dangerous, but I could live with that. I told him it was raining, and he said he promised his wife they'd go sailing and this was their last day. Another red flag."

"Why?"

"Because he's doing it for her, not because he wants to. He's waited until the last minute, and he's dragging the poor woman out in the rain. Sounds like a jerk."

"Well, he's trying to honor a promise."

Kaatje rolled her eyes and continued, "He had a dismissive attitude. Like he knew more about sailing in the rain than I did."

"Are you saying he insulted you?" Kaatje wouldn't have taken the Queen of The Netherlands sailing if she'd wounded her pride.

"No, I wasn't insulted. But when people act like that, they're usually hard to please. I didn't want to spend the day sailing in a chilly rain and then have him try to weasel out of paying."

Laurie didn't have a response. It was ridiculous to refuse a client because of a guess about his attitude. Maybe the guy was a jerk, but it seemed equally likely that he was really trying to make his wife happy. Maybe the wife insisted that she wanted to go in the rain. But it was clear Kaatje wasn't going to change her mind, as she was now lying down, fully immersed in her book.

—⁂—

Kaatje tried her best to focus, but she couldn't get more than a sentence read before she lost her concentration. It didn't help that Laurie was banging around, looking for something to do, but that wasn't the problem. Maybe she was being unreasonable. It was nice to cherry pick customers, but things had been slow. Six hundred bucks wasn't going to make them sink or swim, but it added up. Maybe Laurie had a point about not judging clients before you met them.

Still, there was something galling about having to let any pushy guy on *The Flying Dutchwoman*. Laurie still seemed to think of her as a business, but she was also home. And no one wanted an unpleasant person in her home for the better part of the day.

Laurie pulled out her laptop and started powering it up. She looked bored and cranky, and Kaatje couldn't stand seeing her that way when she could easily fix it. She got up and went over to her, and began caressing the back of her neck. "Want to go to the movies?"

"No, I don't think so."

"Want me to admit I was wrong in telling that guy he couldn't sail today?"

Laurie turned and looked at her suspiciously for a few seconds. "I don't want you to do things just because I think you should. I only want you to…

be a little more open-minded about your clients. It's very easy to misjudge someone based on a two-minute phone call."

"You're probably right. I'll call him back and see if he's still interested."

She hit the "recent calls" button and dialed the number while Laurie slid a hand up her shorts and tickled along the edge of her panties. Being flexible might be a good idea for many reasons.

—•••—

Five hours later Kaatje stood nose to nose with Frank, while his wife, Margaret sat at the table in the cockpit, with Laurie trying to offer some sympathy. Margaret was crying, and from the looks of things, she had plenty to cry about. Kaatje and Frank were both drenched, rain running down the hoods of their slickers, and pelting their bare legs. "I'm not paying because I didn't get to sail!" he bellowed.

"I can't guarantee wind, and I told you clearly that the wind tends to die in this kind of rain."

"A good sailor would have known where to go to find what wind was available."

"We went to where the wind might have been, if there had been any. But there wasn't a whiff."

"If that was such a good place why weren't there any other boats out there?"

"Because it's *raining*," she shouted, cranking her voice up to a level Laurie had never heard. "There's not another boat out today. I only took you because you were so insistent."

"That's stupid! You can't let the customer make that decision. You're the one who's supposed to know the conditions, not me."

"Get off my boat," Kaatje said, her voice low and rough. She stood there for a moment, with Laurie silently pleading for her to not send Frank over the lifelines. Then her head moved quickly to the left and she whistled, using a couple of fingers in her mouth, something Laurie didn't know she could do. A dinghy turned and headed for *The Flying Dutchman*.

When it got alongside, Kaatje said, "Jimmy, will you take these people to shore?"

"Sure. What's wrong with your dinghy?"

"Nothing." She turned and went into the cabin, shutting the sliding door behind her.

Laurie was afraid to go into the cabin, but it couldn't be avoided. She'd gotten involved in something she thought she knew, but obviously did not. Sliding the door open, she spied Kaatje lying on the cushion by the table, reading a book. She looked perfectly calm, and when the door opened, she looked at Laurie and gave her a half smile. "I'm not kidding when I say this, so listen closely."

Laurie walked over to her, ready to be chewed out.

"He was a three on a scale of ten." Then she chuckled and went back to reading, not mentioning the topic again.

By the fourth consecutive day of rain, Laurie was ready to go into town and help the woman who often sat in a plastic chair on the side of the road, selling a few bananas she'd obviously picked from the plants in her yard. Anything to stay busy. She'd cleaned the galley until it shone, the bathrooms were sparkling and their cabin had been organized as neatly as a hospital operating room. And it was still only ten thirty. Kaatje looked up from her reading, "I can't afford to buy a bigger boat for you to clean."

"I didn't ask for one." Laurie sat on the edge of the banquette and lavished some attention on Kaatje's hair.

"I keep thinking I should get up and help you, but then I reason that'll make you finish faster, and that's the last thing you want."

Pulling on a strand of hair, Laurie said, "It seems like you might be making fun of me."

"Not at all. I'm honestly worried that you're this bored after a couple of days of rain. You're gonna have to find a hobby."

"How about making me in charge of the hull? I talked to the owner of *Viking Wing* the other day and he said he cleans his hull every week."

Kaatje twisted her head until she could see Laurie's eyes. "What do you know about cleaning hulls?"

"Nothing. But if there's a book about it I could learn it."

"How would you stay underwater to get to the bottom? Can you hold your breath long enough to make any progress?"

"I'm not sure," she said, tentatively. "Is it hard?"

"Do you know how to avoid touching a live wire?"

She gulped. "That'd be in the book. I'm *sure* that'd be in the book."

Kaatje pushed herself into a sitting position, grasped Laurie by the shoulders and pulled her close. She spoke into her ear. "Are you unhappy, Moppie?"

"Hey, I meant to tell you that I looked the word up and it means 'mop'!"

"It's a common pet name. An endearment. But maybe I was thinking of you swabbing the decks…which I'm sure will be next."

Laurie put her arm around Kaatje's shoulders and hugged her tightly. "I'm not unhappy. How could I be? I'm in love with a fantastic woman, I know what my sexual orientation is, I live in a tropical paradise, and I don't have to work fifteen hours a day. You'd be insane to be unhappy."

Quietly, with a playful spirit, Kaatje said, "Maybe you're insane."

"No, I'm not. I just need to be busier. I need something to do. Something that's mine." She sat up straighter. "How about accounting? I'm really good at that."

Looking away, Kaatje made a few noises and scratched her head.

"How do you do your accounting now?"

"I throw everything into a big envelope and give it to my accountant once a year." She grinned, eyes twinkling. "That's the best way, right?"

"How do you do projections?"

"Projections are…?"

"One of the tools you should use to plan. You have to be able to anticipate your income to make sure you have the money to pay your expenses. Not to mention unexpected repairs or replacement costs. How do you do that?"

"Uhm…I see how much money I have left at the end of the season after I've contracted for my boat repairs. Then I put some of that in savings and spend the rest in The Netherlands." She shrugged, looking completely unconcerned. "It's worked fine."

"But that's…pure happenstance! I could set you up with a system that would allow you to budget for major expenses and keep track of everything routine. Wouldn't you feel better having more financial information?"

"To be honest…no. I try to be thrifty all year 'round. I might not know where every dollar is, but I know I'm always going to look for a bargain. That's all I can do."

"But what if you don't have enough money to do critical repairs?"

"Then I'd sell the boat and work for someone else. I don't like to worry about things like that. They're out of my control."

"No they're not," Laurie insisted. "Not if you carefully budget for everything."

Kaatje slapped her leg and got up. "I know you're trying to help, but I want to handle my money my way for now. Let's talk about it in a few months. Maybe I'll be more reasonable." She walked over to where she'd stowed her laptop and carried it back. "Here's something we can do. I want to start sending out e-mails to everyone who has sailed with me, reminding them of what a good time they had." She grinned adorably. "Can you help me put something together?"

"Sure. Let's find some pictures of the boat and some of your spectacular sunsets. We'll embed those to make it pretty."

"Hey, you *do* know what you're doing."

"I sure do. You can go read if you want to." She batted her eyes playfully. "I don't work well with others."

—⁓—

The weather cleared the next day and they had an excellent week of sailing. A full boat, good passengers and light breezes. The weather was fantastic and Kaatje said she'd never had a week as nice. That's why it puzzled Laurie all the more that she was still at loose ends. She was busy, interacting with the clients, taking a turn at the wheel, serving lunch, cleaning up, and going snorkeling. She was ridiculously fond of Kaatje, finding herself charmed by everything from her smile to the way she hugged her pillow when she slept. There wasn't a valid reason not to be blissful, but blissful she was not.

They'd invited the Hoogebooms for another sunset sail, and as they got ready Kaatje said, "I've never had my parents out more than once in a year. You're a good influence on me."

"Why've you not had them more often? They seem to really appreciate it."

"Yeah," she said pensively. "I guess I assumed my dad would pick on me about something or other. But he doesn't do that when you're here. They both treat me more like an adult."

"I'm glad. You are an adult." She went to her and slipped her arms around Kaatje's waist. "A beautiful adult." They started to kiss but Kaatje's phone went off, signaling their guests were at the dock.

Kaatje grabbed a handful of Laurie's butt and pinched it. "We'll be naked adults the second they leave."

The Hoogebooms were precisely on time and they sailed off into the sunset just as planned. Kaatje had a half glass of wine, but everyone else drank more freely.

Antonia asked, "How is it going being away from your big corporate family, Laurie?"

Kaatje answered for her. "It's hard for her. She's used to being ridiculously busy and being on the boat is starting to drive her a little nuts."

Feigning outrage, Laurie said, "It's not making me nuts. It's just an adjustment."

"Of course it is. I've worked with people who've had to move here for business, and leaving their country is probably similar to what you've done," Antonia said.

"I haven't even thought about leaving my home," Laurie admitted. "I wasn't very connected to LA, and Cincinnati hasn't been home for a very long time."

"It sounds as though your company was a substitute for your home."

"I don't think that's true. Being at Luxor was like being on a football team that wins the Super Bowl. Hundreds of people work together, everyone from ticket sellers to people who do publicity. And when you win, it feels like the whole group has accomplished something. But when the season's over you move on. You have to start all over again to accomplish the next goal."

"I don't follow American football, but when people are on a team that has worked together well, I know they often stay close their whole lives. You must miss them."

Mentally cursing herself for allowing tears to come to her eyes, Laurie nodded. "I…I miss the camaraderie. I had a lot of friends, and some people I spent every day with for years. But more than that, I miss having something I have to get done. I've always been self-motivated, and there just isn't enough here for me to be responsible for."

"I had to grab her by the shorts to stop her from scraping the hull during a storm," Kaatje said dryly.

"That's an unpleasant job, and possibly dangerous, especially if you have to check the sacrificial anodes. Besides, you use ablative paint, don't you, Kaatje?"

"I won't let her do it alone, Dad. Don't worry about it."

Laurie exchanged looks with Antonia. "I guess it's best. I have no idea what they're talking about."

"If you're not going to start cleaning hulls, what will you do to stay busy?" Antonia asked.

"I don't have a clue. I suppose I'll just try to acclimate. I keep reminding myself that only a fool would look for things to do when she's surrounded by such perfection."

"You're my fool," Kaatje said, her look conveying her love.

Antonia said quietly, "Give it time, but don't ignore your feelings. This is a massive adjustment, Laurie. It will take a long while to feel like you belong here. It's a new way of life, a new country, a new partner. That's a huge amount of change."

"Then she has to get used to Amsterdam, where we should head pretty soon," Kaatje said. "The tourists are drying up faster than ever this year. I've heard of five or six guys who're going to pack up and move to another island."

"You have enough savings to weather the slowdown, don't you?" Theo asked. "I know you can't take on any more debt."

Kaatje answered, surprisingly, in Dutch. Laurie had no idea what she said, but Theo responded sharply. They went back and forth a few times until Antonia moved over near Kaatje and stroked her back while father and daughter glared at each other. Kaatje had very few faults, but getting angry when someone told her what to do would always be one of them.

—⁓—

After they got into bed that night, Kaatje rolled onto her side and lay there, not showing any sign of being awake. But Laurie knew she was still upset and didn't want to talk about it. She considered letting it slide, but eventually couldn't resist. "Are you mad at me and your dad or just your dad?"

"Just my dad," Kaatje grunted. "He had to go out of his way to tell me he wouldn't give me another loan, and that I'd better have some savings."

"He loaned you the money for the boat?"

"No, his bank did." She rolled over and lay on her back, staring at the ceiling. "I had to go through the usual approval process. I don't think he helped a bit. But his bank offered the best rate, and that's where I went. He acts like it's his own money and he's the one who decides everything." She almost spat out, "He's not even on the loan committee."

"Try not to let it get to you. He cares about your security, that's all."

"I don't need him to care about my security. I need him to leave me to my own business and him stick to his."

Laurie snuggled into Kaatje's reluctant embrace. "I know." She rubbed her belly, trying to get her to limber up and accept some affection.

"Are you ready to go to Amsterdam now?" Her tone was just as cold as it had been when she talked about her father.

"We don't have to decide that tonight."

Kaatje pulled away, got up and sat on a small chair in the corner. "Yes, we do. I'm ready to go. If you weren't here, I'd get online and make my reservations now."

"Uhm…" That familiar fist was back, gripping her entrails like a vice. "How long do you want to be gone?"

"Through November for sure. I'd like to get busy and find clients for December since I've had some very lucrative Christmas sails. I really need to hustle to make money next year or I *might* wind up selling the boat."

Ignoring that element of the issue, Laurie focused on the timing. "My sabbatical will be up before then. I'd…I think I've got to figure out something to do before I leave here."

Coldly, Kaatje said, "Meaning?"

"It's like your mom said, I've got to take some time to get comfortable. That'll be hard to do in Amsterdam."

"Why? That's where we'll spend at least three months every year. You have to be comfortable in Europe, too."

"I know, I know." The walls were closing in. The cabin was stuffy and she had to throw the sheet off to cool her body down. "What about the idea I proposed?"

Kaatje shook her head firmly. "I'm not going to buy another boat. It's out of the question. This island doesn't need more boats, it needs fewer. There are probably twenty of us competing for every client."

"But you're better at this than many of these guys. If we had two boats we could take bigger groups. We could specialize in long sails to multiple islands. There isn't a lot of that offered here."

"That's because it's impossible to stay busy. There isn't an angle you can think of that someone else hasn't already thought of. You're not the first smart person to come to the Caribbean and try to find a way to make a good living, you know."

"I know that, but I'm pretty good at figuring out how to take a process and make it better and more profitable."

Kaatje got up and headed for the galley. "Fine. Now you just have to find a process that isn't *The Flying Dutchwoman*."

Laurie lay there and stared after her. Kaatje was rarely sharp or testy. Clearly, her father had upset her. But there was more to it than that. Laurie got up and put on a T-shirt and shorts and went into the galley. Kaatje wasn't there, but the sliding doors to the cockpit were open. She was sitting, stark naked, in the captain's chair, staring moodily out at the lights of town.

Laurie stood behind her and put her hands on her chilled shoulders. "Talk to me. I don't want to take over your business, but if I'm going to be your partner, I *do* want to help you."

"I know." She patted her hand, then turned and kissed it. "But I can't have you get too involved. Maybe later, after you really know how to sail and what the market's like. But now you're just guessing at things, and that makes me feel like you assume I haven't thought of those ideas. It's insulting."

"Okay." She sat down, now a few feet away. "I can understand that. If you'd made obvious suggestions about my project, I would have been irritated. But I think it's clear I've got to find something to do here. And if you don't want me helping with the boat…"

"I do want you to help. If you learn how to sail you could eventually be an equal partner. Then maybe we could get a second boat. But that would take years, Laurie, and I don't see you having the patience for that."

"Why would it take years? You know how hard I can work."

Kaatje let out a long breath. "You learn by doing. You can't know what to do in a bad storm until you've been through many of them. Books don't substitute for experience."

"I'm not sure that's true. There have to be simulations we could work on."

"Of course there are. But acting like there's a man overboard isn't the same as *having* a man overboard. You have to train your reflexes and your nerves as well as your knowledge. It's more complicated than it looks."

"Okay, okay. If we don't have time for me to learn to sail, I'll try to find a regular job on the island."

"We've been through this. There isn't anything on the island as complex or difficult as what you've been doing. Your project was as big as our national budget."

"Well, have you given any thought to what Fernando said?"

Kaatje got up and walked over to sit next to Laurie. "I have. If you can find a job where I can work—sailing—I'll go wherever you want. Any country on earth."

That was such a stunning capitulation that Laurie's chest tightened. Kaatje loved her island in the way many people loved their kids. It took a moment to come up with words to acknowledge her offer. "That's a huge sacrifice. Huge."

Kaatje looked at her with love filling her eyes. "I'd do anything to be with you. But I have to be able to stay busy, since you'll be gone all day…at least."

Smiling, Laurie said, "I know. The only thing Fernando thought might work would be to have me running the Miami theme park. We could finagle a way to have you run your business under a shell corporation in my name or something like that. It could work."

"But I'd have to leave the country every six months."

"Yes, but winter is prime season for charter sailing in Miami. You could spend summers with your family."

"Without you." She gazed at Laurie in the dark, her eyes seeming to penetrate the dim light.

"I'd take my vacation then."

"The person who runs the park is going to take a long vacation in the summer? Ask the person who runs it now how that would go over."

Laurie turned and put her hands on Kaatje's bare thighs and squeezed. "We could work it out. It's better than being apart all of the time, isn't it?"

"Is that what it's really down do?" Kaatje asked, sounding tired. "I get six months or nothing?"

"It's no better for me!" Years and years of training herself to be calm flew away in the breeze. Her face was hot, her gut bursting with feelings she'd learned to tamp down. But she couldn't control them now. They'd taken on a life of their own, and they scared her to death. "I want to be with you every moment, but I don't have anything to *do*. I can't make idle conversation with strangers all day. It's not challenging enough for me. I want to accomplish something, make something work better, have something to show for my day."

"Then get a job!" She got up and went to the starboard side and leaned against her chair. "There are jobs here. They're not like the one you had, but it's a job and it would keep you busy. Go work for my father. He'd love you."

"We talked about that," she said quietly, ignoring the outraged look on Kaatje's face. "But the only jobs he ever has available are clerical." She looked into Kaatje's face, seeing, even in the dark, that it had colored. "I can't do a job I could have mastered in high school! I could have been the CEO of a multi-billion dollar corporation someday, Kaatje. I still don't think you know how big a job I left for you."

"I think I do," she replied, her voice like ice. "And I think you want to go back to it. I believe you love me, but I also believe you love your job, and don't want to leave it."

"It's not the job! The job was killing me. It's the sense of accomplishment, the working with the team, the exhilaration from doing something next to impossible. I was never bored. Not for one second—"

"Not like you are here."

Laurie stopped, her heart racing. It was time to face, then tell the truth. "I *am* bored. Not with you," she said fervently. "But with taking clients out. It's like I'm always on vacation, but there are other people around. I don't like that," she said quietly. "I want a job and an apartment or a house. I need more space. I need to get away from the boat after being on it all day." She almost choked on the last sentence, but it was time to get it all out. "I need high-speed internet. I know it's stupid, but that's how I relax. You read books, I read business news on the Internet. But your satellite connection is awfully slow. Most of the time I don't even bother, but it's driving me crazy!" There. It was out. She was a shallow woman who needed mindless surfing on the Internet to feel complete.

Kaatje gazed at her for a long, long time. Finally, she said, "Okay. Figure out a way to allow me to work in Miami or anywhere else that has a body of water and I'll do it. But I have to get a green card. I'm not willing to only see you for six months." She stuck her jaw out and crossed her arms over her chest, looking like a battlefield commander. "That's my best offer."

―

Laurie spent a solid week and untold hundreds of dollars on phone calls to the US. Kaatje didn't ask for updates, but things were vaguely stilted between them. One night, lying in bed after making love, Kaatje said quietly, "If it's too hard to get me a work permit, I'll just hang out in the US or wherever you want to be. I'd rather work but it's not as elemental to my personality as it is to yours." Laurie pulled her close and kissed her, relief flooding her. Kaatje was truly a fantastic partner. She was proud and independent, but still willing to be fully dependent financially—just to stay together. What a gift she was.

―

It took a few more days, but Laurie finally had enough information so they could discuss all of their options. They set up a nice dinner, with candlelight, in the cockpit, while half a mile out at sea. They both knew this was going to be a turning point, but neither knew the outcome.

Laurie started to speak, after carefully apportioning their food between their plates. She took a drink of wine and let it roll. "Here's what I think we can get."

Kaatje took a sip of wine, and Laurie could see her swallow nervously.

"The easiest thing is to get you admitted to a university. You could study anything that interested you. Oceanography…uhm…anything."

Kaatje nodded, not saying a word.

"If that doesn't interest you, I can get you a work permit fairly easily. You could do almost anything at Luxor. Hospitality, customer relations… there are hundreds of jobs. But you have to really do the job. It can't be a way to just get in and run your business."

Again, a nod.

"A work permit is easy, but a green card is tough. But if we can figure out a way to convince the government you have skills the US needs, we can do it. One way is to work for a few years for Luxor, in a job they have trouble filling. Once you've done that, you can quit and do anything you want. You can have your business legally, and stay with me forever." She didn't reveal how many strings she had to pull to get that promise from various levels of the bureaucracy. She knew Kaatje wouldn't be impressed that the CEO himself had given the final approval, just to keep Laurie.

"How many years would that take?"

Glumly, Laurie said, "No one could give me a firm date."

"Years?"

"Yeah, definitely years."

"Ten years?"

Laurie shook her head. "They wouldn't give me a guess."

"Is there a guarantee I'd get the green card?"

Damn her and her perceptive questions! "Not really a guarantee. You never know what's going to happen with immigration. And there's a big backlog of applicants. You'd probably be in the…unskilled labor category." She swallowed at even having to say that. "That makes it take longer."

"Those don't sound like very good options." Kaatje finally took a bite of her food, and a memory flooded Laurie's mind of their first night together. This was just how Kaatje had looked that night when she thought Laurie wanted to leave; guarded, suspicious, and hurt. "I don't want to be a student, but even if I did, wouldn't we be right back to this point when I graduated?"

"Uhm, yeah, I guess." She brightened. "But I'd have four more years of work behind me and I'd have more savings. I could probably retire."

"At thirty-six?" Kaatje's look said it all. "You're saying that in four years it won't bore you to sit on my boat and talk with strangers?"

"Look," she said, her voice rising, "I'm doing everything I can to make this work!"

Kaatje threw down her fork and leaned over the table. They were almost eye to eye and Kaatje's gaze was smoking hot. "No you haven't. There's one thing you need to do. Change! You promised me you wanted to quit. You promised you'd be happy with me. You have to work on changing. It's not going to be fast, and it's not going to be easy, but this is where we have to be, and you have to adapt!"

"That's not fair!" Laurie jumped up and Kaatje did the same. "You want me to quit my job and do what you want, but when I ask you to do the same you won't!"

"It's not the same at all. I want you to spend your days with me, working at something you could come to love. You want me to quit what I love and do something I don't have any interest in. And you'll keep right on working ungodly hours. So I'll be there mainly for you to sleep with. When you're not sleeping on the sofa in your office." She turned and went into the cabin, emerging a few minutes later with her snorkel, mask and a powerful flashlight. She was naked and looked like she wanted to physically fight the first person she encountered. "I'm not punishing you, but I need to be alone." With that, she jumped into the water, and Laurie watched her light slowly fade away in the dark, still water.

———

Kaatje was gone longer than was kind. Laurie was mad with worry, but she didn't have the skills to jump in and look for her, which was folly anyway. After an hour, Kaatje's light shown just off the bow of the boat, and Laurie realized she'd probably been very close for most of the time. There was no way she would have missed the light drawing near, so Kaatje had obviously just turned it on. She swam around to the stern and climbed the ladder, no longer looking angry. She dropped her gear and stared at Laurie whose eyes were red from crying. "It's not going to work. You might as well go back now."

Ignoring her dry clothes, Laurie grabbed her and hung on for dear life. "Don't say that. Please don't say that."

"It's the truth. I'm going to go to The Netherlands as soon as I can. You can go with me or…" She collapsed in tears, with Laurie joining her as their hearts broke together.

CHAPTER TWENTY-THREE

THE ONLY THING Laurie was sure of was that she didn't want to go to Holland. She hoped to spend much time there in the future, but for now, she had to make a decision about Luxor. Being in Holland wouldn't help her do that. For now, they were out of options.

It took a couple of days to get a flight to Cincinnati, and things were surprisingly calm between them. Kaatje wasn't much of a fighter, and that was very reassuring. But she looked so sad and brokenhearted that Laurie could barely stand to look at her. They kept busy taking people out. Since most of the boats had gone down island, everyone who wanted to sail seemed to call. That was a big blessing, because sitting on the boat trying not to cry was too much to ask for.

The day before she was to leave, Laurie caught Kaatje as she was exiting the shower. They hadn't made love since they'd decided to part, but she couldn't bear to think that they'd already had their last time together.

She put her hands on Kaatje's bare shoulders and started when Kaatje turned and looked at one hand as though she were considering whether to allow it to stay. But her head slowly turned back towards Laurie and she grasped her in a feverish embrace. In seconds they were on the bed, with Kaatje yanking on the panties that Laurie was wearing. She pulled hard and they snapped, then were flung aside, forgotten.

Kaatje lay atop Laurie's body, covering her completely—hands holding hands, legs pinning legs beneath her. "I never want to let you go," she whispered hoarsely. "I love you with my whole soul."

"I love you too," Laurie cried, trying not to sob. She buried her face in Kaatje's shoulder and tried to breathe in her soothing scent.

Kaatje gently grasped her face and turned it until their noses touched. "Work on coming back to me. Work as hard as you can."

"I will. I swear I will."

Then, neither needing to speak, they began to make love. They'd learned each other's bodies and hearts. Words were truly superfluous.

—⁓—

The next morning, a cab met Laurie on the dock, the same dock where she and Kaatje had met. They stood there in the blazing sun, neither able to speak. There was little left to say. If she went back to Luxor, they were through. That was a no-brainer. But it wasn't clear they'd make it if she quit Luxor. It was obvious she didn't make a good first mate.

Kaatje tossed the bags in the back of the van, then stood there with her hands in the pockets of her shorts. She looked like she was going to cry, but her eyes were dry. Apparently there were only so many tears in the human body. Putting her head against Kaatje's chest was both reassuring and terrifying. What if this was the last time that strong heartbeat thrummed in her ear? Kaatje tenderly kissed the top of her head, then stepped back, her expression now a blank mask. "Be safe," she said, her voice strained.

"I will." The door closed and she turned her head so she didn't have to see Kaatje's beautiful image getting smaller and smaller.

—⁓—

Much later that day, after a change in Miami, Laurie landed in Cincinnati. She craved advice like a drug, and desperately hoped her mother could help. They could have talked more on the phone, but with Kaatje always being around it was hard to let loose and get everything off her chest. Being there in person would surely help. It simply had to.

She was surprised to see just her Mom waiting for her in the car. "Where are the girls?" They'd always come to the airport to pick her up and would fight over who got to sit with her in the back.

"It's a school night, honey. They have to be in bed by nine."

"Oh. I forgot. It seems like the middle of summer to me."

"I bet it does. Are you sad?" She put her hand on Laurie's shoulder.

"If this is sad, I hope I never get depressed."

—⁓—

There was nothing to do the next day. Everyone was at work, leaving hours of time to obsess. On her second day, Laurie went to the office with her mom, the office manager of the family lighting business. She was determined to fill her day with something—even if it meant dusting the display fixtures as she'd done when she was a child.

She actually did spend two hours dusting, but her mother was finally able to take time out for lunch. They went to a local restaurant to avoid being interrupted by the constantly ringing phone.

Her mom had been suitably sympathetic and a very willing ear the first evening, but now she was full of questions. "Tell me about your offer to buy another boat," she said, picking at her salad.

"I told you about it weeks ago—the first time Kaatje shot me down. I'd sell my house and use the proceeds to buy a second catamaran. We could get one as nice as *The Flying Dutchwoman* if we bought one a few years old. I'd captain that one and we'd try to find bigger groups to take longer trips. There's a lot more money in that."

"And why doesn't Kaatje want that?"

"I told you, Mom. She says it'd be double the work for her, since I'm not a real sailor, and she's sure there isn't enough business to keep both boats busy. She says it'd be a lot more worry for a small profit."

"And why do you think you know more than she does about her business?"

Laurie stabbed a French fry with her fork. "Don't think I didn't notice how you framed that question. It's not that I know more than she does. But she doesn't think big. She leaves money on the table all of the time." She adopted what she thought was a pretty good imitation of Kaatje's Caribbean/Dutch/English accent. "I don't take clients if I don't like them. Life's too short to deal with idiots." She shook her head. "Can you imagine how broke you'd be if that's how you ran your business?"

"No, but if I could afford to, I'd do it in a minute."

"Well, I don't think you can run a business like you do your personal life. I bet dad agrees with me."

"I'm sure he does. That's why he works seventy hours a week. That's also why I have to light a stick of dynamite under him to get him to take a vacation."

"A business is a hard thing to be responsible for, Mom. He has a lot of people who depend on him."

Becky looked like she was going to make a snappish reply, but she sat quietly for a few moments. "He's almost sixty. Our house is paid off, our kids are grown, and there's plenty of money in the college fund for our grandkids. What are we working for? When do we get to do what *I* want?"

Touched, Laurie reached out and covered her mother's hand with her own. "What *do* you want?"

"I want to be with Kaatje," she said, smirking. She pulled her hand away and added, "I don't want to have sex with a woman, but I'd love to live in the Caribbean and The Netherlands and travel around Europe. I've never even been to Canada."

"You were in Japan."

"Yes, we were, and I loved it. But we only saw a bit of Osaka and the park…which was wonderful, honey. You know how proud I am of you. But I want more out of life than making sure the people of Cincinnati have adequate lighting in their homes. I want to travel and get up late and do something I can feel a little embarrassed about. I've never done one thing I'd be afraid to tell my mother. That's an awful thing to admit."

"Are you…unhappy?"

"Well…" Becky took a long breath. "I could be happier. Work is the way I make money. It doesn't give me true happiness."

"It does me," Laurie said sadly. "It truly does."

"Then you might as well be honest with Kaatje and let her find someone who shares her values."

"I share her values!"

"No, on a very important level, you don't. If you really loved her, you'd put her first. It's that simple. You're not treating Kaatje any differently than you did Colin. I hate to say this, honey, but I don't think you're the kind of person who can be in a relationship. You should just have some flings with other workaholics."

Laurie's eyes filled with tears, and she struggled valiantly to control them. "How can you say that?"

Becky reached over and grasped her hand, squeezing it tightly. "I hate to hurt you, baby. I'm just being as honest as I can be. Kaatje is waiting for you to make up your mind, and I hate to see her get more hurt than she already is."

"But you don't mind hurting me!"

"Yes, I do. Of course I do. But you'll be fine. You'll get a new project and you won't notice the years flying by. Kaatje's not like that. It will take her a long time to get over you."

"God damn it, Mom! You make it sound like I have no soul."

"Not at all, honey. You're a very caring, very loyal woman. But if you *can* let Kaatje go over a job...you *should*...for *her* sake."

―⁂―

They'd spoken every day, but the conversations were short and not very sweet. Kaatje had pulled way back, exposing very little of her soft side. That night, Laurie reached her when Kaatje was already in bed, and she could clearly imagine just how she looked—naked, hair mussed, her beautiful eyes heavy with sleep. "Hi, I just wanted to check in."

"Hi. I've got about two minutes of sentience left. I had a boat full of kids. Well, just four, but it seemed like twenty."

"Well, I didn't have anything to say. Other than I miss you."

"That's good." The emotion in that sentence couldn't have filled an eyedropper. "A buddy is going to give the boat its checkup, so I'm flying out tomorrow. I got a surprisingly good last-minute fare."

"Wow, that's fast. I thought you were going to go down island."

"I was. But they're predicting a mild hurricane season. I'm gonna take a risk." Her voice grew quiet. "I need to get out of here."

"Okay." Laurie did her best to keep her tears in check. "I guess I won't be able to talk to you tomorrow."

"No, I got a non-stop. I'll be in the air all day." There was a strained silence. "Look, it's expensive to call Holland, and not much is going on. Let's just…check in when we have something to report."

Laurie couldn't reply. She bit her lip and found herself rocking back and forth, trying to soothe herself with a hug. How could Kaatje not even want to talk any more? Were they enemies now?

"Hey," Kaatje said, her own voice rough with emotion. "It doesn't make sense to talk every day. It's screwing with my emotions. I stare at the phone all day hoping you'll call to say you're coming ho—back."

"I'm so sorry, Kaatje. If I could put it into words, you'd know how much I want to be with you. It's just…"

"I know. Call me when you make up your mind…one way or the other."

"You can always call me." She realized as it came out how rude that sounded. Like she was a bigger person. "No matter what happens, I love you and I care for you. If you need to talk, no one understands this better than I do."

Letting out a big breath, Kaatje said, "I appreciate that. But…"

"All right. I'll call you soon."

"Okay. Bye."

No proclamations of love, no sweet words, not even a wish for a good night's sleep. It was a very steep drop from love to loss.

⁓

After four days with her family, Laurie had to get back to LA. She'd been bored silly bumping around at the store during the day, and her nieces were now old enough to be involved in after-school sports and music lessons. That left her with a ton of time to sulk and mourn, and those were two of her least favorite pastimes.

A day after arriving back in LA, she arranged to meet Fernando for a drink after work. Knowing his habits, she told him to call her when he was in his car, headed for the bar. At seven thirty she heard his sheepish voice ask, "How about dinner instead of drinks?"

"Is that okay with Marisol?"

"Oh, sure. She and the kids ate at six. Now they're all at a basketball practice. I swear, the boys are always gone now that they're in middle school."

"I know how it feels. My nieces didn't sit next to me waiting for me to read to them when I was there. It seems they've learned how to do that all on their own."

"Ingrates," Fernando said, only partially sounding like he was teasing.

—∞—

They settled on a little Mexican dive not far from the office. The food was mediocre, but it was close and they made their tortillas on site, which was a big plus. Fernando had been there so many times he knew the menu by heart and Laurie always let him order for her.

They sipped their margaritas and sampled the surprisingly spicy guacamole. "New cook?" she asked.

"Yeah. The food's better. This guy knows how to use spices." He loaded up another corn chip and took a bite. "You don't look happy. Being in love isn't easy, is it."

"No." She took a bite as well. "It always was before."

"Until your boyfriends broke up with you," he said, his dark eyes glimmering in the candlelight.

"Yeah, that part sucked, but things were good while we were together."

"I understand. Marisol is the only woman I've ever known who doesn't give me a hard time about work."

"She knew you before you started dating, and she's a team member. There were no surprises."

"Yeah, that's part of it. Maybe that's what you need. Find a nice woman here at Luxor, then you'll both know how demanding these jobs are. It's much easier that way."

"But I don't want another woman," she said earnestly. "I want Kaatje."

"She seems great, not to mention pretty. But you can't sit on a boat for months at a time." He laughed, clearly amused at the very thought. "You might be able to run one of our cruise ships, but even that would bore you."

"No, I could do that. But when they have a senior VP running a cruise ship, Honey Bear will be pole dancing on board every night."

"Yuck. That bear is not hot!" He laughed, then sat there contemplatively. "Do you really miss her?"

"More than I can ever say."

"Then suck it up and go back to her. I'd quit if I could."

She peered at him closely. "Would you really?"

"Hell, yes. You know my plan. Once our stock is at the right price and my retirement account is fat enough, I'm gone."

"I thought you were gone at fifty, no matter what."

"Well, that's what I'd like, but I can't do that if the stock price is down. If I'm never going to work again, I need to have a cushion."

"And what will you do when you retire?"

He grinned, looking relaxed and happy. "Spend a lot more time with Marisol and the boys. That's the biggest item on my agenda."

"Yeah, what else?"

"Spend more time with my parents in Puebla."

She didn't comment that his father was over seventy and not in the best of health. "What else?"

"I'll work on my golf game. I've never had time to get as good as I know I can be. And I might buy a boat. I've got those jet skis, but a boat would be more fun. The boys would like it too."

"That sounds good, but could it keep you happy?"

"Oh, sure. I'd love to sit under the avocado tree out in my parents' backyard and just watch the world go by. I could do that for hours."

Laurie looked at him, noting how happy he seemed when lost in that dream. But his kids would be in college when he was fifty, his parents would probably be dead, and he and Marisol would be riding around alone in a powerboat. That would keep him busy for about a week. And he would never, ever have the patience to play golf, a sport he was dreadful at. They were far too much alike, and the thought chilled her to the bone.

—∾—

They ate and were lingering over shots of Kahlua when Fernando said, "Corporate wants you to make a decision soon. If they're going to go to bat for Kaatje, they need to get on it. If not…they want you to take on another project."

"I know." She leaned over and rested her head on her folded hands. "I just don't know what I want to do—if I come back. Will they give me another month?"

"Probably." He rolled his eyes. "Of course they will. But then they'll want you to hit the ground running. I've got some options if you want to hear them."

"No, not now. I have to make up my mind about Luxor or Kaatje. If it's Luxor, I want to be picky this time, because I'm gunning for the top."

"That sounds fair. While you're deciding, why don't you think of what it is about your past assignments that you liked. That might help you narrow things down if you decide to come back."

She grinned at him. "I've been making decisions that way since I could write. I'll start on it tonight."

—∾—

There was no job in the world that was equivalent to Kaatje. It seemed like such a no-brainer. But it wasn't. Loving someone and making a life together was more than attraction and shared interests and similar moral codes. The quotidian struggles and joys of work and accomplishment meant so much more than they should. But it was true. Hard to admit, but true. Many marriages seemed to be between people who were once powerfully attracted to each other, but after that rush of emotions died down, there was little left. And Kaatje was too wonderful a woman to be stuck in that situation. If they couldn't both be fulfilled, they'd have to break up. It was horrible to consider, but the only fair option.

Introspection and soul searching weren't fun, and they took a surprisingly long time. But Fernando had made a good suggestion. She would think of parts of jobs, skills, tasks and concepts that made work fun. Knowing what made work elemental to her personality would make it easier to figure out if there was any way to find what she needed in Kaatje's world.

The final list took three days, but there were threads that carried through. She liked being in charge, making changes, streamlining processes, working as part of a team that she led, and having a budget that she controlled. She didn't like needless reporting, status meetings, people who didn't understand her job trying to implement changes, and most of all—needless reporting. She knew that was at the top and bottom of the list, but it had been the bane of her existence. No one liked working all day then having to tell people what they'd done, but she hated it more than most. The higher she'd gone in the organization, the more she'd hated it.

Looking back, she realized that all Fernando did was plan for the long term, write and demand that others write status reports, and go to meetings. He was one hundred percent desk bound, and she knew she'd be the same in a year or two at the most. That was chilling, but it was a fact of life. The higher you went the less you actually did. Your salary went up, as did your responsibilities, but you could do little about the actual work. All you could do was write reports explaining why people two, three, or six levels below you had messed something up or had done something well. Usually the former. She would hate that kind of job, but there was no other kind at Luxor or any other major corporation. And that sucked.

―――

Fernando called two days later, at the impolite hour of seven in the morning. "I hate to do this to you, but I can only get you an extension on your sabbatical if you'll commit to a new project. Actually…" he paused, and she knew it was bad news, "Warren would like you to fly down to Miami and meet with Ken Stopack. They're reorganizing and they're thinking of having all the hotels and resorts report to him. He needs a deputy and Warren thinks you're the right person. The job would fill out your experience, since you haven't ever had a big staff reporting to you."

Her stomach sank, but a chill of excitement also chased down her spine. "Big is right. What's the headcount?"

"Around a hundred thousand."

"That's a very, very big staff. When does he want me to do this?"

"He'd like your thoughts by Monday."

"This is Wednesday," she said flatly. "I'm supposed to make up my mind about my whole future in two business days?"

He chuckled. "I don't think Warren knows you're making a decision about your whole future. He thinks it's just a step on your career ladder. He probably thinks you'll be upset to leave LA, but that's about it."

"I'd leave LA for a good pizza. But I'm really not ready to make a decision, Fernando. Is there any way to hold off on this?"

"Sure. You tell me how to get Warren off an idea he's latched onto." He waited a few seconds. "Got anything?"

"No. I'll think about it and let you know by the end of the day."

"Which part? The job or the trip to Miami?"

"The latter. I've gotta go. I need to clear my mind and think about my life."

"This is an executive VP job, Laurie. Not right now, of course. But you could be an EVP by the time you're thirty-four. That's young enough to hold on for the brass ring, my friend."

She got into her car and started to drive. Her mind wandered, thinking of the massive responsibilities that running twenty or thirty hotels would be. Since she'd only worked with the hotels in Osaka, she honestly didn't know what the hotel inventory was. She'd have each of those twenty or thirty hotel managers reporting directly to her. Each of them would have ten or fifteen direct reports, and each of them would have significantly more. The five resorts made the number of reports jump into the stratosphere. A hundred thousand souls who would ultimately be her responsibility. That number was ridiculously large and made her stomach hurt just to think of it.

In her current job, she had indirect responsibility for thousands, but direct supervision of only a few. Running the hotels and resorts would mean all of the things she liked would be further diminished and all of the things she hated would be amplified. But doing it well would get her promoted quickly. It looked good for Luxor to have more women EVPs, and she could use that to her benefit. Then she'd be made president of a division. There were only five divisions, and she'd only have to outwork and outlast four other people to have a chance at being CEO.

She'd driven so far that she realized she was on the outskirts of Santa Barbara. Winding her way along unfamiliar streets, she followed her nose and headed for the ocean. Eventually she found a parking lot and left the car, then made her way to the harbor. As she walked along, the salty air brought back a sense memory. Kaatje lying on the hammock on her boat, suntanned legs stretched out, cap pulled low on her head. She was dozing and looked befuddled when she woke. But even though she was groggy, she defended herself and her work choices that day almost a year ago. Kaatje knew who she was, and she wouldn't give up on the things she needed. Heaven knew that list had shrunk as she'd tried to figure out ways for them to stay together, but once she got down to the vital things, she wouldn't budge.

Neither of them could compromise any more. They each had needs that were entirely independent of each other, and they had to meet those needs or break up. Losing her would be like losing a limb. It would be possible to go on, but things would never, ever be the same without her.

Dazed and aching with sorrow, Laurie walked around for a long time, finally seeing a sign that read "Kayak Rentals."

In a few minutes she was outfitted with an orange boat, a life vest and a paddle. She'd had to bluff her way into convincing the young man at the counter of her proficiency, but she was a good swimmer and had grown very comfortable in the ocean.

He helped her into the boat, and she conducted herself respectably as she paddled away, leaving him none the wiser that this was her first time in a kayak.

She'd been told to stay close, and that wasn't a hard commandment to honor. The water was much darker and choppier than the Caribbean, and it didn't smell as good, either. But that was probably because of all of the huge yachts, or diesel gulpers as Kaatje called them, that her little harbor was thankfully lacking. Laurie's mind kept going back to Miami. Living there would make her just an hour or two from Kaatje by air. Maybe they could work something out. They could be together for six months in the states, then Laurie could visit every weekend during the rest of the year. If Kaatje truly loved her why wouldn't six months together every year be better than none?

It took just a few moments to admit that taking weekends off was a dream that would never be a reality. No one at her level worked five days a week. It was possible to be in the office only five days, but was being on the phone or on her computer the other two days the same as truly being with Kaatje? Kaatje wouldn't think so, and who could blame her. No, every visit would require a lot of planning and she'd be stressed the whole time. Still, the job in Miami was intriguing, and was the next step in the plan she'd been working towards since the day she received her MBA.

Paddling around, staying alert to moving boats, she got into a nice rhythm. Being second in hotels and resorts would be a big deal, and her next promotion would be a slam dunk. But what would being an EVP really mean? What had Kaatje asked? Something about wondering if more windows in your office made you happier? Of course they didn't. What made a person happy was an accumulation of all of the little things that gave you satisfaction. If the things on her list were present she'd be happy making twenty thousand and having no title at all, much less an EVP.

The thought of hotels in Miami, Madrid, Osaka, Los Angeles and San Diego was sobering. All of those people. All of the problems. All of those reports. And she wouldn't personally be able to change a light bulb, or a sheet, or adjust the temperature in a shower head. Thousands and thousands of rooms, each with a hundred different issues that could, and would arise. And all she could do was take responsibility for the errors and rely on someone to fix them properly. From high up in an office building miles from the nearest hotel.

She stared at the choppy water, and saw the list she'd made make perfect sense. It was crazy to even consider the job in Miami. Almost nothing on her list was there. She didn't need that much money, or that much responsibility. What she needed was Kaatje, and how she'd get her suddenly seemed so obvious that she could have kicked herself for not having thought of it earlier. She quickly paddled back to the dock, paid for the kayak, and sprinted to the quiet of her car. Not even checking the time, she dialed St. Maarten, and reached him at home.

"Hello, Theo, it's Laurie. I've got an idea, and I need to pick your brain for a while. Is this a good time?"

Chapter Twenty-Four

THREE DAYS LATER, Laurie sat on a bench near the Hoogeboom home. She'd been waiting for more than two hours, but it was a nice fall day in Amsterdam and she was so busy practicing her speech that she was able to endure the passing time. Still, the waiting was horrible. Her stomach was in knots and every dark head that appeared on the street made her heart skip. Finally, the prettiest dark head appeared, but it was accompanied by another woman.

If she's dating someone already I'm going to throw myself into that canal. Rather than see something that would truly make her want to end it all, she got to her feet and strode across the street. Kaatje turned and met her gaze when they were about twenty feet away. "Laurie!" she said with a remarkably heavy Dutch accent. She looked at the woman she was walking with and said a few quick sentences in Dutch. Without being introduced, the woman smiled and waved at Laurie, hugged Kaatje and took off. Laurie didn't even turn to see where she went. She just took a sheet of paper from her jacket pocket and presented it.

Kaatje took it from her tentatively, and read it, a smile starting to form on her lips. "Your resignation," she said, as if in awe.

"That's a copy. I sent the original from Schiphol," she said, smiling. "I wanted to make it clear how serious I was. I thought sending it from another continent would make a statement."

"Are you…" She looked around. "Staying here or did you just deliver this…" She looked adorably confused.

"My suitcases are over there."

Kaatje looked across the street. "Three bags?"

"I'm going to need a lot of stuff if we're staying for a while. It gets cold here, you know."

Kaatje dove for her. She held her so tightly that all either of them could do was make soft grunts of pain. "Come inside. We have a lot to talk about." Kaatje dashed across the street and grappled with the bags, with Laurie taking the heaviest one from her. "It's a long walk up those stairs. I've got to get in practice."

They made it up the three flights, with Laurie having to stop and remove her jacket after the first. When they got inside Kaatje just stood there, looking expectant. No kiss, and not a word.

Laurie reached out and removed Kaatje's jacket, then took her hand and walked over to a pair of chairs that allowed a view of the city. They sat, with neither speaking for a few moments, as Laurie tried to make her brain follow the script she'd been rehearsing.

"Here's the whole thing," she began, knowing that wasn't the right opening. "I knew that if I lived on the boat and didn't have my own thing, I'd start to resent you."

Nodding, Kaatje said, "That's what my mother said."

"She's right. Eventually I would have started to pick on you and we'd fight. And eventually you'd kick me off the boat."

"I'd never do that," Kaatje said solemnly. "Once we made a commitment to each other, we'd find a way around our problems."

"But it's better to make sure you don't have any big ones right at the start, isn't it?"

She nodded. "Of course. Much better." As they spoke her Dutch accent faded and she started to sound more like herself.

"I knew I had to figure out a way to get my work needs met, and I've spent a lot of time figuring out what those needs are."

"Did you spend more time than you did on figuring out you were a lesbian?" That adorable half grin would have weakened her knees if she'd been standing.

"Yes, as a matter of fact. Three whole days. But even when I had the facts in front of me, I couldn't put things together."

"What did you learn? I need to know."

"It's simple. I'm a striver. I've got to have something to fix. Something to work at. I have to keep my mind busy, and I've got to be in charge."

"Then how can you leave your job? I'm certain there isn't a job anywhere on St. Maarten that will be as challenging as what you had."

"That's where you're wrong. Jobs aren't more challenging as you go up. There's just more pressure. You get more money and prestige, and you have more to lose. You think about your salary and your bonus and your stock options and you realize how hard it is to find another job that will reward you like that if you lose the one you're in."

"Then how can you leave?"

"I realized that it isn't the title and the money that compel me. It's the actual job. The things I like best are troubleshooting and running things properly. I really need to be in charge, and I'm going to finally make that happen. I'm buying a small hotel not far from Simpson Bay."

"A hotel…" Kaatje looked dumbfounded.

"Yes. I've learned a lot about hotel management, and what I've learned can be perfectly put to use on a small scale. And having it be small scale will let me…and us…have a life."

"But what if…how did…Simpson Bay?"

"Well, this deal might not work out. I called your father a couple of days ago and asked him if he knew of any place that was small and in trouble. He told me about the Cupecoy Cove—"

"That place?" Kaatje made a face.

"Yep. Thirty rooms. It's a two star hotel now. My goal would be to make it twenty big rooms and get a five star rating Your dad says it's in bad shape, and the owners are barely making it. But it's on the ocean, which is worth a lot, and it's not ancient. Your dad thinks the owners would take a rock-bottom price to walk away."

"My father," she said, as if the word had just then reached her brain.

"Yes," she said, laughing at her vacant expression. "When I figured out that running a hotel would be perfect for me, I called him immediately. His bank holds the loan, and he's on the job now, trying to feel them out."

"I can't believe you called my dad."

"And then I called your mom."

"My mother?" It looked as though her eyes would pop out.

"Yep. I wanted to make sure you hadn't started dating anyone." Kaatje paled. "She assured me you were a long way from dating."

Her eyes darkened. "I'm not sure I ever would have."

Needing desperately to take that sad look from her eyes, Laurie fished in her pocket and removed a bracelet-sized bunch of braided silver strands. "If you'll marry me, I'll be your date 'til death do us part." She slipped the bracelet onto Kaatje's left wrist.

"It's…what is it?" she asked, holding it up to the window. "It looks like a part of the rigging on my boat."

"It is." Laurie snugged it up and showed how it should look. "We'll have them soldered on us. They're just like the stays on your boat." She'd waited too long already. She had to kiss the wonder-filled face that glowed from the late morning light. They slid from their chairs, winding up kneeling on the floor, holding each other tightly.

"I love you," Kaatje whispered.

Laurie kissed her gently. "And I love you. Will you marry me?"

Kaatje looked at the bracelet, smiling so brightly her grin competed with the fall sun. "Maybe. I have more questions before I can decide. Let's go for a sail."

―――

It took a while to arrange to get the keys for Kaatje's brother's boat, but by early afternoon they were cruising along the canals of Amsterdam. Kaatje steered, and Laurie cuddled up against her, feeling that even an extra inch was too much distance between them.

"This is something that dawned on me during the flight over here," Laurie said. "I love *The Flying Dutchwoman*, but I want to have a house. I need the space and I desperately need a faster Internet connection." She batted her eyes at Kaatje. "Can you give in and live on land?"

Kaatje spared a long gaze. "I know this sounds silly, but that will be hard for me. I'm much happier on water than land."

"I knew you liked living on the boat…"

"It's more than a preference, but I'll give it up for you. But I don't think there's any way I can pay for half of a mortgage."

"We'll argue about money later, but I assume I can buy a house for what I sell my condo for. It's already on the market," she added, smiling slyly.

"It is? What if I didn't say 'yes?' What would you do then?"

"Nothing different. I realized that I love St. Maarten as well as you and the boat. I'm going to buy a little hotel even if you won't marry me. But I hope you know I'll never give up chasing you."

"You don't have to chase me," Kaatje said, tears forming in her eyes. "You know how much I love you, but how can I be sure this will work for you? I couldn't stand it if we married and you got as involved in a little hotel as you did with Luxor."

"That will be my challenge," Laurie admitted. "I don't mean to brag, but I've never failed at anything I put my whole heart into. And my whole heart is devoted to you." They kissed, their lips pressed against each other until an insistent horn made Kaatje steer away from a passing boat.

"Maybe we'd better kiss back at the apartment," she said, waving guiltily at the annoyed sailor.

"We can kiss for years and years and—"

"I need more assurances," Kaatje said. "This is a very big part of your personality. The excitement will fade, and then we're going to have to be sure we can live together. And I need *time* with you. Not excuses about the laundry not having the sheets ready for the next guest."

Nodding, Laurie said, "I've thought about it endlessly, and here's why I think this will be easier. I won't have to do status reports. That would save me hours—literally hours a day. No meetings unless I call them." She made a contented purring sound in the back of her throat. "You have no idea how delicious an idea that is. I'm the queen of the brief meeting. When we were really down to it in Osaka, I had meetings in my office, after having the chairs taken out. People really get down to business when they have to stand." She grinned, thinking of her own ingenuity.

"But…I think you liked being that busy. That's what I'm worried about."

"Wrong. I know myself well when it comes to work. I don't like to be at work all hours of the night. I'm certain of that. If I'm really in charge, I'll control my work day and get home on time. I know how to delegate, and I got even better at it near the end in Osaka."

"Are you sure?" Kaatje was begging her for reassurance.

"Yes. I'm certain. I was exhausted. Mentally and physically exhausted. There was nothing fun about that last year. And you met me when things were just getting to their worst point. For the first few years at Luxor, I went out a lot, took classes, exercised…all kinds of normal things and I was really happy. But then the extra work had to be done, and I never break a promise. I said I could handle it, and I did." Even now she was remarkably proud of the job she'd done.

"But what if you backslide? I don't want to fight. I really hate that."

Laurie thought for a minute. "How about this? You keep track of when I get home. I'll try to leave work by five, but for every day I'm home after five thirty, I'll give you a thousand dollars. I won't make nearly as much as I have in the past, and giving away a thousand dollars will make me think long and hard about whether that extra work is worth it."

Kaatje squawked, "I don't want your money and I don't want to be your supervisor."

"Just for a while. As a training tool. Once I have a goal, I'll work like a dog to meet it. And getting home on time will be the best goal I've ever had."

"I could take your money if we kept it in a travel fund. That would help pay for some of the trips I'm going on…hopefully with you." She grinned, clearly teasing.

"Excellent idea. I promise I'll close the hotel in September and October. Every year. It's already on the business website I've mocked up. And I'm pretty sure you could talk me into staying abroad until right before Thanksgiving if you tried just a little bit."

"Can I see the engagement bracelet again?"

She'd had to take it off earlier because it was too large and would easily slip off and be lost. Laurie put it on her again, and Kaatje kept gazing at it, then turned and headed back to port.

"Where are we going?"

"To a jewelry store. I want to have it soldered today." She gave Laurie a luminescent smile. "Are you ready to take the leap?"

"Of course. But these are for when we get married."

"We'll get wedding bands too." She shook her arm, with the bracelet sliding up and down, glinting in the sun. "This is our pledge to each other. It has nothing to do with the legalities of marriage. Our promises will all be bound up in these stays." She sighed. "That's the best word I've ever heard. Laurie will stay…with me."

Chapter Twenty-Five

Laurie sat in front of her computer at the big, modern desk that took up a good portion of their guest room. Kaatje was draped over an upholstered chair, head dangling over one arm, legs over the other. Few people seemed less comfortable in an apartment with normal furniture than she did. She rarely sat upright on their chairs or sofa, but her inability to conform to design aesthetics seemed limited to St. Maarten. In Holland, she acted as though furniture was a perfectly normal part of her life, and her head was always significantly higher than her feet when seated. She was an endless series of contradictions. Really cute contradictions.

Even though she had trouble being upright, no one could say Kaatje was not a good sport when it came to the apartment. She didn't complain about Laurie's desire for a good-sized, two-bedroom place, even though she didn't spend much time in it. Somehow, they wound up on the boat nearly every night, with the gentle rocking of *The Flying Dutchwoman* quickly lulling both of them to sleep.

The apartment had become a good transitional object for Laurie. It was, in essence, hers alone, and she'd filled it with things that made it seem like home. It wasn't just an apartment, like her place in LA had been. It reflected her personality—her newly developing personality—and it helped her feel like she belonged on the island.

They'd met in the apartment after work that night. As usual, Kaatje had ridden her bike over and made dinner. They'd been working in the office since Laurie finished cleaning the kitchen, but now Kaatje seemed itchy to get back on the boat, so Laurie hurried with the paperwork. "Okay, the last question is whether we've lived under the same roof for the past three years." She turned and gave Kaatje a wry grin. "We've lived under two roofs and one deck. That counts, right?"

"That definitely counts. Hey, we're going to Holland to file the naturalization papers, aren't we?"

"Yeah. I'm already shopping online for tickets. I can leave right after Labor Day."

"How about staying to see Sinterklaas arrive?"

"Mmm, I should say 'no,' but I guess I can trust my staff to handle the Thanksgiving crowd."

"Great. The kids would love to have us stay for that."

"Every year we stay a little longer, you know. Not that I'm complaining."

Kaatje grinned at her. "I think you love Holland as much as I do. How much is in our vacation account?"

"I know you want to call it 'Laurie's punishment for getting home late' account, but I'm glad you can contain yourself." Quietly, she grumbled, "I would have had to pay that much in one month if I'd stayed at Luxor. I think I've been exemplary." She logged into their bank account and reported, "Thirty-two thousand, four hundred and sixty-seven dollars. I think we can afford to go," she added dryly.

"You *have* been exemplary, but it's cool to have a lot of money in our trip account. Let's spend a few days in Spain. It's time for another trip to see your former overlord. Thijs has been dropping hints every time we talk."

"He doesn't do that with me."

"He's still a little shy around you. Plus, he tries to be careful to speak at your level…which is really, really good for someone who's only been studying Dutch for two years," she added hastily.

"I had a feeling you told the kids to take it easy on me. Roos says things like, 'Are you healthy? I am well. My school is fun,' and I know she could probably give me her assessment on *Macbeth* or the next national election."

"She likes that you've learned the language. She says you'll feel more like a native if you read some of our classic novels in Dutch."

"My Staatsexamen Nederlands als Tweede Taal diploma says I'm fully integrated into Dutch life. And if a bureaucrat says it, it must be true." She got up and went over to Kaatje, taking her hand and pulling her into a sitting position. "I think we're done. Let's go back to the boat and celebrate Dutch style."

"What's Dutch style?"

Acting as though she were stunned, Laurie stared at her. "And you call yourself a citizen. Everyone knows the Dutch are the best lovers in the world. I want to practice a little more in case I have to show my goods during my naturalization ceremony."

Kaatje took her in her arms, hugging her tightly. "That won't be for months. We have plenty of time to practice. But it couldn't hurt to get to work." They kissed, kindling a tiny flame that would soon glow brightly. "I love you," she whispered.

"*Ik hou ook van jou. Dat zal ik altijd blijven doen.*"

Kaatje grinned at her lovingly. "I will love you always too."

"Can I trust a woman who can't sit upright in a chair?"

"Yes, Moppie, you can trust me even though I can't sit up. My heart belongs to you from any and all directions." She slid off the chair, taking Laurie with her onto the floor. "I like this one," she said, looking lecherous.

"It is pretty nice. Lots of room to move around." She stroked Kaatje's tanned cheek, thrilling to the glint in her beautiful eyes.

"We don't have to rush to get back to the boat. Let's enjoy our apartment for a while." She stretched out on the thick area rug. "We have a nice ceiling in here. Why don't you look at it while I attend to a few things?"

The way Kaatje tossed off such silly comments was definitely part of her charm. That plus a million other things. "If you'd spent the whole day thinking about it you couldn't have come up with a better idea." Laurie tilted her head and kissed Kaatje's smooth lips. That first intent kiss still sent a thrill through her body. There was no doubt that one particular Dutch woman was the best lover in the world—for her alone.

THE END

By Susan X Meagher

Novels

Arbor Vitae
All That Matters
Cherry Grove
Girl Meets Girl
The Lies That Bind
The Legacy
Doublecrossed
Smooth Sailing

Serial Novel

I Found My Heart In San Francisco
Awakenings: Book One
Beginnings: Book Two
Coalescence: Book Three
Disclosures: Book Four
Entwined: Book Five
Fidelity: Book Six
Getaway: Book Seven
Honesty: Book Eight
Intentions: Book Nine
Journeys: Book Ten
Karma: Book Eleven

Anthologies

Undercover Tales
Outsiders

To purchase these books go to *www.briskpress.com*
Author website *www.susanxmeagher.com*